THE METTLE OF A MAN

"You two!" My voice rang in the echoing emptiness of the building. "Get out in the open! Start now or start shootin'!"

My hands were wide, fingers spread, and right then it did not matter to me which way they came for the devil was in me. Men who lurked in dark stalls did not appeal to me, nor the men who hired them.

They came out slowly, hands raised. One was a big man with black hair and unshaven jowls. The other had the cruel, flat face of an Apache. "Suppose I'd come shootin'?" the black-haired man sneered.

"Then they'd be plantin' you at sundown." My eyes held him. "If you don't believe that, cut loose your wolf right now."

That stopped him. He didn't know how much of it I could back up and weren't anxious to find out. . . .

Bantam Books by Louis L'Amour
Ask your bookseller for the books you have missed

THE TRAIL TO CRAZY MAN

Louis L'Amour

BANTAM BOOKS

TORONTO • NEW YORK • LONDON • SYDNEY • AUCKLAND

THE TRAIL TO CRAZY MAN

A Bantam Book / published by arrangement with
the author
Bantam edition / September 1986
Cover artwork by Frank McCarthy.

ISBN 0-553-26392-7

Published simultaneously in the United States and Canada

Bantam Books are published by Bantam Books, Inc. Its trademark, consisting of the words "Bantam Books" and the por-
trayal of a rooster, is Registered in U.S. Patent and Trademark
Office and in other countries. Marca Registrada. Bantam
Books, Inc., 666 Fifth Avenue, New York, New York 10103.

PRINTED IN THE UNITED STATES OF AMERICA

O   0 9 8 7 6 5 4 3 2 1

Contents

FOREWORD

The Trail to Crazy Man contains three novel-length stories I wrote not quite four decades ago for publication in "pulp" magazines long before my first book was released. (I had been working on a novel of the sea when I went into the army for World War II, but it was never completed.) Longer on action than on characterization or background, these "magazine novels" are chapters from my early writing history. In creating them, I became so involved with my characters that their lives were still as much a part of me as I was of them long after the issues in which they appeared became collector's items. Pleased as I was about how I brought the characters and their adventures of life in the pages of the magazines, I still wanted the reader to know more about my people and why they did what they did.

So, years later, after establishing myself as an author of books, I went back and revised and expanded these magazine works ito full-length novels I published as paperbacks with different titles.

The stories in this book, as well as those in *The Rider of the Ruby Hills*, a companion paperback of four more of my "magazine novels" that Bantam is simultaneously publishing, have long been the subject of great speculation by my avid readers. People are curious about how my paperback novels evolved from my "magazine novels" and have very much wanted to read these early versions that I've collected here in book form for the very first time.

"The Trail to Crazy Man," the lead story, begins at sea, as many American life stories did, and proceeds to the Rocky Mountain region. It is the original telling of the novel *Crossfire Trail*. "Riders of the Dawn" later became *Silver Canyon* in a somewhat longer version. "Showdown on the Hogback" was slightly expanded to *Showdown at Yellow Butte*.

The "pulp" action magazines in which these stories were first published were available on every newsstand throughout the twenties, thirties, and forties. They offered readers a wide variety of stories, from western, mystery, romance, science fiction, air, and sea backgrounds. They also offered a substantial market for a working writer. Many of us honed our skills in the "pulps," often writing under pseudonyms, before going on to other genres or literary forms. The essentials demanded by our editors were action and color, but, above all, one had to tell a story with a beginning, a middle, and an end. And the story had to *move*.

In those years, before paperback books and then television rendered them obsolete seemingly in a matter of days, the action-adventure magazines could be found in every bunkhouse or ship's forecastle, being read by the very men of whom the stories were told.

For a writer who had to make a living from his work, they were a rich lode. The pay was small, but if he could write enough he might make ends meet, even though the payment usually started at a half cent per word and rarely got above two cents a word.

Fortunately, I had lived a life of action and knew the sort of men and women I was to write about. I had been over the country, worked in the mines and lumber camps, on ranches and construction outfits, and knew the people and the language. Much of what I was to write about had happened to me, so I knew how men felt and how they reacted.

One does not suddenly become a good writer. No matter how much innate talent one has, skills must be developed and then sharpened by practice. As I have said elsewhere, a writer never knows enough and is never good enough.

The reading public is much more aware than some imagine, and among them are experts in almost any field one can name.

No field of writing demands more intimate knowledge than stories of the frontier. Conditions were changing rapidly: towns grew and died. New styles of rifles and pistols were constantly coming into being. Saddles were always being altered, and the ropes used in California were different from those used in Texas or Montana. Clothing changed, too, from any castoff or otherwise available garment to apparel designed for specific conditions and types of work.

Frontier terrain varied considerably, and nothing could

be taken for granted. To speak of "desert" is not enough, for a desert in Arizona can be much different from one in California.

Oddly enough, many people do not consider California to be "western," yet only Texas surpassed it in numbers of cattle on the range, and no greater ropers existed than the Californios with ropes so long that few Texans would attempt to use them. Los Angeles was as wild and rough as Dodge City and Deadwood.

A writer must know and understand to interpret, and the greatest of writers are those who understand human nature the best. For, in the last analysis, stories are about people, their ideas, emotions, characteristics, and how they react to stress.

Research is essential, and I have always done my own. I have no staff, not even a secretary. If mistakes are made, they are my mistakes, to be blamed upon no one else. I do not feel that I should trust research that has been filtered through somebody else's mind. I want to find the facts myself, weigh them with my own experience, and share them with you in stories like those you are about to read.

AUTHOR'S NOTE
THE TRAIL TO CRAZY MAN

It was "Crazy Woman" in the original story I turned in, but the editor decided he preferred to call it "Crazy Man." I made no protest, as I was glad to sell the story and get the check that resulted. Crazy Woman Creek is in the Hole-in-the-Wall Country not far from the town of Kaycee, where Nate Champion cashed in his checks.

For many years this was the heart of Sioux Country, and later a hangout for outlaws who rode up the Middle Fork of the Powder River and through the Hole-in-the-Wall into the country beyond. The ranchers there were on friendly terms with the outlaws of the Butch Cassidy Wild Bunch.

As with the Charles Rodney of this story, many a man rode away from home and never returned. Traveling was hard and always dangerous. If a man was carrying money, he had to ride with care, as only too many were prepared to take it from him.

There are some baking-powder cans filled with gold cached someplace up on the Crazy Woman, but nobody knows exactly where, or even where to start looking.

The Trail to Crazy Man

Chapter 1
Shanghaied

In the dank, odorous forecastle, a big man with wide shoulders sat at a scarred mess table, his feet spread to brace himself against the roll of the ship. A brass hurricane lantern, its light turned low, swung from a beam overhead, and in the vague light the big man studied a worn and sweat-stained chart.

There was no sound in the forecastle but the distant rustle of the bow wash about the hull, the lazy creak of the square-rigger's timbers, a few snores from sleeping men, and the hoarse, rasping breath of a man who was dying in the lower bunk.

The big man who bent over the chart wore a slipover jersey with alternate red and white stripes, a broad leather belt and a brass buckle, and coarse jeans. On his feet were woven leather sandals of soft, much-oiled leather. His hair was shaggy and uncut, but he was clean-shaven except for a mustache and burnsides.

The chart he studied showed the coast of northern California. He marked a point on it with the tip of his knife and then checked the time with a heavy gold watch. After a swift calculation, he folded the chart and replaced it in an oilskin packet with other papers and tucked the packet under his jersey, above his belt.

Rising, he stood for an instant, canting to the roll of the ship, staring down at the white-haired man in the lower bunk. There was that about the big man to make him stand out in any crowd. He was a man born to command, not only because of his splendid physique and the strength of his character, but because of his personality.

He knelt beside the bunk and touched the dying man's wrist. The pulse was feeble. Rafe Caradec crouched there, waiting, watching, thinking.

In a few hours at most, possibly even in a few minutes,

3

this man would die. In the long year at sea his health had broken down under forced labor and constant beatings, and this last one had broken him up internally. When Charles Rodney was dead he, Rafe Caradec, would do what he must.

The ship rolled slightly, and the older man sighed and his lids opened suddenly. For a moment he stared upward into the ill-smelling darkness. Then his head turned. He saw the big man crouched beside him, and he smiled. His hand fumbled for Rafe's.

"You—you've got the papers? You won't forget?"

"I won't forget."

"You must be careful."

"I know."

"See my wife, Carol. Explain to her that I didn't run away, that I wasn't afraid. Tell her I had the money and was comin' back. I'm worried about the mortgage I paid. I don't trust Barkow."

The man lay silent, breathing deeply, hoarsely. For the first time in three days he was conscious and aware.

"Take care of 'em, Rafe," he said. "I've got to trust you! You're the only chance I have! Dyin' ain't bad, except for them. And to think—a whole year has gone by. Anything may have happened!"

"You'd better rest," Rafe said gently.

"It's late for that. He's done me in this time. Why did this happen to me, Rafe? To us?"

Caradec shrugged his powerful shoulders. "I don't know. No reason, I guess. We were just there at the wrong time. We took a drink we shouldn't have taken."

The old man's voice lowered. "You're goin' to try—tonight?"

Rafe smiled then. "Try? Tonight we're goin' ashore, Rodney. This is our only chance. I'm goin' to see the captain first."

Rodney smiled and lay back, his face a shade whiter, his breathing more gentle.

A year they had been together, a brutal, ugly, awful year of labor, blood, and bitterness. It had begun, that year, one night in San Francisco in Hongkong Bohl's place on the Barbary Coast. Rafe Caradec was just back from Central America with a pocketful of money. His latest revolution was cleaned up, and the proceeds were mostly in his pocket, with some in the bank.

The months just past had been jungle months, dripping jungle, fever ridden and stifling with heat and humidity. It had been a period of raids and battles, but finally it was over, and Rafe had taken his payment in cash and moved on. He had been on the town, making up for lost time—Rafe Caradec, gambler, soldier of fortune, wanderer of the far places.

Somewhere along the route that night he had met Charles Rodney, a sun-browned cattleman who had come to Frisco to raise money for his ranch in Wyoming. They had had a couple of drinks and dropped in at Hongkong Bohl's dive. They'd had a drink there, too, and when they awakened it had been to the slow, long roll of the sea, and the brutal voice of Bully Borger, skipper of the *Mary S*.

Rafe had cursed himself for a tenderfoot and a fool. To have been shanghaied like any drunken farmer! He had shrugged it off, knowing the uselessness of resistance. After all, it was not his first trip to sea.

Rodney had been wild. He had rushed to the captain and demanded to be put ashore, and Bully Borger had knocked him down and booted him senseless while the mate stood by with a pistol. That had happened twice more, until Rodney returned to work almost a cripple and frantic with worry over his wife and daughter.

As always, the crew had split into cliques. One of these consisted of Rafe, Rodney, Roy Penn, Rock Mullaney and Tex Brisco. Penn had been a law student and occasional prospector. Mullaney was an able-bodied seaman, hard-rock miner, and cowhand. They had been shanghaied in Frisco in the same lot with Rafe and Rodney. Tex Brisco was a Texas cowhand who had been shanghaied from a waterfront dive in Galveston, where he had gone to look at the sea.

Finding a friend in Rafe, Rodney had told him the whole story of his coming to Wyoming with his wife and daughter, of what drouth and Indians had done to his herd, and how finally he had mortgaged his ranch to a man named Barkow.

Rustlers had invaded the country, and he had lost cattle. Finally reaching the end of his rope he had gone to San Francisco to get a loan from an old friend. In San Francisco, surprisingly, he had met Barkow and some others, and paid off the mortgage. A few hours later, wandering into Hong-kong Bohl's place, which had been recommended to him by Barkow's friends, he had been doped, robbed, and shanghaied.

*   *   *

When the ship returned to Frisco after a year, Rodney had demanded to be put ashore, and Borger had laughed at him. Then Charles Rodney had tackled the big man again, and that time the beating had been final. With Rodney dying, the *Mary S.* had finished her loading and slipped out of port so he could be conveniently "lost at sea."

The cattleman's breathing had grown gentler, and Rafe leaned his head on the edge of the bunk, dozing.

Rodney had given him a deed to the ranch, a deed that gave him a half share, the other half belonging to Rodney's wife and daughter. Caradec had promised to save the ranch if he possibly could. Rodney had also given him Barkow's signed receipt for the money.

Rafe's head came up with a jerk. How long he had slept he did not know, yet. . . . He stiffened as he glanced at Charles Rodney. The hoarse, rasping breath ws gone; the even, gentle breath was no more. Rodney was dead.

For an instant, Rafe held the old man's wrist. Then he drew the blanket over Rodney's face. Abruptly, then, he got up. A quick glance at his watch told him they had only a few minutes until they would sight Cape Mendocino. Grabbing a small bag of things off the upper bunk, he turned quickly to the companionway.

Two big feet and two hairy ankles were visible on the top step. They moved, and step by step a man came down the ladder. He was a big man, bigger than Rafe, and his small, cruel eyes stared at him and then at Rodney's bunk.

"Dead?"

"Yes."

The big man rubbed a fist along his unshaven jowl. He grinned at Rafe.

"I heard him speak about the ranch. It could be a nice thing, that. I heard about them ranches. Money in 'em." His eyes brightened with cupidity and cunning. "We share an' share alike, eh?"

"No." Caradec's voice was flat. "The deed is made out to his daughter and me. His wife is to share, also. I aim to keep nothin' for myself."

The big man chuckled hoarsely. "I can see that!" he said. "Josh Briggs is no fool, Caradec! You're intendin' to get it all for yourself. I want mine!" He leaned on the handrail of the ladder. "We can have a nice thing, Caradec. They said there was trouble over there? Huh! I guess we can handle any trouble, an' make some ourselves."

"The Rodneys get it all," Rafe said. "Stand aside. I'm in a hurry."

Briggs's face was ugly. "Don't get high an' mighty with me!" he said roughly. "Unless you split even with me, you don't get away. I know about the boat you've got ready. I can stop you there, or here."

Rafe Caradec knew the futility of words. There are some natures to whom only violence is an argument. His left hand shot up suddenly, his stiffened fingers and thumb making a V that caught Briggs where his jawbone joined his throat.

The blow was short, vicious, unexpected. Briggs's head jerked back, and Rafe hooked short and hard with his right, following through with a smashing elbow that flattened Briggs's nose and showered him with blood.

Rafe dropped his bag and then struck, left and right to the body, then left and right to the chin. The last two blows cracked like pistol shots. Josh Briggs hit the foot of the ladder in a heap, rolled over, and lay still, his head partly under the table. Rafe picked up his bag and went up the ladder without so much as a backward glance.

Chapter II
Retribution

On the dark deck Rafe Caradec moved aft along the starboard side. A shadow moved out from the mainmast.

"You ready?"

"Ready, Rock."

Two more men got up from the darkness near the foot of the mast, and all four hauled the boat from its place and got it to the side.

"This the right place?" Penn asked.

"Almost." Caradec straightened. "Get her ready. I'm going to call on the old man."

In the darkness he could feel their eyes on him. "You think that's wise?"

"No, but he killed Rodney. I've got to see him."

"You goin' to kill Borger?"

It was like them that they did not doubt he could if he wished. Somehow he had always impressed men so, that what he wanted to accomplish, he would accomplish.

"No, just a good beatin'. He's had it comin' for a long time."

Mullaney spat. He was a stocky, muscular man. "You're cussed right he has! I'd like to help."

"No, there'll be no help for either of us. Stand by and watch for the mate."

Penn chuckled. "He's tied up aft, by the wheel."

Rafe Caradec turned and walked forward. His soft leather sandals made no noise on the hardwood deck or on the companionway as he descended. He moved like a shadow along the bulkhead and saw the door of the captain's cabin standing open. He was inside and had taken two steps before the captain looked up.

Bully Borger was big, almost a giant. He had a red beard around his jawbone under his chin. He squinted from cold, gray eyes at Rafe.

"What's wrong?" he demanded. "Trouble on deck?"

"No, Captain," Rafe said shortly, "there's trouble here. I've come to beat you within an inch of your life, Captain. Charles Rodney is dead. You ruined his life, Captain, and then you killed him."

Borger was on his feet, catlike. Somehow, he had always known this moment would come. A dozen times he had told himself he should kill Caradec, but the man was a seaman, a first-class, able-bodied seaman, and in the lot of shanghaied crews there were few. So he had delayed.

He lunged at the drawer for his brass knuckles.

Rafe had been waiting for that, poised on the balls of his feet. His left hand dropped to the captain's wrist in a grip like steel, and his right hand sank to the wrist in the captain's middle. It stopped Borger, that punch did, stopped him flat-footed for only an instant, but that instant was enough. Rafe's head darted forward, butting the bigger man in the face, and Rafe felt the bones crunch under his hard skull.

Yet the agony gave Borger a burst of strength, and he tore the hand with the knucks loose and got his fingers through their holes. He lunged, swinging a roundhouse blow that would have dropped a bull elephant. Rafe went under the swing, his movements timed perfectly, his actions almost negligent. He smashed left and right to the wind. The punches drove wind from Borger's stomach, and he doubled up, gasping.

Rafe dropped a palm to the back of the man's head and

shoved down hard. At the same instant, his knee came up, smashing Borger's face into a gory pulp.

Bully Borger, the dirtiest fighter on many a waterfront, staggered back, moaning with pain. His face expressionless, Rafe Caradec stepped in and threw punches with both hands, driving, wicked punches that had the power of those broad shoulders behind them, and timed with the rolling of the ship. Left, right, left, right, blows that cut and chopped like meat cleavers. Borger tottered and fell back across the settee.

Rafe wheeled to see Penn's blond head in the doorway. Roy Penn stared at the bloody hulk and then at Rafe.

"Better come on. The cape's showing off the starboard bow."

When they had the boat in the water, they slid down the rope one after the other. Then Rafe slashed it with his belt knife, and the boat dropped back. The black bulk of the ship swept by them. Her stern lifted and then sank. Rafe, at the tiller, turned the bow of the boat toward the monstrous blackness of the cape.

Mullaney and Penn got the sail up when the mast was stepped, and then Penn looked around at Rafe.

"That was mutiny, you know."

"It was," Rafe said calmly. "I didn't ask to go aboard, and knockout drops in a Barbary Coast dive ain't my way of askin' for a year's job!"

"A year?" Penn swore. "Two years and more, for me. For Tex, too."

"You know this coast?" Mullaney asked.

Rafe nodded. "Not well, but there's a place just north of the cape where we can run in. To the south the sunken ledges and rocks might tear our bottom out, but I think we can make this other place. Can you all swim?"

The mountainous headland loomed black against the gray-turning sky of the hours before daybreak. The seaward face of the cape was rocky and waterworn along the shoreline. Rafe, studying the currents and the rocks, brought the boat neatly in among them and headed for a boulder-strewn gray beach where water curled and left a white ruffle of surf.

They scrambled out of the boat and threw their gear on the narrow beach.

"How about the boat?" Tex demanded. "Do we leave it?"

"Shove her off, cut a hole in the bottom, and let her sink," Rafe said.

When the hole had been cut, they let the sea take the boat offshore a little, watching it fill and sink. Then they picked up their gear. Rafe Caradec led them inland, working along the shoulder of the mountain. The northern slope was covered with brush and trees, and afforded some concealment. Fog was rolling in from the sea, and soon the gray, cottony shroud of it had settled over the countryside.

When they had several miles behind them, Rafe drew to a halt. Penn opened the sack he was carrying and got out some bread, figs, coffee, and a pot.

"Stole 'em out of the captain's stores," he said. "Figured we might as well eat."

"Got anything to drink?" Mullaney rubbed the dark stubble on his wide jaws.

"Uh-huh. Two bottles of rum. Good stuff from Jamaica."

"You'll do to ride the river with," Tex said, squatting on his heels. He glanced up at Rafe. "What comes now?"

"Wyomin', for me." Rafe broke some sticks and put them into the fire Rock was kindling. "I made my promise to Rodney, and I'll keep it."

"He trusted you." Tex studied him thoughtfully.

"Yes. I'm not goin' to let him down. "Anyway," he added, smiling, "Wyomin's a long way from here, and we should be as far away as we can. They may try to find us. Mutiny's a hangin' offense."

"Ever run any cattle?" Tex wanted to know.

"Not since I was a kid. I was born in New Orleans, grew up near San Antone. Rodney tried to tell me all he could."

"I been over the trail to Dodge twice," Tex said, "and to Wyomin' once. I'll be needin' a job."

"You're hired," Rafe said, "if I ever get the money to pay you."

"I'll chance it," Tex Brisco agreed. "I like the way you do things."

"Me for the goldfields in Nevada," Rock said.

"That's good for me," Penn said. "If me and Rock don't strike it rich we may come huntin' a feed."

There was no trail through the tall grass but the one the mind could make, or the instinct of the cattle moving toward water. Yet as the long-legged zebra dun moved along the flank of the little herd, Rafe Caradec thought he was coming home.

This was a land for a man to love, a long, beautiful land of rolling grass and trees, of towering mountains pushing their dark peaks against the sky, and the straight, slim beauty of lodgepole pines.

He sat easy in the saddle, more at home than in many months, for almost half his life had been lived astride a horse. He liked the dun, which had an easy, space-eating stride. He had won the horse in a poker game in Ogden, and won the saddle and bridle in the same game. The new Winchester '73, newest and finest gun on the market, he had bought in San Francisco.

A breeze whispered in the grass, turning it to green and shifting silver as the wind stirred along the bottomland. Rafe heard the gallop of a horse behind him and reined in, turning. Tex Brisco rode up alongside.

"We should be about there, Rafe," he said, digging in his pocket for the makings. "Tell me about that business again, will you?"

Rafe nodded. "Rodney's brand was one he bought from an hombre named Shafter Mason. It was the Bar M. He had two thousand acres in Long Valley that he bought from Red Cloud, paid him good for it, and he was runnin' cattle on that, and some four thousand acres outside the valley. His cabin was built in the entrance to Crazy Man Canyon.

"He borrowed money from, and mortgaged the land to, a man named Bruce Barkow. Barkow's a big cattleman down here, tied in with three or four others. He has several gunmen workin' for him, and Rodney never trusted him, but he was the only man around who could loan him the money he needed."

"What's your plan?" Brisco asked, his eyes following the cattle.

"Tex, I haven't got one. I couldn't plan until I saw the lay of the land. The first thing will be to find Mrs. Rodney and her daughter, and from them, learn what the situation is. Then we can go to work. In the meantime, I aim to sell these cattle and hunt up Red Cloud."

"That'll be tough," Tex suggested. "There's been some Injun trouble, and he's a Sioux. Mostly, they're on the prod right now."

"I can't help it, Tex," Rafe said. "I've got to see him, tell him I have the deed, and explain so's he'll understand. He might turn out to be a good friend, and he would certainly make a bad enemy."

"There may be some question about these cattle," Tex suggested drily.

"What of it?" Rafe shrugged. "They are all strays. We culled them out of canyons where no white man has been in years, and slapped our own brand on 'em. We've driven them two hundred miles, so nobody here has any claim on them. Whoever started cattle where we found these left the country a long time ago. You remember what that old trapper told us?"

"Yeah," Tex agreed. "Our claim's good enough." He glanced again at the brand and then looked curiously at Rafe. "Man, why didn't you tell me your old man owned the C Bar? My uncle rode for 'em a while! I heard a lot about 'em! When you said to put the C Bar on these cattle you could have knocked me down with an ax! Why, Uncle Joe used to tell me all about the C Bar outfit! The old man had a son who was a ringtailed terror as a kid. Slick with a gun. . . . Say!" Tex Brisco stared at Rafe. "You wouldn't be the same one, would you?"

"I'm afraid I am," Rafe said. "For a kid I was too slick with a gun. Had a run-in with some old enemies of Dad's, and when it was over, I hightailed for Mexico."

"Heard about it."

Tex turned his sorrel out in a tight circle to cut a steer back into the herd, and they moved on.

Rafe Caradec rode warily, with an eye on the country. This was all Indian country, and the Sioux and Cheyennes had been hunting trouble ever since Custer had ridden into the Black Hills, which was the heart of the Indian country and almost sacred to the plains tribes. This was the near end of Long Valley, where Rodney's range had begun. It could be no more than a few miles to Crazy Man Canyon and his cabin.

Rafe touched a spur to the dun and cantered toward the head of the drive. There were three hundred head of cattle in this bunch, and when the old trapper had told him about them, curiosity had impelled him to have a look. In the green bottom of several adjoining canyons these cattle, remnants of a herd brought into the country several years before, had looked fat and fine.

It had been brutal, bitter work, but he and Tex had rounded up and branded the cattle. Then they had hired two drifting cowhands to help them with the drive.

He passed the man riding point and headed for the strip of trees where Crazy Man Creek curved out of the canyon and turned in a long sweeping semicircle out to the middle of the valley and then down its center, irrigating some of the finest grassland he had ever seen. Much of it, he noted, was subirrigated from the mountains that lifted on both sides of the valley.

The air was fresh and cool after the long, hot drive over the mountains and desert. The heavy fragrance of the pines and the smell of the long grass shimmering with dew lifted to his nostrils. He moved the dun down to the stream and sat his saddle while the horse dipped its muzzle into the clear, cold water of the Crazy Man.

When the gelding lifted his head, Rafe waded him across the stream and climbed the opposite bank. Then he turned upstream toward the canyon.

Chapter III
Ann Rodney

The bench beside the stream, backed by its stand of lodgepole pines, looked just as Rodney had described it. Yet as the cabin came into sight, Rafe's lips tightened with apprehension, for there was no sign of life. The dun, feeling his anxiety, broke into a canter.

One glance sufficed. The cabin was empty and evidently had been so for a long time.

Rafe was standing in the door when Tex rode up. Brisco glanced around and then at Rafe.

"Well," he said, "looks like we've had a long ride for nothin'."

The other two hands rode up—Johnny Gill and Bo Marsh, both Texans. With restless saddles, they had finished a drive in the Wyoming country, then headed west, and had ridden clear to Salt Lake. On their return they had run into Rafe and Tex, and hired on to work the herd east to Long Valley.

Gill, a short, leather-faced man of thirty, stared around.

"I know this place," he said. "Used to be the Rodney ranch. Feller name of Dan Shute took over. Rancher."

"Shute, eh?" Tex glanced at Caradec. "Not Barkow?"

Gill shook his head. "Barkow made out to be helpin' Rodney's womenfolks, but he didn't do much good. Personal, I never figgered he cut no great swath a-tryin'. Anyway, this here Dan Shute is a bad hombre."

"Well," Rafe said casually, "maybe we'll find out how bad. I aim to settle right here."

Gill looked at him thoughtfully. "You're buyin' yourself a piece of trouble, mister," he said. "But I never cottoned to Dan Shute, myself. You got any rightful claim to this range? This is where you was headed, ain't it?"

"That's right," Rafe said, "and I have a claim."

"Well, Bo," Gill said, hooking a leg over the saddle horn, "want to drift on, or do we stay and see how this gent stacks up with Dan Shute?"

Marsh grinned. He had a reckless, infectious grin. "Sure, Johnny," he said. "I'm for stayin' on. Shute's got him a big red-headed hand ridin' for him that I never liked, no ways."

"Thanks, boys," Rafe said. "Looks like I've got an outfit. Keep the cattle in pretty close the next few days. I'm ridin' in to Painted Rock."

"That town belongs to Barkow," Gill advised. "Might pay you to kind of check up on Barkow and Shute. Some of the boys talkin' around the chuckwagon sort of figgered there was more to that then met the eye. That Bruce Barkow is a right important gent around here, but when you read his sign, it don't always add up."

"Maybe," Rafe suggested thoughtfully, "you'd better come along. Let Tex and Marsh worry with the cattle."

Rafe Caradec turned the dun toward Painted Rock. Despite himself, he was worried. His liking for the little cattleman Rodney had been very real, and he had come to know and respect the man while aboard the *Mary S*. In the weeks that had followed the flight from the ship, he had been considering the problem of Rodney's ranch so much that it had become much his own problem.

Now, Rodney's worst fears seemed to have been realized. The family had evidently been run off their ranch, and Dan Shute had taken possession. Whether there was any connection between Shute and Barkow remained to be seen, but Caradec knew that chuckwagon gossip can often come close to the truth and that cowhands could many times see men more clearly than people who saw them only on their good behavior or when in town.

As he rode through the country toward Painted Rock, he studied it curiously and listened to Johnny Gill's comments. The little Texan had punched cattle in here two seasons and knew the area better than most.

Painted Rock was the usual cow town. A double row of weather-beaten, false-fronted buildings, most of which had never been painted, and a few scattered dwellings, some of logs, most of stone. There was a two-story hotel and a stone building, squat and solid, whose sign identified it as the Painted Rock Bank.

Two buckboards and a spring wagon stood on the street, and a dozen saddle horses stood three-footed at hitching rails. A sign ahead of them and cater-cornered across from the stage station told them that here was the National Saloon.

Gill swung his horse in toward the hitching rail and dropped to the ground. He glanced across his saddle at Caradec.

"The big hombre lookin' us over is the redhead Bo didn't like," he said in a low voice.

Rafe did not look around until he had tied his own horse with a slipknot. Then he hitched his guns into place on his hips. He was wearing two walnut-stocked pistols, purchased in Frisco. He wore jeans, star boots, and a buckskin jacket.

Stepping up on the boardwalk, Rafe glanced at the burly redhead. The man was studying them with frank curiosity.

"Howdy, Gill," he said. "Long time no see."

"Is that bad?" Gill said, and shoved through the doors into the dim, cool interior of the National.

At the bar, Rafe glanced around. Two men stood nearby drinking. Several others were scattered around at tables.

"Red-eye," Gill said, and then in a lower tone, "Bruce Barkow is the big man with the black mustache, wearin' black and playin' poker. The Mexican-lookin' hombre across from him is Dan Shute's gunslingin' *segundo*, Gee Bonaro."

Rafe nodded and lifted his glass. Suddenly, he grinned.

"To Charles Rodney!" he said clearly.

Barkow jerked sharply and looked up, his face a shade paler. Bonaro turned his head slowly, like a lizard watching a fly.

Gill and Rafe both tossed off their drinks, and ignored the stares.

"Man," Gill said, grinning, his eyes dancing, "you don't waste no time, do you?"

Rafe Caradec turned. "By the way, Barkow," he said, "where can I find Mrs. Rodney and her daughter?"

Bruce Barkow put down his cards. "If you've got any business," he said smoothly, "I'll handle it for 'em!"

"Thanks," Rafe said. "My business is personal, and with them."

"Then," Barkow said, his eyes hardening, "you'll have trouble! Mrs. Rodney is dead. Died three months ago."

Rafe's lips tightened. "And her daughter?"

"Ann Rodney," Barkow said carefully, "is here in town. She is to be my wife soon. If you've got any business—"

"I'll transact it with her!" Rafe said sharply.

Turning abruptly, he walked out the door, Gill following. The little cowhand grinned, his leathery face folding into wrinkles that belied his thirty-odd years.

"Like I say, Boss," he chuckled, "you sure throw the hooks into 'em!" He nodded toward a building across the street. "Let's try the Emporium. Rodney used to trade there, and Gene Baker, who runs it, was a friend of his."

The Emporium smelled of leather, dry goods, and all the other varied and exciting smells of a general store. Rafe rounded a bale of jeans and walked back to the long counter backed by shelves holding everything from pepper to rifle shells.

"Where can I find Ann Rodney?" he asked.

The white-haired proprietor gave him a quick glance and then nodded to his right. Rafe turned and found himself looking into the large, soft, dark eyes of a slender, yet beautifully shaped girl in a print dress. Her lips were delicately lovely. Her dark hair was gathered in a loose knot at the nape of her neck. She was so lovely that it left him a little breathless.

She smiled, and her eyes were questioning. "I'm Ann Rodney," she said. "What is it you want?"

"My name is Rafe Caradec," he said gently. "Your father sent me."

Her face went white to the lips and she stepped back suddenly, dropping one hand to the counter as though for support.

"You come—from my *father*? Why, I—"

Bruce Barkow, who had apparently followed them from the saloon, stepped in front of Rafe, his face flushed with anger.

"You've scared her to death?" he snapped. "What do you mean, comin' in here with such a story? Charles Rodney has been dead for almost a year!"

Rafe's eyes measured Barkow, his thoughts racing. "He has? How did he die?"

"He was killed," Barkow said, "for the money he was carryin', it looked like. Barkow's eyes suddenly turned triumphant. "Did you kill him?"

Rafe was suddenly aware that Johnny Gill was staring at him, his brows drawn together, puzzled and wondering. Gill, he realized, knew him but slightly and might easily become suspicious of his motives.

Gene Baker also was studying him coldly, his eyes alive with suspicion. Ann Rodney stared at him, as if stunned by what he had said and somehow uncertain.

"No," Rafe said coolly, "I didn't kill him, but I'd be plumb interested to know what made you believe he was dead."

"Believe he was dead?" Barkow laughed harshly. "I was with him when he died! We found him beside the trail, shot through the body by bandits. I brought back his belongings to Miss Rodney."

"Miss Rodney," Rafe began, "if I could talk to you a few minutes—"

"No!" she whispered. "I don't want to talk to you! What can you be thinking of? Coming to me with such a story? What is it you want from me?"

"Somehow," Rafe said quietly, "you've got hold of some false information. Your father has been dead for no more than two months."

"Get out of here!" Barkow ordered, his hand on his gun. "You're torturin' that poor young lady! Get out, I say! I don't know what scheme you've cooked up, but it won't work! If you know what's good for you, you'll leave this town while the goin' is good!"

Ann Rodney turned sharply around and ran from the store, heading for the storekeeper's living quarters.

"You'd better get out, mister," Gene Baker said harshly. "We know how Rodney died. You can't work no under-

handed schemes on that young lady. Her pa died, and he
talked before he died. Three men heard him."

Rafe Caradec turned and walked outside, standing on
the boardwalk, frowning at the skyline. He was aware that
Gill had moved up beside him.

"Boss," Gill said, "I ain't no lily, but neither am I takin'
part in no deal to skin a young lady out of what is hers by
rights. You'd better throw a leg over your saddle and get!"

"Don't jump to conclusions, Gill," Rafe advised, "and
before you make any change in your plans, suppose you talk to
Tex about this? He was with me, an' he knows all about Rodney's death as well as I do. If they brought any belongin's of his
back here, there's somethin' more to this than we believed."

Gill kicked his boot toe against a loose board. "Tex was
with you? Durn it, man! What of that yarn of theirs? It don't
make sense!"

"That's right," Caradec replied, "it don't, and before it
will we've got to do some diggin'. Johnny," he added, "suppose I told you that Barkow back there held a mortgage on
the Rodney ranch, and Rodney went to Frisco, got the money,
and paid it in Frisco—then never got home?"

Gill stared at Rafe, his mouth tightening. "Then nobody
here would know he ever paid that mortgage but Barkow?
The man he paid it to?"

"That's right."

"Then I'd say this Barkow was a sneakin' polecat!" Gill
said harshly. "Let's brace him!"

"Not yet, Johnny. Not yet!"

A horrible thought had occurred to him. He had antici-
pated no such trouble, yet if he explained the circumstances
of Rodney's death and was compelled to prove them, he would
be arrested for mutiny on the high seas—a hanging offense!

Not only his own life depended on silence, but the
lives of Brisco, Penn, and Mullaney.

Yet there must be a way out. There had to be.

Chapter IV
A Gunman Backs Down

As Rafe Caradec stood there in the bright sunlight he began
to understand a lot of things, and wonder about them. If

some of the possessions of Charles Rodney had been returned to Painted Rock, it implied that those who had returned them knew something of the shanghaiing of Rodney.

How else could they have come by his belongings?

Bully Borger had shanghaied his own crew with the connivance of Hongkong Bohl. Had he taken Rodney by suggestion? Had the man been marked for him? Certainly, it would not be the first time somebody had got rid of a man in such a manner. If that were the true story, it would account for some of Borger's animosity when he had beaten Rodney.

No doubt they had all been part of a plan to make sure that Charles Rodney never returned to San Francisco alive, or to Painted Rock. Yet believing such a thing and proving it were two vastly different things. Also, it presented a problem of motive. Land was not scarce in the West, and much of it could be had for the taking. Why, then, people would ask, would Barkow go to such efforts to get one piece of land?

Rafe had Barkow's signature on the receipt, but that could be claimed to be a forgery. First, a motive beyond the mere value of two thousand acres of land and the money paid on the debt must be established. That might be all, and certainly men had been killed for less, but Bruce Barkow was no fool. Nor was he a man who played for small stakes.

Rafe Caradec lighted a cigarette and stared down the street. He must face another fact. Barkow was warned. Whatever he was gambling for, including the girl, was in danger now and would remain in peril as long as Rafe Caradec remained alive and in the country. That fact stood out cold and clear. Barkow knew by now that he must kill Rafe Caradec.

Rafe understood the situation perfectly. His life had been lived among men who played ruthlessly for the highest stakes. It was no shock to him that men would stoop to killing, or a dozen killings, if they could gain a desired end. From now on he must ride with cat eyes, always aware, and always ready.

Sending Gill to find and buy two packhorses, Rafe turned on his heel and went into the store. Barkow was gone, and Ann Rodney was still out of sight.

Baker looked up, and his eyes held no welcome.

"If you've got any business here," he said, "state it and get out. Charles Rodney was a friend of mine."

"He needed some smarter friends," Rafe replied shortly. "I came here to buy supplies, but if you want to, start askin' yourself some questions. Who profits by Rodney's death? What evidence have you got besides a few of his belongin's, which might have been stolen, that he was killed a year ago? How reliable were the three men who were with him? If he went to San Francisco for the money, what were Barkow and the others doin' on the trail?"

"That's neither here nor there," Baker said roughly. "What do you want? I'll refuse no man food."

Coolly, Caradec ordered what he wanted, aware that Baker was studying him. The man seemed puzzled.

"Where you livin'?" Baker asked suddenly. Some of the animosity seemed to have gone from his voice.

"At the Rodney cabin on the Crazy Man," Caradec said. "I'm stayin', too, till I get the straight of this. If Ann Rodney is wise she won't get married or get rid of any rights to her property till this is cleared up."

"Shute won't let you stay there."

"I'll stay." Rafe gathered up the boxes of shells and stowed them in his pockets. "I'll be right there. While you're askin' yourself questions, ask why Barkow, who holds a mortgage that he claims is unpaid on the Rodney place, lets Dan Shute take over?"

"He didn't want trouble because of Ann," Baker said defensively. "He was right nice about it. He wouldn't foreclose. Givin' her a chance to pay up."

"As long as he's goin' to marry her, why should he foreclose?" Rafe turned away from the counter. "If Ann Rodney wants to see me, I'll tell her all about it, anytime. I promised her father I'd take care of her, and I will, whether she likes it or not! Also," he added, "any man who says he talked to Rodney as he was dyin' *lies!*"

The door closed at the front of the store, and Rafe Caradec turned to see the dark, Mexican-looking gunman Gill had indicated in the National Saloon—the man known as Gee Bonaro.

Bonaro came toward him, smiling and showing even white teeth under a thread of mustache.

"Would you repeat that to me, Señor?" he asked pleasantly, a thumb hooked in his belt.

"Why not?" Rafe said sharply. He let his eyes, their contempt unveiled, go over the man slowly from head to foot and then back. "If you was one of 'em that said that, you're a liar! And if you touch that gun I'll kill you!"

Gee Bonaro's spread fingers hovered over the gun butt, and he stood flat-footed, an uncomfortable realization breaking over him. This big stranger was not frightened. In the green eyes was a coldness that turned Bonaro a little sick inside. He was uncomfortably aware that he stood, perilously, on the brink of death.

"Was you one of 'em?" Rafe demanded.

"*Si, Señor*," Bonaro's tongue touched his lips.

"Where was this supposed to be?"

"Where he died, near Pilot Peak, on the trail."

"You're a white-livered liar, Bonaro. Rodney never got back to Pilot Peak. You're bein' trapped for somebody else's gain, and if I was you I'd back up and look the trail over again." Rafe's eyes held the man. "You say you saw him. How was he dressed?"

"Dressed?" Bonaro was startled and confused. Nobody had asked such a thing. He had no idea what to say. Suppose the same question was answered in a different way by one of the others? He wavered and was lost. "I—I don't know. I—"

He looked from Baker to Caradec and took a step back, his tongue at his lips, his eyes like those of a trapped animal. He was confused. The big man facing him somehow robbed him of his sureness, his poise. And he had come here to kill him.

"Rodney talked to me only a few weeks ago, Bonaro," Rafe said coldly. "Think! How many others did he talk to? You're bein' mixed up in a cold-blooded killin', Bonaro! Now turn around and get out! And get out fast!"

Bonaro backed up, and Rafe took a forward step. Wheeling, the man scrambled for the door.

Rafe turned and glanced at Baker. "Think that over," he said coolly. "You'll take the word of a coyote like that about an honset man! Somebody's tryin' to rob Miss Rodney, and because you're believin' that cock-and-bull story you're helpin' it along."

Gene Baker stood stock-still, his hands still flat on the counter. What he had seen, he would not have believed. Gee Bonaro had slain two men since coming to Painted Rock, and here a stranger had backed him down without lifting a hand or moving toward a gun. Baker rubbed his ear thoughtfully.

Johnny Gill met Rafe in front of the store with two packhorses. A glance told Caradec that the little cowhand had bought well. Gill glanced questioningly at Rafe.

"Did I miss somethin'? I seen that gunhand *segundo* of Shute's coming out of that store like he was chased by the devil. You and him have a run-in?"

"I called him and he backed down," Rafe told Gill. "He said he was one of the three who heard Rodney's last words. I told him he was a liar."

Johnny drew the rope tighter. He glanced out of the corner of his eye at Rafe. This man had come into town and put himself on record for what he was and what he planned faster than anybody he had ever seen.

"Shucks," Johnny said, grinning at the horse, "why go back to Texas? There'll be ruckus enough here, ridin' for that hombre!"

The town of Painted Rock numbered exactly eighty-nine inhabitants, and by sundown the arrival of Rafe Caradec and his challenge to Gee Bonaro was the talk of all of them. It was a behind-the-hand talking, but the story was going the rounds, as was the story that Charles Rodney was alive—or had been alive until recently.

By nightfall Dan Shute heard that Caradec had moved into the Rodney house on Crazy Man, and an hour later he stormed furiously into his bunkhouse and given Bonaro a tongue-lashing that turned the gunman livid with anger.

Bruce Barkow was worried, and he made no pretense of not being so in his conference with Shute. The only hopeful note was that Caradec had said that Rodney was dead.

Gene Baker, sitting in his easy chair in his living quarters behind the store, was uneasy. He was aware that his silence was worrying his wife. He was also aware that Ann was silent herself, an unusual thing, for the girl was usually gay and full of fun and laughter.

The idea that there could have been anything wrong about the story told by Barkow, and Bonaro had never entered the storekeeper's head. He had accepted the story as others had, for many men had been killed along the trails or had died in fights with Indians. It was another tragedy of the westward march, and he had done what he could—he and his wife had taken Ann Rodney into their home and loved her as their own child.

Now this stranger had come with his questions. Despite Baker's irritation that the matter had come up at all, and despite his outward denials of truth in what Caradec had said, he was aware of an inner doubt that gnawed at the walls of his confidence in Bruce Barkow.

Whatever else he might be, Gene Baker was a fair man. He was forced to admit that Bonaro was not a man in whom reliance could be placed. He was a known gunman and a suspected outlaw. That Shute had hired him was bad enough in itself, yet when he thought of Shute, Baker was again uneasy. The twin ranches of Barkow and Shute surrounded the town on three sides. Their purchases represented no less than fifty percent of the storekeeper's business, and that did not include what the hands bought on their own.

The drinking of the hands from the ranches supported the National Saloon, too, and Gene Baker, who for all his willingness to live and let live was a good citizen, or believed himself to be, found himself examining a situation he did not like. It was not a new situation in Painted Rock, and he had been unconsciously aware of it for some time, yet while aware of it he had tacitly accepted it. Now there seemed to be a larger rat in the woodpile, or several of them.

As Baker smoked his pipe, he found himself realizing with some discomfort and growing doubt that Painted Rock was completely subservient to Barkow and Shute. Pod Gomer, who was town marshal, had been nominated for the job by Barkow at the council meeting. Joe Benson of the National had seconded the motion, and Dan Shute had calmly suggested that the nomination be closed, and Gomer was voted in.

Gene Baker had never liked Gomer, but the man was a good gunhand and certainly unafraid. Baker had voted with the others, as had Pat Higley, another responsible citizen of the town.

In the same manner, Benson had been elected mayor of the town, and Roy Gargan had been made judge.

Remembering that the town was actually in the hands of Barkow and Shute, Baker also recalled that at first the tactics of the two big ranchers had caused grumbling among the smaller holders of land. Nothing had ever been done, largely because one of them, Stu Martin, who talked the loudest, had been killed in a fall from a cliff. A few weeks later another small rancher, Al Chase, had mistakenly tried to draw against Bonaro and had died.

Looked at in that light, the situation made Baker uneasy. Little things began to occur to him that had remained unconsidered, and he began to wonder just what could be done about it even if he knew for sure the way Rodney had been killed. Not only was he dependent on Shute and Barkow for business, but Benson, their partner and friend, owned the freight line that brought in his supplies.

Law was still largely a local matter. The Army maintained a fort not too far away, but the soldiers were busy keeping an eye on the Sioux and their allies, who were becoming increasingly restive, what with the booming gold camps at Bannack and Alder Gulch, Custer's invasion of the Black Hills, and the steady roll of wagon trains over the Bozeman and Laramie trails.

If there was trouble here, Baker realized with a sudden sickening fear, it would be settled locally. And that meant it would be settled by Dan Shute and Bruce Barkow.

Yet even as he thought of that, Baker recalled the tall man in the black, flat-crowned hat and buckskin jacket. There was something about Rafe Caradec that was convincing, something that made a man doubt he would be controlled by anybody or anything, anytime or anywhere.

Chapter V
Wounded Squaw

Rafe rode silently alongside Johnny Gill when they moved out of Painted Rock, trailing the two packhorses. The trail turned west by south and crossed the north fork of Clear Creek. They turned then along a narrow path that skirted the huge boulders fringing the mountains.

Gill turned his head slightly. "Might not be a bad idea to take to the hills, Boss," he said carelessly. "There's a trail up thataway—ain't much used, either."

Caradec glanced quickly at the little puncher and then nodded. "All right," he said. "Lead off, if you want."

Johnny was riding with his rifle across his saddle, and his eyes were alert. That, Rafe decided, was not a bad idea. He jerked his head back toward Painted Rock.

"What you think Barkow will do?"

Gill shrugged. "No tellin', but Dan Shute will know what to do. He'll be gunnin' for you if you've sure enough got the straight of this. What you figger happened?"

Rafe hesitated, and then he said carefully, "What happened to Charles Rodney wasn't any accident. It was planned and carried out mighty smooth." He waited while the horse took a half dozen steps and then looked up suddenly. "Gill, you size up like a man to ride the river with. Here's the story, and if you ever tell it, you'll hang four good men."

Briefly and concisely, he outlined the shanghaiing of Rodney and himself, the events aboard ship, and the escape.

"See?" he added. "It must have looked foolproof to them. Rodney goes away to sea and never comes back. Nobody but Barkow knows that mortgage was paid, and what did happen was somethin' they couldn't plan for and probably didn't even think about."

Gil nodded. "Rodney must have been tougher than anybody figgered," he said admiringly. "He never quit tryin', you say?"

"Right. He had only one idea, it looked like, and that was to live to get home to his wife and daughter. If," Rafe added, "the wife was anything like the daughter, I don't blame him!"

The cowhand chuckled. "Yeah, I know what you mean. She's pretty as a baby in a red hat."

"You know, Gill," Rafe said speculatively, "there's one thing that bothers me. Why do they want that ranch so bad?"

"That's got me wonderin', too," Gill agreed. "It's a good ranch, mostly, except for that land at the mouth of the valley. Rises there to a sort of a dome, and the Crazy Man swings around it. Nothin' much grows there. The rest of it's a good ranch."

"Say anything about Tex or Bo?" Caradec asked.

"No," Gill said. "It figgers like war, now. No use lettin' the enemy know what you're holdin'."

The trail they followed left the grasslands of the creek bottom and turned back up into the hills to a long plateau. They rode on among the tall pines, scattered here and there with birch and aspen along the slopes.

A cool breeze stirred among the pines, and the horses walked along slowly, taking their time, their hoofbeats soundless on the cushion of pine needles. Once the trail wound down the steep side of a shadowy canyon, weaving back and forth, finally reaching bottom in a brawling, swift-running stream. Willows skirted the banks, and while the horses were drinking, Rafe saw a trout leap in a pool above the rapids. A brown thrasher swept a darting red-brown arrow past his head, and he could hear yellow warblers gossiping among the willows.

He himself was drinking when he saw the sand crumble from a spot on the bank and fall with a tiny splash into the creek.

Carefully, he got to his feet. His rifle was in his saddle boot, but his pistols were good enough for anything he could see in this narrow place. He glanced casually at Gill, and the cowhand was tightening his cinch, all unaware.

Caradec drew a long breath and hitched up his trousers. Then he hooked his thumbs in his belt near the gun butts. He had no idea who was there, but that sand had not fallen without a reason. In his own mind he was sure that someone was standing in the willow thicket across and downstream, above where the sand had fallen.

Someone was watching them.

"Ready?" Johnny suggested, looking at him curiously.

"Almost," Rafe drawled casually. "Sort of like this little place. It's cool and pleasant. Sort of place a man might like to rest a while, and where a body could watch his back trail, too." He was talking at random, hoping Gill would catch on. The puncher was looking at him intently, now. "At least," Rafe added, "it would be nice here if a man *was* alone. He could think better."

It was then his eye caught the color in the willows. It was a tiny corner of red, a bright, flaming crimson, and it lay where no such color should be.

That was not likely to be a cowhand, unless he was a Mexican or a dude, and they were scarce in this country. It could be an Indian.

If whoever it was had planned to fire, a good chance had been missed while he and Gill drank. Two well-placed shots would have done for them both. Therefore it was logical to discount the person in the willows as an enemy. Or if so, it was a patient enemy.

To all appearances, whoever lay in the willows preferred to remain unseen. It had all the earmarks of being someone or something trying to avoid trouble.

Gill was quiet and puzzled. Catlike, he watched Rafe for some sign to indicate what the trouble was. A quick scanning of the brush had revealed nothing, but Caradec was not a man to be spooked by a shadow.

"You speak Sioux?" Rafe asked casually.

Gill's mouth tightened. "A mite. Not so good, maybe."

"Speak loud and say we are friends."

Johnny Gill's eyes were wary as he spoke. There was no sound, no reply.

"Try it again," Rafe suggested. "Tell him we want to talk. Tell him we want to talk to Red Cloud, the great chief."

Gill complied, and there was still no sound. Rafe looked up at him.

"I'm goin' to go over into those willows," he said softly. "Something's wrong."

"You watch yourself!" Gill warned. "The Sioux are plenty smart."

Moving slowly, so as to excite no hostility, Rafe Caradec walked his horse across the stream and then swung down. There was neither sound nor movement from the willows. He walked back among the slender trees, glancing around. Yet even then, close as he was, he might not have seen her had it not been for the red stripes. Her clothing blended perfectly with the willows and flowers along the stream bank.

She was a young squaw, slender and dark, with large intelligent eyes. One look told Rafe that she was frightened speechless, and knowing what had happened to squaws found by some of the white men, he could understand.

Her legs were outstretched, and from the marks on the grass and the bank of the stream, he could see she had been dragging herself. The reason was plain to see. One leg was broken just below the knee.

"Johnny," he said, not too loud, "here's a young squaw. She's got a busted leg."

"Better get away quick!" Gill advised. "The Sioux are plenty mean where squaws are concerned."

"Not till I set that leg," Rafe said.

"Boss," Gill advised worriedly, "don't do it. She's liable to yell like blazes if you lay a hand on her. Our lives won't be worth a nickel. We've got troubles enough without askin' for more."

Rafe walked a step nearer and smiled at the girl. "I want to fix your leg," he said gently, motioning to it. "Don't be afraid."

She said nothing, staring at him as he walked up and knelt down. She drew back from his touch, and he saw then she had a knife. He smiled and touched the break with gentle fingers.

"Better cut some splints, Gill," he said. "She's got a bad break. Just a little jolt and it might pop right through the skin."

Working carefully, he set the leg. There was no sound from the girl, no sign of pain. Gill shook his head wonderingly.

"Nervy, ain't she?" Rafe suggested.

Taking the splints Gill had cut, he bound them on her leg.

"Better take the pack off that paint and split it between the two of us and the other horse," he said. "We'll put her up on the horse."

When they had her on the paint's back, Gill asked her, in Sioux:

"How far to Indian camp?"

She looked at him and then at Rafe. Then she spoke quickly to him.

Gill grinned. "She says she talks to the chief. That means you. Her camp is about an hour south and west; in the hills."

"Tell her we'll take her most of the way."

Rafe swung into the saddle, and they turned their horses back into the trail. Rafe rode ahead, the squaw and the packhorse following and Johnny Gill, rifle still across the saddle bows, bringing up the rear.

They had gone no more than a mile when they heard voices. Then three riders swung around a bend in the trail, reining in sharply. Tough-looking, bearded men, they stared from Rafe to the Indian girl. She gasped suddenly, and Rafe's eyes narrowed a little.

"See you got our pigeon!" A red-bearded man rode toward them, grinning. "We been a-chasin' her for a couple of hours. Pretty thing, ain't she?"

"Yeah." A slim, wiry man with a hatchet face and a cigarette dangling from his lips was speaking. "Glad you found her. We'll take her off your hands now."

"That's all right," Rafe said quietly. "We're taking her back to her village. She's got a broken leg."

"Takin' her back to the village?" Red exclaimed. "Why, we cut that squaw out for ourselves and we're slappin' our own brand on her. You get your own squaws." He nodded toward the hatchet-faced man. "Get that lead rope, Boyne."

"Keep your hands off that rope!" Rafe's voice was cold.

"You blasted fools will get us all killed! This girl's tribe would be down on your ears before night!"

"We'll take care of that!" Red persisted. "Get her, Boyne!"

Rafe smiled suddenly. "If you boys are lookin' for trouble, I reckon you've found it. I don't know how many of you want to die for this squaw, but any time you figger to take her away from us, some of you'd better start sizin' up grave space."

Boyne's eyes narrowed wickedly. "Why, he's askin' for a ruckus, Red! Which eye shall I shoot him through?"

Rafe Caradec sat his horse calmly, smiling a little. "I reckon," he said, "you boys ain't any too battle wise. You're bunched too much. Now, from where I sit, all three of you are dead in range and grouped nice for even one gun shootin', an' I'm figurin' to use two." He spoke to Gill. "Johnny," he said quietly, "suppose these hombres start smokin' it, you take that fat one. Leave the redhead and this Boyne for me."

The fat cowhand shifted in his saddle uncomfortably. He was unpleasantly aware that he had turned his horse so he was sideward to Gill, and while presenting a fair target himself, would have to turn half around in the saddle to fire.

Boyne's eyes were hard and reckless. Rafe knew he was the one to watch. He wore his gun slung low, and that he fancied himself as a gunhand was obvious. Suddenly Rafe knew the man was going to draw.

"Hold it!" The voice cut sharply across the air like the crack of a whip. "Boyne, keep your hand shoulder high! You, too, Red! Now turn your horses with your knees and start down the trail. If one of you even looks like you wanted to use a gun, I'll open up with this Henry and cut you into little pieces."

Boyne cursed wickedly. "You're gettin' out of it easy this time!" he said viciously. "I'll see you again!"

Rafe smiled. "Why, sure, Boyne! Only next time you'd better take the rawhide lashin' off the butt of your Colt. Mighty handy when ridin' over rough country, but mighty unhandy when you need your gun in a hurry!"

Chapter VI
Horse Trade

With a startled gasp, Boyne glanced down. The rawhide thong was tied over his gun to hold it in place. His face two shades whiter than a snake's belly, he turned his horse with his knees and started the trek down trail.

Bo Marsh stepped out of the brush with his rifle in his hands. He was grinning.

"Hey, Boss! If I'd known that six-gun was tied down, I'd have let you mow him down! That skunk needs it. That's Lem Boyne. He's a gunslinger for Dan Shute."

Gill laughed. "Man! Will our ears burn tonight! Rafe's run two of Shute's boys into the ground today!"

Marsh grinned. "Figgered you'd be headed home soon, and I was out after a deer." He glanced at the squaw with the broken leg. "Got more trouble?"

"No," Rafe said. "Those hombres had been runnin' this girl down. She busted her leg gettin' away, so we fixed it up. Let's ride."

The trail was smoother now and drifted casually from one canyon to another. Obviously it had been a game trail that had been found and used by Indians, trappers, and wandering buffalo hunters before the coming of the cowhands and trail drivers.

When they were still several miles from the cabin on the Crazy Man, the squaw spoke suddenly. Gill looked over at Rafe.

"Her camp's just over that rise in a draw," he said.

Caradec nodded. Then he turned to the girl. She was looking at him, expecting him to speak.

"Tell her," he said, "that we share the land Rodney bought from Red Cloud. That we share it with the daughter of Rodney. Get her to tell Red Cloud we will live on the Crazy Man, and we are a friend to the Sioux, that their women are safe with us, that their horses will not be stolen, and that we are a friend to the warriors of Red Cloud and the great chiefs of the Sioux people."

Gill spoke slowly, emphatically, and the girl nodded. Then she turned her horse and rode up through the trees.

"Boss," Johnny said, "she's got our best horse. That's the one I give the most money for!"

Rafe grinned. "Forget it. The girl was scared silly but wouldn't show it for anything. It's a cheap price to pay to get her home safe. Like I said, the Sioux make better friends than enemies."

When the three men rode up, Tex Brisco was carrying two buckets of water to the house. He grinned at them.

"That grub looks good!" he told them. "I've eaten so much antelope meat, the next thing you know I'll be boundin' along over the prairie myself!"

While Marsh got busy with the grub, Johnny told Tex about the events of the trip.

"Nobody been around here," Brisco said. "Yesterday I seen three Injuns, but they was off a couple of miles and didn't come this way. Today there hasn't been nobody around."

During the three days that followed the trip to Painted Rock, Rafe Caradec scouted the range. There were a lot of Bar M cattle around, and most of them were in fairly good shape. His own cattle were mingling freely with them. The range would support many more head than it carried, however, and toward the upper end of Long Valley was almost untouched. There was much good grass in the mountain meadows, also, and in several canyons south of the Crazy Man.

Johnny Gill and Bo Marsh explained the lay of the land as they knew it.

"North of here," Gill said, "back of Painted Rock, and mostly west of there, the mountains rise up nigh onto nine thousand feet. Good huntin' country, some of the best I ever seen. South, toward the end of the valley, the mountains thin out. There's a pass through to the head of Otter Creek, and that country west of the mountains is good grazin' land and nobody much in there yet. Injuns got a big powwow grounds over there.

"Still further south, there's a long red wall, runnin' pretty much north and south. Only one entrance in thirty-five miles. Regular hole in the wall. A few men could get into that hole and stand off an army, and if they wanted to hightail it, they could lose themselves in that back country."

Rafe scouted the crossing toward the head of Otter Creek and rode down the creek to the grasslands below. This would be good grazing land, and mentally he made a note to make some plans for it.

He rode back to the ranch that night, and when he was sitting on the stoop after the sun was down, he looked around at Tex Brisco. "You been over the trail from Texas?" he asked.

"Uh-huh."

"Once aboard ship you was tellin' me about a stampede

you had. Only got back about sixteen hundred head of a two-thousand-head herd. That sort of thing happen often?"

Tex laughed. "Shucks, yes! Stampedes are regular things along the trail. You lose some cattle, you maybe get more back, but there's plenty of maverick stock runnin' on the plains south of the Platte—all the way to the Canadian, as far as that goes."

"Reckon a few men could slip over there and round up some of that stock?"

Brisco sat up and glanced at Rafe. "Sure could. Wild stuff, though, and it would be a man-sized job."

"Maybe," Caradec suggested, "we'll try and do it. It would be one way of gettin' a herd pretty fast, or turnin' some quick money."

They were days of hard, driving labor. Always, one man stayed at the cabin keeping a sharp lookout for any of the Shute or Barkow riders. Caradec knew they would come, and when they did come they would be riding with only one idea in mind—to get rid of him.

In the visit to Painted Rock he had laid his cards on the table, and they had no idea how much he knew or what his story of Charles Rodney could be. Rafe Caradec knew Barkow was worried, and that pleased him. Yet while the delayed attack was a worry, it was also a help.

There was some grumbling from the hands, but he kept them busy cutting hay in the meadows and stacking it. Winter in this country was going to be bad—he needed no weather prophet to tell him that—and he had no intention of losing a lot of stock.

In a canyon that branched off from the head of Crazy Man, he had found a warm spring. There was small chance of it freezing, yet the water was not too hot to drink. In severe cold it would freeze, but otherwise it would offer an excellent watering place for his stock. They made no effort to bring hay back to the ranch, but stacked it in huge stacks back in the canyons and meadows.

There had been no sign of Indians, and Rafe avoided their camp. Yet once when he did pass nearby, there was no sign of them. It seemed as if they had moved out and left the country.

Then one night he heard a noise at the corral and the snorting of a horse. Instantly he was out of bed and had his boots on when he heard Brisco swearing in the next room.

They got outside in a hurry, fearing someone was rustling their stock. In the corral they could see the horses, and there was no one nearby.

Bo Marsh had walked over to the corral, and suddenly he called out.

"Boss! Lookit here!"

They all trooped over and then stopped. Instead of five horses in the corral, there were ten!

One of them was the paint they had loaned the young squaw, but the others were strange horses, and every one a picked animal.

"Well, I'll be durned!" Gill exploded. "Brung back our own horse and an extra for each of us. Reckon that big black is for you, Boss."

By daylight, when they could examine the horses, Tex Brisco walked around them admiringly.

"Man," he said, "that was the best horse trade I ever heard of! There's four of the prettiest horses I ever laid an eye on! I always did say the Sioux knowed horseflesh, and this proves it. Reckon your bread cast on the water sure come back to you, Boss!"

Rafe studied the valley thoughtfully. They would have another month of good haying weather if there was no rain. Four men could not work much harder than they were, but the beaver were building their houses bigger and in deeper water, and from that and all other indications the winter was going to be hard.

He made his decision suddenly. "I'm ridin' to Painted Rock. Want to come along Tex?"

"Yeah." The Texan looked at him calculatingly. "Yeah, I'd like that."

"How about me?" Bo asked, grinning. "Johnny went last time. I could sure use a belt of that red-eye the National peddles, and maybe a look around town."

"Take him along, Boss," Johnny said. "I can hold this end. If he stays he'll be ridin' me all the time, anyway."

"All right. Saddle up first thing in the mornin'."

"Boss—" Johnny threw one leg over the other and lighted his smoke. "One thing I better tell you. I hadn't said a word before, but two, three days ago when I was down to the bend of the Crazy Man I run into a couple of fellers. One of 'em was Red Blazer, that big galoot who was with Boyne. Remember?"

* * *

Rafe turned around and looked down at the little leather-faced cowhand.

"Well," he said, "what about him?"

Gill took a long drag on his cigarette. "He told me he was carryin' a message from Trigger Boyne and that Trigger was goin' to shoot on sight, next time you showed up in Painted Rock."

Rafe reached over on the table and picked up a piece of cold cornbread.

"Then I reckon that's what he'll do," he said. "If he gets into action fast enough."

"Boss," Marsh pleaded, "if that redheaded Tom Blazer, brother to the one you had the run-in with—if he's there, I want him."

"That the one we saw on the National stoop?" Rafe asked Gill.

"Uh-huh. There's five of them brothers. All gun toters."

Gill got up and stretched. "Well, I'll have it pretty lazy while you hombres are down there dustin' lead." He added, "It would be a good idea to sort of keep an eye out. Gee Bonaro's still in town and feelin' mighty mad."

Rafe walked outside, strolling toward the corral. Behind him, Marsh turned to Gill.

"Reckon he can sling a gun?"

Tex chuckled. "Mister, that hombre killed one of the fastest, slickest gun throwers that ever came out of Texas, and done it when he was no more than sixteen, down on the C Bar. And also, while I've never seen him shoot, if he can shoot like he can fistfight, Mr. Trigger Boyne had better grab hisself an armful of horseflesh and start makin' tracks for the blackest part of the Black Hills—*fast*!"

Chapter VII
Challenge Accepted

Nothing about the town of Painted Rock suggested drama or excitement. It lay sprawled comfortably in the morning sunlight in an elbow of Rock Creek. A normally roaring and plunging stream, the creek had decided here to loiter a while, enjoying the warm sun and the graceful willows that lined the banks.

Behind and among the willows the white, slender trunks of the birch trees marched in neat ranks, each tree so like its neighbor that it was almost impossible to distinguish between them. Clumps of mountain alder, yellow rose, puffed clematis, and antelope bush were scattered along the far bank of the stream and advanced up the hill beyond in skirmishing formation.

In a few weeks now the aspen leaves would be changing, and Painted Rock would take on a background of flaming color—a bank of trees, rising toward the darker growth of spruce and fir along the higher mountainside.

Painted Rock's one street was the only thing about the town that was ordered. It lay between two neat rows of buildings that stared at each other across a long lane of dust and, during the rainy periods, of mud.

At any time of day or night a dozen saddle horses would be standing three-legged at the hitching rails, usually in front of Joe Benson's National Saloon. A buckboard or a spring wagon would also be present, usually driven by some small rancher in for his supplies. The two big outfits sent two wagons together, drawn by mules.

Bruce Barkow sat in front of the sheriff's office this morning, deep in conversation with Pod Gomer. It was a conversation that had begun over an hour before.

Gomer was a short, thickset man, almost as deep from chest to spine as from shoulder to shoulder. He was not fat and was considered a tough man to tangle with. He was also a man who liked to play on the winning side, and long ago he had decided there was only one side to consider in this fight—the side of Dan Shute and Bruce Barkow.

Yet he was a man who was sensitive to the way the wind blew, and he frequently found himself puzzled when he considered his two bosses. There was no good feeling between them. They met on business and pleasure and saw things through much the same eyes, but each wanted to be kingpin. Sooner or later, Gomer knew, he must make a choice between them.

Barkow was shrewd, cunning. He was a planner and a conniver. He was a man who would use any method to win, but in most cases he kept himself in the background of

anything smacking of crime or wrongdoing. Otherwise, he
was much in the foreground.

Dan Shute was another type of man. He was tall and
broad of shoulder. Normally he was sullen, hard-eyed, and
surly. He had little to say to anyone and was more inclined to
settle matters with a blow or a gun than with words. He was
utterly cold-blooded, felt slightly about anything, and would
kill a man as quickly and with as little excitement as he would
brand a calf.

Barkow might carve a notch on his gun butt. Shute
wouldn't even understand such a thing.

Shute was a man who seemed to be without vanity, and
such men are dangerous. For the vanity is there, only sub-
merged, and slow-burning, deep fires of hatred smolder within
them until suddenly they burst into flame and end in sudden,
dramatic, and ugly violence.

Pod Gomer understood little of Dan Shute. He understood the man's complex character just enough to know that
he was dangerous, that as long as Shute rode along, Barkow
would be top dog, but that if ever Barkow incurred Shute's
resentment, the deep-seated fury of the gunman would brush
his partner aside as he would swat a fly. In a sense, both men
were using each other, but of the two, Dan Shute was the
man to be reckoned with.

Yet Gomer had seen Barkow at work. He had seen how
deviously the big rancher planned, how carefully he made
friends. At the fort, they knew and liked him, and what little
law there was outside the town of Painted Rock was in the
hands of the commanding officer at the fort. Knowing this,
Bruce Barkow had made it a point to know the personnel
there, and to plan accordingly. . . .

The big black that Rafe was riding was a powerful horse,
and he let the animal have its head. Behind him in single file
trailed Tex Brisco and Bo Marsh.

Rafe Caradec was thinking as he rode. He had seen too
much of violence and struggle to fail to understand men who
lived along the frontier. He had correctly gauged the kind of
courage Gee Bonaro possessed, yet he knew the man was
dangerous and if the opportunity offered would shoot instantly.

Trigger Boyne was another proposition. Boyne was reckless, wickedly fast with a gun, and the type of man who
would fight at the drop of a hat, and had his own ready to

drop on the slightest pretext. Boyne liked the name of being a gunman, and he liked being top dog. If Boyne had sent a warning to Caradec it would be only because he intended to back up that warning.

Rafe took the black along the mountain trail, riding swiftly. The big horse was the finest he had ever had between his knees. When a Sioux gave gifts, he apparently went all the way. A gift had been sent to each of the men on the Crazy Man, which was evidence that the Sioux had looked them over at home.

The black had a long, space-eating stride that seemed to put no strain on his endurance. The horses given to the others were almost as good. There were not four men in the mountains mounted as well, Rafe knew.

He rounded the big horse into the dusty street of Painted Rock and rode down toward the hitching rail at a spanking trot. He pulled up and swung down, and the other men swung down alongside him.

"Just keep your eyes open," Rafe said guardedly. "I don't want trouble. But if Boyne starts anything, he's my meat."

Marsh nodded and walked up on the boardwalk alongside of Brisco, who was sweeping the street with quick, observant eyes.

"Have a drink?" Rafe suggested, and led the way inside the National.

Joe Benson was behind the bar. He looked up warily as the three men entered. He spoke to Bo and then glanced at Tex Brisco. He placed Tex as a stranger, and his mind leaped ahead. It took no long study to see that Tex was a hard character and a fighting man.

Joe was cautious and shrewd. Unless he was mistaken, Barkow and Shute had their work cut out for them. These men didn't look like the sort to back water for anything or anyone. The town's saloonkeeper-mayor had an uncomfortable feeling that a change was in the offing, yet he pushed the feeling aside with irritation.

That must not happen. His own future and his own interests were too closely allied to those of Barkow and Shute.

Of course, when Barkow married the Rodney girl, that would give them complete title to the ranch. That would leave them in the clear, and these men, if alive, could be run off the ranch with every claim to legal process.

Caradec tossed off his whiskey and looked up sharply. His glance pinned Joe Benson to the spot.

"Trigger Boyne sent word he was looking for me," he said abruptly. "Tell him I'm in town—ready!"

"How should I know Trigger better than any other man who comes into this bar?" Benson demanded.

"You know him. Tell him."

Rafe hitched his guns into a comfortable position and strode through the swinging doors. There were a dozen men in sight, but none of them resembled Boyne or either of the Blazers he had seen.

He started for the Emporium. Behind him Tex stopped by one of the posts that supported the wooden awning over the walk and leaned a negligent shoulder against it, a cigarette drooping from the corner of his mouth.

Bo Marsh sat back in a chair against the wall, his interested eyes sweeping the street. Several men who passed spoke to him and glanced at Tex Brisco's tall, lean figure.

Rafe opened the door of the Emporium and strode inside. Gene Baker looked up, frowning when he saw him. He was not glad to see Rafe, for the man's words on his previous visit had been responsible for some doubts and speculations.

"Is Ann Rodney in?"

Baker hesitated. "Yes," he said finally. "She's back there."

Rafe went around the counter toward the door, hat in his left hand.

"I don't think she wants to see you," Baker advised.

"All right," Rafe said. "We'll see."

He pushed past the screen and stepped into the living room beyond.

Ann Rodney was sewing, and when the quick step sounded, she glanced up. Her eyes changed. Something inside her seemed to turn over slowly. This big man who had brought such disturbing news affected her as no man ever had. Considering her engagement to Bruce Barkow, she didn't like to feel that way about any man. Since he had last been here she had worried a good deal about what he had said and her reaction to it. Why would he come with such a tale? Shouldn't she have heard him out?

Bruce said no, that the man was an impostor and someone who hoped to get money from her. Yet she knew something of Johnny Gill, and she had danced with Bo Marsh. She knew that these men were honest, as much as she had known of them. They had been liked and respected in Painted Rock.

"Oh," she said, rising. "It's you."

Rafe stopped in the center of the room, a tall, picturesque figure in his buckskin coat and with his waving black hair. He was, she thought, a handsome man. He wore his guns low and tied down, and she knew what that meant.

"I was goin' to wait," he said abruptly, "and let you come to me and ask questions, if you ever did. But when I thought it over, rememberin' what I'd promised your father, I decided I must come back now, lay all my cards on the table, and tell you what happened."

She started to speak, and he lifted his hand. "Wait, I'm goin' to talk quick, because in a few minutes I have an appointment outside that I must keep. Your father did not die on the trail back from California. He was shanghaied in San Francisco—taken aboard a ship while unconscious and forced to work as a seaman. I was shanghaied at the same time and place. Your father and I in the months that followed were together a lot. He asked me to come here, to take care of you and his wife and to protect you. He died of beatin's he got aboard ship, just before the rest of us got away from the ship. I was with him when he died, settin' beside his bed. Almost his last words were about you."

Ann Rodney stood very still, staring at him. There was a ring of truth in the rapidly spoken words, yet how could she believe this? Three men had told her they saw her father die, and one of them was the man she was to marry, the man who had befriended her, who had refused to foreclose on the mortgage he held and take from her the last thing she possessed in the world.

"What was my father like?" she asked.

"Like?" Rafe's brow furrowed. "How can anybody say what any man is like? I'd say he was about five feet eight or nine. When he died his hair was almost white, but when I first saw him he had only a few gray hairs. His face was a heap like yours. So were his eyes, except they wasn't so large nor so beautiful. He was a kind man who wasn't used to violence, I think, and he didn't like it. He planned well and thought well, but the West was not the country for him, yet. Ten years from now, when it has settled more, he'd have been a leadin' citizen. He was a good man and a sincere man."

"It sounds like him," Ann said hesitantly, "but there is nothing you could not have learned here or from someone who knew him."

"No," he said frankly. "That's so. But there's somethin' else you should know. The mortgage your father had against his place was paid."

"What?" Ann stiffened. "Paid? How can you say that?"

"He borrowed the money in Frisco and paid Barkow with it. He got a receipt for it."

"Oh, I can't believe that! Why, Bruce would have—"

"Would he?" Rafe asked gently. "You sure?"

She looked at him. "What was the other thing?"

"I have a deed," he said, "to the ranch, made out to you and to me."

Her eyes widened and then hardened with suspicion. "So? Now things become clearer. A deed to my father's ranch made out to you and to me! In other words, you are laying claim to half of my ranch?"

"Please—" Rafe said. "I—"

She smiled. "You needn't say anything more, Mr. Caradec. I admit I was almost coming to believe there was something in your story. At least, I was wondering about it, for I couldn't understand how you hoped to profit from any such tale. Now it becomes clear. You are trying to get half my ranch. You have even moved into my house without asking permission.

She stepped to one side of the door.

"I'm sorry, but I must ask you to leave! I must also ask you to vacate the house on Crazy Man, at once! I must ask you to refrain from calling on me again or from approaching me."

"Please!" Rafe said. "You're jumpin' to conclusions. I never aimed to claim any part of the ranch! I came here only because your father asked me to."

"Good day, Mr. Carradec!" Ann still held the curtain.

He looked at her, and for an instant their eyes held. She was first to look away. He turned abruptly and stepped through the curtain, and as he did the door opened and he saw Bo Marsh.

Marsh's eyes were excited and anxious. "Rafe," he said, "that Boyne hombre's in front of the National. He wants you!"

"Why, sure," Rafe said quietly. "I'm ready."

He walked to the front door, hitching his guns into place. Behind him, he heard Ann Rodney asking Baker:

"What did he mean that Boyne was waiting for him?"

Baker's reply came to Rafe as he stepped out into the morning light.

"Trigger Boyne's goin' to kill him, Ann. You'd better go back inside!"

Rafe smiled slightly. Kill him? Would that be it? No man knew better than he the tricks that destiny plays on a man or how often the right man dies at the wrong time and place. A man never wore a gun without inviting trouble, he never stepped into a street and began the gunman's walk without the full knowledge that he might be a shade too slow, that some small thing might disturb him just long enough!

Chapter VIII
Duel of Painted Rock

Morning sun was bright, and the street lay empty of horses and vehicles. A few idlers loafed in front of the stage station, but all of them were on their feet.

Rafe Caradec saw his black horse switch his tail at a fly, and he stepped down in the street. Trigger Boyne stepped off the boardwalk to face him, some distance off. Rafe did not walk slowly, he made no measured, quiet approach. He started to walk toward Boyne, going fast.

Trigger stepped down into the street easily, casually. He was smiling. Inside, his heart was throbbing, and there was a wild reckless eagerness within him. This one he would finish off fast. This would be simple, easy.

He squared in the street, and suddenly the smile was wiped from his face. Caradec was coming toward him, shortening the distance at a fast walk. That rapid approach did something to the calm on Boyne's face and in his mind. It was wrong. Caradec should have come slowly. He should have come poised and ready to draw.

Knowing his own deadly marksmanship, Boyne felt sure he could kill this man at any distance. But as soon as he saw that walk, he knew that Caradec was going to be so close in a few more steps that he himself would be killed.

It is one thing to know you are to kill another man, quite

a different thing to know you are to die yourself. Why, if
Caradec walked that way he would be so close he couldn't
miss!

Boyne's legs spread and the wolf sprang into his eyes,
but there was panic there, too. He had to stop his man, get
him now. His hand swept down for his gun.

Yet something was wrong. For all his speed he seemed
incredibly slow, because that other man, that tall, moving
figure in the buckskin coat and black hat, was already shooting.

Trigger's own hand moved first, his own hand gripped the
gun butt first, and then he was staring into a smashing,
blossoming rose of flame that seemed to bloom beyond the
muzzle of that big black gun in the hands of Rafe Caradec.
Something stabbed at his stomach, and he went numb to his
toes.

Stupidly he swung his gun up, staring over it. The gun
seemed awfully heavy. He must get a smaller one. That gun
opposite him blossomed with rose again, and something struck
him again in the stomach. He started to speak, half turning
toward the men in front of the stage station, his mouth
opening and closing.

Something was wrong with him, he tried to say. Why,
everyone knew he was the fastest man in Wyoming, unless it
was Shute! Everyone knew that! The heavy gun in his hand
bucked and he saw the flame stab at the ground. He dropped
the gun, swayed, and then fell flat on his face.

He would have to get up. He was going to kill that
stranger, that Rafe Caradec. He would have to get up.

The numbness from his stomach climbed higher, and he
suddenly felt himself in the saddle of a bucking horse, a
monstrous and awful horse that leaped and plunged, and it
was going up! Up! Up!

Then it came down hard, and he felt himself leave the
saddle, all sprawled out. The horse had thrown him, bucked
him off into the dust. He closed his hands spasmodically.

Rafe Caradec stood tall in the middle of the gunman's
walk, the black, walnut-stocked pistol in his right hand. He
glanced once at the still figure sprawled in the street, and
then his eyes lifted, sweeping the walks in swift, accurate
appraisal. Only then, some instinct prodded his subconscious
and warned him. There was the merest flicker of a curtain,
and in the space between the curtain and the edge of the
window, the black muzzle of a rifle!

His .44 lifted and the heavy gun bucked in his hand just as flame leaped from the rifle barrel and he felt quick, urgent fingers pluck at his sleeve. The .44 jolted again, and a rifle rattled on the shingled porch roof. The curtain made a tearing sound, and the head and shoulders of a man fell through, toppling over the sill. Overbalanced, the heels came up and the man's body rolled over slowly, seemed to hesitate, and then rolled over again, poised an instant on the edge of the roof, and dropped soddenly into the dust.

Dust lifted from around the body and then settled back. Gee Bonaro thrust hard with one leg, and his face twisted a little.

In the quiet street there was no sound, no movement.

For the space of a full half minute, the watchers held themselves, shocked by the sudden climax, stunned with unbelief. Trigger Boyne had been beaten to the draw and killed. Gee Bonaro had made his try and died.

Rafe Caradec turned slowly and walked back to his horse. Without a word he swung into the saddle. He turned the horse and, sitting tall in the saddle, swept the street with a cold, hard eye that seemed to stare at each man there. Then, as if by his own wish, the black horse turned. Walking slowly, his head held proudly, he carried his rider down the street and out of town.

Behind him, coolly and without smiles, Bo Marsh and Tex Brisco followed. Like him, they rode slowly, and like him they rode proudly. Something in their bearing seemed to say, "We were challenged. We came. You see the result."

In the window of the National, Joe Benson chewed his mustache. He stared at the figure of Trigger Boyne with vague disquiet, and then irritation.

"Cuss it!" he muttered under his breath. "You was supposed to be a gunman. What in thunder was wrong with you?"

A bullet from Boyne's gun, or from Bonaro's for that matter, could have ended it all. A bullet now could settle the whole thing, quiet the gossip, remove the doubts, and leave Barkow free to marry Ann, and the whole business could go forward. Instead, they had failed.

It would be a long time now, Benson knew, before it was all over. A long time. Barkow was slipping. The man had better think fast and get something done. Rafe Caradec must die.

* * *

The Fort Laramie Treaty of 1868 had forbidden white men to enter the Powder River country, yet gold discoveries brought prospectors north in increasing numbers. Small villages and mining camps had come into existence. Following them, cattlemen discovered the rich grasses of northern Wyoming. A few herds came over what later was to be known as the Texas Trail.

Indian attacks and general hostility caused many of these pioneers to retreat to more stable localities, but a few of the more courageous had stayed on. Prospectors had entered the Black Hills following the Custer expedition in 1874, and the Sioux, always resentful of any incursion upon their hunting grounds or any flaunting of their rights, were preparing to do something more than talk.

The names of such chiefs as Red Cloud, Dull Knife, Crazy Horse, and the medicine man Sitting Bull came more and more into frontier gossip. A steamboat was reported to be en route up the turbulent Yellowstone, and river traffic on the upper Mississippi was an accepted fact. There were increasing reports of gatherings of Indians in the hills, and white men rode warily, never without arms.

Cut off from contact with the few scattered ranchers, Rafe Caradec and his riders heard little of the gossip except what they gleaned from an occasional prospector or wandering hunter. Yet no gossip was needed to tell them how the land lay.

Twice they heard sounds of rifle fire, and once the Sioux ran off a number of cattle from Shute's ranch, taking them from a herd kept not far from Long Valley. Two of Shute's riders were killed. None of Caradec's cattle were molested. He was left strictly alone. Indians avoided his place, no matter what their mission.

Twice, riders from the ranch went to Painted Rock. Each time they returned they brought stories of an impending Indian outbreak. A few of the less courageous ranchers sold out and left the country. In all this time, Rafe Caradec lived in the saddle, riding often from dawn until dusk, avoiding the tangled brakes, but studying the lay of the land with care.

There was, he knew, some particular reason for Bruce Barkow's interest in the ranch that belonged to Ann Rodney. What that reason was, he must know. Without it, he knew he could offer no real reason why Barkow would go to the lengths he had gone to get a ranch that was on the face of things of no more value than any piece of land in the country, most of which could be had for the taking. . . .

Ann spent much of her time alone. Business at the store was thriving, and Gene Baker and his wife, and often Ann as well, were busy. In her spare time the thought kept returning to her that Rafe Caradec might be honest.

Yet she dismissed the thought as unworthy. If she admitted even for an instant that he was honest, she must also admit that Bruce Barkow was dishonest—a thief and possibly a killer. Yet somehow the picture of her father kept returning to her mind. It was present there on one of the occasions when Bruce Barkow came to call.

A handsome man, Barkow understood how to appeal to a woman. He carried himself well, and his clothes were always the best in Painted Rock. He called this evening looking even better than he had on the last occasion, his black suit neatly pressed, his mustache carefully trimmed.

They had been talking for some time when Ann mentioned Rafe Caradec.

"His story sounded so sincere!" she said, after a minute. "He said he had been shanghaied in San Francisco with Father and that they had become acquainted on the ship."

"He's a careful man," Barkow commented, "and a dangerous one. He showed that when he killed Trigger Boyne and Bonaro. He met Boyne out on the range, and they had some trouble over an Indian girl."

"An Indian girl?" Ann looked at him questioningly.

"Yes." Barkow frowned as if the subject was distasteful to him. "You know how some of the cowhands are—always running after some squaw. They have stolen squaws, kept them for a while, and then turned them loose or killed them. Caradec had a young squaw, and Boyne tried to argue with him to let her go. They had words, and there'd have been a shooting then if one of Caradec's other men hadn't come up with a rifle, and Shute's boys went away."

Ann was shocked. She had heard of such things happening and was well aware of how much trouble they caused. That Rafe Caradec would be a man like that was hard to believe. Yet, what did she know of the man?

He disturbed her more than she allowed herself to believe. Despite the fact that he seemed to be trying to work some scheme to get all or part of her ranch, and despite all she had heard of him at one time or another from Bruce, she couldn't make herself believe that all she heard was true.

That he appealed to her she refused to admit. Yet when with him, she felt drawn to him. She liked his rugged masculinity, his looks, and his voice, and was impressed with his sincerity. Yet the killing of Boyne and Bonaro was the talk of the town.

The Bonaro phase of the incident she could understand from the previous episode in the store. But no one had any idea of why Boyne should be looking for Caradec. The solution now offered by Barkow was the only one. A fight over a squaw! Without understanding why, Ann felt vaguely resentful.

For days a dozen of Shute's riders hung around town. There was talk of lynching Caradec, but nothing came of it. Ann heard the talk and asked Baker about it.

The old storekeeper looked up, nodding.

"There's talk, but it'll come to nothin'. None of these boys aim to ride out there to Crazy Man and tackle that crowd. You know what Gill and Marsh are like. They'll fight, and they can. Well, Caradec showed what he could do with a gun when he killed those two in the street. I don't know whether you saw that other feller with Caradec or not, the one from Texas. Well, if he ain't tougher than either Marsh or Gill, I'll pay off! Notice how he wore his guns? Nope, nobody'll go looking for them. If they got their hands on Caradec, that would be somethin' else."

Baker rubbed his jaw thoughtfully. "Unless they are powerful lucky, they won't last long, anyway. That's Injun country, and Red Cloud or Man Afraid of His Horse won't take kindly to white men livin' there. They liked your pa, and he was friendly to 'em."

As a result of his conversations with Barkow, Sheriff Pod Gomer had sent messages south by stage to Cheyenne and the telegraph. Rafe Caradec had come from San Francisco, and Bruce Barkow wanted to know who and what he was. More than that, he wanted to find out how he had been allowed to escape the *Mary S*. With that in mind he wrote to Bully Borger.

Barkow had known nothing about Caradec when the deal was made, but Borger had agreed to take Charles Rodney to sea and let him die there, silencing the truth forever. Allowing Rafe Caradec to come ashore with his story was not keeping the terms of the bargain. If Caradec had actually been aboard the ship and left it, there might be something in that to make him liable to the law.

Barkow intended to leave no stone unturned. And in the meanwhile, he spread his stories around about Caradec's reason for killing Boyne.

Chapter IX
Oil!

Caradec went on with his haying. The nights were already growing more chill. At odd times when not haying or handling cattle, he and the boys built another room to the cabin and banked the house against the wind. Fortunately, its position was sheltered. Wind would not bother them greatly where they were, but there would be snow and lots of it.

Rafe rode out each day and several times brought back deer or elk. The meat was jerked and stored away. Gill got the old wagon Rodney had brought from Missouri and made some repairs. It would be the easiest way to get supplies out from Painted Rock. He worked over it and soon had it in excellent shape.

On the last morning of the month, Rafe walked out to where Gill was hitching a team to the wagon.

"Looks good," he agreed. "You've done a job on it, Johnny."

Gill looked pleased. He nodded at the hubs of the wheels. "Notice 'em? No squeak!"

"Well, I'll be hanged!" Rafe looked at the grease on the hubs. "Where'd you get the grease?"

"Sort of a spring back over in the hills. I brung back a bucket of it."

Rafe Caradec looked up sharply. "Johnny, where'd you find that spring?"

"Why"—Gill looked puzzled—"it's just a sort of hole like, back over next to that mound. You know, in that bad range. Ain't much account down there, but I was down there once and found this here spring. This stuff works as well as the grease you buy."

"It should," Rafe said dryly. "It's the same stuff!"

He caught up the black and threw a saddle on it. Within

an hour he was riding down toward the barren knoll Gill had mentioned. What he found was not a spring, but a hole among some sparse rushes, dead and sick looking. It was an oil seepage.

Oil!

Swiftly his mind leaped ahead. This, then, could be the reason why Barkow and Shute were so anxious to acquire title to this piece of land, so anxious that they would have a man shanghaied and killed. Caradec recalled that Bonneville had reported oil seepages on his trip through the state some forty years or so before, and there had been a well drilled in the previous decade.

One of the largest markets for oil was the patent medicine business, for it was the main ingredient in so-called British Oil.

The hole in which the oil was seeping in a thick stream, might be shallow, but sounding with a six-foot stick found no bottom. Rafe doubted if it was much deeper. Still, there would be several barrels here, and he seemed to recall some talk of selling oil for twenty dollars the barrel.

Swinging into the saddle, he turned the big black down the draw and rode rapidly toward the hills. This could be the reason, for certainly it was reason enough. The medicine business was only one possible market, for machinery of all kinds needed lubricants. There was every chance that the oil industry might really mean something in time.

If the hole was emptied, how fast would it refill? And how constant was the supply? On one point he could soon find out.

He swung the horse up out of the draw, forded the Crazy Man, and cantered up the hill to the cabin. As he reined in and swung down at the door he noticed two strange horses.

Tex Brisco stepped to the door, his face hard.

"Watch it, Boss!" he said sharply.

Pod Gomer's thickset body thrust into the doorway.

"Caradec," he said calmly, "you're under arrest."

Rafe swung down, facing him. Two horses. Who had ridden the other one?

"For what?" he demanded.

His mind was racing. The mutiny? Had they found out about that?

"For killin'. Shootin' Bonaro."

"*Bonaro?*" Rafe laughed. "You mean for defendin' myself? Bonaro had a rifle in that window. He was all set to shoot me!"

Gomer nodded coolly. "That was most folks' opinion, but it seems nobody *saw* him aim any gun at you. We've only got your say-so. When we got to askin' around, it begun to look sort of funny like. It appears to a lot of folks that you just took that chance to shoot him and get away with it. Anyway, you'd be better off to stand trial."

"Don't go, Boss," Brisco said. "They don't ever aim to have a trial."

"You'd better not resist," Gomer replied calmly. "I've got twenty Shute riders down the valley. I made 'em stay back. The minute any shootin' starts, they'll come a-runnin', and you all know what that would mean."

Rafe knew. It would mean the death of all four of them and the end to any opposition to Barkow's plans. Probably, that was what the rancher hoped would happen.

"Why, sure, Gomer," Caradec said calmly. "I'll go."

Tex started to protest, and Rafe saw Gill hurl his hat into the dust.

"Give me your guns then," Gomer said, "and mount up."

"No." Rafe's voice was flat. "I keep my guns till I get to town. If that bunch of Shute's starts anything, the first one I'll kill will be you, Gomer!"

Pod Gomer's face turned sullen. "You ain't goin' to be bothered. I'm the law here. Let's go!"

"Gomer," Tex Brisco said viciously, "if anything happens to him I'll kill you and Barkow both!"

"That goes for me, too!" Gill said harshly.

"And me!" Marsh put in. "I'll get you if I have to drygulch you, Gomer."

"Well, all right!" Gomer said angrily. "It's just a trial. I told 'em I didn't think much of it, but the judge issued the warrant."

He was scowling blackly. It was all right for them to issue warrants, but if they thought he was going to get killed for them, they were bloody well wrong!

Pod Gomer jammed his hat down on his head. This was a far cry from the coal mines of Lancashire, but sometimes he wished he was back in England. There was a look in Brisco's eyes he didn't like.

"No," he told himself, "he'll be turned loose before I take a chance. Let Barkow kill his own pigeons. I don't want these Bar M hands gunnin' for *me!*"

The man who had ridden the other horse stepped out of the cabin, followed closely by Bo Marsh. There was no smile on the young cowhand's face. The man was Bruce Barkow.

For an instant, his eyes met Caradec's. "This is just a formality," Barkow said smoothly. "There's been some talk around Painted Rock, and a trial will clear the air a lot. Of course if you're innocent, Caradec, you'll be freed."

"You sure of that?" Rafe's eyes smmiled cynically. "Barkow, you hate me and you know it. If I ever leave that jail alive, it won't be your fault."

Barkow shrugged. "Think what you want," he said indifferently. "I believe in law and order. We've got a nice little community at Painted Rock, and we want to keep it that way. Boyne had challenged you, and that was different. Bonaro had no part in the fight."

"No use arguin' that here," Gomer protested. "Court's the place for that. Let's go."

Tex Brisco lounged down the steps, his thumbs hooked in his belt. He stared at Gomer.

"I don't like you," he said coolly. "I don't like you a bit. I think you're yellow as a coyote. I think you bob every time this here Barkow says bob."

"Gomer's face whitened, and his eyes shifted.

"You've got no call to start trouble!" he said. "I'm doin' my duty."

"Let it ride," Caradec told Tex. "There's plenty of time."

"Yeah," Tex drawled, his hard eyes on Gomer, "but just for luck I'm goin' to mount and trail you into town, keepin' to the hills. If that bunch of Shute riders gets fancy, I'm goin' to get myself a sheriff, and"—his eyes shifted—"maybe another hombre."

"Is that a threat?" Barkow asked contemptuously. "Talk is cheap."

"Want to see how cheap?" Tex prodded. His eyes were ugly and he was itching for a fight. It showed in every line of him. "Want me to make it expensive?"

Bruce Barkow was no fool. He had not seen Tex Brisco in action, yet there was something chill and deadly about the tall Texan. Barkow shrugged.

"We came here to enforce the law. Is this resistance, Caradec?"

"No," Rafe said. "Let's go."

The three men turned their horses and walked them down the trail toward Long Valley. Tex Brisco threw a saddle on his horse and mounted. Glancing back, Pod Gomer saw the Texan turn his horse up a trail into the trees. He swore viciously.

Caradec sat his horse easily. The trouble would not come now. He was quite sure the plan had been to get him away and then claim the Shute riders had taken him from the law. Yet he was as sure it would not come to that now. Pod Gomer would know that Brisco's Winchester was within range. Also, Rafe was still wearing his guns.

Rafe rode warily, lagging a trifle behind the sheriff. He glanced at Barkow, but the rancher's face was expressionless. Ahead of them, in a tight bunch, waited the Shute riders.

The first he recognized were the Blazers. There was another man, known as Joe Gorman, whom he also recognized. Red Blazer started forward abruptly.

"He come, did he?" he shouted. "Now we'll show him!"

"Get back!" Gomer ordered sharply.

"Huh?" Red glared at Gomer. "Who says I'll get back! I'm stringin' this hombre to the first tree we get to!"

"You stay back!" Gomer ordered. "We're takin' this man in for trial!"

Red Blazer laughed. "Come on, boys!" he yelled. "Let's hang the skunk!"

"I wouldn't, Red," Rafe Caradec said calmly. "You've overlooked somethin'. I'm wearin' my guns. Are you faster than Trigger Boyne?"

Blazer jerked his horse's head around, his face pale but furious.

"Hey!" he yelled. "What the devil is this? I thought—"

"That you'd have an easy time of it?" Rafe shoved the black horse between Gomer and Barkow, pushing ahead of them. He rode right up to Blazer and let the big black shove into the other horse. "Well, get this Blazer! Any time you kill me you'll do it with a gun in your hand, savvy? You're nothin' but a lot of lynch-crazy coyotes! Try it, cuss it! Try it now, and I'll blow you out of that saddle so full of lead you'll sink a foot into the ground!"

Rafe's eyes swept the crowd.

"Think this is a joke? That goes for any of you! And as for Gomer, he knows that if you hombres want any trouble, he gets it, too! There's a man up in the hills with a Winchester, and if you don't think he can empty saddles, start somethin'. That Winchester carries sixteen shots, and I've seen him empty it and get that many rabbits! I'm packing two guns. I'm askin' you now, so if you want any of what I've got, start the ball rollin'. Maybe you'd get me, but I'm tellin' you there'll be more dead men around here than you can shake a stick at!"

Joe Gorman spoke quickly. "Watch it, boys! There is an hombre up on the mountain with a rifle! I see him!"

"What the blue blazes is this?" Red Blazer repeated.

"The fun's over," Rafe replied shortly. "You might as well head for home and tell Dan Shute to kill his own wolves. I'm wearin' my guns and I'm goin' to keep 'em. I'll stand trial, but you know and I know that Bonaro got what he was askin' for." Caradec turned his eyes on Blazer. "As for you, stay out of my sight! You're too blasted willin' to throw your hemp over a man you think is helpless! I don't like skunks and never did!"

"You can't call me a skunk!" Blazer bellowed.

Rafe stared at him. "I just did," he said calmly.

Chapter X
The Trial

For a full minute their eyes held. Rafe's hand was on his thigh within inches of his gun. If it came to gunplay now, he would be killed, but Blazer and Barkow would go down, too, and there would be others. He had not exaggerated when he spoke of Tex Brisco's rifle shooting. The man was a wizard with the gun.

Red Blazer was trapped. White to the lips, he stared at Rafe and could see cold, certain death looking back at him. He could stand it no longer.

"Why don't some of you do somethin'?" he bellowed.

Joe Gorman spat. "You done the talkin', Red."

"Tarnation with it!"

Blazer swung his horse around, touched spurs to the animal, and raced off at top speed.

Bruce Barkow's hand hovered close to his gun. A quick draw, a shot, and the man would be dead. Just like that. His lips tightened, and his elbow crooked. Gomer grabbed his wrist.

"Don't Bruce! Don't! That hombre up there. . . . Look!"

Barkow's head swung. Brisco was in plain sight, his rifle resting over the limb of a tree. At that distance, he could not miss. Yet he was beyond pistol range, and while some of the riders had rifles, they were out in the open without a bit of cover.

Barkow jerked his arm away and turned his horse toward town. Rafe turned the black and rode beside him. He said nothing, but Barkow was seething at the big man's obvious contempt.

Rafe Caradec had outfaced the lot of them. He had made them look fools. Yet Barkow remembered as well as each of the riders remembered that Rafe had fired but three shots in the street battle, that all the shots had scored, and that two men had died.

When the cavalcade reached the National, Rafe turned to Pod Gomer.

"Get your court goin'," he said calmly. "We'll have this trial now."

"Listen here!" Gomer burst out, infuriated. "You can do things like that too often! We'll have our court when we get blamed good and ready!"

"No," Rafe said, "you'll hold court this afternoon—now. You haven't got any calendar to interfere. I have business to attend to that can't wait, and I won't. You'll have your trial today, or I'll leave and you can come and get me."

"Who you tellin' what to do?" Gomer said angrily. "I'll have you know—"

"Then you tell him, Barkow. Or does he take his orders from Shute? Call that judge of yours and let's get this over."

Bruce Barkow's lips tightened. He could see that Gene Baker and Ann Rodney were standing in the doorway of the store, listening.

"All right," Barkow said savagely. "Call him down here."

Not much later Judge Roy Gargan walked into the stage station and looked around. He was a tall, slightly stooped man with a lean, hangdog face and round eyes. He walked up to the table and sat down in the chair behind it. Bruce Barkow took a chair to one side, where he could see the judge.

Noting the move, Rafe Caradec sat down where both men were visible. Barkow, nettled, shifted his chair irritably. He glanced up and saw Ann Rodney come in, accompanied by Baker and Pat Higley. He scowled again. Why couldn't they stay out of this?

Slowly, the hangers-on around town filed in. Joe Benson came in and sat down close to Barkow. They exchanged looks. Benson's questioning glance made Barkow furious. If they wanted so much done, why didn't someone do something beside him?

"I'll watch from here," drawled a voice.

Barkow's head came up. Standing in the window behind and to the right of the judge was Tex Brisco. At the same instant Barkow noted him, the Texan lifted a hand.

"Hi, Johnny! Glad to see yuh!"

Bruce Barkow's face went hard. He saw Johnny Gill and, beside him, Bo Marsh. If anything rusty was pulled in this courtroom the place would be a shambles. Maybe Dan Shute was right, after all. If they were going to be crooked, why not drygulch the fellow and get it over? All Barkow's carefully worked out plans to get Caradec had failed.

There had been three good chances: resistance, which would warrant killing in attempting an arrest; attempted escape, if he so much as made a wrong move; and lynching by the Shute riders. At every point they had been outguessed.

Judge Gargan slammed a six-shooter on the table.

"Order!" he proclaimed. "Court's in session! Reckon I'll appoint a jury. Six men will do. I'll have Joe Benson, Tom Blazer, Sam Mawson, Doc Otto, and—"

"Joe Benson's not eligible," Caradec interrupted.

Gargan frowned. "Who's runnin' this court?"

"Supposedly," Rafe said quietly, "the law. Supposedly, the interests of justice. Joe Benson was a witness to the shootin', so he'll be called on to give testimony."

"Who you tellin' how to run this court?" Gargan demanded belligerently.

"Don't the defendant even have a chance to defend himself?" Caradec asked gently. He glanced around at the crowd. "I think you'll all agree that a man on trial for his life should have a chance to defend himself, that he should be allowed to call and question witnesses, and that he should have an attorney. But since the court hasn't provided an attorney, and because I want to, I'll act for myself. Now"—he looked around—"the judge picked three members of the jury. I'd like to pick out three more. I'd like Pat Higley, Gene Baker, and Ann Rodney as members of the jury."

"What?" Gargan roared. "I'll have no woman settin' on no jury in my court! Why, of all the—"

Rafe said smoothly, "It kind of looks like your honor does not know the law in Wyomin'. By an act approved in December eighteen sixty-nine, the first territorial legislature granted equal rights to women. Women served on juries in Laramie in eighteen seventy, and one was servin' as justice of the peace that year."

Gargan swallowed and looked uncomfortable. Barkow sat up and started to say something, but before he could open his mouth, Caradec was speaking again.

"As I understand, the attorney for the state and the defense attorney usually select a jury. As the court has taken it upon himself to appoint a jury, I was just suggestin' the names of three reputable citizens I respect. I'm sure none of these three can be considered friends of mine, sorry as I am to say it.

"Of course," he added, "if the court objects to these three people—if there's somethin' about their characters I don't know, or if they are not good citizens, then I take back my suggestion." He turned to look at Bruce Barkow. "Or maybe Mr. Barkow objects to Ann Rodney servin' on the jury?"

Barkow sat up, flushing. Suddenly, he was burning with rage. This whole thing had got out of hand. What had happened to bring this about? He was acutely conscious that Ann was staring at him, her eyes wide, a flush mounting in her cheeks at his hesitation.

"No!" he said violently. "No, of course no. Let her sit, but let's get this business started."

Pod Gomer was slumped in his chair, watching cynically. His eyes shifted to Barkow with a faintly curious expression. The planner and schemer had missed out on this trial. It had been his idea to condemn the man in public and then see to it that he was hanged.

"You're actin' as prosecutin' attorney?" Gargan asked Barkow.

The rancher got to his feet, cursing the thought that had given rise to this situation. That Rafe Caradec had won the first round he was unpleasantly aware. Somehow they had never contemplated any trouble on the score of the jury. In the few trials held thus far the judge had appointed the jury and there had been no complaint. All the cases had gone off as planned.

"Your honor," he began, "and lady and gentlemen of the jury. You all know none of us here are lawyers. This court is bein' held only so's we can keep law and order in this community, and that's the way it will be till the county is organized. This prisoner was in a gunfight with Lemuel Boyne, known as Trigger. Boyne challenged him—some of you know the reason for that—and Caradec accepted. In the fight out in the street, Caradec shot Boyne and killed him.

"In almost the same instant, he lifted his gun and shot Gee Bonaro, who was innocently watchin' the battle from his window. If a thing like this isn't punished, any gunfighter is apt to shoot anybody he don't like at any time, and nothin' done about it. We've all heard that Caradec claims Bonaro had a rifle and was about to shoot at him, which was a plumb good excuse, but a right weak one. We know this Caradec had words with Bonaro at the Emporium and almost got into a fight then and there. I say Caradec is guilty of murder in the first degree and should be hung."

Barkow turned his head and motioned to Red Blazer.

"Red, you get up there and tell the jury what you know."

Red strode up to the chair that was doing duty for a witness stand and slouched down in the seat. He was unshaven, and his hair was uncombed. He sprawled his legs out and stuck his thumbs in his belt. He rolled his quid in his jaws and spat.

"I seen this here Caradec shoot Boyne," he said, "then he ups with his pistol and cut down on Bonaro, who was a-standin' in the window, just a-lookin'."

"Did Bonaro make any threatenin' moves toward Caradec?"

"Him?" Red's eyes opened wide. "Shucks, no. Gee was just a-standin' there. Caradec was afraid of him an' seen a chance to kill him and get plumb away."

Rafe looked thoughtfully at Barkow. "Is the fact that the

witness was not sworn in the regular way in this court? Or is his conscience delicate on the subject of perjury?"

"Huh?" Blazer sat up. "What'd he say?"

Barkow flushed. "It hasn't usually been the way here, but— "

"Swear him in," Caradec said calmly, "and have him say under oath what he's just said."

He waited until this was done, and then as Red started to get up Rafe motioned him back.

"I've got a few questions," he said.

"Huh?" Red demanded belligerently. "I don't have to answer no more questions."

"Yes, you do." Rafe's voice was quiet. "Get back on that witness stand!"

"Do I have to?" Blazer demanded of Barkow, who nodded.

If there had been any easy way out, he would have taken it, but there was none. He was beginning to look at Rafe Caradec with new eyes.

Rafe got up and walked over to the jury.

"Lady and gentlemen," he said, "none of you know me well. None of us, as Barkow said, know much about how court business should be handled. All we want to do is get at the truth. I know that all of you here are busy men. You're willin' and anxious to help along justice and the beginnin's of law hereabouts, and all of you're honest men. You want to do the right thing. Red Blazer has just testified that I shot a man who was makin' no threatenin' moves, that Bonaro was standing in a window, just watching."

Caradec turned around and looked at Blazer thoughtfully. He walked over to him, squatted on his haunches, and peered into his eyes, shifting first to one side and then the other. Red Blazer's face flamed.

"What's the matter?" he blared. "You gone crazy?"

"No," Caradec said. "Just lookin' at your eyes. I was just curious to see what kind of eyes a man had who could see through a shingle room and a ceilin'."

"Huh?" Blazer glared.

The jury sat up, and Barkow's eyes narrowed. The courtroom crowd leaned forward.

"Why, Red, you must have forgot," Rafe said. "You were in the National when I killed Boyne. You was standin' behind Joe Benson. You were the first person I saw when I looked around. You could see me, and you could see Boyne—but you couldn't see the second-story window across the street!"

Somebody whooped, and Pat Higley grinned.

"I reckon he's right," Pat said coolly. "I was standin' right alongside of Red."

"That's right!" somebody from back in the courtroom shouted. "Blazer tried to duck out without payin' for his drink, and Joe Benson stopped him!"

Everybody laughed, and Blazer turned fiery red, glaring back into the room to see who the speaker was, and not finding him.

Rafe turned to Barkow and smiled.

"Have you got another witness?"

Chapter XI
Case Dismissed

Despite herself, Ann Rodney found herself admiring Rafe Caradec's composure, his easy manner. Her curiosity was stirred. What manner of man was he? Where was he from? What background had he? Was he only a wanderer, or was he something more, different? His language, aside from his characteristic Texas drawl, and his manner, spoke of refinement, yet she knew of his gun skill as exhibited in the Boyne fight.

"Tom Blazer's my next witness," Barkow said. "Swear him in."

Tom Blazer, a hulking redhead even bigger than Red, took the stand. Animosity glared from his eyes.

"Did you see the shootin'?" Barkow asked.

"You're darned right I did!" Tom declared, staring at Rafe. "I seen it, and I wasn't inside no saloon! I was right out in the street!"

"Was Bonaro where you could see him?"

"He sure was!"

"Did he make any threatenin' moves?"

"Not any!"

"Did he lift a gun?"

"He sure didn't!"

"Did he make any move that would give an idea he was goin' to shoot?"

"Nope. Not any." As Tom Blazer answered each question he glared triumphantly at Caradec.

Barkow turned to the jury. "Well, there you are. I think that's enough evidence. I think—"

"Let's hear Caradec ask his questions," Pat Higley said. "I want both sides of this yarn."

Rafe got up and walked over to Tom Blazer, Then he looked at the judge.

"Your honor, I'd like permission to ask one question of a man in the audience. He can be sworn or not, just as you say."

Gargan hesitated uncertainly. Always before, things had gone smoothly. Trials had been railroaded through and objections swept aside, and the wordless little ranchers or other objectors to the rule of Barkow and Shute had been helpless. This time, preparations should have been more complete. He didn't know what to do.

"All right," he said, his misgiving showing in his expression and tone.

Caradec turned to look at a short, stocky man with a brown mustache streaked with gray.

"Grant," he said, "what kind of a curtain have you got over that window above your harness and saddle shop?"

Grant looked up. "Why, it ain't rightly no curtain," he said frankly. "It's a blanket."

"You keep it down all the time? The window covered?"

"Uh-huh. Sure do. Sun gets in there otherwise and makes the floor hot and she heats up the store thataway. Keepin' that window covered keeps her cooler."

"It was covered the day of the shootin'?"

"Sure was."

"Where did you find the blanket after the shootin'?"

"Well, she laid over the sill, partly inside, partly outside."

Rafe turned to the jury. "Miss Rodney, and gentlemen, I believe the evidence is clear. The window was covered by a blanket, when Bonaro fell after I shot him, he tumbled across the sill, tearin' down the blanket. Do yuh agree?"

"Sure!" Gene Baker found his voice. The whole case was only too obviously a frame up to get Caradec. It was like Bonaro to try a sneak killing, anyway. "If that blanket hadn't been over the window, then he couldn't have fallen against it and carried part out with him!"

"That's right." Rafe turned on Tom Blazer. "Your eyes

seem to be as amazin' as your brother's. You can see through a wool blanket!"

Blazer sat up with a jerk, his face dark with sullen rage. "Listen!" he said. "I'll tell you—"

"Wait a minute!" Rafe whirled on him and thrust a finger in his face. "You're not only a perjurer but a thief! What did you do with that Winchester Bonaro dropped out of the window?"

"It wasn't no Winchester!" Blazer blared furiously. "It was a Henry!"

Then, seeing the expression on Barkow's face, and hearing the low murmur that swept the court, he realized what he had said. He started to get up and then sank back, angry and confused.

Rafe Caradec turned toward the jury.

"The witness swore that Bonaro had no gun, yet he just testified that the rifle Bonaro dropped was a Henry. Gentlemen and Miss Rodney, I'm goin' to ask that you recommend the case be dismissed and also that Red and Tom Blazer be held in jail to answer charges of perjury!"

"What?" Tom blazer came out of the witness chair with a lunge. "Jail? Me? Why, you—"

He leaped, hurling a huge red-haired fist in a round-house swing. Rafe Caradec stepped in with a left that smashed Blazer's lips and then a solid right that sent him crashing to the floor.

He glanced at the judge.

"And that, I think," he said quietly, "is contempt of court!"

Pat Higley got up abruptly. "Gargan, I reckon you better dismiss this case. You haven't got any evidence or anything that sounds like evidence, and I guess everybody here heard about Caradec facin' Bonaro down in the store. If he wanted to shoot him, there was his chance."

Gargan swallowed. "Case dismissed!" he said.

He looked up at Bruce Barkow, but the rancher was walking toward Ann Rodney. She glanced at him. Then her eyes lifted, and beyond him she saw Rafe Caradec.

How fine his face was! It was a rugged, strong face. There was character in it and sincerity. . . . She came to with a start. Bruce was speaking to her.

"Gomer told me he had a case," Barkow said, "or I'd

never have been a party to this. He's guilty as he can be, but he's smooth."

Ann looked down at Bruce Barkow, and suddenly his eyes looked different to her than they ever had before.

"He may be guilty of a lot of things," she said tartly, "but if ever there was a cooked-up, dishonest case, it was this one. And everyone in town knew it! If I were you, Bruce Barkow, I'd be ashamed of myself!"

Abruptly she turned her back on him and started for the door. Yet as she went she glanced up, and for a brief instant her eyes met those of Rafe Caradec, and something within her leaped. Her throat seemed to catch. Head high, she hurried past him into the street. The store seemed a long distance away. . . .

When Bruce Barkow walked into Pod Gomer's office, the sheriff was sitting in his swivel chair. In the big leather armchair across the room Dan Shute was waiting.

He was a big man, with massive shoulders, powerfully muscled arms, and great hands. A shock of dusky blond hair covered the top of his head, and his eyebrows were the color of corn silk. He looked up as Barkow came in, and when he spoke his voice was rough.

"You sure played hob!"

"The man's smart, that's all!" Barkow said. "Next time we'll have a better case."

"Next time?" Dan Shute lounged back in the big chair, the contempt in his eyes unconcealed. "There ain't goin' to be a next time. You're through, Barkow . From now on this is my show, and we run it my way. Caradec needs killin', and we'll kill him. Also, you're goin' to foreclose that mortgage on the Rodney place.

"No"—he held up a hand as Barkow started to speak— "you wait. You was all for pullin' this slick stuff. Winnin' the girl, gettin' the property the easy way, the legal way. To blazes with that! This Caradec is makin' a monkey of you! You're not slick! You're just a country boy playin' with a real smooth lad!

"To blazes with that smooth stuff! You foreclose on that mortgage and do it plumb quick. I'll take care of Mr. Rafe Caradec! With my own hands or guns if necessary. We'll clean that country down there so slick of his hands and cattle they won't know what happened!"

"That won't get it," Barkow protested. "You let me handle this. I'll take care of things!"

Dan Shute looked up at Barkow, his eyes sardonic. "I'll run this show. You're takin' the back seat, Barkow, from now on. All you've done is make us out fumblin' fools! Also," he added calmly, "I'm takin' over that girl."

"*What?*" Barkow whirled, his face livid. In his wildest doubts of Shute, and he had had many of them, this was one thing that had never entered his mind.

"You heard me," Shute replied. "She's a neat little lady, and I can make a place for her out to my ranch. You messed up all around, so I'm takin' over."

Barkow laughed, but his laugh was hollow, with something of fear in it. Always before, Dan Shute had been big, silent, and surly, saying little, but letting Barkow plan and plot and take the lead. Bruce Barkow had always thought of the man as a sort of strong-arm squad to use in a pinch. Suddenly he was shockingly aware that this big man was completely sure of himself, that he held him, Barkow, in contempt. He would ride roughshod over everything.

"Dan," Barkow protested, trying to keep his thoughts ordered, "you can't play with a girl's affections. She's in love with me! You can't do anything about that. You think she'd fall out of love with one man, and—?"

Dan Shute grinned. "Who said anything about love? You talk about that all you want. Talk it to yourself. I want the girl, and I'm goin' to have her. It doesn't make any difference who says no, and that goes for Gene Baker, her, or you."

Bruce Barkow stood flat-footed and pale. Suddenly he felt sick and empty. Here it was, then. He was through. Dan Shute had told him off, and in front of Pod Gomer. Out of the tail of his eye he could see the calm, yet cynical expression on Gomer's face.

He looked up, and he felt small under the flat, ironic gaze of Shute's eyes.

"All right, Dan, if that's the way you feel. I expect we'd better part company."

Shute chuckled, and his voice was rough when he spoke.

"No," he said, "we don't part company. You sit tight. You're holdin' that mortgage, and I want that land. You had a good idea there, Barkow, but you're too weak-kneed to swing it. I'll swing it, and maybe if you're quiet and obey orders, I'll see you get some of it."

Bruce Barkow glared at Shute. For the first time he knew what hatred was. Here, in a few minutes, he had been destroyed. This story would go the rounds, and before nightfall everyone in town would know that Barkow had been swept aside by Dan Shute, big, slow-talking Dan Shute, with his hard fists and his guns. Crushed, Barkow stared at Shute with hatred livid in his eyes.

"You'll go too far!" he said viciously.

Shute shrugged. "You can live an' come out of this with a few dollars," he said calmly, "or you can die. I'd just as soon kill you, Barkow, as look at you." He picked up his hat. "We had a nice thing. That shanghaiin' idea was yours. Why you didnt' shoot him, I'll never know. If you had, this Caradec would never have run into him at all and would never have come in here, stirrin' things up. You could have foreclosed that mortgage, and we could be makin' a deal on that oil now."

"Caradec don't know anything about that," Barkow protested.

"Like sin he don't!" Dan Shute sneered. "Caradec's been watched by my men for days. He's been wise there was somethin' in the wind and he's scouted all over that place. Well, he was down to the knob the other day, and he took a long look at that oil seepage. He's no fool, Barkow."

Bruce Barkow looked up. "No," he replied suddenly, "he's not, and he's a hand with a gun, too, Dan! He's a hand with a gun! He took Boyne!"

Shute shrugged. "Boyne was nothin'! I could have spanked him with his own gun. I'll kill Caradec someday, but first I want to beat him. To beat him with my own hands!"

He heaved himself out of the chair and stalked outside. For an instant, Barkow stared after him. Then his gaze shifted to Pod Gomer.

The sheriff was absently whittling a small stick.

"Well," he said, "he told you."

Chapter XII
"I Think I'll Kill Bruce Barkow!"

Hard and grim, Barkow's mouth tightened. So Gomer was in it, too. He started to speak, then hesitated. Like Caradec, Gomer was no fool, and he, too, was a good hand with a gun. Barkow shrugged.

"Dan sees things wrong," he said. "I've still got an ace in the hole." He looked at Gomer. "I'd like it better if you were on my side."

Pod Gomer shrugged. "I'm with the winner. My health is good. All I need is more money."

"You think Shute's the winner?"

"Don't you?" Gomer asked. "He told you plenty, and you took it."

"Yes, I did, because I know I'm no match for him with a gun. Nor for you." He studied the sheriff thoughtfully. "This is goin' to be a nice thing, Pod. It would split well, two ways."

Gomer got up and snapped his knife shut. "You show me the color of some money," he said, "and Dan Shute out, and we might talk. Also," he added, "if you mention this to Dan, I'll call you a liar in the street or in the National. I'll make you use that gun."

"I won't talk," Barkow said. "Only, I've been learnin' a few things. When we get answers to some of the messages you sent, and some I sent, we should know more. Borger wouldn't let Caradec off that ship willingly after he knew Rodney. I think he deserted. I think we can get something on him for mutiny, and that means hangin'."

"Maybe you can," Gomer agreed. "You show me you're holdin' good cards, and I'll back you to the limit."

Bruce Barkow walked out on the street and watched Pod Gomer's retreating back. Gomer, at least, he understood. He knew the man had no use for him, but if he could show evidence that he was to win, then Gomer would be a powerful ally. Judge Gargan would go as Gomer went and would always adopt the less violent means.

The cards were on the table now. Dan Shute was running things. What he would do, Barkow was not sure. He realized suddenly, with no little trepidation, that after all his association with Shute he knew little of what went on behind the hard brutality of the rancher's face. Yet he was not a man to lag or linger. What he did would be sudden, brutal, and thorough, but it would make a perfect shield under which he, Barkow, could operate and carry to fulfillment his own plans.

Dan Shute's abrupt statement of his purpose in regard to Ann Rodney had jolted Barkow. Somehow, he had taken Ann for granted. He had always planned a marriage. That he wanted her land was true. Perhaps better than Shute he knew what oil might mean in the future, and Barkow was a farsighted man. But Ann Rodney was lovely and interesting. She would be a good wife for him.

There was one way he could defeat Dan Shute on that score—to marry Ann at once.

True, it might precipitate a killing, but already Bruce Barkow was getting ideas on that score. He was suddenly less disturbed about Rafe Caradec than about Dan Shute. The rancher loomed large and formidable in his mind. He knew the brutality of the man, had seen him kill, and knew with what coldness he regarded people and animals.

Bruce Barkow made up his mind. Come what may, he was going to marry Ann Rodney.

He could, he realized, marry her and get her clear away from here. His mind leaped ahead. Flight to the northwest to the gold camps would be foolhardy, and to the Utah country would be as bad. In either case, Shute might and probably would overtake him. There remained another way out, and one that Shute probably would never suspect—he could strike for Fort Phil Kearney not far distant and then, with or without a scouting party for escort, could head across country and reach the Yellowstone. Or he might even try the nearer Powder River.

A steamer had ascended the Yellowstone earlier that year, and there was every chance that another would come. If not, with a canoe or barge they could head downstream until they encountered such a boat and buy passage to St. Louis.

Ann and full title to the lands would be in his hands then, and he could negotiate a sale or leasing of the land from a safe distance. The more he thought of this, the more he was positive it remained the only solution for him.

Let Gomer think what he would. Let Dan Shute believe him content with a minor role. He would go ahead with his plans, then strike suddenly and swiftly, and be well on his way before Shute realized what had happened. Once he made the fort, he would be in the clear. Knowing the officers as well as he did, he was sure he could get an escort to the river.

He had never seen the Yellowstone, nor did he know much about either that river or the Powder River. But they had been used by many men as a high road to the West, and he could use a river as an escape to the East.

Carefully he considered the plan. There were preparations to be made. Every angle must be considered. At his ranch were horses enough. He would borrow Baker's buckboard to take Ann for a ride. Then, at his ranch, they would mount and be off. With luck they would be well on their way before anyone so much as guessed what had happened.

Stopping by the store, he bought ammunition from Baker. He glanced up to find the storekeeper's eyes studying him, and he didn't like the expression.

"Is Ann in?" he asked.

Baker nodded and jerked a thumb toward the curtain. Turning, Barkow walked behind the curtain and looked at Ann, who arose as he entered. Quickly, he sensed a coolness that had not been there before. This was no time to talk of marriage. First things first.

He shrugged shamefacedly. "I suppose you're thinkin' pretty bad of me," he suggested ruefully. "I know now I shouldn't have listened to Dan Shute or to Gomer. Pod swore he had a case, and Shute claims Caradec is a crook and a rustler. If I had realized, I wouldn't have had any hand in it."

"It was pretty bad," Ann agreed as she sat down and began knitting. "What will happen now?"

"I don't know," he admitted, "but I wish I could spare you all this. Before it's over, I'm afraid, there'll be more killin's and trouble. Dan Shute is plenty aroused up. He'll kill Caradec."

She looked at him. "You think that will be easy?"

Surprised, he nodded. "Yes. Dan's a dangerous man, and a cruel and brutal one. He's fast with a gun, too."

"I thought you were a friend to Dan Shute?" she asked, looking at him hard. "What's changed you, Bruce?"

He shrugged. "Oh, little things. He showed himself up today. He's brutal, unfeelin'. He'll stop at nothin' to gain his ends."

"I think he will," Ann said composedly. "I think he'll stop at Rafe Caradec."

Barkow stared at her. "He seems to have impressed you. What makes you think that?"

"I never really saw him until today, Bruce," she admitted. "Whatever his motives, he is shrewd and capable. I think he is a much more dangerous man than Dan Shute. There's something behind him, too. He has background. I could see it in his manner more than his words. I wish I knew more about him."

Nettled at her defense of the man, and her apparent respect for him, Bruce shrugged his shoulders.

"Don't forget, he probably killed your father."

She looked up. "Did he, Bruce?"

Her question struck fear from him. Veiling his eyes, he shrugged again.

"You never know." He got up. "I'm worried about you, Ann. This country is going to be flamin' within a few days or weeks. If it ain't the fight here it'll be the Indians. I wish I could get you out of it."

"But this is my home!" Ann protested. "It is all I have!"

"Not quite all." Her eyes fell before his gaze. "Ann, how would you like to go to St. Louis?"

She looked up, startled. "To St. Louis? But how—"

"Not so loud!" He glanced apprehensively at the door. There was no telling who might be listening. "I don't want anybody to know about it unless you decide, and nobody to know till after we're gone. But Ann, we *could* go. I've always wanted to marry you, and there's no time better than now."

She got up and walked to the window. St. Louis. It was another world. She hadn't seen a city in six years, and after all, they had been engaged for several months now.

"How would we get there?" she asked, turning to face him.

"That's a secret!" He laughed. "Don't tell anybody about it, but I've got a wonderful trip planned for you. I always wanted to do things for you, Ann. We could go away and be married within a few hours."

"Where?"

"By the chaplain at the fort. One of the officers would stand up with me, and there are a couple of officers' wives there, too."

"I don't know, Bruce," she said hesitantly. "I'll have to think about it."

He smiled and kissed her lightly. "Then think fast, honey. I want to get you away from all this trouble, and quick."

When he got outside in the street, he paused, smiling with satisfaction.

"I'll show that Dan Shute a thing or two!" he told himself grimly. "I'll leave him standin' here flat-footed, holdin' the bag. I'll have the girl and the ranch, and won't be within miles of this place!"

Abruptly, he turned toward the cabin where he lived.

Dan Shute, who had been leaning against the door of the building next door, straightened thoughtfully and snapped his cigarette into the dust. He had seen the satisfied smile on Barkow's face, and knew he had been inside for some time.

Dan Shute stood on the boardwalk, staring into the dust, his big hands on his hips above the heavy guns, his gray hat pulled low, a stubble of corn-white beard along his hard jaws.

"I think," he said to himself, looking up, "I'll kill Bruce Barkow!" He added, "And I'm goin' to like the doin' of it!"

Chapter XIII
Warning!

Gene Baker was sweeping his store and the stoop in front of it when he saw a tight little cavalcade of horsemen trot around the corner into the street.

It was the morning after the fiasco of the trial, and he had been worried and irritated while wondering what the reaction would be from Barkow and Shute. Then word had come to him of the break between the two at Gomer's office.

Dan Shute, riding a powerful gray, was in the van of the bunch of horsemen. He rode up to the stoop of Baker's store and reined in. Behind him were Red and Tom Blazer, Joe Gorman, Fritz Handl, Fats McCabe, and others of the hard bunch that trailed with Shute.

"Gene," Shute said abruptly, resting his big hands on the pommel of the saddle, "don't sell any more supplies to Caradec or any of his crowd." He added harshly, "I'm not askin' you. I'm tellin' you. And if you do I'll put you out of business and run you out of the country. You know I don't make threats. The chances are Caradec won't be alive by daybreak anyway, but just in case, you've been told!"

Without giving Baker a chance to reply, Dan Shute touched spurs to his horse and led off down the south trail toward the Crazy Man.

The door slammed behind Baker.

"Where are they going?" Ann wanted to know, her eyes wide. "What are they going to do?"

Gene stared after them bleakly. This was the end of something.

"They are goin' after Caradec and his crowd, Ann."

"What will they do to him?"

Something inside her went sick and frightened. She had always been afraid of Dan Shute. The way he looked at her made her shrink. He was the only human being of whom she had ever been afraid. He seemed without feeling, without decency, without regard for anything but his own immediate desires.

"Kill him," Baker said. "They'll kill him. Shute's a hard man, and with him along, that's a mighty wicked lot of men."

"But can't someone warn him?" Ann protested.

Baker glanced at her. "So far as we know, that Caradec is a crook and maybe a killer, Ann. You ain't gettin' soft on him, are you?"

"No!" she exclaimed, startled. "Of course not! What an idea! Why, I've scarcely talked to him!"

Yet there was a heavy, sinking feeling in her heart as she watched the riders disappear in the dust along the southward trail. If there was only something she could do! If she could warn them!

Suddenly she remembered the bay horse her father had given her. Because of the Indians, she had not been riding in a long time, but if she took the mountain trail . . .

Hurrying through the door she swiftly saddled the bay. There was no thought in her mind. She was acting strictly on impulse, prompted by some memory of the way the hair swept back from Rafe's brow, and the look in his eyes when he met her gaze.

She told herself she wanted to see no man killed, that Bo Marsh and Johnny Gill were her friends. Yet even in her heart she knew the excuse would not do. She was thinking of Rafe, and only of Rafe.

The bay was in fine shape and impatient after his long

restraint in the corral. He started for the trail eagerly, and his
ears pricked up at every sound. The leaves had turned to red
and gold now, and in the air there was a hint of frost. Winter
was coming. Soon the country would be blanketed inches
deep under a thick covering of snow.

Hastily, Ann's mind leaped ahead. The prairie trail, which
the Shute riders had taken, swept wide into the valley, then
crossed the Crazy Man, and turned to follow the stream up
the canyon. By cutting across over the mountain trail, there
was every chance she could beat them to the ranch.

In any case, her lead would be slight, because of the
start the bunch had.

The trail crossed the mountainside through a long grove
of quaking aspens, their leaves shimmering in the cool wind,
dark green above, a gray below. Now, with oncoming autumn, most of the leaves had turned to bright yellow intermixed
with crimson, and here and there among the forest of mounting color were the darker arrowheads of spruce and lodgepole
pine.

Once, coming out in a small clearing, she got a view of
the valley below. She had gained a little, but only a little.
Frightened, she touched spurs to the bay, and the little horse
leaped ahead and swept down through the woods at a rapid
gallop.

Ahead, there was a ledge. It was still a good six miles off,
however, but from there she could see the canyon of the
Crazy Man and the upper canyon. A rider had told her that
Caradec had been putting up hay in the wind-sheltered upper canyon and was obviously planning on feeding his stock
there by the warm spring.

She recalled it because she remembered it was something her father had spoken of doing. There was room in the
upper valley for many cattle, and if there was hay enough for
them, the warm water would be a help. With only a little
help the cattle could survive even the coldest winter.

Fording the stream where Caradec had encountered the
young squaw, she rode higher on the mountain, angling
across the slope under a magnificent stand of lodgepole pine.
It was a splendid avenue of trees, all seemingly of the same
size and shape, as though cast from a mold.

Once she glimpsed a deer, and another time in the distance in a small, branching valley she saw a small bunch of

elk. This was her country. No wonder her father had loved it, wanted it, worked to get and to keep it.

Had he paid the mortgage? But why wouldn't Bruce have told her if he had? She could not believe him dishonest or deceitful. And certainly he had made no effort to foreclose, but had been most patient and thoughtful with her.

What would he think of this ride to warn a man he regarded as an enemy? But she could not sit idly by and know men were about to be killed. She would never forgive herself if that happened and she had made no effort to avert it.

Too often she had listened to her father discourse on the necessity for peace and consideration of the problems of others. She believed in that policy wholeheartedly, and the fact that occasionally violence was necessary did not alter her convictions one whit. No system of philosophy or ethics, no growth of government, no improvement in living, came without trial and struggle. Struggle, she had often heard her father say, quoting Hegel, was the law of growth.

Without giving too much thought to it, she understood that such men as Rafe Caradec, Trigger Boyne, Tex Brisco, and others of their ilk were needed. For all their violence, their occasional heedlessness and their desire to go their own way, they were men building a new world in a rough and violent land where everything tended to extremes. Mountains were high, the prairies wide, the streams roaring, the buffalo by the thousand and tens of thousands. It was a land where nothing was small, nothing was simple. Everything, the lives of men and the stories they told, ran to extremes.

The bay pony trotted down the trail and then around a stand of lodgepole. Ann brought him up sharply on the lip of the ledge that had been her first goal.

Below her, a vast and magnificent panorama, lay the ranch her father had pioneered. The silver curve of the Crazy Man lay below and east of her, and opposite her ledge was the mighty wall of the canyon. From below, a faint thread of smoke among the trees marked the cabin.

Turning her head, she looked west and south into the upper canyon. Far away, she seemed to see a horseman moving, and the black dot of a herd. Turning the bay, she started west, riding fast. If they were working the upper canyon she still had a chance.

An hour later, the little bay showing signs of his rough

traveling, she came down to the floor of the canyon. Not far away, she could see Rafe Caradec moving a bunch of cattle into the trees.

He looked around at her approach, and the black, flat-crowned hat came off his head. His dark, wavy hair was plastered to his brow with sweat, and his eyes were gray and curious.

"Good mornin'!" he said. "This is a surprise!"

"Please!" she burst out. "This isn't a social call! Dan Shute's riding this way with twenty men or more. He's going to wipe you out!"

Rafe's eyes sharpened. "You sure?" She could see the quick wonder in his eyes at her warning. Then he wheeled his horse and yelled, "Johnny! Johnny Gill! Come a-runnin'!"

Jerking his rifle from his boot, he looked at her again. He put his hand over hers suddenly, and she started at his touch.

"Thanks, Ann," he said simply. "You're regular!"

Then he was gone, and Johnny Gill was streaking after him. As Gill swept by, he lifted a hand and waved.

There they went. And below were twenty men, all armed. Would they come through alive? She turned the bay and, letting the pony take his own time, started him back over the mountain trail. . . .

Rafe Caradec gave no thought to Ann's reason for warning him. There was no time for that. Tex Brisco and Bo Marsh were at the cabin. They were probably working outside, and their rifles would probably be in the cabin and beyond them. If they were cut off from their guns, the Shute riders would mow them down, kill them at long range with rifle fire.

Rafe heard Gill coming up and slacked off a little to let the little cowhand draw alongside.

"Shute!" he said. "And about twenty men. I guess this is the payoff!"

"Yeah!" Gill yelled.

Rifle fire came to them suddenly—a burst of shots, and then a shot that might have been from a pistol. Yet that was sheer guesswork, Rafe knew, for distinguishing the two was not easy, especially at this distance.

Their horses rounded the entrance and raced down the main canyon toward the cabin on the Crazy Man, running neck and neck. A column of smoke greeted them, and they could see riders circling and firing.

"The trees on the slope!" Rafe yelled, and raced for them.

He reached the trees with the black at a dead run and hit the ground before the animal had ceased to move. He raced to the rocks at the edge of the trees. His rifle lifted and settled, his breath steadied, and the rifle spoke.

A man shouted and waved an arm, and at the same moment, Gill fired. A horse went down. Two men, or possibly three, lay sprawled in the clearing before the cabin.

Were Tex and Bo already down? Rafe steadied himself and squeezed off another shot. A saddle emptied. He saw the fallen man lunge to his feet and then spill over on his face. Coolly then, and taking their time, he and Gill began to fire. Another man went down, and rifles began to smoke in their direction. A bullet clipped the leaves overhead, but too high.

Rafe knocked the hat from a man's head and as the fellow sprinted for shelter, dropped him. Suddenly, the attack broke and he saw the horses sweeping away from them in a ragged line. Mounting, Rafe and Gill rode cautiously toward the cabin.

There was no cabin. There was only a roaring inferno of flames. There were five sprawled bodies now, and Rafe ran toward them. A Shute rider—another. Then he saw Bo.

The boy was lying on his face with a dark, spreading stain on the back on his shirt. There was no sign of Tex.

Rafe dropped to his knees and put a hand over the young cowhand's heart. It was still beating!

Gently, with Johnny lending a hand, he turned the boy over. Then, working with the crude but efficient skill picked up in war and struggle in a half dozen countries, he examined the wounds.

"Four times!" he said grimly. Suddenly, he felt something mount and swell within him, a tide of fierce, uncontrollable anger!

Around one bullet hole in the stomach, the cloth of the cowhand's shirt was smoldering!

"I seen that!" It was Tex Brisco, his face haggard and smoke grimed. "I seen it! I know who done it! He walked up while the kid was layin' there and stuck a gun against his stomach and shot! He didn't want the kid to go quick, he wanted him to die slow and hard!"

"Who done it?" Gill demanded fiercely. "I'll get him now! Right now!"

Brisco's eyes were red and inflamed. "Nobody gets him but me. This kid was your pard, but I *seen* it!" He turned abruptly on Rafe. "Boss, let me go to town. I want to kill me a man!"

"It won't do, Tex," Caradec said quietly. "I know how you feel, but the town will be full of 'em. They'll be celebratin'. They burned our cabin and ran off some cattle, and they got Bo. It wouldn't do!"

"Yeah." Tex spat. "I know. But they won't be expectin' any trouble now. We've been together a long time, Boss, but if you don't let me go, I'll quit!"

Rafe looked up from the wounded man.

"All right, Tex. I told you I know how you feel. But if somethin' should happen—who did it?"

"Tom Blazer. That big redhead. He always hated the kid. Shute shot the kid down and left him lay. I was out back in the woods lookin' for a pole to cut. They rode up so fast the kid never had a chance. He was hit twice before he knew what was goin' on, and then again when he started toward the house. After the house was afire, Tom Blazer walked up, and the kid was conscious. Tom said somethin' to Bo, shoved the gun against him, and pulled the trigger." He stared miserably at Bo. "I was out of pistol range. Took me a few minutes to get closer. Then I got me two men before you rode up."

Wheeling, he headed toward the corral.

Rafe had stopped the flow of blood, and Johnny had returned with a blanket from a line back of the house.

"Reckon we better get him over in the trees, Boss," Gill said.

Chapter XIV
"I've Come for You, Tom!"

Easing the cowboy to the blanket with care, Rafe and Johnny carried Bo into the shade in a quiet place under the pines.

Caradec glanced up as they put him down. Tex Brisco was riding out of the canyon. Johnny Gill watched him go.

"Boss," Gill said, "I wanted like blazes to go, but I ain't the man Brisco is. Rightly, I'm a quiet man, but that Texan is a wolf on the prowl. I'm some glad I'm not Tom Blazer right now!"

He looked down at Bo Marsh. The young cowhand's face was flushed, his breathing hoarse.

"Will he live, Rafe?" Johnny asked softly.

Caradec shrugged. "I don't know," he said honestly. "He needs better care than I can give him. He studied the situation thoughtfully. "Johnny," he said, "you stay with him. Better take time to build a lean-to over him in case of rain or snow. Get some fuel, too."

"What about you?" Johnny asked. "Where you goin'?"

"To the fort. There's an Army doctor there, and I'll go get him."

"Reckon he'll come this far?" Johnny asked doubtingly.

"He'll come!"

Rafe Caradec mounted the black and rode slowly away into the dusk. It was a long ride to the fort, and even if he got the doctor it might be too late. That was a chance he would have to take. There was small danger of an attack now.

Yet it was not a return of Dan Shute's riders that disturbed him, but a subtle coolness in the air, a chill that was of more than autumn. Winters in this country could be bitterly cold, and all the signs gave evidence this one would be the worst in years, and they were without a cabin. He rode on toward the fort, with the thought that Tex Brisco now must be nearing town.

It was growing late, and Painted Rock lay swathed in velvety darkness when Tex Brisco walked his horse down to the edge of town. He stopped across the bend of the stream from town and left his horse among the trees there. He would have a better chance of escape from across the stream than from the street, and by leaving town on foot, he could create some doubt as to his whereabouts.

He was under no misapprehension as to the problem he faced. Painted Rock would be filled to overflowing with Shute and Barkow riders, many of whom knew him by sight. Yet though he could vision their certainty of victory and their numbers, and was well aware of the reckless task he had chosen, he knew they would not be expecting him or any riders from Crazy Man.

He tied his horse loosely to a bush among the trees and

crossed the stream on a log. Once across, he thought of his spurs. Kneeling down, he unfastened them from his boots and hung them over a root near the end of the log. He wanted no jingling spurs to give his presence away at an inopportune moment.

Carefully avoiding any lighted dwellings, he made his way through the scattered houses to the back of the row of buildings along the street. He was wearing the gun he usually wore, and for luck he had taken another from his saddlebags and thrust it into his waist band.

Tex Brisco was a man of the frontier. From riding the range in south and west Texas, he had drifted north with trail herds. He seen some of the days around the beginning of Dodge and Ellsworth and some hard fighting down in the Nations and with rustlers along the border.

He was an honest man, a sincere man. He had a quality to be found in many men of his kind and period—a quality of deep-seated loyalty that was his outstanding trait.

Hard and reckless in demeanor, he rode with dash and acted with a flair. He had at times been called a hard case. Yet no man lived long in a dangerous country if he were reckless. There was a place always for courage, but intelligent courage, not the heedlessness of a harebrained youngster.

Tex Brisco was twenty-five years old, but he had been doing a man's work since he was eleven. He had walked with men, ridden with men, and fought with men as one of them. He had asked no favors and been granted none. Now, at twenty-five, he was a seasoned veteran. He was a man who knew the plains and the mountains, knew cattle, horses, and guns. He possessed a fierce loyalty to his outfit and to his friends.

Shanghaied, he had quickly seen that the sea was not his element. He had concealed his resentment and gone to work, realizing that safety lay along that route. He had known his time would come. It had come when Rafe Caradec came aboard, and all his need for friendship, for loyalty, and for a cause had been tied to the big, soft-spoken stranger.

Now Painted Rock was vibrant with danger. The men who did not hate him in Painted Rock were men who would not speak for him or act for him. It was like Tex Brisco that he did not think in terms of help. He had his job, he knew his problem, and he knew he was the man to do it.

The National Saloon was booming with sound. The tinny jangle of an out-of-tune piano mingled with hoarse laughter, shouts, and the rattle of glasses. The hitching rail was lined with horses.

Tex walked between the buildings to the edge of the dark and empty street. Then he walked up to the horses and, speaking softly, made his way along the hitching rail, turning every slipknot into a hard knot.

The Emporium was dark except for a light in Baker's living quarters, where he sat with his wife and Ann Rodney.

The stage station was lighted by the feeble glow of a light over a desk as the station agent worked late over his books.

It was a moonless night, and the stars were bright. Tex lighted a cigarette, loosened his guns in his holsters, and studied the situation. The National was full. To step into that saloon would be suicide, and Tex had no such idea in mind. It was early, and he would have to wait.

Yet might it not be the best way, if he stepped in? There would be a moment of confusion. In that instant he could act.

Working his way back to a window, he studied the interior. It took him several minutes to locate Tom Blazer. The big man was standing by the bar with Fats McCabe. Slipping to the other end of the window, Tex could see that no one was between them and the rear door.

He stepped back into the darkest shadows and, leaning against the building, finished his cigarette. When it was down to a stub, he threw it on the ground and carefully rubbed it out with the toe of his boot. Then he pulled his hat low and walked around to the rear of the saloon.

There was some scrap lumber there, and he skirted the rough pile, avoiding some bottles. It was cool out here, and he rubbed his fingers a little, working his hands to keep the circulation going. Then he stepped up to the door and turned the knob. It opened under his hand, and if it made a sound, it went unheard.

Stepping inside, he closed the door after him, pleased that it opened outward.

In the hurly-burly of the interior one more cowhand went unseen. Nobody even glanced his way. He sidled up to the bar and then reached over under Tom Blazer's nose, drew the whiskey bottle toward him, and poured a drink into a glass just rinsed by the bartender.

Tom Blazer scarcely glanced at the bottle, for other bottles were being passed back and forth. Fats McCabe stood beside Tom, also not noticing Tex.

"That bastard Marsh!" Tom said thickly. "I got him! I been wantin' him a long time! You should have seen the look in his eyes when I shoved that pistol against him and pulled the trigger!"

Tex's lips tightened, and he poured his glass full once more. He left it sitting on the bar in front of him.

His eyes swept the room. Dan Shute was not here, and that worried him. He would have felt better to have had the rancher under his eyes. Bruce Barkow was here, though, and Pod Gomer. Tex moved over a little closer to McCabe.

"That'll finish 'em off!" McCabe was saying. "When Shute took over I knew they wouldn't last long! If they get out of the country, they'll be lucky. They've no supplies now, and it will be snowin' within a few days. The winter will get 'em if we don't, or the Injuns."

Tex Brisco smiled grimly. "Not before I get you!" he thought. "That comes first."

The piano was banging away with "Oh, Susanna!" and a bunch of cowhands were trying to sing it. Joe Benson leaned on his bar talking to Pod Gomer. Barkow sat at a table in the corner, staring morosely into a glass. Joe Gorman and Fritz Handl were watching a poker game.

Tex glanced again at the back door. No one stood between the door and himself. Well, why wait?

Just then Tom Blazer reached for the bottle in front of Tex, and Tex pulled it away from his hand.

Tom stared. "Hey, what you tryin' to do?" he demanded belligerently.

"I've come for you, Tom," Tex said. "I've come to kill a skunk that shoots a helpless man when he's on his back. How are you against standin' men, Blazer?"

"Huh?" Tom Blazer said stupidly.

Then he realized what had been said, and he thrust his big face forward for a closer look. The gray eyes he saw were icy, the lantern-jawed Texan's face was chill as death, and Tom Blazer jerked back. Slowly, his face white, Fats McCabe drew aside.

To neither man came the realization that Tex Brisco was alone. All they felt was the shock of his sudden appearance, here, among them.

Brisco turned, stepping one step away from the bar.

"Well, Tom," he said quietly, his voice just loud enough to carry over the sound of the music, "I've come for you."

Riveted to the spot, Tom Blazer felt an instant of panic. Brisco's presence here had the air of magic, and Tom was half frightened by the sheer unexpectedness of it.

Sounds in the saloon seemed to die out, although they still went full blast, and Tom stared across that short space like a man in a trance, trapped and faced with a fight to the death. There would be no escaping this issue, he knew. He might win and he might lose, but it was here, now, and he had to face it. And he realized suddenly that it was a choice he had no desire to make.

Wouldn't anyone notice? Why didn't Fats say something? Tex Brisco stood there, staring at him.

"You've had your chance," Tex said gently. "Now I'm goin' to kill you!"

The shock of the word "kill" snapped Tom Blazer out of it. He dropped into a half crouch, and his lips curled in a snarl of mingled rage and fear. His clawed hand swept back for his gun.

In the throbbing and rattle of the room, the guns boomed like a crash of thunder. Heads whirled, and liquor-befuddled brains tried to focus eyes. All they saw was Tom Blazer sagging back against the bar, his shirt darkening with blood and the strained, foolish expression on his face like that of a man who had been shocked beyond reason.

Facing the room was a lean, broad-shouldered man with two guns, and as they looked, he swung a gun at Fats McCabe.

Instinctively, at the boom of guns, McCabe's brain reacted, but a shade slow. His hand started for his gun. It was an involuntary movement that had he had but a moment's thought would never have been made. He had no intention of drawing. All he wanted was out, but the movement of his hand was enough. It was too much.

Tex Brisco's gun boomed again, and Fats toppled over on his face. Then Tex opened up, and three shots, blasting into the brightly lighted room, brought it to complete darkness. Brisco faded into that darkness, swung the door open, and vanished as a shot clipped the air over his head.

He ran hard for fifty feet and then ducked into the shadow of a barn, threw himself over a low corral fence, and ran across the corral in a low crouch. Shouts and orders sounded, and then the crash of glass came from the saloon.

The door burst open again, and he could have got another man, but only to have betrayed his position. He crawled through the fence and keeping close to a dark house, ran swiftly to its far corner. He paused there, breathing heavily. So far, so good.

From here on he would be in comparative light, but the distance was enough now. He ran on swiftly for the river. Behind him he heard curses and yells as men found their knotted bridle reins. At the end of the log, Tex retrieved his spurs. Then, gasping for breath from his hard run, he ran across the log and started for his horse.

He saw it suddenly, and then he saw something else.

Chapter XV
Through the Dark

In the dim light, Tex recognized Joe Gorman by his hat. Joe wore his hat brim rolled to a point in front.

"Hi, Texas!" Gorman said. Tex could see the gun in his hand, waist high and leveled on him.

"Hi, Joe. Looks like you smelled somethin'."

"Yeah"—Joe nodded—"I did at that. I live in one of those houses over there with some of the other boys. Happened to see somebody ride up here in the dark, and got curious. When you headed for the saloon, I got around you and went in. Then I saw you come in the back door. I slipped out just before the shootin' started so's I could beat you back here in case you got away."

"Too bad you missed the fun," Brisco said quietly.

Behind him, the pursuit seemed to have gained no direction as yet. His mind was on a hair trigger, watching for a break. Which of his guns was still loaded? He had forgotten whether he put the loaded gun in the holster or in his belt.

"Who'd you get?" asked Gorman.

"Tom Blazer. Fats McCabe, too."

"I figgered Tom. I told him he shouldn't have shot the kid. That was a low-down trick. But why shoot Fats?"

"He acted like he was reachin' for a gun."

"Huh. Don't take a lot to get a man killed, does it?"

Brisco could see in the dark enough to realize that Gorman was smiling a little.

"How do you want it, Tex? Should I let you have it now, or save you for Shute? He's a bad man, Tex."

"I think you'd better slip your gun in your holster and walk back home, Joe," Tex said. "You're the most decent one of a bad lot."

"Maybe I want the money I'd get for you, Tex. I can use some."

"Think you'd live to collect?"

"You mean Caradec? He's through, Brisco. Through. We got Bo. Now we got you. That leaves only Caradec and Johnny Gill. They won't be so tough."

"You're wrong, Joe," Tex said quietly. "Rafe could take the lot of you, and he will. But you bought into my game yourself, I wouldn't ask for help, Joe. I'd kill you myself."

"You?" Gorman chuckled with real humor. "And me with the drop on you? Not a chance! Why, Tex, *one* of these slugs would get you, and if I have to start blastin', I'm goin' to empty the gun before I quit."

"Uh-huh," Tex agreed. "You might get me. But I'll get you, too."

Joe Gorman was incredulous. "You mean, get me before I could shoot?" He repeated, "Not a chance!"

The sounds of pursuit were coming closer. The men had a light now and had found his tracks.

"Toward the river. I'll be a coon!" a voice yelled. "Let's go!"

Here it was! Joe Gorman started to yell and then saw the black figure ahead of him move, and his gun blazed. Tex felt the shocking jolt of a slug, and his knees buckled, but his gun was out and he triggered two shots, fast. Joe started to fall, and he fired again, but the hammer fell on an empty chamber.

Tex jerked the slipknot in his reins loose and dragged himself into the saddle. He was bleeding badly. His mind felt hazy, but he saw Joe Gorman move on the ground, and heard him say:

"You did it, cuss you! You did it!"

"So long, Joe!" Tex whispered hoarsely.

He walked the horse for twenty feet and then started moving faster. His brain was singing with a strange noise, and his blood seemed to drum in his brain. He headed up the tree-covered slope, and the numbness crawled up his legs.

He fought like a cornered wolf against the darkness that crept over him.

"I can't die—I can't!" he kept saying in his brain. "Rafe'll need help! I can't!"

Fighting the blackness and numbness, he tied the bridle reins to the saddle horn, and thrust both feet clear through the stirrups. Sagging in the saddle, he got his handkerchief out and fumbled a knot, tying his wrists to the saddle horn.

The light glowed and died, and the horse walked on, weaving in the awful darkness, weaving through a world of agony and the soft clutching hands that seemed to be pulling Tex down, pulling him down.

The darkness closed in around him, but under him he seemed still to feel the slow plodding of the horse. . . .

Roughly, the distance to the fort was seventy miles, a shade less perhaps. Rafe Caradec rode steadily into the increasing cold of the wind. There was no mistaking the seriousness of Bo's condition. The young cowhand was badly shot up and weak from loss of blood. Despite the amazing vitality of frontier men, his chance was slight unless his wounds had proper care.

Bowing his head to the wind, Rafe headed the horse down into a draw and its partial shelter. There was no use thinking of Tex. Whatever had happened in Painted Rock had happened by now, or was happening. Brisco might be dead. He might be alive and safe, even now heading back to the Crazy Man. Or he might be wounded and in need of help.

Tex Brisco was an uncertainty now, but Bo Marsh hung between life and death. Hence there was no choice.

The friendship and understanding between the lean, hard-faced Texan and Rafe Caradec had grown aboard ship. And Rafe was not one to take lightly the Texan's loyalty in joining him in his foray into Wyoming.

Now Brisco might be dead, killed in a fight he would never have known but for Rafe. Yet Tex would have had it no other way. His destinies were guided by his loyalties. Those loyalties were his life, his religion, his reason for living.

Yet despite his worries over Marsh and Brisco, Rafe found his thoughts returning again and again to Ann Rodney. Why had she ridden to warn them of the impending attack? Had it not been for that warning, the riders would have wiped out Brisco at the same time they got Marsh, and would have followed it up to find Rafe and Johnny back in the canyon. It would have been, or could have been, a clean sweep.

Why had Ann warned them? Was it because of her dislike of violence and killing? Or was there some other, some deeper feeling?

Yet how could that be? What feeling could Ann have for any of them, believing as she seemed to believe that he was a thief or worse? The fact remained that she had come, that she had warned them.

Remembering her, he recalled the flash of her eyes, the proud lift of her chin, the way she walked.

He stared grimly into the night and swore softly. Was he in love?

"Who knows?" he demanded viciously of the night. "And what good would it do if I was?"

He had never seen the fort, yet knew it lay between the forks of the Piney and its approximate location. His way led across the billowing hills and through a country marked by small streams lined with cottonwood, box elder, willow, choke-cherry, and wild plum. That this was the Indian country, he knew. The unrest of the tribes was about to break into open warfare, and already there had been sporadic attacks on haying or woodcutting parties, and constant attacks were being made on the Missouri steamboats far to the north.

Red Cloud, most influential chieftain among the Sioux, had tried to hold the tribes together, and despite the continued betrayal of treaties by the white man, had sought to abide by the code laid down for his people. With Man Afraid of His Horse, the Oglala chief, Red Cloud, was the strongest of all the Sioux leaders, or had been.

With Custer's march into the Black Hills and the increasing travel over the Laramie and Bozeman trails, the Sioux were growing restless. The Sioux medicine man Sitting Bull was indulging in war talk, and was aided and abetted by two powerful warriors, skilled tacticians and great leaders—Crazy Horse and Gall.

No one in the West but understood that an outbreak of serious nature was overdue.

Rafe Caradec was aware of all this. He was aware, too, that it would not be an easy thing to prevail upon the doctor to leave the fort or upon the commandant to allow him to leave. In the face of impending trouble, the doctor's place was with the Army. . . .

News of the battle on the Crazy Man, after Ann's warning, reached her that evening. The return of the triumphant Shute riders was enough to tell her what had happened. She heard them ride into the street, heard their yells and their shouts.

She heard that Bo Marsh was definitely dead. Even some of the Shute riders were harsh in their criticism of Tom Blazer for that action.

While the Shute outfit had ridden away following their attack, fearful of the effects of the sharpshooting from the timber, they were satisfied. Winter was coming on, and they had destroyed the cabin on the Crazy Man and killed Bo Marsh. Mistakenly, they also believed they had killed Brisco and wounded at least one other man.

Sick at heart, Ann had walked back into her room and stood by the window. Suddenly she was overwhelmed by the desire to get away, to escape all this sickening violence, the guns, the killings, the problems of frontier life. Back east, there were lovely homes along quiet streets, slow-running streams, men who walked quietly on Sunday mornings. There were parties, theaters, friends, and homes.

Her long ride had tired her. The touch of Rafe Caradec's hand, the look in his eyes, had given her a lift. Something had sparked within her, and she felt herself drawn to him, yearning toward him with everything feminine that was within her. Riding away, she had heard the crash of guns, shouts, and yells. Had she been too late?

There had been no turning back. She had known there was nothing she could do. Her natural good sense had told her that she would only complicate matters if she tried to stay. Nor did she know now what she would have done if she had stayed?

Where was her sympathy? With Shute's riders? Or with this strange, tall young man who had come to claim half her ranch and tell fantastic stories of knowing her father aboard a ship?

Every iota of intelligence she had told her the man was all wrong, that his story could not be true.

Bruce Barkow's story of her father's death had been the true one.

What reason for him to lie?

Why would he want to claim her land when there was so much more to be had for the taking?

Her father had told her, and Gene Baker had agreed, that soon all this country would be open to settlement, and there would be towns and railroads here. Why choose one piece of land, a large section of it worthless, when the hills lay bare for the taking?

Standing by the window and looking out into the darkness, Ann knew suddenly she was sick of it all.

She would get away, go back east. Bruce was right.

It was time she left here, and when he came again, she would tell him she was ready.

He had been thoughtful and considerate. He had protected her, been attentive and affectionate. He was a man of intelligence, and he was handsome. She could be proud of him.

She stifled her misgivings with a sudden resolution and hurriedly began to pack.

Chapter XVI
One by One

Vaguely Ann had sensed Barkow's fear of something, but she believed it was fear of an attack by Indians. Word had come earlier that day that the Oglala were gathering in the hills and that there was much war talk among them. That it could be Dan Shute whom Barkow feared, Ann had no idea.

She had completed the packing of the few items she would need for the trip when she heard the sound of gunfire from the National.

The shots brought her to her feet with a start, her face pale. Running into the living room, she found that Gene Baker had caught up his rifle. She ran to Mrs. Baker, and the two women stood together, listening.

Baker looked at them. "Can't be Indians," he said, after a moment. "Maybe some wild cowhand celebratin'."

They heard excited voices and yells. Baker went to the door, hesitated, and then went out. He was gone several minutes before he returned. His face was grave.

"It was that Texas rider from the Crazy Man," he said.

"He stepped into the back door of the National and shot it out with Tom Blazer and Fats McCabe. They are both dead."

"Was he alone?" Ann asked quickly.

Baker nodded, looking at her somberly. "They are huntin' him now. He won't get away, I'm afraid."

"You're *afraid* he won't?"

"Yes, Ann," Baker said, "I am. That Blazer outfit's poison. All of that Shute bunch, far as that goes. Tom killed young Bo Marsh by stickin' a pistol against him whilst he was lyin' down."

The flat bark of a shot cut across the night air, and they went rigid. Two more shots rang out.

"Guess they got him," Baker said. "There's so many of them, I figgered they would."

Before the news reached them of what had actually happened, daylight had come. Ann Rodney was awake after an almost sleepness night. Tex Brisco, she heard, had killed Joe Gorman when Gorman had caught him at his horse. Tex had escaped, but from all the evidence, he was badly wounded. They were trailing him by the blood from his wounds.

First it had been Bo Marsh, and now Brisco. Was Johnny Gill alive? Was Rafe? If Rafe was alive, then he must be alone, harried like a rabbit by hounds.

Restless, Ann paced the floor. Shute riders came and went in the store. They were buying supplies and going out in groups of four and five, scouring the hills for Brisco or any of the others of the Crazy Man crowd.

Bruce Barkow came shortly after breakfast. He walked into the store. He looked tired and worried.

"Ann," he said abruptly, "if we're goin', it'll have to be today. This country is goin' to the wolves. All they think about now is killin'. Let's get out."

She hesitated only an instant. Something inside her seemed lost and dead.

"All right, Bruce. We've planned it for a long time. It might as well be now."

There was no fire in her, no spark. Barkow scarcely heeded that. She would go, and once away from here and married, he would have title to the land, and Dan Shute for all his talk and harsh ways would be helpless.

"All right," he said. "We'll leave in an hour. Don't tell anybody. We'll take the buckboard like we were goin' for a drive, as we often do."

She was ready, so there was nothing to do after he had gone.

Baker seemed older, worried. Twice riders came in, and each time Ann heard that Tex Brisco was still at large. His horse had been trailed, seemingly wandering without guidance, to a place on a mountain creek. There the horse had walked into the water, and no trail had been found to show where he had left it. He was apparently headed for the high ridges, south by west.

Nor had anything been found of Marsh or Gill. Shute riders had returned to the Crazy Man, torn down the corral, and hunted through the woods, but no sign had been found beyond a crude lean-to where the wounded man had evidently been sheltered. Marsh, if dead, had been buried and the grave concealed. Nothing had been found of any of them, although one horse had ridden off to the northeast, mostly east.

One horse had gone east! Ann Rodney's heart gave a queer leap. East would mean toward the fort! Perhaps. . . . But she was being foolish. Why should it be Caradec rather than Gill, and why to the fort? She expressed the thought, and Baker looked at her.

"Likely enough one of 'em's gone there. If Marsh ain't dead, and the riders didn't find his body, chances are he's mighty bad off. The only doctor around is at the fort."

The door to the store opened, and Baker went in, leaving the living room. There was a brief altercation, and then the curtain was pushed aside and Ann looked up.

A start of fear went through her.

Dan Shute was standing in the door. For a wonder, he was clean-shaven except for his mustache. He looked at her with his queer, gray-white eyes.

"Don't you do nothin' foolish," he said, "like tryin' to leave here. I don't aim to let you."

Ann got up, amazed and angry. "You don't aim to let me?" she flared. "What business is it of yours?"

Shute stood there with his big hands on his hips, staring at her insolently.

"Because I want to make it my business," he said. "I've told Barkow where he stands with you. If he don't like it he can say so and die. I ain't particular. I just wanted you should know that from here on you're my woman."

"Listen here, Shute!" Baker flared. "You can't talk to a decent woman that way!"

"Shut your mouth!" Shute said, staring at Baker. "I talk the way I please. I'm tellin' her. If she tries to get away from here, I'll take her out to the ranch now. If she waits"—he looked her up and down coolly—"I may marry her. Don't know why I should." He added, glaring at Baker, "You butt into this and I'll smash you. She ain't no woman for a weak sister like Barkow. I guess she'll come to like me all right. Anyway, she'd better." He turned toward the door. "Don't get any ideas. I'm the law here, and the only law."

"I'll appeal to the Army!" Baker declared.

"You do," Shute said, "and I'll kill you. Anyway, the Army's goin' to be some busy. A bunch of Sioux raided a stage station way south of here last night. Killed three men and then ran off the stock. Two men were killed havin' over on Otter last night. A bunch of soldiers havin' not far from the Piney were fired on and one man wounded. The Army's too busy to bother with the likes of you. Besides," he added, grinning, "the commandin' officer said that in case of Injun trouble, I was to take command at Painted Rock and make all preparations for defense."

He turned and walked out of the room. They heard the front door slam, and Ann sat down, suddenly.

Gene Baker walked to the desk and got out his gun. His face was stiff and old.

"No, not that," Ann said. "I'm leaving, Uncle Gene."

"Leavin'? How?" He turned on her, his eyes alert.

"With Bruce. He's asked me several times. I was going to tell you, but nobody else. I'm all packed."

"Barkow, eh?" Gene Baker stared at her. "Well, why not? He's half a gentleman, anyway. Shute is an animal and a brute."

The back door opened gently. Bruce Barkow stepped in. "Was Dan here?"

Baker explained quickly. "Better forget that buckboard idea," he said, when Barkow had explained the plan. "Take the horses and go by the river trail. Leave at noon when everybody will be eatin'. Take the Bannock Trail, and then swing north and east and cut around toward the fort. They'll think you're tryin' for the goldfields."

Barkow nodded. He looked stiff and pale, and he was wearing a gun.

It was almost noon.

When the streets were empty, Bruce Barkow went out back to the barn and saddled the horses. There was no one in sight. The woods along the creek were only a hundred yards away.

Walking outside, the two got into their saddles and rode at a walk, the dust muffling the beat of the horses' hoofs, to the trees. Then they took the Bannock Trail. Two miles out, Barkow rode into a stream and then led the way north.

Once away from the trail they rode swiftly, keeping the horses at a rapid trot. Barkow was silent, and his eyes kept straying to the back trail. Twice they saw Indian sign, but their escape had evidently been made successfully, for there was no immediate sound of pursuit.

Bruce Barkow kept moving, and as he rode, his irritation, doubt, and fear began to grow more and more obvious. He rode like a man in the grip of deadly terror. Ann, watching him, wondered.

Before, Shute had tolerated Barkow. Now a definite break had been made, and with each mile of their escape, Barkow became more frightened. There was no way back now. He would be killed on sight, for Dan Shute was not a man to forgive or tolerate such a thing.

It was only on the girl's insistence that he stopped for a rest and to give the horses a much needed blow. They took it, while Ann sat on the grass and Bruce paced the ground, his eyes searching the trail over which they had come. When they were in the saddle again, he seemed to relax, to come to himself. Then he looked at her.

"You must think I'm a coward," he said, "but it's just that I'm afraid of what Shute would do if he got his hands on you. And I'm no gunfighter. He'd kill us both."

"I know." She nodded gravely.

This man who was to be her husband impressed her less at every moment. Somehow, his claim that he was thinking of her failed to ring with sincerity. Yet with all his faults, he was probably only a weak man, a man cut out for civilization and not for the frontier.

They rode on, and the miles piled up behind them. . . .

Rafe Caradec awakened with a start to the sound of a bugle. It took him several seconds to realize that he was in bed at the fort. Then he remembered. The commanding officer had refused to allow the surgeon to leave before morn-

ing, and then only with an escort. With Lieutenant Bryson
and eight men they would form a scouting patrol, circle
around by Crazy Man, and then cut back toward the fort.

The party at the fort was small, for the place had been
abandoned several years before and had been utilized only
for a few weeks as a base for scouting parties when fear of an
Indian outbreak began to grow. It was no longer an established post, but merely a camp.

Further to the south there was a post at Fort Fetterman,
named for the leader of the troops trapped in the Fetterman
Massacre. A wagon train had been attacked within a short
distance of Fort Phil Kearney and a group of seventy-nine
soldiers and two civilians were to march out to relieve them
under command of Major James Powell, a skilled Indian
fighter. However, Brevet Lieutenant Colonel Fetterman had
used his rank to take over command and had ridden out.

Holding the fighting ability of the Indians in contempt,
Fetterman had pursued some of them beyond a ridge. Firing
had been heard, and when other troops were sent out from
the fort they discovered Fetterman and his entire command
wiped out, about halfway down the ridge.

The wagon train they had gone to relieve reached the
fort later, unaware of the encounter on the ridge.

Getting into his clothes, Rafe hurried outside. The first
person he met was Bryson.

"Good morning, Caradec!" Bryson said, grinning. "Bugle
wake you up?"

Caradec nodded. "It isn't the first time."

"You've been in the service then?" Bryson asked, glancing at him quickly.

"Yes," Rafe glanced around the stockade. "I was with
Sully. In Mexico for a while, too, and Guatemala."

Bryson glanced at him. "Then you're *that* Caradec? Man,
I've heard of you! Major Skehan will be pleased to know.
He's an admirer of yours, sir!"

He nodded toward two weary, dust-covered horses.

"You're not the only arrival from Painted Rock," Bryson
said. "Those horses came in last night. Almost daylight, in
fact, with two riders. A chap named Barkow and a girl.
Pretty, too, the lucky dog!"

Rafe turned on him, his eyes sharp. "A woman? A girl?"

Bryson looked surprised. "Why, yes. Her name's Rodney. She—"

"Where is she?" Rafe snapped. "Where is she now?"

Bryson smiled slightly. "Why, that's her over there! A friend of yours?"

But Rafe was gone.

Ann was standing in the door of one of the partly reconstructed buildings, and when she saw him, her eyes widened.

"Rafe! You, here? Then you got away?"

"I came after a doctor for Marsh. He's in a bad way." He tossed the remark aside, studying her face. "Ann, what are you doing here with Barkow?"

His tone nettled her. "Why? How does it concern you?"

"Your father asked me to take care of you," he said, "and if you married Bruce Barkow, I certainly wouldn't be doin' it!"

"Oh?" Her voice was icy. "Still claiming you knew my father? Well, Mr. Caradec, I think you'd be much better off to forget that story. I don't know where you got the idea, or how, or what made you believe you could get away with it, but it won't do! I've been engaged to Bruce for months. I intend to marry him now. There's a chaplain here. Then we'll go on to the river and down to St. Louis. There's a steamer on the way up that we can meet."

"I won't let you do it, Ann," Rafe said harshly.

Her weariness, her irritation, and something else brought quick anger to her face and lips.

"You won't *let* me? You have nothing to do with it! It simply isn't any of your business! Now, if you please, I'm waiting for Bruce. Will you go?"

"No," he said violently, "I won't! I'll say again what I said before. I knew your father. He gave me a deed givin' us the ranch. He asked me to care for you. He also gave me the receipt that Bruce Barkow gave him for the mortgage money. I wanted things to be different, Ann. I—"

"Caradec!" Bryson called. "We're ready!"

He glanced around. The small column awaited him, and his horse was ready. For an instant he glanced back at the girl. Her jaw was set, her eyes blazing.

"Oh, what's the use?" he flared. "Marry who you blasted well please!"

Wheeling, he walked to his horse and swung into the saddle, riding away without a backward glance.

Chapter XVII
The Killer

Lips parted to speak, Ann Rodney stared after the disappear-
ing riders. Suddenly all her anger was gone. She found
herself gazing at the closing gate of the stockade and fighting
a mounting sense of panic.

What had she done? Suppose what Rafe had said was the
truth? What had he ever done to make her doubt him?

Confused, puzzled by her own feelings for this stranger
of whom she knew so little, yet who stirred her so deeply,
she was standing there, one hand partly upraised, when she
saw two men come around the corner of the building. Both
wore the rough clothing of miners.

They paused near her, one a stocky, thickset man with a
broad, hard jaw, the other a slender, blond young man.

"Ma'am," the younger man said, "we just come in from
the river. The major was tellin' us you were goin' back that
way?"

She nodded dumbly and then forced herself to speak.
"Yes, we are going to the river with some of the troops. Or
that has been our plan."

"We come up the Powder from the Yellowstone, ma'am,"
the young man said, "and if you could tell us where to find
your husband, we might sell him our boats."

She shook her head. "I'm not married yet. You will have
to see my fiancé, Bruce Barkow. He's in the mess hall."

The fellow hesitated, turning his hat in his hand. "Ma'am,
they said you was from Painted Rock. Ever hear tell of a man
named Rafe Caradec over there?"

She stiffened. "Rafe Caradec?" She looked at him quickly.
"You know him?"

He nodded, pleased by her sudden interest.

"Yes, ma'am. We were shipmates of his. Me and my
partner over there, Rock Mullaney. My name is Penn, ma'am—
Roy Penn."

Suddenly, her heart was pounding. She looked at him
and bit her underlip. Then she said carefully, "You were on a
ship with him?"

"That's right."

Penn was puzzled, and he was growing wary. After all,
there was the manner of their leaving. Of course, that was

months ago, and they were far from the sea now, but that still hung over them.

"Was there—aboard that ship—a man named Rodney?"

Ann couldn't look at them now. She stared at the stockade, almost afraid to hear their reply. Vaguely, she realized that Bruce Barkow was approaching.

"Rodney? Surest thing you know! Charles Rodney. Nice fellow, too. He died off the California coast after—" He hesitated. "Ma'am, you ain't no relation of his now?"

"I'm Charles Rodney's daughter."

"Oh?" Then Penn's eyes brightened. "Say, then you're the girl Rafe was lookin' for when he come over here! Will you think of that!" He turned. "Hey, Rock! This here's that Ann Rodney, the girl Rafe came here to see! You know, Charlie's daughter!"

Bruce Barkow stopped dead still. His dark face was suddenly wary.

"What was that?" he said sharply. "What did you say?"

Penn stared at him. "No reason to get excited, mister. Yeah, we knew this young lady's father on board ship. He was shanghaied out of San Francisco!"

Bruce Barkow's face was cold. Here it was, at the last minute. This did it. He was trapped now. He could see in Ann's face the growing realization of how he had lied, how he had betrayed her, and even—he could see that coming into her eyes, too—the idea that he had killed her father.

Veins swelled in his forehead and throat. He glared at Penn, half crouching, like some cornered animal.

"You're a liar!" he snarled.

"Don't call me that!" Penn said fiercely. "I'm not wearing a gun, mister!"

If Barkow heard the last words they made no impression. His hand was already sweeping down. Penn stepped back, throwing his arms wide, and Bruce Barkow, his face livid with the fury of frustration, whipped up a gun and shot him twice through the body. Penn staggered back, uncomprehending, staring.

"No—gun!" he gasped. "I don't—gun."

He staggered into an Army wagon, reeled, and fell headlong.

Bruce Barkow stared at the fallen man, and then his contorted face turned upward. On the verge of escape and success he had been trapped, and now he had become a killer!

* * *

Wheeling, he sprang into the saddle. The gate was open for a wood wagon, and he whipped the horse through it, shouting hoarsely. Men had rushed from everywhere, and Rock Mullaney, staring in shocked surprise, could only fumble at his belt. He wore no gun either.

He looked up at Ann. "We carried rifles," he muttered. "We never figgered on no trouble!" Then he rubbed his face, sense returning to his eyes. "Ma'am, what did he shoot him for?"

She stared at him, humbled by the grief written on the man's hard, lonely face.

"That man, Barkow, killed my father!" she said.

"No, ma'am. If you're Charlie Rodney's daughter, Charlie died aboard ship, with us."

She nodded. "I know, but Barkow was responsible. Oh, I've been a fool! An awful fool!"

An officer was kneeling over Penn's body. He got up, glanced at Mullaney, and then at Ann.

"This man is dead," he said.

Resolution came suddenly to Ann. "Major," she said, "I'm going to catch that patrol. Will you lend me a fresh horse? Ours will still be badly worn-out after last night."

"It wouldn't be safe, Miss Rodney," he protested. "It wouldn't at all. There's Indians out there. How Caradec got through, or you and Barkow, is beyond me." He gestured to the body. "What do you know about this?"

Briefly, concisely, she explained, telling all. She made no attempt to spare herself or to leave anything out. She outlined the entire affair, taking only a few minutes.

"I see." He looked thoughtfully at the gate. "If I could give you an escort, I would, but—"

"If she knows the way," Mullaney said, "I'll go with her. We came down the river from Fort Benton, then up the Yellowstone and the Powder. We thought we would come and see how Rafe was gettin' along. If we'd knowed there was trouble we'd have come before."

"It's as much as your life is worth, man," the major warned.

Mullaney shrugged. "Like as not, but my life has had chances taken with it before. Besides"—he ran his fingers over his bald head—"there's no scalp here to attract Injuns!"

Well mounted, Ann and Mullaney rode swiftly. The

patrol would be hurrying because of Bo Marsh's serious condition, but they should overtake them, and following was no immediate problem.

Mullaney knew the West and had fought before in his life as a wandering jack-of-all-trades. He was not upset by the chance they were taking. He glanced from time to time at Ann, and then rambling along, he began to give her an account of their life aboard ship, of the friendship that had grown between her father and Rafe Caradec, and of all Rafe had done to spare the older man work and trouble.

He told him how Rafe had treated Rodney's wounds when he had been beaten, how he saved food for him, and how close the two had grown. Twice, noting her grief and shame, he ceased talking, but each time she insisted on his continuing.

"Caradec?" Mullaney said finally. "Well, I'd say he was one of the finest men I've known. A fighter, he is! The lad's a fighter from way back! You should have seen the beatin' he gave that Borger! I got only a glimpse, but Penn told me about it. And if it hadn't been for Rafe none of us would have got away. He planned it, and he carried it out. He planned it before your father's last trouble—the trouble that killed him— but when he saw your father would die, he carried on with it."

They rode on in silence. All the time, Ann knew now, she should have trusted her instincts. Always they had warned her about Bruce Barkow; always they had been sure of Rafe Caradec. As she sat in the jury box and watched him talk, handling his case, it had been his sincerity that impressed her, even more than his shrewd handling of questions.

He had killed men, yes. But what men! Bonaro and Trigger Boyne, both acknowledged and boastful killers of men themselves. Men unfit to walk in the tracks of such as Rafe. She had to find him! She must!

The wind was chill, and she glanced at Mullaney.

"It's cold!" she said. "It feels like snow!"

He nodded grimly. "It does that!" he said. "Early for it, but it happened before. If we get a norther now—" He shook his head.

They made camp while it was still light, and Mullaney built a fire of dry sticks that gave off almost no smoke. Water was heated, and they made coffee. While Ann was fixing the little food they had, he rubbed the horses down with handsful of dry grass.

"Can you find your way in the dark?" he asked her.

"Yes, I think so. It is fairly easy from here, for we have the mountains. That highest peak will serve as a landmark unless there are too many clouds."

"All right," he said, "we'll keep movin'."

She found herself liking the burly seaman and cowhand. He helped her smother the fire and wipe out traces of it.

"If we can stick to the trail of the soldiers," he said, "it'll confuse the Injuns. They'll think we're with their party."

They started on. Ann led off, keeping the horses at a fast walk. Night fell, and with it the wind grew stronger. After an hour of travel, Ann reined in.

Mullaney rode up beside her. "What's the matter?"

She indicated the tracks of a single horse crossing the route of the soldiers.

"You think it's this Barkow?" He nodded as an idea came. "It could be. The soldiers don't know what happened back there. He might ride with 'em for protection."

Another thought came to him. He looked at Ann keenly.

"Suppose he'd try to kill Caradec?"

Her heart jumped. "Oh, no!" She was saying no to the thought, not to the possibility. She knew it was a possibility. What did Bruce have to lose? He was already a fugitive, and another killing would make it no worse. And Rafe Caradec had been the cause of it all.

"He might," she agreed. "He might, at that." . . . .

Miles to the west, Bruce Barkow, his rifle across his saddle, leaned into the wind. He had followed the soldiers for a way, and the idea of a snipe shot at Caradec stayed in his mind. He could do it, and they would think the Indians had done it.

But there was a better way, a way to get at them all. If he could ride on ahead and reach Gill and Marsh before the patrol did, he might kill them and then get Caradec when he approached. If then he could get rid of Shute, Gomer would have to swing with him to save something from the mess. Maybe Dan Shute's idea was right, after all! Maybe killing was the solution.

Absorbed by the possibilities of the idea, Barkow turned off the route followed by the soldiers. There was a way that could make it safer and somewhat faster. He headed for the old Bozeman Trail, now abandoned.

He gathered his coat around him to protect him from the increasing cold. His mind was fevered with worry and with doubt of himself, and mingled with it was hatred of Caradec, Shute, Ann Rodney, and everyone and everything. He drove on into the night.

Twice, he stopped to rest. The second time he started on it was turning gray with morning, and as he swung into the saddle, a snowflake touched his cheek.

He thought little of it. His horse was uneasy, though, and anxious for the trail. Snow was not a new thing, and Barkow scarcely noticed as the flakes began to come down thicker and faster.

Gill and the wounded man had disappeared, he knew. Shute's searchers had not found them near the house. Bruce Barkow had visited that house many times before the coming of Caradec, and he knew the surrounding hills well. About a half mile back from the house, sheltered by a thick growth of lodgepole pine, was a deep cave among some rocks. If Johnny Gill had found that cave, he might have moved Marsh there.

It was, at least, a chance.

Bruce Barkow was not worried about the tracks he was leaving. Few Indians would be moving in this inclement weather. Nor would the party from the fort have come this far north. From the route they had taken, he knew they were keeping to the low country.

He was nearing the first range of foothills now, the hills that divided Long Valley from the open plain that sloped gradually away to the Powder and the old Bozeman Trail. He rode into the pines and started up the trail, intent upon death. His mind was sharpened like that of a hungry coyote. Cornered and defeated for the prize himself, his only way out, either for victory or revenge, lay in massacre, in wholesale killing.

It was like him that having killed once, he did not hesitate to accept the idea of killing again.

He did not see the big man on the gray horse who fell in behind him. He did not glance back over his trail, although by now the thickening snow had obscured the background so much that the rider, gaining slowly on him through the storm, would have been no more than a shadow.

To the right, behind the once bald and now snow-covered dome, was the black smear of seeping oil. Drawing abreast of it, Bruce Barkow reined in and glanced down.

Here it was, the cause of it all, the key to wealth, to everything a man could want. Men had killed for less; he could kill for this. He knew where there were four other such seepages, and the oil sold from twenty dollars to thirty dollars the barrel.

He got down and stirred it with a stick. It was thick now, thickened by cold. Well, he still might win.

Then he heard a shuffle of footsteps in the snow and looked up. Dan Shute's figure was gigantic in the heavy coat he wore, sitting astride the big horse. He looked down at Barkow, and his lips parted.

"Tried to get away with her, did you? I knew you had coyote in you, Barkow."

His hand came up, and in the gloved hand was a pistol. In a sort of shocked disbelief, Bruce Barkow saw the gun lift. His own gun was under his short, thick coat.

"No!" he gasped hoarsely. "Not that! *Dan!*"

The last word was a scream, cut sharply off by the sharp, hard bark of the gun. Bruce Barkow folded slowly and, clutching his stomach, toppled across the black seepage, staining it with a slow shading of red.

For a minute, Dan Shute sat his horse, staring down. Then he turned the horse and moved on. He had an idea of his own. Before the storm began, from a mountain ridge he picked out the moving patrol. Behind it were two figures. He had a hunch about those two riders, striving to overtake the patrol.

He would see.

Chapter XVIII
Hunters in the Snow

Pushing rapidly ahead through the falling snow, the patrol came up to the ruins of the cabin on the Crazy Man on the morning of the second day out from the Fort. Steam rose from the horses, and the breath of horses and men fogged the air.

There was no sign of life. Rafe swung down and stared

about. The smooth surface of the snow was unbroken, yet he could see that much had happened since he had started his trek to the fort for help. The lean-to, not quite complete, was abandoned.

Lieutenant Bryson surveyed the scene thoughtfully.

"Are we too late?" he asked.

Caradec hesitated, staring around. There was no hope in what he saw.

"I don't think so," he said. "Johnny Gill was a smart hand. He would figger out somethin', and besides, I don't see any bodies."

In his mind, he surveyed the canyon. Certainly, Gill could not have gone far with the wounded man. Also, it would have to be in the direction of possible shelter. The grove of lodgepoles offered the best chance. Turning, he walked toward them. Bryson dismounted his men and they started fires.

Milton Waitt, the surgeon, stared after Rafe and then walked in his tracks. When he came up with him, he suggested:

"Any caves around?"

Caradec paused, considering that. "There may be. None that I know of, though. Still, Johnny prowled in these rocks a lot and may have found one. Let's have a look." Then a thought occurred to him. "They'd have to have water, Doc. Let's go to the spring."

There was ice over it, but the ice had been broken and had frozen again. Rafe indicated it.

"Somebody drank here since the cold set in."

He knelt and felt of the snow with his fingers, working his way slowly around the spring. Suddenly he stopped.

"Found something?" Waitt watched curiously. This made no sense to him.

"Yes. Whoever got water from the spring splashed some on this side. It froze. I can feel the ice it made. That's a fair indication that whoever got water came from that side of the spring."

Moving around, he kept feeling of the snow.

"Here." He felt again. "There's an icy ring where he set the bucket for a minute. Water left on the bottom froze." He straightened, studying the mountainside. "He's up there somewheres. He's got a bucket, and he's able to come down here for water, but findin' him'll be the devil's own job. He'll need fuel, though. Somewhere he's been breakin' sticks and collectin' wood, but wherever he does it won't be close to his shelter. Gill's too smart for that."

Studying the hillside, Rafe indicated the nearest clump of trees.

"He wouldn't want to be out in the open on this snow any longer than he had to," he said thoughtfully, "and the chances are he'd head for the shelter of those trees. When he got there, he would probably set the bucket down while he studied the back trail and made sure he hadn't been seen."

Waitt nodded, his interest aroused.

"Good reasoning, man. Let's see."

They walked to the clump of trees, and after a few minutes of search, Waitt found the same kind of icy frozen place just under the thin skimming of snow.

"Where do we go from here?" he asked.

Rafe hesitated, studying the trees. A man would automatically follow the line of easiest travel, and there was an opening between the trees. He started on and then stopped.

"This is right. See? There's not so much snow on this branch. There's a good chance he brushed it off in passin'."

It was mostly guesswork, he knew. Yet after they had gone three hundred yards Rafe looked up and saw the cliff pushing its rocky shoulder in among the trees. At its base was a tumbled cluster of gigantic boulders and broken slabs.

He led off for the rocks, and almost the first thing he saw was a fragment of loose bark lying on the snow and a few crumbs of dust such as is sometimes found between bark and tree. He pointed it out to Waitt.

"He carried wood this way."

They paused there, and Rafe sniffed the air. There was no smell of woodsmoke. Were they dead? Had cold done what rifle bullets couldn't do? No, he decided, Johnny Gill knew too well how to take care of himself.

Rafe walked between the rocks, turning where it felt natural to turn. Suddenly, he saw a tipped-up slab of granite leaning against a larger boulder. It looked dry underneath. He stooped and glanced in. It was dark and silent, yet some instinct seemed to tell him it was not so empty as it appeared.

He crouched in the opening, leaving light from outside to come in first along one wall, then another. His keen eyes picked out a damp spot on the leaves. There was no place for a leak, and the wind had been in the wrong direction to blow in here.

"Snow," he said. "Probably fell off a boot."

They moved into the cave, bending over to walk. Yet it was not really a cave at first, merely a slab of rock offering partial shelter.

About fifteen feet further along, the slab ended under a thick growth of pine boughs and brush that formed a canopy overhead, which offered almost as solid shelter as the stone itself. Then, in the rock face of the cliff, they saw a cave, a place gouged by wind and water long since, and completely obscured behind the boulders and brush from any view but where they stood.

They walked up to the entrance. The overhang of the cliff offered a shelter that was all of fifty feet deep, running along one wall of a diagonal gash in the cliff that was invisible from outside. They stepped in on the dry sand and had taken only a step when they smelled wood smoke. At almost the same instant, Johnny Gill spoke.

"Hi, Rafe!" He stepped down from behind a heap of debris against one wall of the rock fissure. "I couldn't see who you were till now. I had my rifle ready so's if you was the wrong one I could plumb discourage you." His face looked drawn and tired. "He's over here, Doc," Gill continued, "and he's been delirious all night."

While Waitt was busy over the wounded man, Gill walked back up the cave with Rafe.

"What's happened," Gill asked. "I thought they'd got you."

"No, they haven't, but I don't know much of what's been goin' on. Ann's at the fort with Barkow. Says she's goin' to marry him."

"What about Tex?" Gill asked quickly.

Rafe shook his head, scowling. "No sign of him. I don't know what's come off at Painted Rock. I'm leavin' for there as soon as I've told the Lieutenant and his patrol where Doc is. You'll have to stick here because the Doc has to get back to the fort."

"You goin' to Painted Rock?"

"Yes. I'm goin' to kill Dan Shute."

"I'd like to see that," Gill said grimly, "but watch yourself!" The little cowhand looked at him seriously. "Boss, what about that girl?"

Rafe's lips tightened, and he stared at the bare wall of the cave.

"I don't know," he said grimly. "I tried to talk her out of it, but I guess I wasn't what you'd call tactful."

Gill stuck his thumbs in his belt. "Tell her you're in love with her yourself?"

Caradec stared at him. "Where'd you get that idea?"

"Readin' sign. You ain't been the same since you ran into her the first time. She's your kind of people, Boss."

"Maybe. But looks like she reckoned she wasn't. Never would listen to me give the straight story on her father. Both of us flew off the handle this time."

"Well, I ain't no hand at ridin' herd on womenfolks, but I've seen a thing or two, Boss. The chances are if you'd have told her you're in love with her, she'd never have gone with Bruce Barkow."

Rafe was remembering those words when he rode down the trail toward Painted Rock. What lay ahead of him could not be planned. He had no idea when or where he would encounter Dan Shute. He knew only that he must find him.

After reporting to Bryson so he wouldn't worry about the doctor, Rafe had hit the trail for Painted Rock alone. By now he knew that mountain trail well, and even the steady fall of snow failed to make him change his mind about making the ride.

He was burning up inside. The old, driving recklessness was in him, the urge to be in and shooting. His enemies were in the clear, and all the cards were on the table in plain sight.

Barkow he discounted. Dan Shute was the man to get, and Pod Gomer the man to watch. What he intended to do was high-handed, as high-handed in its way as what Shute and Barkow had attempted, but in Rafe's case the cause was just. . . .

Mullaney had stopped in a wooden draw short of the hills. He stopped for a short rest just before daybreak on that fatal second morning. The single rider had turned off from the trail and was no longer with the patrol. Both he and the girl needed rest, aside from the horses.

He kicked snow away from the grass and then swept some of it clear with a branch. In most places it was already much too thick for that. After he made coffee and they had eaten, he got up.

"Get ready," he said, "and I'll get the horses."

All night he had been thinking of what he would do

when he found Barkow. He had seen the man draw on Penn, and he was not fast. That made it an even break, for Mullaney knew that he was not fast himself.

When he found the horses missing, he stopped. Evidently they had pulled their picket pins and wandered off. He started on, keeping in their tracks. He did not see the big man in the heavy coat who stood in the brush and watched him go.

Dan Shute threaded his way down to the campfire. When Ann looked up at his approach, she thought it was Mullaney, and then she saw Shute.

Eyes wide, she came to her feet. "Why, hello! What are you doing here?"

He smiled at her, his eyes sleepy and yet wary. "Huntin' you. Reckoned this was you. When I seen Barkow I reckoned somethin' had gone wrong."

"You saw Bruce? Where?"

"North a ways. He won't bother you none." Shute smiled. "Barkow was spineless. Thought he was smart. He never was half as smart as that Caradec, nor as tough as me."

"What happened?" Ann's heart was pounding. Mullaney should be coming now. He would hear their voices and be warned.

"I killed him." Shute was grinning cynically. "He wasn't much good." Shute smiled. "Don't be wonderin' about that hombre with you. I led his horses off and turned 'em adrift. He'll be hours catchin' 'em, if he ever does. However, he might come back, so we'd better drift."

"No," Ann said. "I'll wait."

He smiled again. "Better come quiet. If he came back, I'd have to kill him. You don't want him killed, do you?"

She hesitated only a moment. This man would stop at nothing. He was going to take her if he had to knock her out and tie her. Better anything than that. If she appeared to play along, she might have a chance.

"I'll go," she said simply. "You have a horse?"

"I kept yours," he said. "Mount up."

Chapter XIX
Trail of a Lobo

By the time Rafe Caradec was en route to Painted Rock, Dan Shute was riding with his prisoner into the ranch yard of his place near Painted Rock. Far to the south and west, Rock Mullaney long since had come up to the place where Shute had finally turned his horse loose and ridden on, leading the other. Mullaney kept on the trail of the lone horse and came up with it almost a mile further.

Lost and alone in the thickly falling snow, the animal hesitated at his call and then waited for him to catch up. When he was mounted once more, he turned back to his camp, and the tracks, nearly covered, told him little. The girl, accompanied by another rider, had ridden away. She would never have gone willingly.

Mullaney was worried. During their travel they had talked little, yet Ann had supplied a few of the details, and he knew vaguely about Dan Shute and about Bruce Barkow. He also knew, having learned all about that long before reaching the fort, than an Indian outbreak was feared.

Mullaney knew something about Indians and doubted any trouble until spring or summer. There might be occasional shootings, but Indians were not, as a rule, cold-weather fighters. For that he didn't blame them. Yet any wandering hunting or foraging parties must be avoided, and it was probable that any warrior or group of them coming along a fresh trail would follow it and count coup on an enemy if possible.

He knew roughly the direction of Painted Rock, yet instinct told him he had better stick to the tangible and near, so he swung back to the trail of the Army patrol and headed for the pass into Long Valley. . . .

Painted Rock lay still under the falling snow when Rafe Caradec drifted down the street on the big black. He swung down in front of the Emporium and went in.

Baker looked up, and his eyes grew alert when he saw Rafe. At Caradec's question, he told him of what had happened to Tex Brisco so far as he knew, of the killing of Blazer, McCabe, and Gorman, and of Brisco's escape while apparently wounded.

He also told him of Dan Shute's arrival and threat to Ann

and her subsequent escape with Barkow. Baker was relieved to know they were at the fort.

A wind was beginning to moan around the eaves, and they listened a minute.

"Won't be good to be out in that," the storekeeper said gravely. "Sounds like a blizzard comin'. If Brisco's found shelter, he might be all right."

"Not in this cold," Caradec said, scowling. "No man with his resistance lowered by a wound is going to last in this. And it's going to be worse before it's better."

Standing there at the counter, letting the warmth of the big potbellied stove work through his system, Rafe assayed his position. Bo Marsh, while in bad shape, had been tended by a doctor and would have Gill's care. There was nothing more to be done there for the time being.

Ann had made her choice. She had gone off with Barkow, and in his heart he knew that if there was any choice between the two—Barkow or Shute—she had made the better. Yet there had been another choice. Or had there? Yes, she could at least have listened to him.

The fort was far away, and all he could do now was trust to Ann's innate good sense to change her mind before it was too late. In any event, he could not get back there in time to do anything about it.

"Where's Shute?" he demanded.

"Ain't seen him," Baker said worriedly. "Ain't seen hide nor hair of him. But I can promise you one thing, Caradec. He won't take Barkow's runnin' out with Ann lyin' down. He'll be on their trail."

The door opened in a flurry of snow, and Pat Higley pushed in. He pulled off his mittens and extended stiff fingers toward the red swell of the stove. He glanced at Rafe.

"Hear you askin' about Shute?" he asked. "I just seen him, headed for the ranch. He wasn't alone, neither." He rubbed his fingers. "Looked to me like a woman ridin' along."

Rafe looked around. "A woman?" he asked carefully. "Now who would that be?"

"He's found Ann!" Baker exclaimed.

"She was at the fort," Rafe said, "with Barkow. He couldn't take her away from the soldiers."

"No, he couldn't," Baker agreed, "but she might have left on her own. She's a stubborn girl when she takes a notion. After you left she may have changed her mind."

* * *

Rafe pushed the thought away. The chance was too slight. And where was Tex Brisco?

"Baker," he suggested, "you and Higley know this country. You know about Tex. Where do you reckon he'd wind up?"

Higley shrugged. "There's no tellin'. It ain't as if he knew the country, too. They trailed him for a while, and they said it looked like his horse was wanderin' loose without no hand on the bridle. Then the horse took to the water, so Brisco must have come to his sense somewhat. Anyway, they lost his trail when he was ridin' west along a fork of Clear Creek. If he held to that direction it would take him over some plumb high, rough country south of the big peak. If he did get across, he'd wind up somewheres down along Tensleep Canyon, maybe. But that's all guesswork."

"Any shelter that way?"

"Nary a mite. Not if you mean human shelter. There's plenty of timber there, but wolves, too. There's also plenty of shelter in the rocks. The only humans over that way are the Sioux, and they ain't in what you'd call a friendly mood. That's where Man Afraid of His Horse has been holed up."

Finding Tex Brisco would be like hunting a needle in a haystack and worse, but it was what Rafe Caradec had to do. He had to make an effort, anyway. Yet the thought of Dan Shute and the girl returned to him. Suppose it was Ann? He shuddered to think of her in Shute's hands. The man was without a spark of decency or mercy. Not even his best friends would deny that.

"No use goin' out in this storm," Baker said. "You can stay with us, Caradec."

"You've changed your tune some, Baker," Rafe suggested grimly.

"A man can be wrong, can't he?" Baker inquired testily. "Maybe I was. I don't know. Things have gone to perdition around here fast, ever since you came in here with that story about Rodney."

"Well, I'm not stayin'," Rafe told him. "I'm going to look for Tex Brisco."

The door was pushed open and they looked around. It was Pod Gomer. The sheriff looked even squarer and more bulky in a heavy buffalo coat. He cast a bleak look at Caradec and then walked to the fire, sliding out of his overcoat.

"You still here?" he asked, glancing at Rafe out of the corners of his eyes.

"Yes, I'm still here, Gomer, but you're traveling."

"What?"

"You heard me. You can wait till the storm is over. Then get out, and keep movin'."

Gomer turned, his square hard face dark with angry blood.

"You—tellin' me?" he said furiously. "I'm sheriff here!"

"You were," Caradec said calmly. "Ever since you've been here you've been hand in glove with Barkow and Shute, runnin' their dirty errands for them, pickin' up the scraps they tossed you. Well, the fun's over. You slope out of here when the storm's over. Barkow's gone, and within a few hours Shute will be, too."

"Shute?" Gomer was incredulous. "You'd go up against Dan Shute? Why, man, you're insane!"

"Am I?" Rafe shrugged. "That's neither here nor there. I'm talkin' to you. Get out and stay out. You can take your tinhorn judge with you."

Gomer laughed. "You're the one who's through! Marsh dead, Brisco either dead or on the dodge, and Gill maybe dead. What chance have you got?"

"Gill's in as good shape as I am," Rafe said calmly, "and Bo Marsh is gettin' Army care, and he'll be out of the woods, too. As for Tex, I don't know. He got away, and I'm bankin' on that Texan to come out walkin'. How much stomach are your boys goin' to have for the fight when Gill and I ride in here? Tom Blazer's gone, and so are a half dozen more. Take your coat"—Rafe picked it up with his left hand—"and get out. If I see you after this storm, I'm shootin' on sight. Now get!"

He heaved the heavy coat at Gomer, and the sheriff ducked, his face livid.

Yet surprisingly he did not reach for a gun. He lunged and swung with his fist. A shorter man than Caradec, he was wider and thicker, a powerfully built man who was known in mining and trail camps as a rough-and-tumble fighter.

Caradec turned, catching Gomer's right on the cheekbone, but bringing up a solid punch to Gomer's midsection. The sheriff lunged close and tried to butt, and Rafe stabbed him in the face with a left and then smeared him with a hard right.

It was no match. Pod Gomer had fancied himself as a

fighter, but Caradec had too much experience. He knocked
Gomer back into a heap of sacks and then walked in on him
and slugged him wickedly in the middle with both hands.
Gomer went to his knees.

"All right, Pod," Rafe said, panting, "I told you. Get
goin'."

The sheriff stayed on his knees, breathing heavily, blood
dripping from his smashed nose. Rafe Caradec slipped into
his coat and walked to the door.

Outside, he took the horse to the livery stable, brushed
him off, and then gave him a rubdown and some oats.

He did not return to the store, but after a meal, saddled
his horse and headed for Dan Shute's ranch. He couldn't
escape the idea that the rider with Shute might have been
Ann, despite the seeming impossibility of her being this far
west. If she had left the fort within a short time after the
patrol, then it might be.

But there was small chance of that. Barkow would never
return, having managed to get that far away. There was no
one else at the fort to bring her. Scouts had said a party of
travelers were coming up from the river, but there would be
small chance any of them would push on to Painted Rock in
this weather.

Dan Shute's ranch lay in a hollow of the hills near a
curving stream. Not far away the timber ran down to the
plain's edge and dwindled away into a few scattered groves,
blanketed now in snow.

A thin trail of smoke lifted from the chimney of the
house and another from the bunkhouse. Rafe Caradec decided on boldness as the best course, relying on his muffled,
snow-covered appearance to disguise him until within gun
range. He opened a button on the front of his coat so he
could get at a gun thrust into his waistband.

He removed his right hand from its glove and thrust it
deep in his pocket. There it would be warm and at the same
time free to grasp the six-gun when he needed it.

No one showed. It was very cold, and if there was
anyone around and they noticed his approach, their curiosity
did not extend to the point where they would come outside
to investigate.

Rafe rode directly to the house, walked up on the porch,
and rapped on the door with his left hand. There was no
response. He rapped again, much harder.

All was silence. The mounting wind made hearing difficult, but he put his ear to the door and listened. There was
no sound.

He dropped his left hand to the door and turned the
knob. The door opened easily, and he let it swing wide,
standing well out of line. The wind howled in, and a few
flakes of snow, but there was no sound. He stepped inside
and closed the door after him.

His ears tingled with cold, and he resisted a desire to
rub them. Then he let his eyes sweep the wide room. A fire
burned in the huge stone fireplace, but there was no one in
the long room. Two exits from the room were hung with
blankets. There was a table, littered with odds and ends, and
one end held some dirty dishes where a hasty meal had been
eaten. Beneath that spot was a place showing dampness, as
though a pair of boots had shed melting snow.

There was no sound in the long room but the crackle of
the fire and the low moan of the wind around the eaves.
Walking warily, Rafe stepped over a saddle and some bits of
harness and walked across to the opposite room.

He pushed the blanket aside.

The room was empty. He saw an unmade bed of tumbled blankets, and a lamp standing on a table by the bed.

Rafe turned and stared at the other door and then looked
back into the bedroom. There was a pair of dirty socks lying
there, and he stepped over and felt of them. They were damp.

Someone, within the last hour or less, had changed socks
here. Walking outside, he noticed something he had not seen
before. Below a chair near the table was another spot of
dampness. Apparently, two people had been here.

He stepped back into the shadow of the bedroom door
and put his hand in the front of his coat. He hadn't wanted to
reach for that gun, in case anyone was watching. Now, with
his hand on the gun, he stepped out of the bedroom and
walked to the other blanket-covered door. He pushed it
aside.

It was a large kitchen. A fire glowed in the huge sheet-
metal stove, and there was a coffeepot filled with boiling
coffee. Seeing it, Rafe let go of his gun and picked up a cup.
When he had filled it, he looked around the unkempt room.
Like the rest of the house, it was strongly built, but poorly
kept inside. The floor was dirty, and dirty dishes and scraps
of food were around.

He lifted the coffee cup, and then his eyes saw a bit of white. He put down the cup and stepped over to the end of the woodpile.

His heart jumped. It was a woman's handkerchief!

Chapter XX
Missing Girl

Quickly Rafe Caradec glanced around. Again he looked at the handkerchief in his hand and lifted it to his nostrils. There was a faint whiff of perfume—a perfume he remembered only too well.

She had been here, then. The other rider with Dan Shute had been Ann Rodney. But where was she now? Where could she be? What had happened?

He gulped a mouthful of the hot coffee and stared around again. The handkerchief had been near the back door. He put down the coffee and eased the door open. Beyond was the barn and a corral. He walked outside and, pushing through the curtain of blowing snow, reached the corral and then the barn.

Several horses were there. Hurrying along, he found two with dampness marking the places where their saddles had been. One of them he recalled as Ann's horse. He had seen the mount when he had been at the store.

There were no saddles showing any evidence of having been ridden, and the saddles would be sweaty underneath if they had been. Evidently, two horses had been saddled and ridden away from this barn.

Scowling, Rafe stared around. In the dust of the floor he found a small track, almost obliterated by a larger one. Had Shute saddled two horses and taken the girl away? If so, where would he take her, and why? He decided suddenly that Shute had not taken Ann from here. She must have slipped away, saddled a horse, and escaped.

It was a farfetched conclusion, but it offered not only the solution he wanted, but one that fitted with the few facts available. Or at least, with the logic of the situation.

Why would Shute take the girl away from his home ranch? There was no logical reason, especially in such a storm as this when so far as Shute knew there would be no pursuit. Rafe himself would not have done it.

Perhaps he had been overconfident, believing Ann would rather share the warmth and security of the house than face the mounting blizzard.

Only the bunkhouse remained unexplored. There was a chance they had gone there. Turning, Rafe walked to the bunkhouse. Shoving the door open, he stepped inside.

Four men sat on bunks, and one, his boots off and his socks propped toward the stove, stared glumly at him from a chair made of a barrel.

The faces of all the men were familiar, but he could put a name to none of them.

They had seen the right hand in the front of his coat, and they sat quiet, appreciating its significance.

"Where's Dan Shute?" he demanded, finally.

"Ain't seen him," said the man in the barrel chair.

"That go for all of you?" Rafe's eyes swung from one to the other.

A lean, hard-faced man with a scar on his jawbone grinned, showing yellow teeth. He raised himself on his elbow.

"Why, no. It sure don't, pilgrim. I seen him. He rode up here nigh onto an hour ago with that there girl from the store. They went inside. Suppose you want to get killed, you go to the house."

"I've been there. It's empty."

The leaf-faced man sat up. "That right? That don't make sense. Why would a man with a filly like that take off into the storm?"

Rafe Caradec studied them coldly. "You men," he said, "had better sack up and get out of here when the storm's over. Dan Shute's through."

"Ain't you countin' unbranded stock, pardner?" the lean-faced man said, smiling tauntingly. "Dan Shute's able to handle his own troubles. He took care of Barkow."

This was news to Rafe. "He did? How'd you know that?"

"He done told me. Barkow run off with this girl, and Shute trailed him. I didn't only see Shute come back, I talked some with him, and I unsaddled his horses. "He picked up a boot and pulled it on. "This here Rodney girl, she left the fort, runnin' away from Barkow and takin' after the Army patrol that rode out with you. Shute, he seen 'em. He also seen Barkow. He hunted Bruce down and shot him near that

bare dome in your lower valley, and then he left Barkow and
caught up with the girl and this strange hombre with her.
Shute led their horses off and then got the girl while this
hombre was huntin' the horses."

The explanation cleared up several points for Rafe. He
stared thoughtfully around.

"You didn't see 'em leave here?"

"Not us," the lean-faced puncher said drily. "None of us
hired on for punchin' cows or ridin' herd on women in
blizzards. Come a storm, we hole up and set her out. We aim
to keep on doin' just that."

Rafe backed to the door and stepped out. The wind tore
at his garments, and he backed away from the building.
Within twenty feet, it was lost behind a curtain of blowing
snow. He stumbled back to the house.

More than ever, he was convinced that somehow Ann
had escaped. Yet where to look? In this storm there was no
direction, nothing. If she headed for town, she might make
it. However, safety for her would more likely lie toward the
mountains, for there she could improvise shelter and probably could last the storm out. Knowing the country, she would
know how long such storms lasted. It was rarely more than
three days.

He had little hope of finding Ann, yet he knew she
would never return here. Seated in the ranch house, he
coolly ate a hastily picked up meal and drank more coffee.
Then he returned to his horse, which he had led to the
stable. Mounting, he rode into the storm on the way to
town. . . .

Gene Baker and Pat Higley looked up when Rafe Caradec
came in. Baker's face paled when he saw that Rafe was alone.

"Did you find out?" he asked. "Was it Ann?"

Briefly, Rafe explained, telling all he had learned and his
own speculations as to what had happened.

"She must have got plumb away," Higley agreed. "Shute
would never take her away from his ranch in this storm. But
where could she have gone?"

Rafe explained his own theories on that. "She probably
took it for granted he would think she would head for town,"
he suggested, "so she may have taken to the mountains. After
all, she would know that Shute would kill anybody who tried
to stop him."

Gene Baker nodded miserably. "That's right, and what can a body do?"

"Wait," Higley said. "Just wait."

"I won't wait," Rafe said. "If she shows up here, hold her. Shoot Dan if you have too, drygulch him or anything. Get him out of the way. I'm goin' into the mountains. I can at least be lookin', and I might stumble onto some kind of a trail." . . .

Two hours later, shivering with cold, Rafe Caradec acknowledged how foolhardy he had been. His black horse was walking steadily through a snow-covered avenue among the pines, weaving around fallen logs and clumps of brush. He had found nothing that resembled a trail, and twice he had crossed the stream. This, he knew, was also the direction that had been taken by the wounded Tex Brisco.

No track could last more than a minute in the whirling snow-filled world in which Rafe now rode. The wind howled and tore at his garments even here, within the partial shelter of the lodgepoles. Yet he rode on. Then he dismounted and walked ahead, resting the horse. It was growing worse instead of better, yet he pushed on, taking the line of least resistance, sure that this was what the fleeing Ann would have done.

The icy wind ripped at his clothing, at times faced him like a solid, moving wall. The black stumbled wearily, and Rafe was suddenly contrite. The big horse had taken a brutal beating in these last few days, and even its great strength was weakening.

Squinting his eyes against the blowing snow, he stared ahead. He could see nothing, but he was aware that the wall of the mountain was on his left. Bearing in that direction, he came up to a thicker stand of trees and some scattered boulders. He rode on, alert for possible shelter for himself and his horse.

Almost an hour later, he found it, a dry, sandy place under the overhang of the cliff, sheltered from the wind and protected from the snow by the overhang and by the trees and brush that fronted it. Swinging down, Rafe led the horse into the shelter and hastily built a fire.

From the underside of a log he got some bark, great sheets of it, and some fibrous, rotting wood. Then he broke some low branches on the trees, dead and dry. In a few minutes his fire was burning nicely. Then he stripped the

saddle from the horse and rubbed him down with a handful of
crushed bark. When that was done, he got out the nosebag
and fed the horse some of the oats he had appropriated from
Shute's barn.

The next hour he occupied himself in gathering fuel.
Luckily, there were a number of dead trees close by, debris
left by some landslide from up the mountain. He settled
down by the fire and made coffee. Dozing against the rock,
he fed the blaze intermittently, his mind far away.

Somehow, sometime, he fell asleep.

Around the rocks the wind, moaning and whining, sought
with icy fingers for a grasp at his shoulder, at his hands. But
the log burned well, and the big horse stood close, stamping
in the sand and dozing beside the man on the ground.

Once, starting from his sleep, Rafe noticed that the log
had burned until it was out of the fire, so he dragged it
around and then laid another across it. Soon he was again
asleep. . . .

He awakened suddenly. It was daylight, and the storm
was still raging. His fire blazed among the charred embers of
his logs, and he lifted his eyes.

Six Indians faced him beyond the fire, and their rifles
and bows covered him. Their faces were hard and unreada-
ble. Two stepped forward and jerked him to his feet, stripped
his guns from him, and motioned for him to saddle his horse.

Numb with cold, he could scarcely realize what had
happened to him. One of the Indians, wrapped in a worn red
blanket, jabbered at the others and kept pointing to the
horse, making threatening gestures. Yet when Rafe had the
animal saddled, they motioned to him to mount. Two of the
Indians rode up then, leading the horses of the others.

So this was the way it ended. He was a prisoner.

Chapter XXI
"Take Off Your Guns!"

Uncomprehending, Rafe Caradec opened his eyes to darkness. He sat up abruptly and stared around. Then, after a
long minute, it came to him. He was a prisoner in a village of
the Oglala Sioux, and he had just awakened.

Two days before, they had brought him here, bound him hand and foot, and left him in the tepee he now occupied. Several times, squaws had entered the tepee and departed. They had given him food and water.

It was night, and his wrists were swollen from the tightness of the bonds. It was warm in the tepee, for there was a fire, but smoke filled the skin wigwam and filtered but slowly out at the top. He had a feeling it was almost morning.

What had happened at Painted Rock? Where was Ann? And where was Tex Brisco? Had Dan Shute returned?

He was rolling over toward the entrance to catch a breath of fresh air when the flap was drawn back and a squaw came in. She caught him by the collar and dragged him back, but made no effort to molest him. He was more worried about the squaws than the braves, for they were given to torture.

Suddenly, the flap was drawn back again and two people came in—a warrior and a squaw. She spoke rapidly in Sioux and then picked a brand from the fire. As it blazed up, she held it close to his face. He drew back, thinking she meant to sear his eyes. Then, looking beyond the blaze, he saw that the squaw holding it was the Indian girl he had saved from Trigger Boyne!

With a burst of excited talk, she bent over him. A knife slid under his bonds, and they were cut. Chafing his ankles, he looked up. In the flare of the torchlight he could see the face of the Indian man.

He spoke gutturally, but in fair English. "My daughter say you man help her," he said.

"Yes," Rafe replied. "The Sioux are not my enemies, nor am I theirs."

"Your name Caradec." The Indian's statement was flat, not to be contradicted.

"Yes." Rafe stumbled to his feet, rubbing his wrists.

"We know your horse, also the horses of the others."

"Others?" Rafe asked quickly. "There are others here?"

"Yes, a girl who rode your horse, and a man who rode one of ours. The man is much better. He had been injured."

Ann and Tex! Rafe's heart leaped.

"May I see them?" he asked. "They are my friends."

The Indian nodded. He studied Rafe for a minute.

"I think you are good man. My name Man Afraid of His Horse."

The Oglala chief!

Rafe looked again at the Indian. "I know the name. With Red Cloud you are the greatest of the Sioux."

The chief nodded. "There are others. John Grass, Gall, Crazy Horse, many others. The Sioux have many great men."

The girl led Rafe away to a tent where he found Tex Brisco lying on a pile of skins and blankets. Tex was pale, but he grinned when Rafe came in.

"Man," he said, "it's good to see you! And here's Ann!"

Rafe turned to look at her, and she smiled and then held out her hand.

"I have learned how foolish I was. First from Penn and then from Mullaney and Tex."

"Penn? Mullaney?" Rafe squinted his eyes. "Are they here?"

Quickly, Ann explained about Barkow's killing of Penn and her subsequent attempt to overtake Bruce, guided and helped by Rock Mullaney.

"Barkow's dead," Rafe told them. "Shute killed him."

"Ann told me," Tex said. "He had it comin'. Where's Dan Shute now?"

Caradec shrugged. "I don't know, but I'm goin' to find out."

"Please!" Ann came to him. "Don't fight with him, Rafe! There has been enough killing! You might be hurt, and I couldn't stand that."

He looked at her. "Does it matter so much?"

Her eyes fell. "Yes," she said simply, "it does. . . ."

Painted Rock lay quiet in a world of white, its shabbiness lost under the purity of freshly fallen snow. Escorted by a band of the Oglala, Ann, Rafe, and Tex rode to the edge of town and then said a quick good-bye to the friendly warriors.

The street was empty, and the town seemed to have no word of their coming.

Tex Brisco, still weak from loss of blood and looking pale, brought up the rear. With Ann, he headed right for the Emporium. Rafe Caradec rode ahead until they neared the National Saloon. Then he swung to the boardwalk and waited until they had gone by.

Baker came rushing from the store and with Ann's help, got Tex down from the horse and inside.

Rafe Caradec led his own horse down the street and tied

it to the hitching rail. Then he glanced up and down the street, looking for Shute. Within a matter of minutes Dan would know he was back, and once he was aware of it, there would be trouble.

Pat Higley was inside the store when Rafe entered. He nodded at Rafe's story of what had taken place.

"Shute's been back in town," Higley said. "I reckon after he lost Ann in the snowstorm he figgered she would circle around and come back here."

"Where's Pod Gomer?" Rafe inquired.

"If you mean has he taken out, why I can tell you he hasn't," Baker said. "He's been around with Shute, and he's wearin' double hardware right now."

Higley nodded. "They ain't goin' to give up without a fight," he warned. "They're keepin' some men in town, quite a bunch of 'em."

Rafe also nodded. "That will end as soon Shute's out of the way."

He looked up as the door pushed open, and started to his feet when Johnny Gill walked in with Rock Mullaney.

"The soldiers rigged a sled," Gill announced at once. "They're takin' Bo back to the fort, so we reckoned it might be a good idea to come down here and stand by in case of trouble."

Ann came to the door and stood there by the curtain, watching them. Her eyes continually strayed to Rafe, and he looked up, meeting their glance. Ann flushed and looked away and then invited him to join her for coffee.

Excusing himself, he got up and went inside. Gravely, Ann showed him to a chair, brought him a napkin, and then poured coffee for him and put sugar and cream beside his cup. He took the sugar and then looked up at her.

"Can you ever forgive me?" she asked.

"There's nothin' to forgive," he said, "I couldn't blame you. You were sure your father was dead."

"I didn't know why the property should cause all that trouble until I heard of the oil. Is it really worth so much?"

"Quite a lot. Shippin' is the problem now, but that will be taken care of soon, so it could be worth a great deal of money. I expect they knew more about that end of it than we did." Rafe looked up at her. "I never aimed to claim my half of the ranch," he said, "and I don't now. I accepted it just to give me some kind of a legal basis for workin' with you, but now that the trouble is over, I'll give you the deed, the will your father made out, and the other papers."

"Oh, no!" she exclaimed quickly. "You mustn't! I'll need your help to handle things, and you must accept your part of the ranch and stay on. That is," she added, "if you don't think I'm too awful for the way I acted."

He flushed. "I don't think you're awful, Ann," he said clumsily, getting to his feet. "I think you're wonderful. I guess I always have, ever since that first day when I came into the store and saw you."

His eyes strayed, and carried their glance out the window. He came to with a start and got to his feet.

"There's Dan Shute," he said. "I've got to go."

Ann arose with him, white to the lips. He avoided her glance and then turned abruptly toward the door. The girl made no protest, but as he started through the curtain, she said:

"Come back, Rafe. I'll be waiting!"

He walked to the street door, and the others saw him go. Then something in his manner apprised them of what was about to happen. Mullaney caught up his rifle and started for the door also, and Baker reached for a scattergun.

Rafe Caradec glanced quickly up the snow-covered street. One wagon had been down the center of the street about daybreak, and there had been no other traffic except for a few passing riders. Horses stood in front of the National and the Emporium and had kicked up the snow, but otherwise it was an even, unbroken expanse of purest white.

Rafe stepped out on the porch of the Emporium. Dan Shute's gray was tied at the National's hitching rail, but Shute was nowhere in sight. Rafe walked to the corner of the store, his feet crunching on the snow. The sun was coming out, and the snow might soon be gone. As he thought of that, a drop fell from the roof overhead and touched him on the neck.

Dan Shute would be in the National. Rafe walked slowly down the walk to the saloon and pushed open the door. Joe Benson looked up from behind his bar, and hastily moved down toward the other end. Pod Gomer, slumped in a chair at a table across the room, sat up abruptly, his eyes shifting to the big man at the bar.

Dan Shute's back was to the room. In his short, thick

coat he looked enormous. His hat was off, and his shock of blond hair, coarse and uncombed, glinted in the sunlight.

Rafe stopped inside the door, his gaze sweeping the room in one all-encompassing glance. Then his eyes riveted on the big man at the bar.

"All right, Shute," he said calmly. "Turn around and take it."

Dan Shute turned, and he was grinning. He was grinning widely, but there was a wicked light dancing in his eyes. He stared at Caradec, letting his slow, insolent gaze go over him from head to foot.

"Killin' you would be too easy," he said. "I promised myself that when the time came I would take you apart with my hands and then if there was anything left, shoot it full of holes. I'm goin' to kill you Caradec!"

Out of the tail of his eye, Rafe saw that Johnny Gill was leaning against the jamb of the back door and that Rock Mullaney was just inside of that same door.

"Take off your guns, Caradec, and I'll kill you!" Shute said softly.

"It's their fight," Gill said suddenly. "Let 'em have it the way they want it!"

The voice startled Gomer so that he jerked, and he glanced over his shoulder, his face white. Then the front door pushed open, and Higley came in with Baker. Pod Gomer touched his lips with his tongue and shot a sidelong glance at Benson. The saloonkeeper looked unhappy.

Carefully, Dan Shute reached for his belt buckle and unbuckled the twin belts, laying the big guns on the bar, butts toward him. At the opposite end of the bar, Rafe Caradec did the same. Then, as one man, they shed their coats.

Lithe and broad-shouldered, Rafe was an inch shorter and forty pounds lighter than the other man. Narrow-hipped and lean as a greyhound, he was built for speed, but the powerful shoulders and powerful hands and arms spoke of years of training as well as hard work with a doublejack or an ax, or heaving at the heavy, wet lines of a ship.

Dan Shute's neck was thick, his chest broad and massive. His stomach was flat and hard. His hands were big, and he reeked of sheer animal strength and power. Licking his lips like a hungry wolf, he started forward. He was grinning, and the light was dancing in his hard gray-white eyes.

He did not rush or leap. He walked right up to Rafe, with that grin on his lips, and Caradec stood flat-footed, waiting for him. But as Shute stepped in close, Rafe suddenly whipped up a left to the wind that beat the man to the punch. Shute winced at the blow and his eyes narrowed. Then he smashed forward with his hard skull, trying for a butt.

Rafe clipped him with an elbow and swung away, keeping out of the corner.

Chapter XXII
Man to Man

Still grinning, Dan Shute moved in. The big man was deceptively fast, and as he moved in, suddenly he left his feet and hurled himself feet foremost at Rafe.

Caradec sprang back, but too slow. The legs jackknifed around his, and Rafe staggered and went to the floor! He hit hard, and Dan was the first to move. Throwing himself over, he caught his weight on his left hand and swung with his right. It was a wicked, half-arm blow, and it caught Rafe on the chin. Lights exploded in his brain and he felt himself go down.

Then Shute sprang for him.

Rafe rolled his head, more by instinct than knowledge, and the blow clipped his ear. He threw his feet high and tipped Dan over on his head and off his body. Both men came to their feet like cats and hurled themselves at each other. They struck like two charging bulls with an impact that shook the room.

Rafe slugged a right to the wind and took a smashing blow to the head. They backed off and then charged together, and both men started pitching them—short, wicked hooks thrown from the hips with everything they had in the world in every punch.

Rafe's head was roaring, and he felt the smashing blows rocking his head from side to side. He smashed an inside right to the face, and saw a thin streak of blood on Shute's cheek. He fired his right down the same groove, and it might as well have been on a track. The split in the skin widened and a trickle of blood started. Rafe let go another one to the same spot and then whipped a wicked left uppercut to the wind.

Shute took it coming in and never lost stride. He ducked and lunged, knocking Rafe off balance with his shoulder and then swinging an overhand punch that caught Rafe on the cheekbone. Rafe tried to sidestep and failed, slipping in a wet spot on the floor. As he went down, Dan Shute aimed a teriffic kick at his head that would have ended the fight right there, but half off-balance, Rafe hurled himself at the pivot leg and knocked Dan sprawling.

Both men came up and walked into each other, slugging.

Rafe evaded a kick aimed for his stomach and slapped a palm under the man's heel, lifting it high. Shute went over on his back, and Rafe left the floor in a dive and lit right in the middle of Dan Shute and knocked the wind out of him. But not enough so that Dan's thumb failed to stab him in the eye.

Blinded by pain, Rafe jerked his head away from that stabbing thumb and felt it rip along his cheek. Then he slammed two blows to the head before Shute heaved him off. They came up together.

Dan Shute was bleeding from the cut on his cheek, but he was still smiling. His gray shirt was torn, revealing bulging white muscles. He was not even breathing hard, and he walked into Rafe with a queer little bounce in his step. Rafe weaved right to left and then straightened suddenly and left-handed a stiff one into Shute's mouth.

Dan went under a duplicate punch and slammed a right to the wind that lifted Rafe off the floor. They went into a clinch then, and Rafe was the faster, throwing Dan with a rolling hiplock. He came off the floor fast, and the two went over like a pinwheel, gouging, slugging, ripping, and tearing at each other with fists, thumbs, and elbows.

Shute was up first and Rafe followed, lunging in, but Dan stepped back and whipped up a right uppercut that smashed every bit of sense in Rafe's head into a blinding pinwheel of white light. But he was moving fast and went on in with the impetus of his rush, and both men crashed to the floor.

Up again and swinging, they stood toe to toe and slugged viciously, wickedly, each punch a killing blow. Jaws set, they lashed at each other like madmen. Then Rafe let his right go down the groove to the cut cheek. He sidestepped and let go again, then again and again. Five times straight he hit that split cheek. It was cut deeply now and streaming blood.

Dan rushed and grabbed Rafe around the knees, heaving him clear of the floor. He brought him down with a thunderous crash that would have killed a lesser man.

Rafe got up panting and was set for Shute as he rushed. He split Dan's lips with another left and then threw a right that missed and caught a punch in the middle that jerked his mouth open and brought his breath out of his lungs in one great gasp.

All reason gone, the two men fought like animals, yet worse than animals, for in each man was the experience of years of accumulated brawling and slugging in the hard, tough, wild places of the world. They lived by their strength and their hands and the fierce animal drive that was within them, the drive of the fight for survival.

Rafe stepped in, punching Shute with a wicked, cutting, stabbing left. And then his right went down the line again, and blood streamed from the cut cheek.

They stood, then, facing each other, shirts in ribbons, blood streaked, with arms a-swing. They started to circle, and suddenly Shute lunged. Rafe took one step back and swung a kick from the hips. An inch or so lower down and he would have caught the bigger man in the solar plexus. As it was, the kick struck him on the chest and lifted him clear of the floor. He came down hard, but his powerful arms grabbed Rafe's leg as they swung down, and both men hit the floor together.

Shute sank his teeth into Rafe's leg, and Rafe stabbed at his eye with a thumb. Shute let go and got up, grabbing a chair. Rafe went under it, heard the chair splinter and scarcely realized in the heat of battle that his back had taken the force of the blow. He shoved Dan back and smashed both hands into the big man's body. Then he rolled aside and spilled him with a rolling hiplock.

Dan Shute came up, and Rafe walked in. He stabbed a left to the face, and Shute's teeth showed through his lip, broken and ugly. Rafe set himself and whipped up an uppercut that stood Shute on his toes.

Tottering and punchdrunk, the light of battle still flamed in Shute's eyes. He grabbed a bottle and lunged at Rafe, smashing it down on his shoulder. Rafe rolled with the blow and felt the bottle shatter over the compact mass of the deltoid at the end of his shoulder. Then he hooked a left with that same numb arm, and felt the fist sink into Shute's body.

The strong muscles of that rock-ribbed stomach were yielding now. Rafe set himself and threw a right from the hip to the same place, and Shute staggered, his face greenish white. Rafe walked in and stabbed three times with a powerful, cutting left that left Shute's lips in shreds.

Then, suddenly, calling on some hidden well of strength, Dan dived for Rafe's legs, got him around the knees, and jerked back. Rafe hit the floor on the side of his head, and his world splintered into fragments of broken glass and light, flickering and exploding in a flaming chain reaction.

He rolled over, took a kick on the chest, and then staggered up as Shute stepped in, drunk with a chance of victory. Heavy, brutal punches smashed him to his knees, but Rafe staggered up. A powerful blow brought him down again, and he lunged to his feet.

Again he went to his knees, and again he came up. Then he uncorked one of his own, and Dan Shute staggered. But Dan had shot his bolt. Head ringing, Rafe Caradec walked in, grabbed the bigger man by the shirt collar and belt, right hand at the belt, and then turned his back on him and jerked down with his left hand at the collar and heaved up with the right. He got his back under him and then hurled the big man like a sack of wheat!

Dan Shute hit the table beside which Gene Baker was standing, and both went down in a heap. Suddenly, Shute rolled over and came to his knees, his eyes blazing. Blood streamed from the gash in his cheek, open now from mouth to ear. His lips were shreds, and a huge blue lump concealed one eye. His face was scarcely human, yet in the remaining eye gleamed a wild, killing, insane light. And in his hands he held Gene Baker's double-barreled shotgun!

He did not speak—just swept the gun up and squeezed down on both triggers!

Yet at the very instant that he squeezed those triggers, Rafe's left hand had dropped to the table near him. With one terriffic heave he spun it toward the kneeling man. The gun belched flame and thunder as Rafe hit the floor flat on his stomach and rolled over to see an awful sight.

Joe Benson, crouched over the bar, took the full blast of buckshot in his face and went over backward with a queer, choking scream.

Rafe heaved himself erect, and suddenly the room was deathly still. Pod Gomer's face was a blank sheet of white horror as he stared at the spot where Benson had vanished.

Staggering, Caradec walked toward Dan Shute. The man lay on his back, arms outflung, head lying at a queer angle.

Mullaney pointed. "The table!" he said. "It busted his neck!"

Rafe turned and staggered toward the door. Johnny Gill caught him there. He slid an arm under Rafe's shoulders and strapped his guns to his waist.

"What about Gomer?" he asked.

Caradec shook his head. Pod Gomer was getting up to face him, and he lifted a hand.

"Don't start anything. I've had enough. I'll go."

Somebody brought a bucket of water, and Rafe fell on his knees and began splashing the ice-cold water over his head and face. When he had dried himself on a towel someone handed him, he started for a coat. Baker had come in with a clean shirt from the store.

"I'm sorry about that shotgun," he said. "It happened so fast I didn't know."

Rafe tried to smile and couldn't. His face was stiff and swollen.

"Forget it," he said. "Let's get out of here."

"You ain't goin' to leave, are you?" Baker asked. "Ann said that she—"

"Leave? Shucks, no! We've got an oil business here, and there's a ranch. While I was at the fort I had a wire sent to the C Bar down in Texas for some more cattle."

Ann was waiting for him, wide-eyed when she saw his face. He walked past her toward the bed and fell across it.

"Don't let it get you, honey," he said. "We'll talk about it when I wake up next week!"

She stared at him and started to speak, and then a snore sounded in the room.

Ma Baker smiled. "When a man wants to sleep, let him sleep, and I'd say he'd earned it!"

AUTHOR'S NOTE
RIDERS OF THE DAWN

No matter how far back one goes, there are always stories of earlier arrivals. For example, in the archives of Paris, there is preserved a map prepared supposedly by Jesuits in 1792 that shows the Black Hills and the Big Horn Mountains. It is a topographical map and remarkably good, but where the Jesuits got their information we do not know.

At Massacre Rocks and several other places in Nevada, there are inscriptions and markings on rock walls that do not resemble anything done by American Indians.

Riders of the Dawn

I

I rode down from the high blue hills and across the brush flats into Hattan's Point, a raw bit of spawning hell, scattered hit or miss along the rocky slope of a rust-topped mesa.

Ah, it's a grand feeling to be young and tough with a heart full of hell, strong muscles, and quick, flexible hands! And the feeling that somewhere in town there's a man who would like to tear down your meat house with hands or gun.

It was like that, Hattan's Point was, when I swung down from my buckskin and gave him a word to wait with. A new town, a new challenge, and if there were those who wished to take me on, let them come and be damned.

I knew the whiskey of this town would be the raw whiskey of the last town and of the towns behind it, but I shoved through the batwing doors and downed a shot of rye and looked around, measuring the men along the bar and at the tables. None of these men did I know, yet I had seen them all before in a dozen towns. There was the big, hard-eyed rancher with the iron-gray hair who thought he was the bull of the woods, and the knifelike man beside him with the careful eyes who would be gunslick and fast as a striking snake.

The big man turned his head toward me, as a great brown bear turns to look at something he could squeeze to nothing if he wished. "Who sent for you?"

There was harsh challenge in the words, the cold demand of a conqueror. I laughed within me. "Nobody sent for me. I ride where I want and stop when I want."

He was a man grown used to smaller men who spoke softly to him, and my answer was irritating. "Then ride on," he said, "for you're not wanted in Hattan's Point."

"Sorry, friend," I said. "I like it here. I'm staying, and maybe in whatever game you're playing, I'll buy chips. I

127

don't like being ordered around by big frogs in such small puddles."

His big face flamed crimson, but before he could answer, another man spoke up, a tall young man with white hair. "What he means is that there's trouble here, and men are taking sides. Those who stand upon neither side are everybody's enemy in Hattan Point."

"So?" I smiled at them all, but my eyes held to the big bull of the woods. "Then maybe I'll choose a side. I always did like a fight."

"Then be sure you choose the right one"—this was from the knifelike man beside the bull—"and talk to me before you decide."

"I'll talk to you," I said, "or any man. I'm reasonable enough. But get this, the side I choose will be the right one!"

The sun was bright on the street, and I walked outside, feeling the warm of it, feeling the cold from my muscles. Within me I chuckled, because I knew what they were saying back there. I'd thrown my challenge at them for pure fun; I didn't care about anyone . . . and then suddenly I did.

She stood on the boardwalk straight before me, slim, tall, with a softly curved body and magnificent eyes and hair of deepest black. Her skin was lightly tanned, her eyes an amazing green, her lips full and rich.

My black leather chaps were dusty, and my gray shirt was sweat stained from the road. My jaws were lean and unshaven, and under my black, flat-crowned hat, my hair was black and rumpled. I was in no shape to meet a girl like that, but there she was, the woman I wanted, my woman.

In two steps I was beside her. "I realize," I said, as she turned to face me, "the time is inopportune. My presence scarcely inspires interest, let alone affection and love, but this seemed the best time for you to meet the man you are to marry. The name is Mathieu Sabre.

"Furthermore—I might as well tell you now—I am of Irish and French extraction, have no money, and have no property but a horse and the guns I wear, but I have been looking for you for years, and I could not wait to tell you that I was here, your future mate and husband." I bowed, hat in hand.

She stared, startled, amazed, and then angry. "Well, of all the egotistical—"

"Ah!" My expression was one of relief. "Those are kind

words, darling, wonderful words! More true romances have begun with those words than any other! And now, if you'll excuse me?"

Taking one step back, I turned, vaulted over the hitching rail, and untied my buckskin. Swinging into the saddle, I looked back. She was standing there, staring at me, her eyes wide, and the anger was leaving them. "Good afternoon," I said, bowing again. "I'll call upon you later!"

It was time to get out and away, but I felt good about it. Had I attempted to advance the acquaintance I should have gotten nowhere, but my quick leaving would arouse her curiosity. There is no trait women possess more fortunate for men than their curiosity.

The livery stable at Hattan's Point was a huge and rambling structure that sprawled lazily over a corner at the beginning of the town. From a bin I got a scoop of corn, and while the buckskin absorbed this warning against hard days to come, I curried him carefully. A jingle of spurs warned me, and when I looked around, a tall, very thin man was leaning against the stall post watching me.

When I straightened up, I was looking into a pair of piercing dark eyes from under shaggy brows that seemed to overhang the long hatchet face. He was shabby and unkempt, but he wore two guns, the only man in town whom I'd seen wearing two except for the knifelike man in the saloon. "Hear you had a run-in with Rud Maclaren."

"Run-in? I'd not call it that. He suggested the country was crowded and that I move on. So I told him I liked it here, and if the fight looked good I might choose a side."

"Good! Then I come right on time! Folks are talkin' about you. They say Canaval offered you a job on Maclaren's Bar M. Well, I'm beatin' him to it. I'm Jim Pinder, ramroddin' the CP outfit. I'll pay warrior wages, seventy a month an' found. All the ammunition you can use."

My eyes had strayed behind him to the two men lurking in a dark stall. They had, I was sure, come in with Pinder. The idea did not appeal to me. Shoving Pinder aside, I sprang into the middle of the open space between the rows of stalls.

"You two!" My voice rang in the echoing emptiness of the building. "Get out in the open! Start now or start shootin'!"

My hands were wide, fingers spread, and right then it

did not matter to me which way they came. There was that old jumping devil in me, and the fury was driving me as it always did when action began to build up. Men who lurked in dark stalls did not appeal to me, nor the men who hired them.

They came out slowly, hands wide. One of them was a big man with black hair and unshaven jowls. He looked surly. The other had a cruel, flat face and looked like an Apache. "Suppose I'd come shootin'?" the black-haired man sneered.

"Then they'd be plantin' you at sundown." My eyes held him. "If you don't believe that, cut loose your wolf right now."

That stopped him. He didn't like it, for they didn't know me and I was too ready. Wise enough to see that I was no half-baked gunfighter, they didn't know how much of it I could back up and weren't anxious to find out.

"You move fast." Pinder was staring at me with small eyes. "Suppose I had cut myself in with Blacky and the Apache?"

My chuckle angered him. "You? I had that pegged, Jim Pinder. When my guns came out you would have died first. You're faster than either of those two, so you'd take yours first. Then Blacky, and after him"— I nodded toward the Apache—"him. He would be the hardest to kill."

Pinder didn't like it, and he didn't like me. "I made an offer," he said.

"And you brought these coyotes to give me a rough time if I didn't take it? Be damned to you, Pinder! You can take your CP outfit and go to blazes!"

His lips thinned down and he stared at me. I've seldom seen such hatred in a man's eyes. "Then get out!" he said. "Get out fast! Join Maclaren, an' you die!"

"Then why wait? I'm not joining Maclaren so far as I know now, but I'm staying, Pinder. Anytime you want what I've got, come shooting. I'll be ready."

"You swing a wide loop for a stranger. You started in the wrong country. You won't live long."

"No?" I gave it to him flat and face up on the table. "No? Well, I've a hunch I'll handle the shovel that throws dirt on your grave, and maybe trigger the gun that puts you there. I'm not asking for trouble, but I like it, so whenever you're ready, let me know."

*   *   *

With that I left them. Up the street, there was a sign:

MOTHER O'HARA'S COOKING
MEALS FOUR BITS

With my gnawing appetite, that looked as likely a direction as any. It was early for supper, and there were few at table: the young man with white hair and the girl I loved . . . and a few scattered others who ate sourly and in silence.

When I shoved the door open and stood there with my hat shoved back on my head and a smile on my face, the girl looked up, surprised, but ready for battle. I grinned at her and bowed. "How do you do, the future Mrs. Sabre? The pleasure of seeing you again so soon is unexpected, but real!"

The man with her looked surprised, and the buxom woman of forty-five or so who came in from the kitchen looked quickly from one to the other of us.

The girl ignored me, but the man with the white hair nodded. "You've met Miss Maclaren, then?"

So, Maclaren it was? I might have suspected as much. "No, not formally. But we met briefly on the street, and I've been dreaming of her for years. It gives me great wonder to find her here, although when I see the food on the table, I don't doubt why she is so lovely if it is here she eats!"

Mother O'Hara liked that. "Sure, an' I smell the blarney in that!" she said sharply. "But sit down, if you'd eat!"

My hat came off, and I sat on the bench opposite my girl, who looked at her plate in cold silence.

"My name is Key Chapin." The white-haired man extended his hand. "Yours, I take it, is Sabre?"

"Matt Sabre," I said.

A grizzled man from the foot of the table looked up. "Matt Sabre from Dodge. Once marshal of Mobeetie, the Mogollon gunfighter."

They all looked from him to me, and I accepted the cup of coffee Mother O'Hara poured. "The gentleman knows me," I said quietly. "I've been known in those places."

"You refused Maclaren's offer?" Chapin asked.

"Yes, and Pinder's, too."

"Pinder?" Chapin's eyes were wary. "Is he in town?"

"Big as life." I could feel the girl's eyes on me. "Tell me what this fight is about?"

"What are most range wars about? Water, sheep, or

grass. This one is water. There's a long valley east of here called Cottonwood Wash, and running east out of it is a smaller valley or canyon called the Two Bar. On the Two Bar is a stream of year-round water with volume enough to irrigate land or water thousands of cattle. Maclaren wants that water. The CP wants it."

"Who's got it?"

"A man named Ball. He's no fighter and has no money to hire fighters, but he hates Maclaren and refuses to do business with Pinder. So there they sit with the pot boiling and the lid about to blow off."

"And our friend Ball is right smack in the middle."

"Right. Gamblers around town are offering odds he won't last thirty days, even money that he'll be dead within ten."

That was enough for now. My eyes turned to the daughter of Rud Maclaren. "You can be buying your trousseau, then," I said, "for the time will not be long."

She looked at me coolly, but behind it there was a touch of impudence. "I'll not worry about it," she said calmly. "There's no weddings in Boot Hill."

They laughed at that, yet behind it I knew there was the feeling that she was right, and yet the something in me that was me, told me no . . . it was not my time to go. Not by gun or horse or rolling river . . . not yet.

"You've put your tongue to prophecy, darlin'," I said, "and I'll not say that I'll not end in Boot Hill, where many another good man has gone, but I will say this, and you sleep on it, daughter of Maclaren, for it's a bit of the truth. Before I sleep in Boot Hill, there'll be sons and daughters of yours and mine on this ground.

"Yes, and believe me"—I got up to go—"when my time comes I'll be carried there by six tall sons of ours, and there'll be daughters of ours who'll weep at my grave, and you with them, remembering the years we've had."

When the door slapped shut behind me, there was silence inside, and then through the thin walls I heard Mother O'Hara speak. "You'd better be buyin' that trousseau, Olga Maclaren, for there's a lad as knows his mind!"

This was the way of it then, and now I had planning to do and my way to make in the world, for though I'd travelled wide and far, in many lands not my own, I'd no money and no home to take her to.

*   *   *

Behind me were wars and struggles, hunger, thirst, and cold, and the deep, splendid bitterness of fighting for a cause I scarcely understood, because there was in me the undying love of a lost cause and a world to win. And now I'd my own to win, and a threshold to find to carry her over.

And then, as a slow night wind moved upon my cheek and stirred the hair above my brow, I found an answer. I knew what I would do, and the very challenge of it sent my blood leaping, and the laughter came from my lips as I stepped into the street and started across.

Then I stopped, for there was a man before me.

He was a big man, towering above my six feet and two inches, broader and thicker than my two hundred pounds. He was a big-boned man and full of raw power, unbroken and brutal. He stood there, wide-legged before me, his face wide as my two hands, his big head topped by a mat of tight curls, his hat missing somewhere.

"You're Sabre?" he said.

"Why, yes," I said, and he hit me.

Never did I see the blow start. Never even did I see the balled fist of him, but it bludgeoned my jaw like an ax butt, and something seemed to slam me behind the knees, and I felt myself going. He caught me again before I could fall and then dropped astride of me and began to swing short, brutal blows to my head with both big fists. All of two hundred and sixty pounds he must have weighed, and none of it wasted by fat. He was naked, raw, unbridled power.

Groggy, bloody, beaten, I fought to get up, but he was astride me, and my arms were pinned to my sides by his great knees. His fists were slugging me with casual brutality. Then suddenly, he got up and stepped back and kicked me in the ribs. "If you're conscious," he said, "hear me. I'm Morgan Park, and I'm the man who marries Olga Maclaren!"

My lips were swollen and bloody. "You lie!" I said, and he kicked me again. Then he stepped over me and walked away, whistling.

Somehow I got my arms under me. Somehow I dragged myself against the stage station wall, and then I lay there, my head throbbing like a great drum, the blood slowly drying on my split lips and broken face. It had been a beating I'd taken, and the marvel of it was with me. I'd not been licked since I was a lad, and never in all my days have I felt such blows as these. His fists were like knots of oak, and the arms behind them like the limbs of a tree.

I had a broken rib, I thought, but one thing I knew. It was time for me to travel. Never would I have the daughter of Maclaren see me like this!

My hands found the building corner, and I pulled myself to my feet. Staggering behind the buildings, I got to the corner of the livery stable. Entering, I got to my horse, and somehow I got the saddle on him and led him out of the door. And then I stepped for an instant, in the light.

Across the way, on the stoop of Mother O'Hara's, was Olga Maclaren!

The light was on my face, swollen, bloody and broken. She stepped down off the porch and came over to me, looking up, her eyes wide with wonder. "So it's you. He found you, then. He always hears, and this always happens. You see, it is not so simple a thing to marry Olga Maclaren!" There seemed almost regret in her voice. "And now you're leaving!"

"Leaving? That I am, but I'll be back!" The words fumbled through my swollen lips. "Have your trousseau ready, daughter of Maclaren! I mean what I say! Wait for me. I'll be coming again, darlin', and when I do it will be first to tear down Morgan Park's great hulk, to rip him with my fists!"

There was coolness in her voice, shaded with contempt. "You boast! All you have done is talk—and take a beating!"

That made me grin, and the effort made me wince, but I looked down at her. "It's a bad beginning, at that, isn't it? But wait for me, darlin', I'll be coming back!"

I could feel her watching me ride down the street.

II

Throughout the night I rode into wilder and wilder country, always with the thought of what faced me. At daybreak I bedded down in a canyon tall with pines, resting there while my side began to mend. My thoughts returned again and again to the shocking power of those punches I had taken. It was true the man had slugged me unexpectedly, and once pinned down I'd had no chance against his great weight. Nonetheless I'd been whipped soundly. Within me there was a gnawing eagerness to go back—and not with guns. This man I must whip with my hands.

The Two Bar was the key to the situation. Could it be had with a gun and some blarney? The beating I'd taken rankled, and the contempt of Olga Maclaren, and with it the memory of the hatred of Jim Pinder and the coldness of Rud Maclaren. On the morning of the third day I mounted the buckskin and turned him toward the Two Bar.

A noontime sun was darkening my buckskin with sweat when I turned up Cottonwod Wash. There was green grass here, and trees, and the water that trickled down was clear and pure. The walls of the wash were high and the trees towered to equal them, and the occasional cattle looked fat and lazy, far better than elsewhere on this range. The path ended abruptly at a gate bearing a large sign in white letters against a black background.

TWO BAR GATE
RANGED FOR A SPENCER .56
SHOOTING GOING ON HERE

Ball evidently had his own ideas. No trespasser who got a bullet could say he hadn't been warned. Beyond this gate a man took his own chances. Taking off my hat, I rose in my stirrups and waved it toward the house.

A gun boomed, and I heard the sharp *whap* of a bullet whipping past. It was a warning shot, so I merely waved once more. That time the bullet was close, so I grabbed my chest with both hands and slid from the saddle to the ground. Speaking to the buckskin, I rolled over behind a boulder. Leaving my hat on the ground in plain sight, I removed a boot and placed it to be seen from the gate. Then I crawled into the brush, from where I could cover the gate.

Several minutes later, Ball appeared. Without coming through the gate, he couldn't see the boot was empty.

He was a tall old man with a white handlebar mustache and shrewd eyes. No fool, he studied the layout carefully, but to all appearances his aim had miscalculated and he had scored a hit. He glanced at the strange brand on the buckskin and at the California bridle and bit. Finally, he opened the gate and came out, and as he moved toward my horse his back turned toward me. "Freeze, Ball! You're dead in my sights!"

He stood still. "Who are you?" he demanded. "What you want with me?"

"No trouble. I came to talk business."

"I got no business with anybody."

"You've business with me. I'm Matt Sabre. I've had a run-in with Jim Pinder and told off Maclaren when he told me to leave. I've taken a beating from Morgan Park."

Ball chuckled. "You say you want no trouble with me, but from what you say, you've had it with everybody else!"

He turned at my word, and I holstered my gun. He stepped back far enough to see the boot, and then he grinned. "Good trick. I'll not bite on that one again. What you want?"

Pulling on my boot and retrieving my hat, I told him. "I've no money. I'm a fighting man and a sucker for the tough side of any scrap. When I rode into Hattan's I figured on trouble, but when I saw Olga Maclaren I decided to stay and marry her, I've told her so."

"No wonder Park beat you. He's run off the local lads." He studied me curiously. "What did she say?"

"Very little, and when I told her I was coming back to face Park again, she thought I was loudmouthed."

"Aim to try him again?"

"I'm going to whip him. But that's not all. I plan to stay in this country, and there's only one ranch in this country I want or would have."

Ball's lips thinned. "This one?"

"It's the best, and anybody who owns it stands in the middle of trouble. I'd be mighty uncomfortable anywhere else."

"What you aim to do about me? This here's my ranch."

"Let's walk up to your place and talk it over."

"We'll talk here." Ball's hands were on his hips, and I had no doubt he'd go for a gun if I made a wrong move. "Speak your piece."

"All right, here it is. You're buckin' a stacked deck. Gamblers are offerin' thirty to one you won't last thirty days. Both Maclaren and Pinder are out to get you. What I want is a fighting, working partnership. Or you sell out and I'll pay you when I can. I'll take over the fight."

He nodded toward the house. "Come on up. We'll talk this over."

Two hours later the deal was ironed out. He could not stay awake every night. He could not work and guard his stock. He could not go to town for supplies. Together we could do all of it.

"You'll be lucky if you last a week," he told me. "When they find out, they'll be fit to be tied."

"They won't find out right away. First I'll buy supplies and ammunition and get back here."

"Good idea. But leave Morgan Park alone. He's as handy with a gun as with his fists."

The Two Bar controlled most of Cottonwood Wash and on its eastern side opened into the desert wilderness with only occasional patches of grass and much desert growth. Maclaren's Bar M and Pinder's CP bordered the ranch on the west, with Maclaren's range extending to the desert land in one portion, but largely west of the Two Bar.

Both ranches had pushed the Two Bar cattle back, usurping the range for their own use. In the process of being pushed north, most of the Two Bar calves had vanished under Bar M or CP brands. "Mostly the CP," Ball advised. "Them Pinders are poison mean. Rollie rode with the James boys a few times, and both of them were with Quantrill. Jim's a fast gun, but nothin' to compare with Rollie."

At daylight, with three unbranded mules to carry the supplies, I started for Hattan's, circling around to hit the trail on the side away from the Two Bar. The town was quiet enough, and the day warm and still. As I loaded the supplies I was sweating. The sweat trickled into my eyes and my side pained me. My face was still puffed, but both my eyes were now open. Leading my mules out of town, I concealed them in some brush with plenty of grass and then returned to Mother O'Hara's.

Key Chapin and Canaval were there, and Canaval looked up at me. "Had trouble?" he asked. "That job at the Bar M is still open."

"Thanks. I'm going to run my own outfit." Foolish though it was; I said it. Olga had come in the door behind me, her perfume told me who it was, and even without it something in my blood would have told me. From that day on she was never to be close to me without my knowledge. It was something deep and exciting that was between us.

"Your own outfit?" They were surprised. "You're turning nester?"

"No. Ranching." Turning, I swept off my hat and indicated the seat beside me. "Miss Maclaren? May I have the pleasure?"

Her green eyes were level and measuring. She hesitated and then shook her head. Walking around the table she seated herself beside Canaval.

Chapin was puzzled. "You're *ranching*? If there's any open range around here, I don't know of it."

"It's a place over east of here," I replied lightly, "the Two Bar."

"What about the Two Bar?" Rud Maclaren had come in. He stood cold and solid, staring down at me.

Olga glanced up at her father, some irony in her eyes. "Mr. Sabre was telling us that he is ranching—on the Two Bar."

"*What?*" Glasses and cups jumped at his voice, and Ma O'Hara hurried in from her kitchen, rolling pin in hand.

"That's right." I was enjoying it. "I've a working partnership with Ball. He needed help and I didn't want to leave despite all the invitations I was getting." Then I added, "A man dislikes being far from the girl he's to marry."

"What's that?" Maclaren demanded, his eyes puzzled.

"Why, Father!" Olga's eyes widened. "Haven't you heard? The whole town is talking of it! Mr. Sabre has said he is going to marry me!"

"I'll see him in hell first!" Maclaren replied flatly. "Young man, you stop using my daughter's name, or you'll face me."

"No one," I said quietly, "has more respect for your daughter's name than I. It's true that I've said she was to be my wife. That is not disrespectful, and it's certainly true. As for facing you, I'd rather not. I'd like to keep peace with my future father-in-law."

Canaval chuckled, and even Olga seemed amused. Key Chapin looked up at Rud. "One aspect of this may have escaped you. Sabre is now a partner of Ball. Why not make it easy for Sabre to stay on and then buy him out?"

Maclaren's head lifted as he absorbed the idea. He looked at Sabre with new interest. "We might do business, young man."

"We might," I replied, "but not under threats. Nor do I intend to sell out my partner. Nor did I take the partnership with any idea of selling out. Tomorrow or the next day I shall choose a building site. Also, I expect to restock the Two Bar range.

"All of which brings me to the point of this discussion. It has come to my attention that the Bar M cattle are trespassing on Two Bar range. You have just one week to remove them. The same goes for the CP. You've been told and you understand. I hope we'll have no further trouble."

Maclaren's face purpled with fury. Before he could find words to reply, I was on my feet. "It's been nice seeing you," I told Olga. "If you care to help plan your future home, why don't you ride over?"

With that I stepped out the door before Maclaren could speak. Circling the building, I headed for my horse.

Pinder's black-haired man was standing there with a gun in his hand. Hatred glared from his eyes. "Figured you pulled a smart one, hey?" he sneered. "Now I'll kill you!"

His finger started to whiten with pressure, and I hurled myself aside and palmed my gun. Even before I could think, my gun jarred in my hand. Once! Twice!

Blacky's bullet had torn my shirt collar and left a trace of blood on my neck. Blacky stared at me and then lifted to his toes and fell, measuring his length upon the hard ground.

Men rushed from the buildings, crowding around. "Seen it!" one man explained quietly. "Blacky laid for him with a drawed gun."

Canaval was among the men. He looked at me with cool, attentive gaze. "A drawn gun? That was fast, man."

Ball was at the gate when I arrived. "Trouble?" he asked quickly.

My account was brief.

"Well, one less for later," said Ball. "If it had to be anybody it's better it was Blacky, but now the Pinders will be after you."

"Where does Morgan Park stand?" I asked. "And what about Key Chapin?"

"Park?" Ball said. "He's fixin' to marry the Maclaren girl. That's where his bread's buttered. He's got him a ranch on the Arizona line, but he don't stay there much. Chapin publishes the *Rider's Voice*, a better newspaper than you'd expect in this country. He's also a lawyer, plays a good hand of poker, an' never carries a gun. If anybody isn't takin' sides, it's him."

Mostly I considered the cattle situation. Our calves had been rustled by the large outfits, and if we were to prosper we must get rid of the stock we now had and get some young stuff. Our cattle would never be in better shape and would get older and tougher. Now was the time to sell. A drive was impossible, for two of us couldn't be away at once, and nobody wanted any part of a job with the Two Bar. Ball was frankly discouraged. "No use, Matt. They got us bottled up. We're through whenever they want to take us."

An idea occurred to me. "By the way, when I was drifting down around Organ Rock the other day, I spotted an outfit down there in the hills. Know 'em?"

Ball's head came up sharply. "Should have warned you. Stay away. That's the Benaras place, the B Bar B brand. There's six in the family that I know of, an' they have no truck with anybody. Dead shots, all of 'em. Few years back some rustlers run off some of their stock. Nobody heard no more about it until Sheriff Will Tharp was back in the badlands east of here. He hadn't seen hide nor hair of man nor beast for miles when suddenly he comes on six skeletons hanging from a rock tower."

"Skeletons?"

Ball took the pipe from his mouth and spat. "Six of 'em, an' a sign hung to 'em readin', 'They rustled B Bar B cows.' Nothin' more."

But quite enough! The Benaras outfit had been let strictly alone after that. Nevertheless, an idea was in my mind, and the very next morning I saddled up and drifted south.

It was wild and lonely country, furrowed and eroded by thousands of years of sun, wind, and rain, a country tumbled and broken as if by an insane giant. There were miles of raw, unfleshed land with only occasional spots of green to break its everlasting reds, pinks, and whites. Like an oasis, there appeared a sudden cluster of trees, green fields, and fat, drifting cattle. "Whoever these folks are, Buck," I commented to my horse, "they work hard."

The click of a drawn-back hammer froze Buck in his tracks, and carefully I kept my hands on the saddle horn. "Goin' somewhere, stranger?" Nobody was in sight among the boulders at the edge of the field.

"Yes. I'm looking for the boss of the B Bar B."

"What might you want with him?"

"Business talk. I'm friendly."

The chuckle was dry. "Ever see a man covered by two Spencers that wasn't friendly?"

The next was a girl's voice. "Who you ridin' for?"

"I'm Matt Sabre, half owner of the Two Bar, Ball's outfit."

"You mean that old coot took a partner? You could be lyin'."

'Do I see the boss?"

"I reckon." A tall boy of eighteen stepped from the rocks. Lean and drawn, his hatchet face looked tough and wise. He carried his Spencer as if it was part of him. He motioned with his head.

The old man of the tribe was standing in front of a house built like a fort. Tall as his son, he was straight as a lodgepole pine. He looked me up and down and then said. "Get down an' set."

A stout, motherly woman put out some cups and poured coffee. Explaining who I was, I said, "We've some fat stock about ready to drive. I'd like to make a swap for some of your young stuff. We can't make a drive, don't dare even leave the place or they'd steal it from us. Our stock is in good shape, but all our young stuff has been rustled."

"You're talkin'." He studied me from under shaggy brows. He looked like a patriarch right out of the Bible, a hard-bitten old man of the tribe who knew his own mind and how to make it stick. He listened as I explained our setup and our plans. Finally, he nodded. "All right, Sabre. We'll swap. My boys will help you drive 'em back here."

"No need for that. Once started down the canyons I'll need no help. No use you getting involved in this fight."

He turned his fierce blue eyes on me. I'm buyin' cows," he said grimly. "Anybody who wants trouble over that, let 'em start it!"

"Now, Paw!" Mother Benaras smiled at me. "Paw figures he's still a-feudin'."

Old Bob Benaras knocked out his pipe on the hearth. "We're beholden to no man, nor will we backwater for any man. Nick, roust out an' get Zeb, then saddle up an' ride with this man. You ride to this man's orders. Start no trouble, but back up for nobody. Understand?"

He looked around at me. "You'll eat first. Maw, set up the table. We've a guest in the house." He looked searchingly at me. "Had any trouble with Jim Pinder yet?"

It made a short tale; then I added, "Blacky braced me in town a few days ago. Laid for me with a drawn gun."

Benaras stared at me, and the boys exchanged looks. The old man tamped tobacco into his pipe. "He had it comin'. Jolly had trouble with that one. Figured soon or late he'd have to kill him. Glad you done it."

All the way back to the Two Bar we watched the country warily, but it was not until we were coming up to the gate that anyone was sighted. Two riders were on the lip of the wash, staring at us through a glass. We passed through the gate and started up the trail. There was no challenge. Nick said suddenly, "I smell smoke!"

Fear went through me like an electric shock. Slapping the spurs to my tired buckskin, I put the horse up the trail at a dead run, Nick and Zeb right behind me. Turning the bend in the steep trail, I heard the crackle of flames and saw the ruins of the house!

All was in ruins, the barn gone, the house a sagging, blazing heap. Leaving my horse on the run I dashed around the house. "Ball!" I yelled. "Ball!" And above the crackle of flames, I heard a cry.

He was back in a niche of rock near the spring. How he had lived this long I could not guess. His clothes were charred and it was obvious he had somehow crawled, wounded, from the burning house. He had been fairly riddled with bullets.

His fierce old eyes were pleading. "Don't let 'em get . . . get the place. Yours . . . it's yours now." His eyes went to Nick and Zeb. "You're witnesses . . . I leave it to him. Never to sell . . . never to give up!"

"Who was it?" For the first time in my life I really wanted to kill. Although I had known this old man for only a few days I had come to feel affection for him and respect. Now he was dying, shot down and left for dead in a blazing house.

"Pinder!" His voice was hoarse. "Jim an' Rollie. Rollie, he . . . he was dressed like you. Never had no chance. Fun-funny thing. I . . . I thought I saw . . . Park."

"Morgan Park?" I was incredulous. "With the Pinders?"

His lips stirred, but he died forming the words. When I got up, there was in me such hatred as I had never believed was possible. "Everyone of them!" I said. "I'll kill every man of them for this!"

"Amen!" Zeb and Nick spoke as one. "He was a good old man. Pappy liked him."

"Did you hear him say Morgan Park was with the Pinders?"

"Sounded like it," Zeb admitted, "but it ain't reasonable. He's thick with the Maclarens. Couldn't have been him."

Zeb was probably right. The light had been bad, and Ball had been wounded. He could have made a mistake.

The stars came out, and night moved in over the hills and gathered black and rich in the canyons. Standing there in the darkness, we could smell the smoke from the burned house and see occasional sparks and flickers of tiny flames among the charred timbers. A ranch had been given me, but I had lost a friend. The road before me stretched dark and long, a road I must walk alone, gun in hand.

III

For two days we combed the draws and gathered cattle, yet at the end of the second day we had but three hundred head. The herds of the Two Bar had been sadly depleted by the rustling of the big brands. On the morning of the third day we started the herd. Neither of the men had questioned me, but now Zeb wanted to know, "You aim to leave the ranch unguarded? Ain't you afraid they'll move in?"

"If they do they can move out or be buried here. That ranch was never to be given up, and believe me, it won't be!"

The canyon channeled the drive, and the cattle were fat and easy to handle. It took us all day to make the drive, but my side pained me almost none at all, and only that gnawing fury at the killers of the old man remained to disturb me. They had left the wounded man to burn, and for that they would pay.

Jonathan and Jolly Benaras helped me take the herd of young stuff back up the trail. Benaras had given me at least fifty head more than I had asked, but the cattle I had turned over to him were as good as money in the bank, so he lost nothing by his generosity.

When we told him what had happened, he nodded. "Jolly was over to Hattan's. It was the Pinders, all right. That

Apache tracker of theirs along with Bunt Wilson and Corby Kitchen an' three others. They were with the Pinders."

"Hear anything about Morgan Park?"

"No. Some say Lyell, that rider of Park's, was in the crowd."

That could have been it. Ball might have meant to tell me it was a rider of Park's. We pushed the young stuff hard to get back, but Jonathan rode across the drag before we arrived. "Folks at your place. Two, three of 'em."

My face set cold as stone. "Bring the herd. I'll ride ahead."

Jonathan's big adam's apple bobbed. "Jolly an' me, we ain't had much fun lately. Can't we ride with you?"

An idea hit me. "Where's their camp?"

"Foot of the hill where the house was. They got a tent."

"Then we'll take the herd. Drive 'em right over the tent!"

Jolly had come back to the drag. He chuckled. "Why, sure!" He grinned at Jonathan. "Won't Nick an' Zeb be sore? Missin' all the fun?"

We started the herd. They were young stuff and still full of ginger, ready enough to run. They came out of the canyon not more than four hundred yards from the camp and above the gate. Then we really turned them loose, shooting and shouting; we started that herd on a dead run for the camp. Up ahead we saw men springing to their feet, and one man raced for his rifle. They hadn't expected me to arrive with cattle, so they were caught completely off guard. Another man made a dive for his horse and the startled animal sprang aside. As he grabbed again, it kicked out with both feet and started to run.

Running full tilt, the herd hit the camp. The man who had lost his horse scrambled atop a large rock, and the others lit out for the cliffs, scattering away from the charging cattle. But the herd went through the camp, tearing up the tent, grinding the food into the earth, smearing the fire, and smashing the camp utensils into broken and useless things under their charging feet.

One of the men who had gotten into the saddle swung his horse and came charging back, his face red with fury. "What goes on here?" he yelled.

                    *   *   *

The horse was a Bar M. Maclaren's men had beaten the CP to it.

Kneeing my horse close to him, I said, "I'm Matt Sabre, owner of the Two Bar, with witnesses to prove it. You're trespassin'. Now light a shuck!"

"I will like hell!" His face was dark with fury. "I got my orders, an' I—"

My fist smashed into his teeth and he left the saddle, hitting the ground with a thud. Blazing with fury, I lit astride him, jerking him to his feet. My left hooked hard to his jaw and my right smashed him in the wind. He went down, but he got up fast and came in swinging. He was a husky man, mad clear through, and for about two minutes we stood toe to toe and swapped it out. Then he started to back up and I caught him with a sweeping right that knocked him to the dust. He started to get up then thought the better of it. "I'll kill you for this!"

"When you're ready!" I said and then turned around. Jonathan and Jolly had rounded up two of the men, and they stood waiting for me. One was a slim, hard-faced youngster who looked like the devil was riding him. The other was a stocky redhead with a scar on his jaw. The redhead stared at me, hatred in his eyes. "You ruined my outfit. What kind of a deal is this?"

"If you ride for a fighting brand you take the good with the bad," I told him. "What did you expect when you came up here, a tea party? You go back and tell Maclaren not to send boys to do a man's job and that the next trespasser will be shot."

The younger one looked at me, sneering. "What if he sends me?" Contempt twisted his lips. "If I'd not lost my gun in the scramble I'd make you eat that."

"Jolly! Lend me your gun!"

Without a word, Jolly Benaras handed it to me.

The youngster's eyes were cold and calculating, but wary now. He suspected a trick, but could not guess what it might be.

Taking the gun by the barrel, I walked toward him. "You get your chance," I said. "I'm giving you this gun, and you can use it any way you like. Try a border roll or shoot through that open-tip holster. Anyway you try it, I'm going to kill you."

*   *   *

He stared at me and then at the gun.

His tongue touched his lips. He wanted that gun more than anything else in the world. He had guts, that youngster did, guts and the streak of viciousness it takes to make a killer, but suddenly he was face to face with it at close range and he didn't like it. He would learn if he lived long enough, but right now he didn't like any part of it. Yet he wore the killer's brand and we both knew it.

"It's a trick," he said. "You ain't that much of a fool!"

"*Fool?*" That brought my own fury surging to the top. "Why, you cheap, phony, would-be badman! I'd give you two guns and beat you any day you like! I'll face you right now. You shove your gun in my belly and I'll shove mine in yours! If you want to die, that makes it easy! Come on, gunslick! What do you say?"

Crazy? Right then I didn't care. His face turned whiter but his eyes were vicious. He was trembling with eagerness to grab that gun. But face to face? Guns shoved against the body? We would both die. We couldn't miss. He shook his head, his lips dry.

My fingers held the gun by the barrel. Tossing it up suddenly I caught it by the butt, and without stopping the motion, I slashed the barrel down over his skull. He hit the dirt at my feet. Turning my back on them I returned the pistol to Jolly.

"You!" I said then to the redhead. "Take off your boots!"

"Huh?" he was startled.

"Take 'em off! Then take his off! When he comes out of it, start walking!"

"*Walkin'?*" Red's face blanched. "Look, man, I'll—"

"You'll walk. All the way back to Hattan or the Bar M. You'll start learnin' what it means to try stealin' a man's ranch."

"It was orders," he protested.

"You could quit, couldn't you?"

His face was sullen. "Wait until Maclaren hears of this! You won't last long! Far as that goes"—he motioned at the still figure on the ground—"he'll be huntin' you now. That's Bodie Miller!"

The name was familiar. Bodie Miller had killed five or six men. He was utterly vicious, and although lacking seasoning, he had it in him to be one of the worst of the badmen.

We watched them start, three men in their sock feet

with twenty miles of desert and mountains before them. Now they knew what they had tackled. They would know what war meant.

The cattle were no cause for worry. They would drift into canyons where there was plenty of grass and water, more than on the B Bar B. "Sure you won't need help?" Jolly asked hopefully. "We'd like to side you."

"Not now. This is my scrap."

They chuckled. "Well," Jolly grinned, "they can't never say you didn't walk in swingin'. You've jumped nearly the whole durned country!"

Nobody knew that better than I, so when they were gone I took my buckskin and rode back up the narrow Two Bar Canyon. It narrowed down and seemed to end. Unless one knew, a glance up the canyon made it appear to be boxed in, but actually there was a turn and a narrower canyon leading into a maze of canyons and broken lava flows. There was an ancient cliff house back there, and in it Ball and I had stored supplies for a last-ditch stand. There was an old kiva with one side broken and room enough to stable the buckskin.

At daybreak I left the canyon behind me, riding watchfully, knowing I rode among enemies. No more than two miles from the canyon toward which I was heading, I rounded a bend and saw a dozen riders coming toward me at a canter. Sighting me, they yelled in chorus, and a shot rang out. Wheeling the buckskin I slapped the spurs to him and went up the wash at a dead run. A bullet whined past my ear, but I dodged into a branch canyon and raced up a trail that led to the top of the plateau. Behind me I heard the riders race past the canyon's mouth. Then there was a shout as a rider glimpsed me, and the wheeling of horses as they turned. By the time they entered the canyon mouth I was atop the mesa.

Sliding to the ground, Winchester in hand, I took a running dive to shelter among some rocks and snapped off a quick shot. A horse stumbled, and his rider went off over his head. I opened up, firing as rapidly as I could squeeze off the shots. They scattered for shelter, one man scrambling with a dragging leg.

Several of the horses had raced away, and a couple of others stood ground hitched. On one of these was a big canteen. A bullet emptied it, and when the other horse turned a few minutes later, I shot into that canteen also.

Bullets ricocheted around me, but without exposing themselves they could not get a good shot at me, while I could cover their hideout without trouble.

A foot showed and I triggered my rifle. A bit of leather flew up and the foot was withdrawn. My position could not have been better. As long as I remained where I was, they could neither advance nor retreat, but were pinned down and helpless. They were without water, and it promised to be an intensely hot day. Having no desire to kill them, I still wished to make them thoroughly sick of the fight. These men enjoyed the fighting as a break in the monotony of range work, but knowing cowhands, I knew they would become heartily sick of a battle that meant waiting, heat, no water, and no chance to fight back.

For some time all was still. Then a man tried to crawl back toward the canyon mouth, evidenlty believing himself unseen. Letting go a shot at a rock ahead of him, I splattered his face with splinters, and he ducked back, swearing loudly.

"Looks like a long hot day boys!" I yelled. "See what it means when you jump a small outfit? Ain't so easy as you figured, is it?"

Somebody swore viciously, and there were shouted threats. My own canteen was full, so I sat back and rolled a smoke. Nobody moved below, but the sun began to level its burning rays into the oven of the canyon mouth. The hours marched slowly by, and from time to time when some thirsty soul grew restive at waiting, I threw a shot at him.

"How long you figure you can keep us here?" one of them yelled. "When we get out, we'll get you!"

"Maybe you won't get out," I yelled back cheerfully. "I like it here. I've got water, shade, grub, and plenty of smokin' tobacco. Also," I added, "I've got better than two hundred rounds of ammunition. You hombres are riding for the wrong spread."

Silence descended over the canyon and two o'clock passed. Knowing they could get no water aggravated their thirst. The sun swam in a coppery sea of heat, and the horizon lost itself in heat waves. Sweat trickled down my face and down my body under the arms. Where I lay, there was not only shade but a slight breeze, but down there, heat would reflect from the canyon walls and all wind would be shut off. Finally, letting go with a shot, I slid back out of sight and got to my feet.

My buckskin cropped grass near some rocks, well under the shade. Shifting my rifle to my left hand I slid down the bank, mopping my face with my right. Then I stopped stock-still, my right hand belt high. Backed up against a rock near my horse was a man I knew at once although I had never seen him—Rollie Pinder!

"You gave them boys hell," he said conversationally, "an' good for 'em. They're Bar M riders. It's a shame it has to end."

"Yeah," I drawled, watching him closely. He could be waiting for only one reason.

"Hear you're mighty fast, but it won't do you any good. I'm Rollie Pinder!"

As he spoke, he grabbed for his gun.

My left hand was on the rifle barrel a few inches ahead of the trigger guard, the butt in front of me, the barrel pointed slightly up. I tilted the gun hard, and the stock struck my hip as my hand slapped the trigger guard and trigger.

Rollie's gun had come up smoking, but my finger closed on the trigger a split second before his slug hit me. It felt as if I had been kicked in the side, and I took a staggering step back, a rock rolling under my foot just enough to throw me out of the line of his second shot.

Then I fired again, having worked the lever unconsciously.

Rollie went back against the rocks and tried to bring his gun up. He fired as I did. The world weaved and waved before me, but Rollie was down on his face, great holes torn in his back where the .44 slugs had emerged. Turning, scarcely able to walk, I scrambled up the incline to my former position. My head was spinning and my eyes refused to focus, but the shots had startled the men and they were getting up. If they started after me now, I was through.

The ground seemed to dip and reel, but I got off a shot, then another. One man went down and the others vanished as if swallowed by the earth. Rolling over, my breath coming in ragged gasps, I ripped my shirttail off and plugged cloth into my wounds. I had to get away at all costs, but I could never climb back up to the cliff house, even if the way were open.

My rifle dragging, I crawled and slid to the buckskin. Twice I almost fainted from weakness. Pain was gripping my vitals, squeezing and knotting them. Somehow I got to my horse, grabbed a stirrup, managed to get a grip on the pommel, and pulled myself into the saddle. Getting my rifle back into its scabbard, I got some piggin strings and tied myself into the saddle. Then I started the buckskin toward the wilderness, and away from my enemies.

Day was shooting crimson arrows into the vast bowl of the sky when my eyes opened again. My head swam with effort, and I stared about, seeing nothing familiar. Buck had stopped beside a small spring in a canyon. There was grass and a few trees, with not far away the ruin of a rock house. On the sand beside the spring was the track of a mountain lion, several deer tracks and what might be a mountain sheep, but no cow, horse, or human tracks.

Fumbling with swollen fingers, I untied the piggin strings and slid to the ground. Buck snorted and sidestepped and then put his nose down to me inquiringly. He drew back from the smell of stale clothes and dried blood, and I lay there, staring up at him, a crumpled human thing, my body raw with pain and weakness. "It's all right, Buck," I whispered. "We'll pull through! We've got to pull through!"

IV

Over me the sky's high gray faded to pink shot with blood-red swords that swept the red into gold. As the sun crept up, I lay there, still beneath the wide sky, my body washed by a sea of dull pain that throbbed and pulsed in my muscles and veins. Yet within beat a deeper, stronger pulse, the pulse of the fighting man that would not let me die without fighting, that would not let me lie long without movement.

Turning over, using hand grasps of grass, I pulled myself to the spring and drank deep of the cool, clear, life-giving water. The wetness of it seemed to creep through all my tissues, bringing peace to my aching muscles and life to my starved body. To live I must drink, and I must eat, and my body must have rest and time to mend. Over and over these thoughts went through my mind, and over and over I said them, staring at my helpless hands.

With contempt I looked at them, hating them for their weakness. And then I began to fight for life in those fingers, willing them to movement, to strength. Slowly my left hand began to stir, to lift at my command, to grasp a stick.

Triumph went through me. I was not defeated! Triumph lent me strength, and from this small victory I went on to another—a bit of broken manzanita placed across the first, a handfull of scraped up leaves, more sticks.

Soon I would have a fire.

I was a creature fighting for survival, wanting only to live and to fight. Through waves of delirium and weakness, I dragged myself to an aspen where I peeled bark for a vessel—fainting there, coming to, struggling back to the place for my fire, putting the bark vessel together with clumsy fingers. With the bark vessel, a sort of box, I dipped into the water but had to drag it to the sand, lacking the strength to lift it up, almost crying with weakness and pain.

Lighting my fire, I watched the flames take hold. Then I got the bark vessel atop two rocks in the fire, and the flames rose around it. As long as the flames were below the water level of the vessel, I knew, the bark would not burn, for the heat was absorbed by the water inside. Trying to push a stick under the vessel I leaned too far and fainted.

When next I opened my eyes the water was boiling. Pulling myself to a sitting position, I unbuckled my thick leather belt and let my guns fall back on the ground. Then, carefully, I opened my shirt and tore off a corner of it. I soaked it in the boiling water and began to bathe my wounds. Gingerly working the cloth plugs free of the wounds, I extracted them. The hot water felt good, but the sight of the wound in my side was frightening. It was red and inflamed, but near as I could see as I bathed it, the bullet had gone through and touched nothing vital. The second slug had gone through the fleshy part of my thigh, and after bathing that wound also, I lay still for a while, regaining strength and soaking up the heat.

Nearby, there was a patch of prickly pear, so I crawled to it and cut off a few big leaves. Then I roasted them to get off the spines and bound the pulp against the wounds. Indians had used it to fight inflammations, and it might help. I found a clump of amolillo and dug some of the roots, scraping them into hot water. They foamed up when stirred, and I drank the foamy water, remembering that the Indians used the drink to carry off clotted blood. A man's bullet wounds healed better after he drank it.

Then I made a meal of squaw cabbage and breadroot,

not wanting to attempt getting at my saddlebags. Yet when evening came and my fever returned, I managed to call Buck to me and loosen the girths. The saddle dropped, bringing with it my bedroll and saddlebags. Then I hobbled Buck and got the bridle off.

The effort exhausted me, so I crawled into my bedroll. My fever haunted the night with strange shapes, and guns seemed to be crashing about me. Men and darkness fought on the edge of my consciousness. Morgan Park . . . Jim Pinder . . . Rud Maclaren . . . and the sharply feral face of Bodie Miller.

The nuzzling of Buck awakened me in the cold light of day. "All right, Buck," I whispered. "I'm awake. I'm alive."

My weakness horrified me. If my enemies found me they would not hesitate to kill me, and Buck must have left a trail easily followed. High up the canyon wall, there was a patch of green, perhaps a break in the rock. Hiding my saddle under some brush and taking with me my bedroll, saddlebags, rifle, and rope, I dragged myself toward an eyebrow of trail up the cliff.

If there was a hanging valley up there it was just what I wanted. The buckskin wandered after me, more from curiosity than anything else. Getting atop a boulder I managed to slide onto his back and then kneed him up the steep trail. A mountain horse, he went willingly, and in a few minutes we had emerged into a high hanging valley.

A great crack in the rock, it was flat floored and high walled, yet the grass was rich and green. Somewhere water was running, and before me was a massive stone tower all of sixty feet high. Blackened by age and by fire, it stood beside a spring, quite obviously the same as that from which I had been drinking below. The hanging valley comprised not over three acres of land, seemingly enclosed on the far side and almost enclosed on the side where I had entered.

The ancient Indians who built the tower had known a good thing when they saw it, for here was shelter and defense, grass, water, and many plants. Beside the tower some stunted maize, long since gone native, showed that there had once been planting here. Nowhere was there any evidence that a human foot had trod here in centuries.

A week went slowly by, and nothing disturbed my camp. Able to walk a few halting steps, I explored the valley. The maize had been a fortunate discovery, for Indians had long used a mush made of the meal as an hourly application for bullet wounds. With this and other remedies my recovery became more rapid. The jerky gave out, but with snared rabbits and a couple of sage hens, I managed. And then I killed a deer, and with the wild vegetables growing about, I lived well.

Yet a devil of impatience was riding me. My ranch was in the hands of my enemies, and each day of absence made the chance of recovery grow less. Then, after two weeks, I was walking, keeping watch from a lookout spot atop the cliff and rapidly regaining strength. On the sixteenth day of my absence I decided to make an effort to return.

The land through which I rode was utterly amazing— towering monoliths of stone, long, serrated cliffs of salmon-colored sandstone, and nothing human. It was almost noon of the following day before the buckskin's ears lifted suddenly. It took several seconds for me to discover what drew his attention, and then I detected a lone rider. An hour later, from a pinnacle of rock near a tiny seep of water, I saw that the rider was drawing near, carefully examining the ground.

A surge of joy went through me. It was Olga Maclaren!

Stepping out from the shadow, I waited for her to see me, and she did, almost at once. How I must look, I could guess. My shirt was heavy with dust, torn by a bullet and my own hands. My face was covered with beard and my cheeks drawn and hollow, but the expression on her face was only of relief. "Matt?" Her voice was incredulous. "You're alive?"

"Did you think I'd die before we were married, daughter of Maclaren? Did you think I'd die before you had those sons I promised? Right now I'm coming back to claim my own."

"Back?" The worry on her face was obvious. "You must never go back! You're believed dead, so you are safe. Go away while there's time!"

"Did you think I'd run? Olga, I've been whipped by Morgan Park, shot by Rollie Pinder, and attacked by the others, but Pinder is dead, and Park's time is coming. No, I made a promise to a fine old man named Ball, another one to myself, and one to you, and I'll keep them all. In my time I've backed up, I've sidestepped, and occasionally I've run, but always to come back and fight again."

She looked at me, and some of the fear seemed to leave

her. Then she shook her head. "But you can't go back now. Jim Pinder has the Two Bar."

"Then he'll move," I promised her.

Olga had swung down from her horse and lifted my canteen. "You've water!" she exclaimed. "They all said no man could survive out there in that waste, even if he was not wounded."

"You believed them?"

"No." She hesitated. "I knew you'd be alive somewhere."

"You know your man, then, Olga Maclaren. Does it mean that you love me, too?"

She hesitated and her eyes searched mine, but when I would have moved toward her she drew back, half frightened. Her lips parting a little, her breast lifting suddenly as she caught her breath. "It isn't time for that now—please!"

It stopped me, knowing what she said was true. "You are sure you weren't trailed?"

She shook her head. "I've been careful. Every day."

"This isn't the first day you looked for me?"

"Oh, no." She looked at me, her eyes shadowed with worry. "I was afraid you were lying somewhere bloody and suffering." Her eyes studied me, noting the torn shirt, the pallor of my face. "And you have been."

"Rollie was good. He was very good."

"Then it *was* you who killed him?"

"Who else?"

"Canaval and Bodie Miller found him after they realized you were gone from the mesa where you had pinned them down. Canaval was sure it had been you, but some of them thought it was the mountain boys."

"They've done no fighting for me, although they wanted to. You'd best start back. I've work to do."

"But you're in no shape! You're sick!" She stared at me.

"I can still fight," I said. "Tell your father you've seen me. Tell him the Two Bar was given me in the presence of witnesses. Tell him his stock is to be off that range—at once!"

"You forget that I am my father's daughter!"

"And my future wife!"

"I've promised no such thing!" she flared. "You know I'd never marry you! I'll admit you're attractive, and you're a devil. But marry you? I'd die first!"

Her breast heaved and her eyes flashed and I laughed at her. "Tell your father, though, and ask him to withdraw from this fight before it's too late." Swinging into the saddle, I added. "It's already too late for you. You love me and you know it. Tell Morgan Park that, and tell him I'm coming back to break him with my hands!"

V

Riding into Hattan's Point, I was a man well known. Rollie Pinder was dead, and they knew whose gun had downed him. Maclaren's riders had been held off and made a laughingstock, and I had taken up Ball's fight to hold his ranch. Some men hated me for this, some admired me, and many thought me a fool.

All I knew was the horse between my knees, the guns on my thighs and the blood of me pounding. My buckskin lifted his head high and moved down the dusty street like a dancer, for riding into this town was a challenge to them all. They knew it and I knew it. Leaving my horse behind Mother O'Hara's, I walked to the saloon and went in.

By then I'd taken time to shave, and though the pallor of sickness was on my face, there was none in my eyes or heart. It did me good to see their eyes widen and to hear my spurs jingle as I walked to the bar. "Rye," I said. "The best you've got."

Key Chapin was there, and sitting with him, Morgan Park. The big man's eyes were cold as they stared at me. "I'm buying, gentlemen," I said, "and that includes you, Morgan Park, although you slug a man when his hands are down."

Park blinked. It had been a long time since anyone had told him off to his face. "And you, Key Chapin. It has always been my inclination to encourage freedom of the press and to keep my public relations on a good basis. And today I might even offer you a news item, something to read like this: Matt Sabre, of the Two Bar, was in town Friday afternoon. Matt is recovering from a bullet wound incurred during a minor dispute with Rollie Pinder, but is returning to the Two Bar to take up where he left off."

Chapin smiled. "That will be news to Jim Pinder. He didn't expect you back."

"He should have," I assured him. "I'm back to punish every murdering skunk who killed old man Ball."

All eyes were on me now, and Park was staring, not

knowing what to make of me. "Do you know who they are?"
Chapin asked curiously.

"Definitely!" I snapped the word. "Every man of them"—
I shifted my eyes to Park—"is known—with one exception.
When Ball was dying he named a man to me. Only I am not
sure."

"Who?" demanded Chapin.

"Morgan Park," I said.

The big man came to his feet with a lunge. His brown
face was ugly with hatred. "That's a lie!" he roared.

My shoulders lifted. "Probably a misunderstanding. I'll
not take offense at your language, Mr. Park, because it is a
dead man you are calling a liar, and not I. Ball might have
meant that one of your riders, a man named Lyell, was there.
He died before he could be questioned. If it is true, I'll kill
you after I whip you."

"Whip me?" Park's bellow was amazed. "*Whip me?* Why,
you—"

"Unfortunately, I'm not sufficiently recovered from my
wounds to do it today, but don't be impatient. You'll get your
bellyful of it when the time comes." Turning my back on
him, I lifted my glass. "Gentlemen, your health!" And then I
walked out of the place.

There was the good rich smell of cooked food and coffee
when I opened the door of Mother O'Hara's. "Ah? It's you,
then! And still alive! Things ain't what they used to be around
here! Warned off by Maclaren, threatened by Jim Pinder,
beaten by Morgan Park, and you're still here!"

"Still here an' stayin', Katie O'Hara," I said, grinning at
her, "and I've just said that and more to Morgan Park."

"There's been men die, and you've had the killin' of
some."

"That's the truth, Katie. I'd rather it never happened,
but it's a hard country and a small chance for a man who
hesitates to shoot when the time comes. All the same, it's a
good country, this. A country where I plan to stay and grow
my children, Katie. I'll go back to the Two Bar, and build my
home there."

"You think they'll let you? You think you can keep it?"

"They'll have no choice."

Behind me a door closed and the voice of Rud Maclaren

was saying, "We'll have a choice. Get out of the country while you're alive!"

The arrogance in his voice angered me, so I turned and faced him. Canaval and Morgan Park had come with him. "The Two Bar is my ranch," I said, "and I'll be staying there. Do you think yourself a king that you can dictate terms to a citizen of a free country? You've let a small power swell your head, Maclaren. You think you have power when all you have is money. If you weren't the father of the girl I'm to marry, Maclaren, I'd break you just to show you this is a free country and we want no barons here."

His face mottled and grew hard. "Marry my daughter? You? I'll see you in hell first!"

"If you see me in hell, Maclaren," I said lightly, "you'll be seeing a married man, because I'm marrying Olga and you can like it or light a shuck! I expect you were a good man once, but there's some that cannot stand the taste of power, and you're one."

My eyes shifted to Morgan Park. "And there's another beside you. He has let his beef get him by too long. He uses force where you use money, but his time is running out, too. He couldn't break me when he had the chance, and when my time comes, I'll break him."

More than one face in the room was approving, even if they glared at me, these two. "The trouble is obvious," I continued. "You've never covered enough country. You think you're sitting in the center of the world, whereas you're just a couple of two-bit operators in a forgotten corner."

Turning my back on them I helped myself to the Irish stew. Maclaren went out, but Park came around the table and sat down, and he was smiling. The urge climbed up in me to bat the big face off him and down him in the dirt as he had me. He was wider than me by inches, and taller. The size of his wrists and hands was amazing, yet he was not all beef, for he had brains and there was trouble in him, trouble for me.

When I returned to my horse, there was a man sitting there. He looked up and I was astonished at him. His face was like that of an unhappy monkey, and he was without a hair to the top of his head. Near as broad in the shoulders as Morgan Park, he was shorter than me by inches. "By the look of you," he said, "you'll be Matt Sabre."

"You're right, man. What is it about?"

"Katie O'Hara was a-tellin' me it was a man you needed at the Two Bar. Now I'm a handy all-around man. Mr. Sabre, a rough sort of gunsmith, hostler, blacksmith, an' carpenter, good with an ax. An' I shoot a bit, know Cornish-style wrestlin', an' am afraid of no man when I've my two hands before me. I'm not so handy with a short gun, but I've a couple of guns of my own that I handle nice."

He got to his feet, and he could have been nothing over five feet four but weighed all of two hundred pounds, and his shirt at the neck showed a massive chest covered with black hair and a neck like a column of oak. "The fact that you've the small end of a fight appeals to me." He jerked his head toward the door. "Katie has said I'm to go to work for you, an' she'd not take it kindly if I did not."

"You're Katie's man, then?"

His eyes twinkled amazingly. "Katie's man? I'm afraid there's no such. She's a broth of a woman, that one." He grinned up at me. "Is it a job I have?"

"When I've the ranch back," I agreed, "you've a job."

"Then let's be gettin' it back. Will you wait for me? I've a mule to get."

The mule was a dun with a face that showed all the wisdom, meanness, and contrariness that have been the traits of the mule since time began. With a tow sack behind the saddle and another before him, we started out of town. "My name is Brian Mulvaney," he said. "Call me what you like."

He grinned widely when he saw me staring at the butts of the two guns that projected from his boot tops. "These," he said, "are the Neal Bootleg pistol, altered by me to suit my taste. The caliber is thirty-five, but good. Now this"—from his waistband he drew a gun that lacked only wheels to make an admirable artillery piece—"this was a Mills seventy-five caliber. Took me two months of work off and on, but I've converted her to a four-shot revolver. A fine gun," he added.

All of seventeen inches long, it looked fit to break a man's wrists, but Mulvaney had powerful hands and arms. No man ever hit by a chunk of lead from that gun would need a doctor.

Four horses were in the corral at the Two Bar, and the men were strongly situated behind a long barricade. Mulvaney grinned at me. "What'd you suppose I've in this sack, laddie?" he demanded, his eyes twinkling. "I, who was a miner also?"

"Powder?"

"Exactly! In those new-fangled sticks. Now unless it makes your head ache too much, help me cut a few o' these sticks in half." When that was done he cut the fuses very short and slid caps into the sticks of powder. "Come now, me boy, an' we'll slip down close under the cover of darkness, an' you'll see them takin' off like you never dreamed!"

Crawling as close as we dared, each of us lit a fuse and hurled a stick of powder. My own stick must have landed closer to them than I planned, for we heard a startled exclamation followed by a yell. Then a terrific explosion blasted the night apart. Mulvaney's followed, and then we hastily hurled a third and a fourth.

One man lunged over the barricade and started straight for us. The others had charged the corral. The man headed our way suddenly saw us, and wheeling, he fled as if the devil was after him. Four riders gripping only mane holds dashed from the corral, and then there was silence. Mulvaney got to his feet chuckling. "For guns they'd have stood until hell froze over, but the powder and the flyin' rocks an' dust scared 'em good. An' you've your ranch back."

We had eaten our midday meal the next day, when I saw a rider approaching. It was Olga Maclaren. "Nice to see you," I said, aware of the sudden tension her presence always inspired.

She was looking toward the foundation we had laid for the new house. It was on a hill with the long sweep of Cottonwod Wash before it. "You should be more careful," she said. "You had a visitor last night."

"We just took over last night," I objected. "Who do you mean?"

"Morgan. He was out here shortly after our boys got home. They met the bunch you stampeded from here."

"He's been puzzling me," I admitted. "Who is he? Did he come from around here?"

"I don't know. He's not talkative, but I've heard him mention places back east. I know he's been in Philadelphia and New York, but nothing else about him except that he goes to Salt Lake and San Francisco occasionally."

"Not back east?"

"Never since we've known him."

"You like him?"

She looked up at me. "Yes, Morgan can be very wonderful. He knows a lot about women and the things that please them." There was a flicker of laughter in her eyes. "He probably doesn't know as much about them as you."

"Me?" I was astonished. "What gave you that idea?"

"Your approach that first day. You knew it would excite my curiosity, a man less sure of himself would never have dared. If you knew no more about women than most western men you would have hung back, wishing you could meet me, or you would have got drunk to work up your courage."

"I meant what I said that day. You're going to marry me."

"Don't say that. Don't even think it. You've no idea what you are saying or what it would mean."

"Because of your father?" I looked at her. "Or Morgan Park?"

"You take him too lightly, Matt. I think he is utterly without scruple. I believe he would stop at nothing."

There was more to come, and I was interested.

"There was a young man here from the East," she continued, "and I liked him. Knowing Morgan, I never mentioned him in Morgan's presence. Then one day he asked me about him. He added that it would be better for all concerned if the man did not come around anymore. Inadvertently I mentioned the young man's name, Arnold D'Arcy.

"When he heard that name he became very disturbed. Who was he? Why had he come here? Had he asked any questions about anybody? Or described anybody he might be looking for? He asked me all those questions, but at the same time I thought little about it. Afterwards I began to believe that he was not merely jealous. Right then I decided to tell Arnold about it when he returned."

"And did you?"

There was a shadow of worry on her face. "No. He never came again." She looked quickly at me. "I've often thought of it. Morgan never mentioned him again, but somehow Arnold hadn't seemed like a man who would frighten easily."

Later, when she was mounting to leave, I asked her, "Where was D'Arcy from? Do you remember?"

"Virginia, I believe. He had served in the Army and before coming west had been working in Washington."

Watching her go, I thought again of Morgan Park. He might have frightened D'Arcy away, but I could not shake off the idea that something vastly more sinister lay behind it. And Park had been close to us during the night. If he had wanted to kill me, it could have been done, but apparently he wanted me alive. Why?

"Mulvaney," I suggested, "if you can hold this place, I'll ride to Silver Reef and get off a couple of messages."

He stretched his huge arms and grinned at me. "Do you doubt it? I'll handle it or them. Go, and have yourself a time."

And in the morning I was in the saddle again.

VI

High noon, and a mountain shaped like flame. Beyond the mountain and around it was a wide land with no horizons, but only the shimmering heat waves that softened all lines to vagueness and left the desert an enchanted land without beginning and without end.

As I rode, my mind studied the problem created by the situation around Cottonwood Wash. There were at least three and possibly four sides to the question. Rud Maclaren with his Bar M, Jim Pinder with his CP, and myself with the Two Bar. The fourth possibility was Morgan Park.

Olga's account of Arnold D'Arcy's disappearance had struck a chord of memory. During ten years of my life I had been fighting in foreign wars, and there had been a military observer named D'Arcy, a Major Leo D'Arcy, who had been in China during the fighting there. It stuck in my mind that he had a brother named Arnold.

It was a remote chance, yet a possiblity. Why did the name upset Park? What had become of Arnold? Where did Park come from? Pinder could be faced with violence and handled with violence. Maclaren might be circumvented.

Morgan Park worried me.

Silver Reef lay sprawled in haphazard comfort along a main street and a few cross streets. There were the usual frontier saloons, stores, churches, and homes. The sign on the Elk Horn Saloon caught my attention. Crossing to it I pushed through the door into the dim interior. While the bartender served me, I glanced around, liking the feel of the place.

"Rye?" The smooth-pated bartender squinted at me.

"Uh-huh. How's things in the mines?"

"So-so. But you ain't no miner." He glanced at my cowhand's garb and then at the guns in their tied-down holsters. "This here's a quiet town. We don't see many gun handlers around here. The place for them is over east of here."

"Hattan's?"

"Yeah. I hear the Bar M an' CP both are hirin' hands. Couple of hombres from there rode into town a few days ago. One of 'em was the biggest man I ever did see."

Morgan Park in Silver Reef! That sounded interesting, but I kept a tight rein on my thoughts and voice. "Did he say anything about what was goin' on over there?"

"Not to me. The feller with him, though, he was inquirin' around for the Slade boys. Gunslicks both of them. The big feller, he never come in here atall. I seen him on the street a couple of times, but he went to the Wells Fargo Bank and down the street to see that shyster, Jake Booker."

"You don't seem to like Booker?"

"Him? He's plumb no good! The man's a crook!"

Once started on Booker, the bartender told me a lot. Morgan Park had been in town before, but never came to the Elk Horn. He confined his visits to the back room of a dive called the Sump or occasional visits to the office of Jake Booker. The only man who ever came with him was Lyell.

Leaving the saloon, I sent off my telegram to Leo D'Arcy. Then I located the office of Booker, spotted the Sump, and considered the situation. Night came swiftly and miners crowded the street, a good-natured shoving, pushing, laughing throng, jamming the saloons and drinking. The crowd relaxed me with its rough good humor, and for the night I fell into it, drifting, joking, listening.

Turning off the street near Louder's store I passed the street lamp on the corner and for an instant was outlined in its radiance. From the shadows, flame stabbed. There was a tug at my sleeve, and then my own gun roared, and as the shot sped, I went after it.

A man lunged from the side of the store and ran staggeringly toward the alley behind it. Pistol ready, I ran after him.

He wheeled, slipped, and was running again. He brought up with a crash against the corral bars and fell. He was crawling to his feet, and I caught a glimpse of his face in the glow from the window. It was Lyell.

One hand at his throat, I jerked him erect. His face was gaunt, and there was blood on his shirtfront. He had been hit hard by my sudden, hardly aimed shot. "Got you, didn't I?"

"Yes, damn you, an' I missed. Put—put me down."

Lowering him to the ground, I dropped to one knee. "I'll get a doctor. I saw a sign up the street."

He grabbed my sleeve. "Ain't no use. I feel it. You got me good. Anyway—" he stared at me—"why should you get a doc for me?"

"I shouldn't. You were in the gang killed Ball."

His eyes bulged. "No! No, I wasn't there! He was a good old man! I wasn't in that crowd."

"Was Morgan Park there?"

His eyes changed, veiled. "Why would he be there? That wasn't his play."

"What's he seeing Booker for? What about Sam Slade?"

Footsteps crunched on the gravel, and a man carrying a lantern came up the alley. "Get a doctor, will you? This man's been shot."

The man started off at a run, and Lyell lay quiet, a tough, unshaven man with brown eyes. He breathed hoarsely for several minutes while I uncovered the wound. Then he spoke. "The Slades are to get Canaval. Park wants you for himself."

"What does he want? Range?"

"No. He—he wants money."

The doctor hurried up with the lantern carrier. Watching him start work, I backed away and disappeared in the darkness. If anybody knew anything about Park's plans it would be Booker, and I had an idea I could get into Booker's office.

Booker's office was on the second floor of a frame building reached by an outside stairway. Once up there, a man would be fairly trapped if anyone came up those stairs. Down the street a music box was jangling, and the town showed no signs of going to sleep. Studying that stairway, I liked no part of it. Booker had many friends here, but I had none, and going up there would be a risk. Then I remembered all the other times I'd had no friends, so I hitched my guns easier on my thighs and went across the street.

Going up the steps two at a time, I paused at the door. Locks were no problem to a man of my experience, and a minute later I was inside a dark office, musty with stale tobacco. Swiftly, I checked the tray on the desk, the top drawer, and then the side drawers, lighting my exploration with a stump of candle. Every sense alert, ears attuned to the slightest sound, I worked rapidly, suddenly coming to an assayer's report. No location was mentioned and no notation was on the sheet, but the ore had been rich, amazingly rich. Then among some older papers at the bottom of a drawer I found a fragment of a letter from Morgan Park, signed with his name.

You have been recommended to me as a man of discretion who could turn over a piece of property for a quick profit and who could handle negotiations with a buyer. I am writing for an appointment and will be in Silver Reef on the 12th. It is essential that this business remain absolutely confidential.

It was little enough, but a hint. I left the assayer's report but pocketed the letter. The long ride had tired me, for my wounds, while much improved, had robbed me of strength. Dousing the candle, I returned it to its shelf. And then I heard a low mutter of voices and steps on the stair!

Backing swiftly, I glanced around and saw a closed door that must lead to an inner room. Stepping through it I closed it just in time. It was a room used for storage. Voices sounded and a door closed. A match scratched, and light showed under the door. "Nonsense! Probably got in some drunken brawl! You're too suspicious, Morgan."

"Maybe, but the man worries me. He rides too much, and he may get to nosing around and finding something."

"Did you see Lyell before he died?"

"No. He shot first, though. Some fool saw him take a bead on somebody. This other fellow followed it up and killed him."

The crabbed voice of Booker interrupted. "Forget him. Forget Sabre. My men are lined up, and they have the cold cash ready to put on the line! We haven't any time for child's play! I've done my part, and now it's up to you! Get Sabre out of the way and get rid of Maclaren!"

"That's not so easy," Park objected stubbornly. "Maclaren is never alone, and if anybody ever shot at him he'd turn the country upside down to find the man. And after he is killed, the minute we step in suspicion will be diverted to us."

"Nonsense!" Booker replied irritably. "Nobody knows we've had dealings. They'll have to settle the estate, and I'll step in as the representative of the buyers. Of course, if you were married to the girl it would simplify things. What's the matter? Sabre cutting in there, too?"

"Shut up!" Park's voice was ugly. "If you ever say a thing like that again, I'll wring you out like a dirty towel, Booker. I mean it."

"You do your part," Booker said, "and I'll do mine. The buyers have the money and they are ready. They won't wait forever."

A chair scraped, and Park's heavy step went to the door and out. There was a faint squeak of a cork twisting in a bottle neck and the gurgle of a poured drink. Then the bottle and glass were returned to the shelf. The light vanished and a door closed. Then footsteps grated on the gravel below. Only a minute behind him, I hurried from the vicinity. Then I paused, sweating despite the cool air. Thinking of what I'd heard, I retrieved my horse and slipped quietly out of town. Bedded down among the clustering cedars, I thought of that and then of Olga, the daughter of Maclaren, of her soft lips, the warmth of her arms, the quick, proud lift of her chin.

Coming home to Cottonwood Wash and the Two Bar with the wind whispering through the greasewood and rustling the cottonwood leaves, I kept a careful watch but saw nobody until Mulvaney himself stepped into sight.

"Had any trouble?" I asked him.

"Trouble? None here," he replied. "Some men came by, but the sound of my Spencer drove them away again." He walked to the door. "There's grub on the table. How was it in Silver Reef?"

"A man killed."

"Be careful, lad. There's too many dying."

When I had explained, he nodded. "Do they know it was you?"

"I doubt it." It felt good to be back on my own place

again, seeing the white-faced cattle browsing in the pasture below, seeing the water flowing to irrigate the small garden we'd started.

"You're tired." Mulvaney studied me. "But you look fit. You've thrown a challenge in the teeth of Park. You'll be backing it up?"

"Backing it up?" My eyes must have told what was in me. "That's one man I want, Mulvaney! He had me down and beat me, and I'll not live free until I whip him or he whips me fair!"

"He's a power of man, lad. I've seen him lift a barrel of whiskey at arm's length overhead. It will be a job to whip him."

"Ever box any, Mulvaney? You told me you'd wrestled Cornish style."

"What Irishman hasn't boxed a bit? Is it a sparrin' mate you're wantin'? Sure an' it would be good to get the leather on my maulies again."

For a week we were at it. Every night we boxed, lightly at first, then faster. He was a brawny man, a fierce slugger and a powerful man in the clinches. On the seventh day we did a full thirty minutes without a break. And in the succeeding days my strength returned and my speed grew greater. The rough and tumble part of it I loved. Nor was I worried about Morgan knowing more tricks than I—the waterfronts are the place to learn the dirty side of fighting. I would use everything I'd learned there, if Morgan didn't fight fair.

It was after our tenth session with the gloves that Mulvaney stripped them off and shook his head admiringly. "Faith, lad, you've a power of muscle behind that wallop of yours! That last one came from nowhere and I felt it clean to my toes! Never did I believe a man lived that could hit like that!"

"Thanks," I said. "I'm ridin' to town tomorrow."

"To fight him?"

"No, to see the girl, Olga Maclaren, to buy supplies, and perhaps to ride him a little. I want him furious before we fight. I want him mad, mad and wild."

He nodded wisely at me. "It'll help, for no man can fight unless he keeps his head. But be careful, lad. Remember they are gunnin' for you, an' there's nothin' that would better please them than to see you dead on the ground."

*　　*　　*

When the buckskin was watered I returned him to the hitch rail and walked into the saloon. Hattan's Point knew that Lyell was dead, but they had no idea who had done it. Key Chapin was the first man I met, and I looked at him, wondering on which side he stood.

He looked at me curiously and motioned toward the chair across the table from him. Dropping into it, I began to build a smoke. "Well, Sabre, you're making quite a name for yourself."

I shrugged. "That's not important. All I want is a ranch."

"All?"

"And a girl."

"One may be as hard to get as the other."

"Maybe. Anyway, I've made a start on the ranch. In fact, I have the ranch and intend to keep it."

"Heard about Lyell?"

"Killed, wasn't he? Somewhere west of here?"

"At Silver Reef. It's a peaceful, quiet town in spite of being a boomtown. And they have a sheriff over there who believes in keeping it peaceful. They tell me he is working hard to find out who killed Lyell."

"It might be anybody. There was a rumor that he was one of the men in the raid on the Ball ranch."

"And which you promised to bury on the spot."

What this was building to I did not know, but I was anxious to find out just where Chapin stood. He would be a good friend to have, and a bad enemy, for his paper had a good deal of influence around town.

"You told me when I first came here that the town was taking sides. Which is your side?"

He hesitated, toying with his glass. "That's a harder question to answer since you came," he replied frankly. "I will say this. I am opposed to violence. I believe now is the time to establish a peaceful community, and I believe it can be done. For that reason I am opposed to the CP outfit, whose code is violence."

"And Maclaren?"

He hesitated again. "Maclaren can be reasoned with at times. Stubborn, yes, but only because he has an exaggerated view of his own rightness. It is not easy to prove him wrong, but it can be done."

"And Park?"

He looked at me sharply, a cool, measuring glance, as if to see what inspired the remark. Then he said, "Morgan Park is generally felt to see things as Maclaren does."

"Is that your opinion?"

He did not answer me, frowning as he stared out the door. Key Chapin was a handsome man and an able one. I could understand how he felt about law and order. Basically, I agreed with him, but when I'm attacked, I can't take it lying down.

"Look, Chapin"—I leaned over the table—"I've known a dozen frontier towns tougher than this one. To each came law and order, but it took a fight to get it. The murderers, cheats, and swindlers must be stamped out before the honest citizens can have peace. And it's peace that I'm fighting for. You, more than anybody else, can build the situation to readiness for it with your paper. Write about it. Get the upright citizens prepared to enforce it, once this battle is over."

He nodded and then glanced at me. "What about you? You're a gunfighter. In such a community, there is no place for such a man."

That made me grin. "Chapin, I never drew a gun on a man in my life who didn't draw on me first, or try to! And while I may be a gunfighter, I'm soon to be a rancher and a solid citizen. Count on me to help."

"Even to stopping this war?"

"What war? Ball had a ranch. He was a peaceful old man who wanted no trouble from anyone, but he was weaker than the Bar M or the CP so he died. He turned the ranch over to me on the condition that I keep it. If protecting one's property is war, then we'll have it for a long time."

"You could sell out."

"Run? Is that what you mean? I never ducked out of a good fight yet, Chapin, and never will. When they stop fighting me, I'll hang up my guns. Until then, I shall continue to fight."

Filling my glass, I added, "Don't look at the overall picture so long that you miss the details."

"What do you mean?"

"Look for motives. What are the origins of this fight? I'd start investigating the participants, and I mean neither Maclaren nor Pinder!"

Getting up, I put my hat on my head and added, "Ever hear of a man named Booker at Silver Reef? A lawyer?"

"He's an unmitigated scoundrel, and whatever he does he's apt to get away with. If there's a loophole in the law he doesn't know, then nobody knows it."

"Then find out why he's interested in this fight, and when the Slade boys drift into this country, ask yourself why they are here. Also, ask yourself why Morgan Park is meeting Booker in secret."

Olga was not in town, so I turned the buckskin toward the Bar M. A cowhand with one foot bandaged was seated on the doorstep when I rode up. He stared, his jaw dropping.

"Howdy," I said calmly, taking out the makings. "I'm visiting on the ranch and don't want any trouble. As far as you boys are concerned, I've no hard feelings."

"*You've* no hard feelin's! What about me? You durned near shot my foot off!"

I grinned at him. "Next time you'll stay under cover. Anyway, what are you gripin' about? You haven't done a lick of work since it happened!"

Somebody chuckled. I looked around and saw Canaval. "I reckon he did it on purpose, Sabre."

"*Purpose?*" The injured man roared. Disgusted, he turned and limped off.

"What you want here, Sabre?" Canaval asked, still smiling.

"Just visiting."

"Sure you're welcome?"

"No, I'm not sure. But if you're wondering if I came looking for trouble, I didn't. If touble comes to me on this ranch now it will be because I'm pushed and pushed hard. If you're the guardian angel of peace, just relax. I'm courtin'."

"Rud won't take kindly to that. He may have me order you off."

"All right, Canaval, if he does, and you tell me to go, I'll go. Only one thing—you keep Park off me. I'm not ready for him, and when it comes I'd rather she didn't see it."

"Fair enough." He tossed his cigarette into the yard. "You'll not be bothered under those circumstances. Only"— he grinned and his eyes twinkled—"you might be wrong about Olga. She might like to see you tangle with Park!"

Starting up the steps, I remembered something. "Canaval!"

He turned sharply, ready on the instant.

"A friendly warning," I said. "Some of the people who don't like me also want your boss out of here. To get him out, you have to go first. If you hear of the Slades in this country, you'll know they've come for you and your boss!"

His eyes searched mine. "The Slades?"

"Yeah, for you and Maclaren. Somebody is saving me for dessert."

He was standing there looking after me when I knocked. Inside a voice answered that set my blood pounding. "Come in!"

VII

As I entered, there was an instant when my reflection was thrown upon the mirror beside hers. Seeing my gaze over her shoulder, she turned, and we stood there, looking at ourselves in the mirror—a tall, dark young man in a dark blue shirt, black silk neckerchief, black jeans, and tied-down holsters with their walnut-stocked guns, and Olga in a sea-green gown, filmy and summery looking.

She turned quickly to face me. "What are you doing here? My father will be furious!"

"He'll have to get over it sometime, and it might as well be right now."

She searched my face. "You're still keeping up that foolish talk? About marrying me?"

"It isn't foolish. Have you started buying your trousseau?"

"Of course not!"

"You'd better. You'll need something to wear, and I won't have much money for a year or two."

"Matt"— her face became serious—"you'd better go. I'm expecting Morgan."

I took her hands. "Don't worry. I promised Canaval there would be no trouble, and there will be none, no matter what Morgan Park wants to do or tries to do."

She was unconvinced and tried to argue, but I was thinking how lovely she was. Poised, her lovely throat bare, she was something to set a man's pulses pounding.

"Matt!" She was angry now. "You're not even listening! And don't look at me like that!"

"How else should a man look at a woman? And why don't we sit down? Is this the way you receive guests at the Bar M? At the Two Bar we are more thoughtful."

"So I've heard!" she said dryly. Her anger faded. "Matt? How do you feel? I mean those wounds—are they all right?"

"Not all right, but much better. I'm not ready for Morgan Park yet, but I will be soon. He won't be missed much when he's gone."

"Gone?" She was surprised. "Remember that I like Morgan."

"Not very much." I shrugged. "Yes, gone. This country isn't big enough to hold both of us even if you weren't in it."

She sat down opposite me, and her face was flushed a little. She looked at me and then looked away, and neither of us said anything for a long minute. "It's nice here," I said at last. "Your father loves this place, doesn't he?"

"Yes, only I wish he would be content and stop trying to make it bigger."

"Men like your father never seem to learn when they have enough."

"You don't talk like a cowhand, Matt."

"That's because I read a book once."

"Key told me you had been all over the world. He checked up on you. He said you had fought in China and South Africa."

"That was a long time ago."

"How did you happen to come west?"

"I was born in the West, and then I always wanted to return to it and have a ranch of my own, but there wasn't anything to hold me down, so I just kept on drifting from place to place. Staying in one place did not suit me unless there was a reason to stay, and there never was—before."

Tendrils of her dark hair curled against her neck. The day was warm, and I could see tiny beads of perspiration on her upper lip. She stood up suddenly, uneasily. "Matt, you'd better go. Father will be coming and he'll be furious."

"And Morgan Park will be coming. And it doesn't matter in the least whether they come or not. I came here to see you, and as long as they stay out of the way there'll be no trouble."

"But, Matt—" She stepped closer to me, and I took her by the elbows. She started to step back, but I drew her to me swiftly. I took her chin and turned her head slightly. She resisted, but the continued pressure forced her chin to come around. She looked at me then, her eyes wide and more beautiful than I would ever have believed eyes could be, and then I kissed her.

We stood there, clinging together tightly, and then she pulled violently away from me. For an instant she looked at me, and then she moved swiftly to kiss me again, and we were like that when hoofs sounded in the yard. Two horses.

We stepped apart, but her eyes were wide and her face was pale when they came through the door, her breast heaving and her white teeth clinging to her lower lip. They came through the door, Rud Maclaren first and then Morgan Park, dwarfing Maclaren in spite of the fact that he was a big man. When they saw me they stopped.

Park's face darkened with angry blood. He started toward me, his voice hoarse with fury. "Get out! Get *out*, I say!"

My eyes went past him to Maclaren.

"Is Park running this place, or are you? It seems to me he's got a lot of nerve, ordering people off the place of Rud Maclaren."

Maclaren flushed. He didn't like my being there, but he disliked Park's usurping of authority even more. "That'll do, Morgan! I'll order people out of my own home!"

Morgan Park's face was ugly at that minute. But before he could speak, Canaval appeared in the door. "Boss, Sabre said he was visitin', not huntin' trouble. He said he would make no trouble and would go when I asked him. He also said he would make no trouble with Park."

Before Maclaren could reply, Olga said quickly, "Father, Mr. Sabre is my guest. When the time comes he will leave. Until then I wish him to stay."

"I won't have him in this house!" Maclaren said angrily. He strode to me, the veins in his throat swelling. "Damn you, Sabre! You've a gall to come here after shootin' my men, stealin' range that rightly belongs to me, an' runnin' my cattle out of Cottonwood!"

"Perhaps," I admitted, "there's something in what you say, but I think we have no differences we can't settle without fighting. Your men came after me first. I never wanted trouble with you, Rud, and I think we can reach a peaceful solution."

It took the fire out of him. He was still truculent, still wanting to throw his weight around, but mollified. Right then I sensed the truth about Rud Maclaren. It was not land and property he wanted so much as to be known as the biggest man in the country. He merely knew of no way to get respect and admiration other than through wealth and power.

Realizing that gave me an opening. "I was talking to Chapin today. If we are going to be safe we must stop all this fighting, and the only way it can be done is through the leadership of the right man. I think you're that man, Maclaren."

He was listening, and he liked what he heard.

"You're the big man of the community," I added. "If you make a move for peace, others will follow."

"The Pinders wouldn't listen!" he protested. "You know that! You killed Rollie, but if you hadn't, Canaval might have. Jim will never rest until you're dead. And he hates me and all I stand for."

Morgan Park was listening, his eyes hard and watchful. He had never imagined that Maclaren and I would talk peace, and if we reached a settlement, his plans were finished.

"If Pinder and the CP were alone they would have to become outlaws to persist in this fight. If the fight continues, all the rustlers in the country will come in here to run off our herds while we fight. Did it ever fail? When honest men fall out, thieves always profit. Moreover, you'll break yourself paying gunman's wages. From now on they'll come higher."

Olga was listening with some surprise and, I believed, with respect. Certainly, I had gone farther than I had ever believed possible. My own instinct is toward fighting, yet I have always been aware of the futility of it. Now I could see that if the fighting ended, all our problems would be simple and easily settled. The joker in the deck was Morgan Park; he had everything to lose by a settlement and nothing to gain.

Park interrupted suddenly. "I wouldn't trust all this talk, Rud. Sabre sounds good, but he's got some trick in mind. What's he planning? What's he trying to cover?"

"Morgan!" Olga protested. "I'm surprised at you! Matt is sincere and you know it."

"I know nothing of the kind," he replied shortly. "I'm surprised that you would defend this—this killer."

He was looking at me as he spoke, and it was then I said the one thing I had wanted to say, the hunch I could not prove. "At least," I replied, "my killings have been in fair fights, by men trying to kill me. I've never killed a man who

had no gun and who would have been helpless against me in
any case!"

Morgan Park stiffened and his face grew livid. Yet I
knew from the way his eyes searched my face that he detected the undercurrent of meaning, and he was trying to
gauge the depth of my knowledge. It was D'Arcy I had in
mind, for D'Arcy had known something about Park and had
been slain for what he knew, or because he might tell others
what he knew. I was sure of that.

"It isn't only rustlers," I continued, to Maclaren, "but
others have schemes they can only bring to success through
trouble here. There are those who wish this fight to continue
so they may get rights and claims they could never secure if
there was peace."

Morgan Park was glaring, fighting for control. He could
see that unless he kept his temper and acted quickly his plans
might be ruined. Something of what I'd said apparently touched
Maclaren, for he was nodding.

"I'll have to think it over," Maclaren said. "This is no
time to make decisions."

"By all means." Turning, I took Olga's arm. "Now if
you'll excuse us?"

Morgan's face was a study in concentrated fury. He
started forward, blood in his eye. Putting Olga hurriedly to
one side, I was ready for him, but Canaval stepped between
us. "Hold it!" Canaval's command stopped Park in his tracks.
"That's all, Park. We'll have no trouble here."

"What's the matter?" he sneered. "Sabre need a nurse-
maid now?"

"No." The foreman was stiff. "He gave me his word, and
I gave mine. As long as he is on this place my word holds. If
the boss wants him to go, he'll go."

In the silence that followed, Maclaren turned to me.
"Sabre, I've no reason to like you, but you are my daughter's
guest and you talk straight from the shoulder. Remain as long
as you like."

Park started to speak, but realized he could do nothing.
He turned his heavy head, staring at me from under heavy
brows. That gaze was cold and deadly. "We can settle our
differences elsewhere, Sabre."

Olga was worried when we got outside. "You shouldn't
have come, Matt. There'll be trouble. Morgan is a bad enemy."

"He was my enemy, anyway. That he is a bad enemy, I know. I think another friend of yours found that out."

She looked up quickly, real fear in her eyes. "What do you mean?"

"Your friend D'Arcy. He comes of a family that does not frighten easily. Did you ever have a note of acknowledgment from him?"

"No."

"Strange. I'd have said such a man would never neglect such an obvious courtesy."

We stood together, then, looking out at the night and the desert, no words between us but needing no words, our hearts beating together, our blood moving together, feeling the newness of love discovered. The cottonwood leaves brushed their pale green hands together, and their muted whispering seemed in tune with our own thoughts. This was my woman, the one I would walk down the years with. The leaves said that and my blood said it, and I knew the same thoughts were in her, reluctant as she might be to admit it.

"This trouble will pass," I said softly, "as the night will pass, and when it has gone, and the winds have blown the dust away, then I shall take you to Cottonwood Wash—to live." Her hand stayed in mine, and I continued. "We'll build something there to last down the years until this will all seem a bad dream, a nightmare dissipated by the morning sunlight."

"But could you ever settle down? Could you stay?"

"Of course. Men don't wander for the love only of wandering, they wander because they are in search of something. A place of one's own, a girl, a job accomplished. It is only you who has mattered since the day I rode into the streets of Hattan's Point and saw you there."

Turning toward her, I took her by the elbows. Her breath caught and then came quickly and deeply. Her lips parted slightly as she came into my arms, and I felt her warm body melt against mine, and her lips were warm and seeking, urgent, passionate. My fingers ran into her hair and along her scalp, and her kisses hurt my lips as mine must have hurt hers. All the fighting, all the waiting, melted into nothingness then.

She pulled back suddenly, frightened yet excited, her breasts rising and falling as she fought for control. "This isn't good! We're—we're too violent. We've got to be more calm."

I laughed then, full of the zest of living and loving and seeing the glory of her there in the moonlight. I laughed and took her arms again. "You're not exactly a calm person."

"I?" A flush darkened her face. "Well, all right then. Neither of us is calm."

"Need we be?" My hands reached for her, and then I heard someone whistling. Irritably, I looked up to hear feet grating on the gravel path.

It was Canaval. "Better ride," he said. "I wouldn't put it past Park to drygulch a man."

"Canaval!" Olga protested. "How can you say that?"

His slow eyes turned to her. "You think so too, ma'am. You always was an uncommon smart girl. You've known him for what he was for a mighty long time." He turned back to me. "Mean what you said back there? About peace and all?"

"You bet I did. What can we gain by fighting?"

"You're right," Canaval agreed; "but there'll be bloodshed before it's over. Pinder won't quit. He hated Rud Maclaren, and now he hates you. He won't back up or quit." Canaval turned to Olga. "Let me talk to Sabre alone, will you? There's something he should know."

"All right." She gave me her hand. "Be careful. And goodnight."

We watched her walk back up the path, and when my eyes turned back to him, his were surprisingly soft. I could see his expression even in the moonlight. "Reminds me of her mother," he said quietly.

"You knew her?" I was surprised.

"She was my sister."

That was something I could never have guessed. "She doesn't know," he explained. "Rud and I used to ride together. I was too fast with a gun and killed a man with too many relatives. I left and Rud married my sister. From time to time we wrote, and when Rud was having trouble with rustlers, I came out to lend a hand. He persuaded me to stay."

He looked around at me. "One thing more. What did you mean about the Slades?"

So I told him in detail of my trip to Silver Reef, the killing of Lyell and the conversation I'd overheard between Park and Booker. Where I had heard the conversation I did not tell him. I only said there was some deal between the two of them that depended upon results to be obtained by Morgan Park.

It was after midnight when I finally left the Bar M, turning off the main trail and cutting across country for the head of Gypsum Canyon.

Mulvaney was waiting for me. "Knowed the horse's walk," he explained. Nodding toward the hills, he added. "Too quiet out there."

The night was clear, wide, and peaceful. Later during the night, I awakened with a start, the sound of a shot ringing in my ears. Mulvaney was sleeping soundly, so I did not disturb him. Afterward, all was quiet, so I dropped off to sleep once more.

In the morning I mentioned it to Mulvaney.

"Did you get up?" he asked.

"Yeah. Went out in the yard and listened, but heard nothing more. Could have been a hunter. Maybe one of the Benaras boys."

Two hours later I knew better. Riding past Maverick Spring I saw a riderless horse grazing near a dark bundle that lay on the grass. The dark bundle was Rud Maclaren, and he was dead.

He had been shot twice from behind, both shots through the head.

He was sprawled on his face, both hands above his head, one knee drawn up. Both guns were in their holsters, and his belt gun was tied down. After one look I stood back and fired three shots as a signal to Mulvaney.

When he saw Maclaren, his face went white and he looked up. "You shouldn't have done it, boy. The country hated him but they respected him, too. They'll hang a man for this!"

"Don't be foolish!" I was irritated, but appalled, too. "I didn't do this! Feel of him! It must have been that shot I heard last night."

"He's cold, all right. This'll blow the lid off, Matt. You'd best rig a story for them. And it had better be good!"

"No rigging. I'll tell the truth."

"They'll hang you, Matt. They'll never believe you didn't do it." He waved a hand around. "He's on your place. The two of you have been feudin'. They'll say you shot him in the back."

Standing over the body with the words of Mulvaney in

my ears, I could see with piercing clarity the situation I was in. What could he have been doing here? Why would he come to my ranch in the middle of the night?

I could see their accusing eyes when the death was reported, the shock to Olga, the reaction of the people, the accusations of Park. Somebody wanted Maclaren dead enough to shoot him in the back. Who?

VIII

Strangely, the morning was cool with a hint of rain. Mulvaney, at my request, had gone to the Bar M to tell Canaval of the killing, and it was up to Canaval to tell Olga. I did not like to think of that. My luck held in one sense, for Jolly Benaras came riding up the wash, and I asked him to ride to Hattan's to report to Key Chapin.

Covering the body with a tarp, I mounted and began to scout the area. How much time I had, I did not know, but it could not be much. Soon they would be arriving from Hattan's, and even sooner from the Bar M. One thing puzzled me. There had been but one shot fired, but there were two bullet holes in Maclaren's skull.

Carefully, I examined the sand under the body and was struck by a curious thing. There was no blood! None on the sand, that is. There was plenty of blood on Rud himself, but all of it, strangely enough, seemed to come from one bullet hole!

There was a confusion of tracks where his horse had moved about while he lay there on the ground, but at this point the wash was sandy, and no definite track could be distinguished. Then horses' hoofs sounded, and I looked up to see five riders coming toward me. The nearest was Canaval, and beside him, Olga. The others were all Bar M riders, and from one glance at their faces I knew there was no doubt in their minds and little reason for speculation that I had killed Rud Maclaren.

Canaval drew up, and his eyes pierced mine, cold, calculating, and shrewd. Olga threw herself from her horse and ran to the still form on the ground. She had refused to meet my eyes or to notice me.

"This looks bad, Canaval. When did he leave the ranch?"

He studied me carefully, as if he were seeing me for the

first time. "I don't know, exactly," he said. "No one heard him go. He must have pulled out sometime after two this morning."

"The shot I heard was close to four." ·

"One shot?"

"Only one—but he's been shot twice." Hesitating a little, I asked, "Who was with him when you last saw him?"

"He was alone. If it's Morgan Park, you are thinkin' of, forget it. He left right after you did. When I last saw Rud he was goin' to his room, feelin' mighty sleepy."

The Bar M riders were circling around. Their faces were cold, and they started an icy chill coming up my spine. These men were utterly loyal, utterly ruthless when aroused. The night before, they had given me the benefit of the doubt, but now they saw no reason to think of any other solution but the obvious one.

Tom Fox, a lean, hard-bitten Bar M man, was staring at me. Coolly, he took a rope from his pommel. "What we waitin' for, men?" he asked bitterly, "There's our man."

Turning, I said, "Fox, from what I hear you're a good man and a good hand. Don't jump to any hasty conclusions. I didn't kill Rud Maclaren and had no reason to. We made peace talk last night an' parted in good spirits."

Fox looked up at Canaval. "That right?"

Canaval hesitated, his expression unchanging. Then he spoke clearly. "It is—but Rud Maclaren changed his mind afterward!"

"Changed his mind?" That I couldn't believe, yet at the expression in Canaval's eyes, I knew he was speaking the truth. "Even so," I added, "how could I be expected to know that? When I left, all was friendly."

"You couldn't know it," Canaval agreed, "unless he got out of bed an' came to tell you. He might have done that, and I can think of no other reason for him to come here. He came to tell you—an' you killed him when he started away."

The hands growled and Fox shook out a loop. It was Olga who stopped them. "No! Wait until the others arrive. If he killed my father, I want him to die! But wait until the others come!"

Reluctantly, Fox drew in his rope and coiled it. Sweat broke out on my forehead. I could fight, and I would if it came to that, but these men only believed they were doing the right thing. They had no idea that I was innocent. My mouth was dry and my hands felt cold. I tried to catch Olga's eye but she ignored me. Canaval seemed studying about something, but he did not speak a word.

The first one to arrive was Key Chapin, and behind him a dozen other men. He looked at me, a quick, worried glance, and then looked at Canaval. Without waiting for questions, the foreman quietly repeated what had happened, telling of the entire evening, facts that could not until then have been known to the men.

"There's one thing," I said suddenly, "that I want to call to your attention."

They looked at me, but there was not a friendly eye in the lot of them. Looking around the circle of their faces, I felt a cold sinking in my stomach, and a feeling came over me. Matt Sabre, I was telling myself, this is the end. You've come to it at last, and you'll hang for another man's crime.

Not one friendly face—and Mulvaney had not returned with the Bar M riders. There was no sign of Jolly Benaras.

"Chapin," I asked, "will you turn Maclaren over?"

The request puzzled him, and they looked from me to the covered body and then to Chapin. He swung down and walked across to the dead man. I heard Olga's breath catch, and then Chapin rolled Maclaren on his back.

He straightened up then, still puzzled. The others looked blankly at me.

"The reason you are so quick to accuse me is that he is here, on my ranch. Well, he was not killed here. *There's no blood on the ground!*"

Startled, they all looked. Before any comment could be made, I continued. "One of the wounds bled badly, and the front of his shirt is dark with blood. The sand would be too, if he'd been killed here. What I am saying is that he was killed elsewhere and then carried here!"

"But why?" Chapin protested.

Canaval said, "You mean to throw guilt onto you?"

"I sure do mean that! Also, that shot I heard fired was shot into him after he was dead!"

Fox shook his head, and sneered. "How could you figure that?"

"A dead man does not bleed. Look at him! All the blood came from one wound!"

Suddenly we heard more horsemen, and Mulvaney returned with his guns and the Benaras boys. Not one, but all of them.

Coolly, they moved up to the edge of the circle.

"We'd be beholden," the older Benaras said loudly, "if you'd all move back. We're friends to Sabre, an' we don't believe he done it. Now give him air an' listen."

They hesitated, not liking it. But their common sense told them that if trouble started now it would be a bloody mess. Carefully, the nearest riders eased back. Whether Olga was listening, I had no idea. Yet it was she whom I wanted most to convince.

"There are other men with axes to grind beside the Pinders and I," I said. "What had I to fear from Rud? Already I had shown I could take care of myself against all of them. Face to face, I was twice the man Rud was."

"You talk yourself up mighty well," Fox said.

"You had your chance in the canyon," I said brutally, "and when I say I can hold this ranch, you know I'm not lying."

Horses came up the trail, and the first faces I recognized were Bodie Miller and the redhead I'd whipped at the Two Bar. Bodie pushed his horse into the circle when he saw me. The devil was riding Bodie again, and I could see from Canaval's face that he knew it.

Right at the moment, Bodie was remembering how I had dared him to gamble at point-blank range. "You, is it?" he said. "I'll kill you one day."

"Keep out of this, Bodie!" Canaval ordered sharply.

Miller's dislike was naked in his eyes. "Rud's dead now," he said. "Maybe you won't be the boss anymore. Maybe she'll want a *younger* man for boss!"

The import of his words was like a blow across the face. Suddenly I wanted to kill him, suddenly I was going to. Canaval's voice was a cool breath of air through my fevered brain. "That will be for Miss Olga to decide." He turned to her. "Do you wish me to continue as foreman?"

"Naturally!" Her voice was cold and even, and in that moment I was proud of her. "And your first job will be to fire Bodie Miller!"

Miller's face went white with fury, and his lips bared back from his teeth. Before he could speak, I interfered. "Don't say it, Bodie! Don't say it!" I stepped forward to face him across Maclaren's body.

The malignancy of his expression was unbelievable. "You an' me are goin' to meet," he said, staring at me.

"When you're ready, Bodie." Deliberately, not wanting the fight here, now, I turned my back on him.

Chapin and Canaval joined me while the men loaded the body into a buckboard. "We don't think you're guilty, Sabre. Have you any ideas?"

"Only that I believe he was killed elsewhere and carried here to cast blame on me. I don't believe it was Pinder. He would never shoot Maclaren in the back."

"You think Park did it?" Canaval demanded.

"Peace between myself and Maclaren would be the last thing he'd want," I said.

Bob Benaras was waiting for me. "You can use Jonathan an' Jolly," he said. "I ain't got work enough to keep 'em out of mischief."

He was not fooling me in the least. "Thanks. I can use them to spell Mulvaney on lookout, and there's plenty of work to do."

For two weeks we worked hard, and the inquest of Rud Maclaren turned up nothing new. There had been no will, so the ranch went to Olga. Yet nothing was settled. Some people believed I had killed Maclaren, most of them did not know, but the country was quiet.

Of Bodie Miller we heard much. He killed a man at Hattan's in a saloon quarrel, shot him before he could get his hand on a gun. Bodie and Red were riding with a lot of riffraff from Hite. The Bar M was missing cattle, and Bodie laughed when he heard it. He pistol-whipped a man in Silver Reef and wounded a man while driving off the posse that came after him.

I worried more about Morgan Park. I had to discover just what his plan was. My only chance was to follow Park every hour of the day and night. I must know where he went, what he was doing, with whom he was talking. One night I waited on a hill above Hattan's watching the house where he lived when in town.

When he came out of the house I could feel the hackles rising on the back of my neck. There was something about him that would always stir me to fury, and it did now. Stifling it, I watched him go to Mother O'Hara's, watched him mount up and ride out of town on the Bar M road. Yet scarcely a dozen miles from town he drew up and scanned his back trail. Safely under cover, I watched him. Apparently satisfied with what he did not see, he turned right along the ridge, keeping under cover. He now took a course that led him into the wildest and most remote corner of the Bar M, that neck of land north of my own and extending far west. His trail led him out upon Dark Canyon Plateau. Knowing little of this area, I closed the distance between us until I saw him making camp.

Before daylight, he was moving again. The sun rose and the day became hot, with a film of heat haze obscuring all the horizons. He seemed headed toward the northwest where the long line of the Sweet Alice Hills ended the visible world. This country was a maze of canyons. To the south it fell away in an almost sheer precipice for hundreds of feet to the bottom of Dark Canyon. There were trails off the plateau, but I knew none of them.

The view was breathtaking, overlooking miles of columned and whorled sandstone, towering escarpments, minarets, and upended ledges. This had once been inhabited country, for there were ruins of cliff dwellings about, and Indian writings.

The trail divided at the east end of the plateau, and the flat rock gave no indication of which fork Park had taken. It looked as though I had lost him. Taking a chance, I went down a steep slide into Poison Canyon and worked back in the direction he must have taken, but the only tracks were of rodents and one of a bighorn sheep. Hearing a sound of singing, I dismounted. Rifle in hand, I worked my way through the rocks and brush.

"No use to shave," the man at the fire said. "We're stuck here. No chance to get to Hattan's now."

"Yeah?" The shaver scoffed. "You see that big feller? Him an' slade are talking medicine. We'll move out soon. I don't want to get caught with no beard when I go to town."

"Who'll care how you look? An' maybe the fewer who know how you look, the better."

"After this show busts open," the shaver replied, "it ain't goin' to matter who knows me! We'll have that town sewed up tighter than a drum!"

"Maybe." The cook straightened and rubbed his back. "Again, maybe not. I wish it was rustlin' cows. Takin' towns can be mighty mean."

"It ain't the town, just a couple of ranches. Only three, four men on the Two Bar, an' about the same on the Bar M. Slade will have the toughest job done afore we start."

"That big feller looks man enough to do it by himself. But if he can pay, his money will look good to me."

"He better watch his step. That Sabre ain't no chicken with a pair of Colts. He downed Rollie Pinder, an' I figure it was him done for Lyell over to the Reef."

"It'll be somethin' when he an' Bodie get together. Both faster than greased lightnin'."

"Sabre won't be around. Pinder figures on raidin' that spread today. Sam wouldn't help him because he'd promised Park. Pinder'll hit 'em about sundown, an' that'll be the end of Sabre."

Waiting no longer, I hurried back to my horse. If Pinder was to attack the Two Bar, Park would have to wait. Glancing at the sun, fear rose in my throat. It would be nip and tuck if I was to get back. Another idea came to me. I would rely on Mulvaney and the Benaras boys to protect the Two Bar. I would counterattack and hit the CP!

When I reached the CP, it lay deserted and still but for the cook, bald-headed and big bellied. He rushed from the door but I was on him too fast, and he dropped his rifle under the threat of my six-gun. Tying him up, I dropped him in a feed bin and went to the house. Finding a can of wagon grease, I smeared it thickly over the floor in front of both doors and more of it on the steps. Leaving the door partly open, I dumped red pepper into a pan and balanced it above the door, where the slightest push would send it cascading over whoever entered, filling the air with fine grains.

Opening the corral, I turned the horses loose and started them down the valley. Digging out all the coffee on the place, I packed it to take away, knowing how a cowhand dearly loves his coffee. It was my idea to make their lives as miserable as possible to get them thoroughly fed up with the fight. Pinder would not abandon the fight, but his hands might get sick of the discomfort.

Gathering a few sticks, I added them to the fire already laid, but under them I put a half dozen shotgun shells. In the tool shed were six sticks of powder and some fuse left from blasting rocks. Digging out a crack at one corner of the fireplace I put two sticks of dynamite into the crack and then ran the fuse within two inches of the fire and covered it with ashes. The shotgun shells would explode and scatter the fire, igniting, I hoped, the fuse.

A slow hour passed after I returned to a hideout in the brush. What was happening at the Two Bar? In any kind of fight, one has to have confidence in those fighting with him, and I had it in the men I'd left behind me. If one of them was killed, I vowed never to stop until all this crowd were finished.

Sweat trickled down my face. It was hot under the brush. Once a rattler crawled by within six or seven feet of me. A packrat stared at me and then moved on. Crows quarreled in the trees over my head. And then I saw the riders.

One look told me. Whatever had happened at the Two Bar, I knew these men were not victorious. There were nine in the group, and two were bandaged. One had his arm in a sling and one had his skull bound up. Another man was tied over a saddle, head and heels hanging. They rode down the hill and I lifted my rifle, waiting for them to get closer to the ranch. Then I fired three times as rapidly as I could squeeze off the shots.

One horse sprang into the air, spun halfway around, scattering the group, and then fell, sending his rider sprawling. The others rushed for the shelter of the buildings, but just as they reached them one man toppled from his horse, hit the dirt like a sack of old clothes, and rolled over in the dust. He staggered to his feet and rushed toward the barn, fell again, and then got up and ran on.

Others made a break for the house, and the first one to hit those greasy steps was Jim Pinder. He hit them running. His feet flew out from under him and he hit the step on his chin!

With a yell, the others charged by him, and even at that distance I could hear the crash of their falling, their angry shouts, and then the roaring sneezes and gasping yells as the red pepper filled the air and bit into their nostrils.

Coolly, I proceeded to shoot out the windows and to knock the hinges off the door, and when Jim Pinder stag-

gered to his feet and reached for his hat, I put a bullet
through the hat. He jumped as if stung and grabbed for his
pistol. He swung it up, and I fired again as he did. What
happened to his shot I never knew, but he dropped the pistol
with a yell and plunged for the door.

One man had ducked for the heavily planked water
trough, and now he fired at me. He was invisible from my
position, but I knew that he was somewhere under the trough,
and so I drilled the trough with two quick shots, draining the
water down upon him. He jumped to escape, and I put a
bullet into the dust to left and right of his position. Like it or
not, he had to lie there while all the water ran over him. A
few scattered shots stampeded their horses, and then I settled down to wait for time to bring the real fireworks.

A few shots came my way after a while, but all were high
or low, and none came close to me.

Taking my time, I loaded up for the second time and
then rolled a smoke. My buckskin was in a low place and had
cover from the shots. There was no way they could escape
from the house to approach me. One wounded man had
fallen near the barn, and I let him get up and limp toward it.
Every once in a while somebody would fall inside the house.
In the clear air I could hear the sound, and each time I
couldn't help but grin.

There was smashing and banging inside the house, and I
could imagine what was happening. They were looking for
coffee and not finding it. A few minutes later a slow trickle of
smoke came out the chimney. My head resting on the palm
of one hand, I took a deep drag on my cigarette and waited
happily for the explosion.

They came, and suddenly. There was the sharp bark of a
shotgun shell exploding and then a series of bangings as the
others went off. Two men rushed from the door and charged
for the barn. Bullets into the dust hurried them to shelter,
and I laid back and laughed heartily. I'd never felt so good in
my life, picturing the faces of those tired, disgruntled men,
besieged in the cabin, unable to make coffee, sliding on the
greasy floor, sneezing from the red pepper, ducking shotgun
shells from the fire.

Not five minutes had passed when the powder went off
with a terrific concussion. I had planted it better than I knew,

for it not only cracked the fireplace but blew a hole in it from which smoke gulped and then trickled slowly.

Rising, I drifted back to my horse and headed for the ranch. Without doubt, the CP outfit was beginning to learn what war meant. Furthermore, I knew my methods were far more exasperating to the cowhands than out-and-out fight. Your true cowhand savors a good scrap, but he does not like discomfort or annoyance, and I knew that going without water, without good food, and without coffee would do more to end the fight than anything else. All the same, as I headed the gelding back toward the Two Bar, I knew that if any of my own boys had been killed I would retaliate in kind. There would be no other answer.

Mulvaney greeted me at the door. "Sure, Matt, you missed a good scrap! We give them lads the fight of their lives!"

Jolly and Jonathan looked up at me, Jolly grinning, the more serious Jonathan smiling faintly. Jolly showed me a bullet burn on his arm, the only scratch any of them had suffered.

They had been watching, taking turnabout, determined they would not be caught asleep while I was gone. The result was that they sighted the CP riders when they were still miles from the headquarters of the Two Bar. The Benaras boys began it with a skirmishers' battle, firing from rocks and brush in a continual running fight. A half dozen times they drove the CP riders to shelter, killing two horses and wounding a man.

They had retreated steadily until in a position to be covered by Mulvaney, who was ready with all the spare arms loaded. From the bunkhouse they stood off the attack. They had so many loaded weapons that there was no break in their fire until the CP retreated.

"Somebody didn't want to fight," Jolly explained. "We seen 'em argufyin', an' then finally somebody else joined in an' they backed out on Pinder. He was almighty sore, believe you me."

Amid much laughter I told them about my own attack on the CP.

Mulvaney ended it suddenly. "Hey!" he turned swiftly. "I forgot to tell you. That catamount of a Bodie Miller done shot Canaval!"

"Is he dead?"

"Not the last we heard, but he's hurt mighty bad. He took four bullets before he went down."

"Miller?"

"Never got a scratch! That kid's plumb poison, I tell you! Poison!"

IX

For a minute I considered that, and liked none of it. Canaval had been a man with whom I could reason. More than that, with Canaval at hand there had always been protection for Ogla.

There was no time to be wasted now. Telling Mulvaney of what I had seen in the canyon, I turned my buckskin toward the Bar M. I wanted first of all to talk with Olga, and second to see Canaval. If the man was alive, I had to talk to him. The gun star of Bodie Miller was rising now, and I knew how he would react. This new shooting would only serve to convince him of his speed. The confidence he had lacked on our first meeting he would now have.

He would not wait long to kill again, and he would seek out some known gunfighter, for his reputation could grow now only by killing the good ones, and Canaval had been one of the fastest around. And who would that mean? Jim Pinder, Morgan Park, or myself. And knowing how he felt about me, I had an idea whom he would be seeking out.

Key Chapin was standing on the wide veranda of the Bar M house when I rode into the yard. Fox was loitering nearby, and he started toward me. "You ain't wanted here, Sabre!" he told me brusquely. "Get off the place!"

"Don't be a fool, man! I've come on business!"

He shook his head stubbornly. "Don't make no difference! Start movin' an' don't reach for a gun! You're covered from the bunkhouse an' the barn!"

"Fox," I persisted, "I've no row with you, and you're the last man in the world I'd like to kill, but I don't like being pushed and you're pushin' me! I've got Bodie Miller an' Morgan Park to take care of, as well as Jim Pinder! So get this straight. If you want to die, grab iron. Don't ride me, Fox, because I won't take it!"

My buckskin started, and Fox, his face a study in conflicting emotion, hesitated. Then a cool voice interposed. "Fox! Step back! Let the gentleman come up!"

It was Olga Maclaren.

Fox hesitated and then stepped back, and I drew up the buckskin for a minute. Fox looked up at me, and our eyes met. "I'm glad of that, Fox," I said. "I'd hate to have killed a man as good as you. They don't come often."

The sincerity in my voice must have reached him, for when I happened to glance back he was staring after me, his face puzzled. As I dismounted, Chapin walked over toward the house.

Olga stood on the steps awaiting me. There was no welcome in her eyes. Her face was cool, composed. "There was something you wanted?"

"Is that my only welcome?"

"What reason have you to expect anything more?"

That made me shrug. "None," I said, "none at all. How's Canaval?"

"Resting."

"Is he better? Is he conscious?"

"Yes to both questions. Can he see anybody? No."

Then I heard him speak. "Sabre? Is that you? Come in!"

Olga hesitated, and for a minute I believed she was going to defy the request. Then with a shrug of indifference she led Chapin and me into the wounded man's room.

The foreman's appearance shocked me. He was drawn and thin, his eyes huge and hollow in the deathly pallor of his face. His hand gripped mine and he stared up at me. "Glad you're here, Sabre," he said abruptly. "Watch that little demon! Oh, he's a fast man! He's blinding! He had a bullet into me before my gun cleared! He's a freak, Sabre!"

"Sure," I agreed, "but that isn't what I came about. I came to tell you again. I had nothing to do with killing Rud Maclaren."

He nodded slightly. "I'm sure of it." I could feel Olga behind me. "I found—tracks. Not yours. Horse tracks, and tracks of a man carrying a heavy burden. Small feet."

Chapin interrupted suddenly. "Sabre, I've a message for you. Picked it up in Silver Reef yesterday." He handed me a telegram, still sealed. Ripping it open, I saw there what I had expected.

MY BROTHER UNHEARD OF IN MANY MONTHS. MORGAN
PARK ANSWERS DESCRIPTION OF PARK CANTWELL, WANTED
FOR MURDER AND EMBEZZLEMENT OF REGIMENTAL FUNDS.
COMING WEST.
LEO D'ARCY
COL. 12TH CAVALRY

Without comment I handed the message back to Chapin,
who read it aloud. Olga grew pale, but she said nothing.

"Know anything about the case?" Canaval asked Chapin.

The editor nodded. "Yes, I do. It was quite an exciting
case at the time. Park Cantwell was a captain in the cavalry.
He embezzled some twenty thousand dollars and then murdered his commanding officer when faced with it. He got
away, was recaptured, and then broke jail and killed two men
in the process. He was last heard of in Mexico."

"Not much chance of a mistake, is there?"

"None, I'd say. Or very slight. Not many men are so big,
and he is a striking character. Out west here he probably
believed he would not be seen. Most of his time he spent on
that lonely ranch of his, and he rarely was around town until
lately. Apparently, if this is true, he hoped to realize enough
money out of this deal of his with Jake Booker to retire in
Mexico or elsewhere. Probably in this remote corner of the
West, he believed he might never be recognized."

"And now?" Olga had returned to the room. "What will
happen?"

Chapin shrugged. "I'll take this meassage to Sheriff Will
Tharp, and then we'll wait for D'Arcy to arrive."

"There's not much else we can do," I agreed.

"What is it Park and Booker want?" Chapin wondered.
"I don't grasp their motive."

"Who does?" I shrugged.

Olga had not looked at me. Several times I tried to catch
her eyes, but she avoided my glance. Her face was quiet,
composed, and she was, as always, perfectly poised. Not by so
much as a flicker of an eyelash did she betray her feelings
toward me, but I found no comfort in that. Whether or not
she believed I had killed her father, she obviously wanted no
part of me.

Discouraged, I turned toward the door.

"Where to now?" Canaval asked.

"Why"—I turned—"I'm heading for town to see Morgan Park. No man ever beat me with his fists yet and walked away scot-free. I'll have the hide off that brute, and now is as good a time as any."

"Leave him alone, Sabre!" Canaval tried to sit up. "I've seen him kill a man with his fists!"

"He won't kill me."

"What is this?" Olga turned around, her eyes blazing. "A cheap, childish desire for revenge? Or are you talking just to make noise? It seems all I've heard you do since you came here is to talk! You've no right to go in there and start trouble! You've no right to fight Morgan Park simply because he beat you! Leave him alone!"

"Protecting him?" My voice was not pleasant. Did she, I wondered, actually love the man? The idea did not appeal to me, and the more it stayed in my mind, the more angry I became.

"No!" she flared. "I am not protecting him! From what I saw of you after that first fight I don't believe it is he who needs the protection!"

She could have said nothing more likely to bring all my own temper to the surface. So when she spoke, I listened, my face stiffening. Then without another word I turned and walked from the room. I went down the steps to my horse, and into the saddle.

The buckskin leaned into the wind and kept the fast pace I set for him. Despite my fury, I kept my eyes open and on the hills. Right then I would have welcomed a fight and any kind of a fight. I was mad all the way through, burning with it.

And perhaps it was lucky that right then I should round a bend of the trail and come into the midst of Jack Slade and his men.

They had not heard me until I rounded the bend, and they were heading the same way I was, toward town. The sudden sound of horse's hoofs turned their heads, and Slade dove for his gun.

He was too late. Mad clear through, the instant I saw them I slammed the spurs into my startled buckskin. The horse gave a lunge, driving between the last two riders and striking Slade's horse with his shoulder. At the same instant, I lashed out with the barrel of my Colt and laid it above the

ear of the nearest rider. He went off his horse as if struck by
lightning, and I swung around, blasting a shot from my belt
that knocked the gun from the hand of another rider. Slade
was fighting his maddened horse, and I leaned over and hit it
a crack with my hat. The horse gave a tremendous leap up
and started to run like a scared rabbit with Slade fighting to
stay in the saddle. He had lost one stirrup when my horse
lunged into his and had not recovered it. The last I saw of
him was his running horse and a cloud of dust. It all
happened in a split second, and one man had a smashed hand,
one was knocked out, and Slade was fighting his horse.

The fourth man had been maneuvering for a shot at me,
but among the plunging horses he was afraid of hitting his
own friends. Wheeling my horse, I fired as he did and both of
us missed. He tried to steady his horse and swung. Buck did
not like it and was fighting to get away. I let him go, taking a
backward shot at the man in the saddle, a shot that must have
clipped his ear, for he ducked like a bee-stung farmer, and
then Buck was laying them down on the trail to town.

Feeding shells into my gun, I let him run. I felt better
for the action and was ready for anything. The town loomed
up, and I rode in and swung down in front of Mother O'Hara's.
Buck's side looked bad, for the spurs had bit deep, and I'm a
man who rarely touches a spur to a horse. After greasing the
wounds and talking Buck into friendship again, I went inside.

There was nobody around, but Katie O'Hara came out of
her kitchen. One look at me and she could see I was spoiling
for trouble. "Morgan Park in town?"

She did not hesitate. "He is that. A moment ago I heard
he was in the saloon."

Morgan Park was there, all right. He was sitting at a
table with Jake Booker, and they both looked up when I
entered. I didn't waste any time. I walked up to them.

"Booker," I said, "I've heard you're a no-account shyster, a sheep-stealin', small-town shyster, at that. But you're
doing business with a thief and a murderer, and the man I'm
going to whip!" With that I grabbed the table and hurled it
out of the way, and then I slapped Morgan Park across the
mouth with my hat.

Morgan Park came off his chair with a roar. He lunged
and came up fast, and I smashed him in the teeth with a left.
His lips flattened and blood showered from his mouth, and

then I threw a right that caught him flush on the chin—and I threw it hard!

He blinked, but he never stopped coming, and he rushed me, swinging with both of those huge, ironlike fists. One of them rang bells on my skull, and the other dug for my midsection with a blow I partially blocked with an elbow. Then I turned with his arm over my shoulder and threw him bodily across the floor against the bar rail. He came up fast, and I nailed him with another left. Then he caught me with both hands, and sparks danced among the stars in my skull. That old smoky taste came up inside of me, and the taste of blood in my mouth, and I walked in smashing with both hands! Something busted on his face, and his brow was cut to the bone. The blood was running all over him.

There was a crowd around, and they were yelling, but I heard no sound. I walked in, bobbing and weaving to miss as many of those jarring, brutal blows as possible, but they kept landing and battering me. He knocked me back into the bar and then grabbed a bottle. He took a terrific cut at my skull and I ducked, smashing him in the ribs. He staggered and sprawled out of balance from the force of his missed swing, and I rushed him and took a flying leap at his shoulders. I landed astride and jammed both spurs into his thighs, and he let out a roar of agony.

I went over his head, lighting on all fours, and he sprang atop my back. I flattened out on the floor with the feeling that he had me. He was yelling like a madman, and he grabbed my hair and began to beat my head against the floor. How I did it I'll never know, but I bowed my back under his weight and forced myself to my hands and knees. He ripped at me with his own spurs, and then I got his leg and threw him off.

Coming up together we circled, more wary now. His shirt was in ribbons, and he was covered with blood. I'd never seen Morgan stripped before. He had a chest and shoulders like a Hercules. He circled and then came into me, snarling. I nailed that snarl into his teeth with both fists, and we stood there swinging free with both hands, rocking with the power of those punches and smelling of sweat, blood, and fury.

He backed up and I went into him. Suddenly he caught my upper arms, and dropping he put a foot in my stomach and threw me over his head!

For a fleeting instant I was flying through the air, and then I lit on a poker table and grabbed the sides with both hands. It went over on top of me, and that was all that saved me as he rushed in to finish me with the boots. I shoved the table at him and came up off the floor, and he hit me again and I went right back down. He dropped a big palm on my head and shoved me at the floor. I sprawled out and he kicked me in the side. It missed my ribs and glanced off my gun belt, and I rolled over and grabbed his boot, twisting hard!

It threw him off balance and he hit the floor, which gave me a chance to get on my feet. I got him just as he was halfway up with a right that knocked him through the door and out onto the porch. I hit the porch in a jump, and he tackled me around the knees. We both were down then, and I slapped him with a cupped hand over his ear and knew from the way he let go that I'd busted an eardrum for him. I dropped him again with a solid right to the chin, and stood back, gasping and pain-wracked, fighting for breath. He got up more slowly, and I nailed him left and right in the mouth and he went down heavily.

Sprawled out, he lay there on the edge of the walk, one hand trailing in the dust, and I stared down at him. He was finished, through! Turning on my heels I walked back inside, and brushing off those who crowded around me I headed for the bar. I took the glass of whiskey that was shoved at me and poured it in my hands and mopped the cuts on the lower part of my face with it. Then I took a quick gulp from another glass they put before me and turned.

Morgan Park was standing three feet away from me, a bloody, battered giant with cold, ugly fury blazing from his eyes. "Give me a drink!" he bellowed.

He picked up the glass and tossed it off. "Another!" he yelled, while I stared at him. He picked that up, lifted it to his lips, and then threw it in my eyes!

I must have blinked, for instead of getting the shot-glass full, I got only part of it, but enough to blind me. And then he stepped close. As I fought for sight I caught a glimpse of his boot toes, wide spread, and I was amazed that such a big man had such small feet. Then he hit me. It felt like a blow from an ax, and it knocked me into the bar. He faced around, taking his time, and smashed one into my body, and I went down, gasping for breath. He kickd at me with the toe of one of those deadly boots that could have put an eye out, but the kick glanced off the side of my head and I went down.

It was my turn to be down and out. Then somebody drenched me with a bucket of water and I looked up. Key Chapin was standing over me, but it was not Key Chapin who had thrown the water. It was Olga.

Right then I was only amazed that she was there at all, and then I got up shakily and somebody said, "There he is!" and I saw Park standing there with his hands on his hips, leering at me, and with the same mutual hatred we went for each other again.

How we did it I don't know. Both of us had taken beatings that would have killed a horse. All I knew was that time for me had stopped. Only one thing remained. I had to whip that man, whip him or kill him with my bare hands, and I was not stopping until I was sure I had done it.

"Stop it, you crazy fools! Stop it or I'll throw you both in jail!" Sheriff Will Tharp was standing in the door with a gun on me. His cold blue eyes were blazing.

Behind him were maybe twenty men staring at us. One of them was Key Chapin. Another was Bodie Miller.

"Take him out of here, then," I said. "If he wants more of this he can have it in the morning."

Park backed toward the door and then turned away. He looked punch-drunk.

After that I sat up for an hour putting hot water on my face.

Then I went to the livery stable and crawled into the loft, taking a blanket with me. I had worn my guns and had my rifle along.

How long I slept I have no idea, except that when I awakened bright sunlight was streaming through the cracks in the walls of the old stable. The loft was like an oven with the heat. Sitting up, I touched my face. It was sore, all right, but felt better. I worked my fingers to loosen them up and then heard a movement and looked around. Morgan Park was on the ladder staring at me. And I knew then that I was not looking at a sane man.

X

He stood there on the ladder in that hot old barn, staring at me with hatred, with a fury that seemed no whit abated from the previous night.

"You back again?" I spoke quietly, yet lay poised for instant movement. I knew now the tremendous vitality that huge body held. "After the way I licked you last night?"

The veins distended in his brow and throat. "Whipped *me*?" His voice was hoarse with anger. "Why, you—" He started over the end of the ladder, and I let him come. Right then I could have cooled him, knocked him off that ladder, but something within me wouldn't allow it. With a lesser man, one I could have whipped easily, I might have done it just to end the fighting, but not with Morgan Park. Right then I knew I had to whip him fairly, or I could never be quite comfortable again.

He straightened from the ladder, and I could see that he was a little stiff. Well, so was I. But my boxing with Mulvaney and the riding I had done had been keeping me in trim. My condition was better than his, almost enough to neutralize his greater size and strength. He straightened and turned toward me. He did not rush, just stood there studying me with cool calculation, and I knew that he, too, had come here to make an end to this fight and to me.

Right then he was studying how best to whip me, and suddenly I perceived his advantage. In the loft—one side open to the barn, the rest of it stacked with hay—I was distinctly at a disadvantage. Here his weight and strength could be decisive. He moved toward me, backing me toward the hay. I feinted, but he did not strike. He merely moved on in, his head hunched behind a big shoulder, his fists before him, moving slightly. Then he lunged. My back came up against the slanting wall of hay and my feet slipped. Off balance, lying against the hay, I had no power in my blows. With cold brutality he began to swing. His eyes were exultant and wicked with sadistic delight. Lights exploded in my brain, and then another punch hit me, and another.

My head spinning, my mouth tasting of smoke, I let myself slide to a sitting position and then threw my weight sidewise against his knees. He staggered, and fearing the fall off the edge of the loft, fought for balance. Instantly, I smashed him in the mouth. He went to his haunches, and I sprang past him, grabbed a rope that hung from the rafters, and dropped to the hard-packed earth of the barn's floor.

He turned and glared at me, and I waited. A man appeared in the door, and I heard him yell, "They're at it again!" And then Morgan Park clambered down the ladder and turned to me.

Now it had to be ended. Moving in quickly, I jabbed a stiff left to his face. The punch landed on his lacerated mouth and started the blood. Circling carefully, I slipped a right and countered with a right to the ribs. Then I hit him, fast and rolling my shoulders, with a left and right to the face. He came in, but I slipped another punch and uppercut hard to the wind. That slowed him down. He hit me with a glancing left and took two punches in return.

He looked sick now, and I moved in, smashing him on the chin with both hands. He backed up, bewildered, and I knocked his left aside and hit him on the chin. He went to his knees and I stepped back and let him get up.

Behind me, there was a crowd and I knew it. Waiting, I let him get up. He wiped off his hands and then lunged at me, head down and swinging! Sidestepping swiftly, I evaded the rush, and when he tried it again I dropped my palm to the top of his head and spun him. At the same instant I uppercut with a wicked right that straightened him up. He turned toward me, and then I pulled the trigger on a high hard one. It struck his chin with the solid thud of the butt end of an ax striking a log.

He fell—not over backwards, but face down. He lay there still and quiet, unmoving. Out cold.

Sodden with weariness and fed up with fighting for once, I turned away from him and picked up my hat and rifle. Nobody said anything, staring at my battered face and torn clothing. Then they walked to him.

At the door I met Sheriff Tharp. He glared at me. "Didn't I tell you to stop fighting in this town, Sabre?"

"What am I going to do? Let him beat my head off? I came here to sleep without interruption, and he followed me, found me this morning." Jerking my head toward the barn's interior, I told him, "You'll find him in there, Tharp."

He hesitated. "Better have some rest, Sabre. Then ride out of town for a few days. Ater all, I have to have peace. I'm arresting Park."

"Not for fighting?"

"For murder. This morning I received an official communication confirming your message."

Actually, I was sorry for Park. No man ever hates a man he has whipped in a hand-to-hand fight. All I wanted now was sleep, food, and gallons of cold spring water. Right then I felt as if it had been weeks since I'd had a decent drink.

Yet all the way to O'Hara's I kept remembering that bucket of water doused over me the night before. Had it really been Olga Maclaren there? Or had I been out of my head from the punches I'd taken?

When my face was washed off I came into the restaurant, and the first person I saw was Key Chapin. He looked at my face and shook his head. "I'd never believe anything human could fight the way you two did!" he exclaimed. "And again this morning! I hear you whipped him good this time."

"Yeah." I was tired of it all. Somberly, I ate breakfast, listening to the drone of voices in my ears.

"Booker's still in town." Chapin was speaking. "What's he after, I wonder?"

Right then I did not care, but as I ate and drank coffee, my mind began to function once more. After all, this was my country. I belonged here. For the first time I really felt that I belonged someplace.

"Am I crazy, or was Olga here last night?"

"She was here, all right. She saw part of your fight."

"Did she leave?"

"I think not. I believe she's staying over at Doc and Mrs. West's place. They're old friends of hers." Chapin knocked out his pipe. "As a matter of fact, you'd better go over there and have him look at those cuts. One of them at least needs some stitches."

"Tharp arrested Park."

"Yes, I know. Park is Cantwell, all right."

Out in the air I felt better. With food and some strong black coffee inside of me I felt like a new man, and the mountain air was fresh and good to the taste. Turning, I started up the street, walking slowly. This was Hattan's. This was my town. Here, in this place, I would remain. I would ranch here, graze my cattle, rear my sons to manhood. Here I would take my place in the world and be something more than the careless, cheerful, trouble-hunting rider. Here, in this place, I belonged.

Doc West lived in a small white cottage surrounded by rose bushes and shrouded in vines. Several tall poplars reached toward the sky, and there was a small patch of lawn inside the white picket fence.

He answered the door at my rap, a tall, austere-looking man with gray hair and keen blue eyes. He smiled at me. "You're Matt Sabre? I was expecting you."

That made me grin. "With a face like this, you should expect me. I took a licking for a while."

"And gave one to Morgan Park. I have just come from the jail, where I looked him over. He has three broken ribs and his jaw is broken."

"No!" I stared at him.

He nodded. "The ribs were broken last night sometime, I'd guess."

"There was no quit in him."

West nodded seriously. "There still isn't. He's a dangerous man, Sabre. A very dangerous man."

That I knew. Looking around, I saw nothing of Olga Maclaren. Hesitating to ask, I waited and let him work on me. When he was finished I got to my feet and buckled on my guns.

"And now?" he asked.

"Back to the Two Bar. There's work to do there."

He nodded, but seemed to be hesitating about something. Then he asked, "What about the murder of Rud Maclaren? What's your view on that?"

Something occurred to me then that I had forgotten. "It was Morgan Park," I said. "Canaval found the footprint of a man nearby. The boots were very small. Morgan Park—and I noticed it for the first time during our fight—has very small feet despite his size."

"You may be right," he agreed, hesitantly. "I've wondered."

"Who else could it have been? I know I didn't do it."

"I don't believe you did, but—" He hesitated and then dropped the subject.

Slowly, I walked out to the porch and stopped there, fitting my hat on my head. It had be done gently, for I had

two good-sized lumps just at my hairline. A movement made
me turn, and Olga was standing in the doorway.

Her dark hair was piled on her head, the first time I had
seen it that way, and she was wearing something green and
summery that made her eyes an even deeper green. For a
long moment neither of us spoke, and then she said, "Your
face—does it hurt very much?"

"Not much. It mostly just looks bad, and I'll probably
not be able to shave for a while. How's Canaval?"

"He's much better. I've put Fox to running the ranch."

"He's a good man." I twisted my hat in my hands.
"When are you going back?"

"Tomorrow, I believe."

How lovely she was! At this moment I knew that I had
never in all my life seen anything so lovely, or anyone so
desirable, or anyone who meant so much to me. It was
strange, all of it. But how did she feel toward me?

"You're staying on the Two Bar?"

"Yes, my house is coming along now, and the cattle are
doing well. I've started something there, and I think I'll stay.
This," I said quietly, "is my home. This is my country. This is
where I belong."

She looked up, and as our eyes met I thought she was
going to speak, but she said nothing. Then I stepped quickly
to her and took her hands. "Olga! You can't really believe
that I killed your father? You can't believe I ever would do
such a thing?"

"No. I never really believed you'd killed him."

"Then—"

She said nothing, not meeting my eyes.

"I want you, Olga. You, more than anything. I want you
on the Two Bar. You are the reason I have stayed here, and
you are the reason I am going to remain."

"Don't. Don't talk like that. We can never be anything
to each other."

"What are you saying? You can't mean that!"

"I do mean it. You—you're violent! You're a killer! You've
killed men here, and I think you live for fighting! I watched
you in that fight with Morgan! You—you actually enjoyed it!"

Thinking that over, I had to agree. "In a way, yes. After
all, fighting has been a necessity too long in the life of men

upon earth. It is not an easy thing to be rid of. Mentally, I know that violence is always a bad means to an end. I know that all disputes should be settled without it. Nevertheless, deep inside me there is something that does like it. It is too old a feeling to die out quickly, and as long as there are men in the world like Morgan Park, the Pinders, and Bodie Miller, there must be men willing and able to fight them."

"But why does it have to be you?" She looked up at me quickly. "Don't fight anymore, Matt! Stay on the Two Bar for a while! Don't come to town! I don't want you to meet Bodie Miller! You mustn't! You mustn't!"

Shrugging, I drew back a little. "Honey, there are some things a man must do, some things he has to do. If meeting Bodie Miller is one of them, I'll do it. Meeting a man who challenges you may seem very foolish to a woman's world, but a man cannot live only among women. He must live with men, and that means he must be judged by their standards, and if I back down for Miller, then I'm through here."

"You can go away! You could go to California. You could go and straighten out some business for me there! Matt, you could—"

"No. I'm staying here."

There were more words and hard words but when I left her I had not changed. Not that I underestimated Miller in any way. I had seen such men before. Billy the Kid had been like him. Bodie Miller was full of salt now. He was riding his luck with spurs. Remembering that sallow face with its hard, cruel eyes, I knew I could not live in the country around Hattan's without facing Miller.

Yet I saw nothing of Bodie Miller in Hattan's, and took the trail for the Two Bar, riding with caution. The chances were he was confident enough now to face me, especially after the smashing I'd taken. Moreover, the Slades were in the country and would be smarting over the beating I had given them.

The Two Bar looked better than anything I had seen in a long time. It was shadowed now with late evening, but the slow smoke lifted straight above the chimney, and I could see the horses in the corral. As I rode into the yard a man materialized from the shadows. It was Jonathan Benaras, with his long rifle.

When I swung down from the saddle he stared at my

face, but said nothing. Knowing he would be curious, I explained simply. "Morgan Park and I had it out. It was quite a fight. He took a licking."

"If he looks worse than you he must be a sight."

"He does, believe me. Anybody been around?"

"Nary a soul. Jolly was down the wash this afternoon. Them cows are sure fattenin' up fast. You got you a mighty fine ranch here. Paw was over. He said if you need another hand you could have Zeb for the askin'."

"Thanks. Your father's all man."

Jonathan nodded. "I reckon. We aim to be neighbors to folks who'll neighbor with us. We won't have no truck with them as walks it high an' mighty. Paw took to you right off. Said you come an' faced him like a man an' laid your cards on the table."

Mulvaney grinned when I walked through the door, and then indicated the food on the table. "Set up. You're just in time."

It was good, sitting there in my own home, seeing the light reflecting from the dishes and feeling the warmth and pleasantness of it. But the girl I wanted to share these things with was not here to make it something more than just a house.

"You are silent tonight," Mulvaney said shrewdly. "Is it the girl, or is it the fight?"

I grinned, and my face hurt with the grinning. "I was thinking of the girl, but not of Park."

"I was wondering about the fight," Mulvaney replied. "I wish I'd been there to see it."

I told them about it, and as I talked I began to wonder what Park would do now, for he would not rest easy in jail, and there was no telling what trick Jake Booker might be up to. And what was it they wanted? Until I knew that, I knew nothing.

The place to look was where the Bar M and the Two Bar joined. And tomorrow I would do my looking, and would do it carefully.

On this ride Mulvaney joined me, and I welcomed the company as well as the Irishman's shrewd brain. We rode east toward the vast wilderness that lay there, east toward the country where I had followed Morgan Park toward his rendezvous with Jack Slade, east toward the maze of canyons, desert, and lonely lands beyond the river.

"See any tracks up that way before?" Mulvaney asked suddenly.

"Some," I admitted, "but I was following the fresh trail. We'll have a look around."

"Think it will be that silver you found out about in Booker's office?"

"Could be. We'll head for Dark Canyon Plateau and work north from there. I think that's the country."

"I'd feel better," Mulvaney admitted after a pause, "if we knew what had become of that Slade outfit. They'll be feelin' none too kindly after the whippin' you gave 'em."

I agreed. Studying the narrowing point, I knew we would soon strike a trail that led back to the northwest, a trail that would take us into the depths of Fable Canyon. Nearing that trail, I suddenly saw something that looked like a horse track. A bit later we found the trail of a single horse, freshly shod and heading northeast—a trail no more than a few hours old!

"Could be one of the Slade outfit," Mulvaney speculated dubiously. "Park's in jail, an' nobody else would come over here."

We fell in behind, and I could see these tracks must have been made during the night. At one place a hoof had slipped and the earth had not yet dried out. Obviously, then, the horse had passed after the sun went down.

We rode with increasing care, and we were gaining. When the canyon branched we found a waterhole where the rider had filled his canteen and prepared a meal. "He's no woodsman, Mulvaney. Much of the wood he used was not good burning wood and some of it green. Also, his fire was in a place where the slightest breeze would swirl smoke in his face."

"He didn't unsaddle," Mulvaney said, "which means he was in a hurry."

This was not one of Slade's outlaws, for always on the dodge, nobody knew better than they how to live in the wilds. Furthermore, they knew these canyons. This might be a stranger drifting into the country looking for a hideout. But it was somewhere in this maze that we would find what it was that drew the interest of Morgan Park.

Scouting around, I suddenly looked up. "Mulvaney! He's whipped up! There's no trial out!"

"Sure an' he didn't take wings to get out of here," Mulvaney growled. "We've gone blind, that's what we've done."

Returning to the spring we let the horse drink while I did some serious thinking. The rock walls offered no route of escape. The trail had been plain to this point and then vanished.

No tracks. He had watered his horse, prepared a meal—and afterward left no tracks. "It's uncanny," I said. "It looks like we've a ghost on our hands."

Mulvaney rubbed his grizzled jaw and chuckled. "Who would be better to cope with a ghost than a couple of Irishmen?"

"Make some coffee, you bogtrotter," I told him. "Maybe then we'll think better."

"It's a cinch he didn't fly," I said later, over coffee, "and not even a snake could get up these cliffs. So he rode in, and if he left, he rode out."

"But he left no tracks, Matt. He could have brushed them out, but we saw no signs of brushing. Where does that leave us?"

"Maybe"—the idea came suddenly—"he tied something on his feet?"

"Let's look up the canyons. He'd be most careful right here, but if he is wearin' somethin' on his feet, the further he goes the more tired he'll be—or his horse will be."

"You take one canyon, an' I'll take the other. We'll meet back here in an hour."

Walking, leading my buckskin. I scanned the ground. At no place was the sand hard packed, and there were tracks of deer, lion, and an occasional bighorn. Then I found a place where wild horses had fed, and there something attracted me. Those horses had been frightened!

From quiet feeding they had taken off suddenly, and no bear or lion would frighten them so. They would leave, but not so swiftly. Only one thing could make wild horses fly so quickly—man!

The tracks were comparatively fresh, and instinct told me this was the right way. The wild horses had continued to run. Where their tracks covered the bottom of the canyon, and where the unknown rider must follow them, I should find a clue. And I did, almost at once.

Something foreign to the rock and manzanita caught my eye. Picking it free of a manzanita branch, I straightened up. It was sheep's wool!

Swearing softly, I swung into the saddle and turned back. The rider had brought sheepskins with him, tied some over his horse's hoofs and some over his own boots, and so left no defined tracks. Mulvaney was waiting for me. "Find anything?"

He listened with interest and then nodded. "It was a good idea he had. Well, we'll get him now!"

The trail led northeast and finally to a high, windswept plateau unbroken by anything but a few towering rocks or low-growing sagebrush. We sat our horses squinting against the distance, looking over the plateau and then out over the vast maze of canyons, a red, corrugated distance of land almost untrod by men. "If he's out there," Mulvaney said, "we may never find him. You could lose an army in that."

"We'll find him. My hunch is that it won't be far." I nodded at the distance. "He had no packhorse and only a canteen to carry water, and even if he's uncommonly shrewd, he's not experienced in the wilds."

Mulvaney had been studying the country. "I prospected through here, boy." He indicated a line of low hills to the east. "Those are the Sweet Alice Hills. There are ruins ahead of us, and away yonder is beef basin."

"We'll go slow. My guess is we're not far behind him."

As if in acknowledgment of my comment, a rifle shot rang out sharply in the clear air! We heard no bullet, but only the shot, and then another, closer, sharper!

"He's not shootin' at us!" Mulvaney said, staring with shielded eyes. "Where is he?"

"Let's move!" I called. "I don't like this spot!"

Recklessly, we plunged down the steep trail into the canyon. Down, down, down! We went racing around elbow turns of the switchback trail, eager only to get off the skyline and into the shelter. If the unknown rider had not fired at us, whom had he fired at?

Who was the rider? Why was he shooting?

XI

Tired as my buckskin was, he seemed to grasp the need for
getting under cover, and he rounded curves in that trail that
made my hair stand on end. At the bottom we drew up in a
thick cluster of trees and brush, listening. Even our horses
felt the tension, for their ears were up, their eyes alert.

All was still. Some distance away a stone rattled. Sweat
trickled behind my ear, and I smelt the hot aroma of dust and
baked leaves. My palms grew sweaty and I dried them, but
there was no sound. Careful to let my saddle creak as little as
possible, I swung down, Winchester in hand. With a motion
to wait, I moved away.

From the edge of the trees I could see no more than
thirty yards in one direction and no more than twenty in the
other. Rock walls towered above, and the canyon lay hot and
still under the midday sun. From somewhere came the sound
of trickling water, but there was no other sound or movement. My neck felt hot and sticky, and my shirt clung to my
shoulders. Shifting the rifle in my hands, I studied the rock
walls with misgiving. Drying my hands on my jeans, I took a
chance and moved out of my cover, moving to a narrow,
six-inch band of shade against the far wall. Easing myself to
the bend of the rock. I peered around.

Sixty yards away stood a saddled horse, head hanging.
My eyes searched and saw nothing, and then, just visible
beyond a white, water-worn boulder, I saw a boot and part of
a leg. Cautiously, I advanced, wary for any trick, ready to
shoot instantly. There was no sound but an occasional chuckle
of water over rocks. Then suddenly I could see the dead man.

His skull was bloody. He had been shot over the eye
with a rifle and at fairly close range. He had probably never
known what hit him. There was vague familiarity to him, and
his skull bore a swelling. This had been one of Slade's men,
whom I had slugged on the trail to Hattan's.

The bullet had struck over the eye and ranged downward,
which meant he had been shot from ambush, from a hiding
place high on the canyon wall. Lining up the position, I
located a tuft of green that might be a ledge.

Mulvaney was approaching me. "He wasn't the man we
followed," he advised. "This one was comin' from the other
way."

"He's one of the Slade crowd. Drygulched."

"Whoever he is," Mulvaney assured me, "we can't take chances. The fellow who killed this man shot for keeps."

We started on, but no longer were the tracks disguised. The man we followed was going more slowly now. Suddenly I spotted a boot print. "Mulvaney!" I whispered hoarsely. "That's the track of the man who killed Rud Maclaren!"

"But Morgan Park is in the hoosegow!" Mulvaney protested.

"Unless he's broken out. But I'd swear that was the track found near Maclaren's body. The one Canaval found!"

My buckskin's head came up and his nostrils dilated. Grabbing his nose, I stifled the neigh, and then stared up the canyon. Less than a hundred yards away a dun horse was picketed near a patch of bunchgrass. Hiding our horses in a box canyon, we scaled the wall for a look around. From the top of the badly fractured mesa we could see all the surrounding country. Under the southern edge of the mesa was a cluster of ancient ruins and beyond them some deep canyons. With my glasses shielded from sun reflection by my hat, I watched a man emerge from a crack in the earth, carrying a heavy sack. Placing it on the ground he removed his coat and with a pick and bar began working at a slab of rock.

"What's he doin'?" Mulvaney demanded, squinting his eyes.

"Pryin' a slab of rock," I told him, and even as I spoke the rock slid, rumbled with other debris, and then settled in front of the crack. After a careful inspection the man concealed his tools, picked up his sack and rifle, and started back. Studying him, I could see he wore black jeans, very dusty now, and a small hat. His face was not visible. He bore no resemblance to anyone I had seen before.

He disappeared near the base of the mountain, and for a long time we heard nothing.

"He's gone," I said.

"We'd best be mighty careful," Mulvaney warned uneasily. "That's no man to be foolin' with, I'm thinkin'!"

A shot shattered the clear, white radiance of the afternoon. One shot, and then another.

We stared at each other, amazed and puzzled. There was no other sound, no further shots. Then uneasily we began our descent of the mesa, sitting ducks if he was waiting for us. To the south and west the land shimmered with heat, looking like a vast and unbelievable city, long fallen to ruin. We slid into the canyon where we'd left the horses, and then the shots were explained.

Both horses were on the ground, sprawled in pools of their own blood. Our canteens had been emptied and smashed with stones. We were thirty miles from the nearest ranch, and the way lay through some of the most rugged country on earth.

"There's water in the canyons," Mulvaney said at last, "but no way to carry it. You think he knew who we were?"

"If he lives in this country he knows that buckskin of mine," I said bitterly. "He was the best horse I ever owned."

To have hunted for us and found us, the unknown man would have had to take a chance on being killed himself, but by this means he left us small hope of getting out alive.

"We'll have a look where he worked," I said. "No use leaving without knowing about that."

It took us all of an hour to get there, and night was near before we had dug enough behind the slab of rock to get at the secret. Mulvaney cut into the bank with his pick. Ripping out a chunk and grabbing it, he thrust it under my eyes, his own glowing with enthusiasm. "Silver!" he said hoarsely. "Look at it! If the vein is like that for any distance, this is the biggest strike I ever saw! Richer than Silver Reef!"

The ore glittered in his hand. There was what had killed Rud Maclaren and all the others. "It's rich," I agreed, "but I'd settle for the Two Bar."

Mulvaney agreed. "But still," he said, "the silver is a handsome sight."

"Pocket it, then," I said dryly, "for it's a long walk we have."

"But a walk we can do!" He grinned at me. "Shall we start now?"

"Tonight," I said, "when the walking will be cool."

We let the shadows grow long around us while we walked and watched the thick blackness choke the canyons and deepen in the shadows of trees. We walked on steadily, with little talk, up Ruin Canyon and over a saddle of the Sweet Alice Hills, and down to the spring on the far side of the hills.

There we rested, and we drank several times. From the stars I could see that it had taken us better than two hours of walking to make less than five miles. But now the trail would be easier along Dark Canyon Plateau—and then I remembered Slade's camp. What if they were back there again, holed up in the same place?

It was a thought, and to go down the canyon toward them was actually none out of the way. Although the walking might be rougher at times, we would have the stream beside us, a thing to be considered. Mulvaney agreed, and we descended into the canyon.

Dark it was there, and quiet except for the rustle of water over stones, and there was a cool dampness that was good to our throats and skins after the heat. We walked on, taking our time, for we'd no records to break. And then we heard singing before we saw the reflection of the fire.

We walked on, moving more carefully, for the canyon walls caught and magnified every sound.

Three men were about the fire, and one of them was Jacke Slade. Two were talking while one man sang as he cleaned his rifle. We reached the edge of the firelight before they saw us, and I had my Winchester on them, and Mulvaney that cannonlike four-shot pistol of his. "Grab the sky, Slade!" I barked the order at him, and his hand dropped and then froze.

"Who is it?" he demanded hoarsely, straining his eyes at us. Our faces being shielded by the brims of our hats, he could not see enough of them. I stepped nearer so the firelight reached under my hat brim.

"It's Matt Sabre," I said, "and I'm not wanting to kill you or anybody. We want two horses. You can lend them to us, or we'll take them. Our horses were shot by the same man that killed your partner."

Slade jerked, his eyes showing incredulity. "Killed? Lott killed?"

"That's right. Intentionally or otherwise he met up with the hombre we were following. He drilled your man right over the eyes. We followed on, and he found where we left our horses and shot them both to leave us afoot."

"Damn a man that'll kill a horse," Slade said. "Who was he?"

"Don't know," I admitted. "Only he leaves a track like Morgan Park. At least, he's got a small foot."

"But Park's in jail," Mulvaney added.

"Not now he isn't," Slade said. "Morgan Park broke jail

within an hour after darkness last night. He pulled one of those iron bars right out of that old wall, stole a horse, and got away. He's on the loose and after somebody's scalp."

Park free! But the man we had followed had not been as big as Park was. I did not tell them that. "How about the horses?" I asked.

"You can have them, Sabre," Slade said grudgingly. "I'm clearing out. I've no stomach for this sort of thing."

"Are they spares?"

Slade nodded. "We've a half dozen extras. In our business it pays to keep fresh horses." He grinned. "No hard feelin's, Sabre?"

"Not me," I said. "Only don't you boys get any wild ideas about jumping game. My trigger finger is right jittery."

Slade shrugged wryly. "With two guns on us? Not likely. I don't know whether your partner can shoot or not, but with a cannon that big he doesn't need to. What kind of gun is that, anyway?"

"She's my own make," Mulvaney said cheerfully, "but the slug kills just as dead."

"Give this hombre an old stovepipe and he'd make a cannon." I told them. "He's a genius with tools."

While Mulvaney got the horses I stood over the camp. "Any other news in town?" I asked Slade.

"Plenty!" he admitted. "Some Army officer came into town claimin' Park killed his brother. Seems a right salty gent, And"—his eyes flickered to mine—"Bodie Miller is talkin' it big around town. He says you're his meat."

"He's a heavy eater, that boy," I said carelessly. "He may tackle something one of these days that will give him indigestion."

Jack Slade shrugged and watched Mulvaney lead the horses up. As we mounted, I glanced back at him. "We'll leave these horses at the corral of the livery stable in town, if you like."

Slade's eyes twinkled a little. "Better not. First time you get a chance take 'em to a corral you'll find in the woods back of Armstrong's. Towns don't set well with me, nor me with them."

The horses were fresh and ready to go, and we let them run. Daylight found us riding up the street of Hattan's, a town that was silent and waiting. The loft was full of hay, and both of us headed for it. Two hours later I was wide awake. Splashing water on my face I headed for O'Hara's. The first person I saw as we came through the door was Key Chapin. Olga Maclaren was with him.

Chapin looked up as we entered. "Sorry, Sabre," he said. "I've just heard."

"Heard what?" I was puzzled.

"That you're losing the Two Bar."

"Are you crazy? What are you talking about?"

"You mean you haven't heard? Jake Booker showed up the other day and filed a deed to the Two Bar. He purchased the rights to it from Ball's nephew, the legitimate heir. He also has laid claim to the Bar M, maintaining that it was never actually owned by Rud Maclaren, but belonged to his brother-in-law, now dead. Booker has found some relative of the brother-in-law and bought his right to the property."

"Well, of all the— That's too flimsy, Chapin. He can't hope to get away with that! What's on his mind?"

Chapin shrugged. "If he goes to court he can make it tough. You have witnesses to the fact that Ball gave you the ranch, but whether that will stand in court, I don't know, especially with a shrewd operator like Booker fighting it. As to Maclaren, it turns out he did leave the ranch to his brother-in-law during a time some years ago when he was suffering from a gunshot wound, and apparently never made another will. What's important right now is that Jake is going to court to get both you and Olga off the ranches, and he plans to freeze all sales, bank accounts, and other money or stock until the case is settled."

"In other words, he doesn't want us to have the money to fight him."

Chapin shrugged. "I don't know what his idea is, but I'll tell you one thing. He stands in well with the judge, who is just about as crooked as he is, and they'll use your reputation against you. Don't think Booker hasn't considered all the angles, and don't think he doesn't know how flimsy his case may be. He'll bolster it every way possible, and he knows every trick in the book."

I sat down. This had come so suddenly that it took the wind out of my sails. "Has this news gone to the Bar M yet? Has it got out to Canaval?"

Chapin shrugged. "Why should it? He was only the

foreman. Olga has been told, and you can imagine how she feels."

My eyes went to hers, and she looked away. Katie O'Hara came in, and I gave her my order for breakfast and tried the coffee she had brought with her. It tasted good.

As I sat there my mind began to work swiftly. There was still a chance, if I figured things right. Jake Booker was no fool. He had not paid out money for those claims unless he believed he could make them stand in court. He knew about how much money I had and knew that Olga Maclaren, with the ranch bank accounts frozen, would be broke. Neither of us could afford to hire an attorney, and so far as that went, there was no attorney within miles able to cope with Booker. What had started as a range war had degenerated into a range steal by a shyster lawyer, and he had arguments that could not be answered with a gun.

"How was Canaval when you left?"

"Better," Olga said, still refusing to meet my eyes.

"What about Morgan Park? I heard he escaped."

"Tharp's out after him now. That Colonel D'Arcy went with him and the posse. There had been a horse left for Park. Who was responsible for that, we don't know, but it may have been one of his own men."

"Where did Tharp go?"

"Toward the ranch, I think. There was no trail they could find."

"They should have gone east, toward Dark Canyon. That's where he'll be."

Chapin looked at me curiously, intently. "Why there?"

"That's where he'll go," I replied definitely. "Take my word for it."

They talked a little between them, but I ate in silence, always conscious of the girl across the table, aware of her every move.

Finishing my meal, I got up and reached for my hat. Olga looked up quickly. "Don't go out there! Bodie Miller is in town!"

"Thanks." Our eyes met and held. Were they saying something to me? Or was I reading into their depths the meaning. I wanted them to hold? "Thanks," I repeated. "I'd prefer not to meet him now. This is no time for personal grudges."

It was a horse I wanted, a better horse than the one borrowed from Slade, which might have been stolen. This, I reflected dryly, would be a poor time to be hung as a horse thief. There was no gate at the corral on this side, so I climbed over, crossing the corral. At the corner I stopped in my tracks. A horse was tied to the corral, a horse stripped but recently of a saddle, a dun horse that showed evidence of hard riding! And in the damp earth near the trough was a boot print. Kneeling, I examined the hocks of the tied horse. From one of them I picked a shred of wool and then another. Spinning around I raced for the restaurant. "Katie!" I demanded. "Who owns that horse? Did you see the rider?"

"If you're thinkin' of Park, that horse couldn't carry him far. An' he would not stay in the town. Not him."

"Did you see anyone else?"

"Nobody—wait a minue! I did so. 'Twas Jake Booker. Not that I saw him with the horse, but a bit before daylight he came around the corner from that way and asked if I'd coffee ready."

Booker! He had small feet. He was in with Park. He wanted Maclaren dead. He had killed Slade's man and shot our horses. Booker had some explaining to do.

Mulvaney was crawling from the loft where I'd slept but was all attention at once. He listened and then ran to the stable office. Waiting only until he was on a horse and racing from town, I started back to O'Hara's. My mind was made up.

The time had come for a showdown, and this time we would all be in in it, and Jake Booker would not be forgotten.

Key Chapin looked up when I came in. "Key," I said quickly, "this is the payoff. Find out for me where Booker is. Get somebody to keep an eye on him. He's not to leave town if he tries. Keep him under observation all the time until Mulvaney gets back from the ranch."

Turning to Olga, I asked her, "How about Canaval? Can he ride yet? Could he stand a buckboard trip?"

She hesitated. "He couldn't ride, but he might stand it in the buckboard."

"Then get him into town, and have the boys come with him, Fox especially. I like that man Fox, and Canaval may need protection. Bring him in, and bring him here."

"What is it? What have you learned?" Chapin demanded.

"About everything I need to know," I replied. "We're going to save the Bar M for Olga, and perhaps we'll save my ranch, too. In any event, we'll have the man who killed Rud Maclaren!"

"What?" Olga's face was pale. "Matt, do you mean that?"

"I do. I only hope that Tharp gets back with Morgan Park, but I doubt if we'll see him again." Turning to Key, who was at the door. "Another thing. We might as well settle it all. Send a rider to the CP and have Jim Pinder in here. Get him here fast. We'll have our showdown the first thing in the morning."

Twice I walked up the street and back. Nowhere was there any sign of Bodie Miller or of Red, his riding partner. The town still had that sense of expectancy that I had noticed upon coming into town. And they were right—for a lot of things were going to happen and happen fast.

Key met me in the saloon. He walked toward me quickly, his face alive with interest. "What have you got in mind, Matt? What are you planning?"

"Several things. In the first place, there has been enough fighting and trouble. We're going to end it right here. We're going to close up this whole range fight. There aren't going to be any halfway measures. How well do you know Tharp?"

"Very well, why?"

"Will he throw his weight with us? It would mean a lot if he would."

"You can bank on him. He's a solid man, Matt. Very solid."

"All right, in the morning then. In the morning we'll settle everything!"

There was a slight movement at the door and I looked up. My pulse almost stopped with the shock of it.

Bodie Miller stood there, his hands on his hips, his lips smiling. "Why, sure!" he said. "If that's what you want. The morning is as good a time as any!"

XII

The sun came up clear and hot. Already at daybreak the sky was without a cloud, and the distant mountains seemed to shimmer in a haze of their own making. The desert lost itself in heat waves before the day had scarce begun, and there was a stillness lying upon both desert and town, a sort of poised awareness without sound.

When I emerged upon the street I was alone. Like a town of ghosts, the street was empty, silent except for the echo of my steps on the boardwalk. Then, as if their sound had broken the spell, the saloon door opened and the bartender emerged and began to sweep off the walk. He glanced quickly around at me, bobbed his head, and then with an uneasy look around, finished his sweeping hurriedly and ducked back inside. A man carrying two wooden buckets emerged from an alley and looked cautiously about. Assured there was no one in sight he started across the street, glancing apprehensively first in one direction, then the other.

Sitting down in one of the polished chairs before the saloon I tipped back my hat and stared at the mountains. In a few minutes or a few hours, I might be dead.

It was not a good morning on which to die—but what morning is? Yet in a few minutes or hours another man and myself would probably meet out there in that street, and we would exchange shots, and one or both of us would die.

A rider came into the street, Mulvaney. He left his horse at the stable and clumped over to me. He was carrying enough guns to fight a war.

"Comin'," Mulvaney said, "the whole kit an' kaboodle of 'em. Be here within the hour. Jolly's already in town. Jonathan went after the others."

Nodding, I watched a woman looking down the street from the second floor. Suddenly she turned and left the window as if she had seen something or been called.

"Eat yet?"

"Not yet."

"Seen Olga? Or Chapin?"

"No."

"If Red cuts in this scrap," Mulvaney said, "he's mine."

"You can have him."

A door slammed somewhere, and then the man with the two wooden buckets hurried fearfully across the street, slopping water at every step. "All right," I said, "we'll go eat."

There was no sign of Bodie Miller or of Jim Pinder. Sheriff Tharp was still out hunting Morgan Park. Unless he got back soon, I'd have to run my show alone.

*   *   *

Mother O'Hara had a white tablecloth over the oilcloth, and her best dishes were out. She brought me coffee and said severely, "You should be ashamed. That girl laid awake half the night, thinkin' of nothin' but you!"

"About *me*?" I was incredulous.

"Yes, about you! Worried fair sick, she is! About you an' that Bodie Miller!"

The door opened and Olga walked in. Her eyes were very green today, and her hair was drawn back to a loose knot at the back of her neck, but curled slightly into two waves on her forehead. She avoided my glance, and it was well she did or I'd have come right out of my chair.

Then men entered the restaurant—Chapin, looking unusually severe, Colonial D'Arcy, and last of all, Jake Booker.

D'Arcy caught my eye, and a slow smile started on his lips. "Sabre! Well, I'm damned! The last time I saw Sabre he was in China!"

He took my hand and we grinned at each other. He was much older than I, but we talked the same language. His hair was gray at the temples. "They say you've had trouble with Cantwell."

"And more to come if the sheriff doesn't get him. Park is mixed up in a shady deal with Jake Booker, the man across the table from me."

"I?" Booker smiled, but his eyes were deadly. "You're mistaken, Mr. Sabre. It is true that Mr. Park asked me to represent him in some trouble he was having, but we've no other connection. None at all."

Jim Pinder stalked in at that moment, but knowing that Mulvaney and Jolly were watching, I ignored him.

"From the conversation I overheard in Silver Reef," I said to Booker, "I gathered you had obtained a buyer for some mining property he expected you to have."

Fury flickered across his face. He had no idea how much I knew.

"It might interest you to know, Booker, that the fighting in this area is over. Pinder is here, and we're having a peace meeting. Pinder is making a deal with us and with the Bar M. The fun's over."

"I ain't said nothin' about no deal," Pinder declared harshly. "I come in because I figured you was ready to sell."

"I might buy, Pinder, but I wouldn't sell. Furthermore, I'm with Chapin and Tharp in organizing this peace move.

You can join or stay out, but if you don't join you'll have to haul supplies from Silver Reef. This town will be closed to you. Each of us who has been in this fight is to put up a bond to keep the peace, effective at daybreak tomorrow. You can join or leave the country."

"After you killed my brother?" Pinder demanded. "You ask for peace?"

"You started the trouble in the livery stable figuring you were tough enough to hire me or run me out of the country. You weren't big enough for fast enough then, and you aren't now. Nobody doubts your nerve. You've too much for your own good, and so have the lot of us, but it gets us nothing but killing and more killing. You can make money on the CP, or you can try to buck the country.

"As for Rollie, he laid for me and he got what he asked for. You're a hard man, Pinder, but you're no fool, and I've an idea you're square. Isn't it true Rollie stared out to get me?"

Pinder hesitated, rubbing his angular jaw. "It is," he said finally, "but that don't make no—"

"It makes a lot of difference," I replied shortly. "Now look, Pinder. You've lost more than you've cost us. You need money. You can't ship cattle. You sign up or you'll never ship any! Everybody here knows you've nerve enough to face me, but everybody knows you'd die. All you'd prove would be that you're crazy. You know I'm the faster man."

He stared stubbornly at the table. Finally he said, "I'll think it over. It'll take some time."

"It'll take you just two minutes," I said, laying it on the line.

He stared hard at me, his knuckles whitening on the arm of the chair. Suddenly, reluctantly, he grinned. Sinking back into his chair, he shrugged. "You ride a man hard, Sabre. All right, peace it is."

"Thanks. Pinder." I thrust out my hand. He hesitated and then took it.

Katie O'Hara filled his cup.

"Look," he said suddenly, "I've got to make a drive. The only way there's water is across your place."

"What's wrong with that? Drive 'em across, and whatever water your herd needs is yours. Just so it doesn't take you more than a week to get 'em across!"

Pinder smiled bleakly, but with humor. "Aw, you know it won't take more than a day!" He subsided into his chair and started on the coffee.

Jake Booker had been taking it all in, looking from one to the other of us with his sharp little eyes.

Canaval opened the door and stepped in, looking pale and drawn, followed by Tom Fox. "Miss Olga could have signed for me," he said. "She's the owner."

"You sign, too," I insisted. "We want to cover every eventuality."

Booker was smiling. He rubbed his lips with his thin, dry fingers. "All nonsense!" he said briskly. "Both the Bar M and the Two Bar belong to me. I've filed the papers. You've twenty-four hours to get off and stay off!"

"Booker," I said, "has assumed we are fools. He believed if he could get a flimsy claim he could get us into court and beat us. Well, this case will never go to court."

Booker's eyes were beady. "Are you threatening me?"

Sheriff Will Tharp came into the room. His eyes rested on Jake, but he said nothing.

"We aren't threatening," I said. "On what does your claim to the Bar M stand?"

"Bill of sale," he replied promptly. "The ranch was actually left to Jay Collins, the gunfighter. He was Maclaren's brother-in-law. His will left all his property to a nephew, and I bought it, including the Bar M and all appurtenances thereto!"

Canaval gave me a brief nod. "Sorry, Jake. You've lost your money. Jay Collins is not dead."

The lawyer jumped as if slapped. "Not *dead*? I saw his grave!"

"Booker," I smiled, "look down the table at Jay Collins!" I pointed to Canaval.

Booker broke into a fever of protest, but I was looking at Olga Maclaren. She was staring at Canaval, and he was smiling.

"Sure, honey," he said. "That's why I knew so much about your mother. She was the only person in the world I ever really loved—until I knew my niece."

Booker was worried now, really worried. In a matter of minutes half his plan had come to nothing. He was shrewd enough to know we would not bluff and that we had proof of what we said.

"As for the Two Bar," I added, "don't worry about it. I've my witnesses that the estate was given me. Not that it will matter to you."

"What's that? What'd you mean?" Booker stared at me.

"Because you were too greedy. You'll never rob another man, Booker. For murder, you'll hang."

He protested, but now he was cornered and frightened. "You killed Rud Maclaren," I told him, "and if that's not enough, you killed one of Slade's men from ambush. We can trail your horse to the scene of the crime, and if you think a western jury won't take the word of an Indian tracker, you're wrong."

"*He* killed Maclaren?" Canaval asked incredulously.

"He got him out of the house on some trumped-up excuse—to show him the silver, or to show him something I was planning—it doesn't matter what excuse was used. He shot him and then loaded him on a horse and brought him to my place. He shot him again, hoping to draw me to the vicinity, as he wanted my tracks around the body."

"Lies!" Booker was recovering his assurance. "Sabre had trouble with Maclaren, not I. We knew each other only by sight. The idea that I killed him is preposterous."

He got to his feet. "In any event, what have the ranches to do with the silver claim of which you speak?"

"Morgan Park found the claim while trailing a man he meant to murder—Arnold D'Arcy, who knew him as Cantwell. Arnold had stumbled upon the old mine. Park murdered him only to find there was a catch in the deal. D'Arcy had already filed on the claim and had done assessment work on it. Legally, there was no way Park could gain possession, and no one legally could work the mine until D'Arcy's claim lapsed. Above all, Park wanted to avoid any public connection with the name of D'Arcy. He couldn't sell the claim, because it wasn't his, but if he could get control of the Bar M and the Two Bar, across which anyone working the claim must go, he could sell them at a fabulous price to an unscrupulous buyer. The new owner of the ranches could work the claim quietly, and by owning the ranches he could deny access to the vicinity, so it would never be discovered what claims were being worked. When D'Arcy's assessment work lapsed, the claims could be filed upon by the new owners."

"Booker was to find a buyer?" asked Tharp.

"Yes. Park wanted money, not a mine or a ranch. Booker,

I believe, planned to be that buyer himself. He wanted possession of the Bar M, so he decided to murder Rud Maclaren."

"You've no case against me that would stand in court!" Booker sneered. "You can prove nothing! What witnesses do you have?"

We had none, of course. Our evidence was a footprint. All the rest of what I'd said was guesswork. Tharp couldn't arrest the man on such slim grounds. We needed a confession.

Tom Fox leaned over the table, his eyes cold. "Some of us are satisfied. We don't need witnesses an' we don't need to hear no more. Some of us are almighty sure you killed Rud Maclaren. Got any arguments that will answer a six-gun? Or a rope?"

Booker's face thinned down, and he crouched back against his chair. "You can't do that! The law! Tharp will protect me!"

Sighting a way clear, I smiled. "That might be, Booker! Confess, and Tharp will protect you! He'll save you for the law to handle. But if you leave here a free man, you'll be on your own."

"An' I'll come after you!" Fox said.

"Confess, Booker," I suggested, "and you'll be safe."

"Aw! Turn him loose!" Fox protested angrily. "No need to have trouble, a trial an' all! Turn him loose! We all know he's a crook, an' we all know he killed Rud Maclaren! Turn him loose!"

Booker's eyes were haunted with fear. There was no acting in Tom Fox, and he knew it. The rest of us might bluff, but not Fox. The Bar M hand wanted to kill him, and given an opportunity, he would.

Right then I knew we were going to win. Jake Booker was a plotter and a conniver, not a courageous man. His mean little eyes darted from Fox to the sheriff. His mouth twitched and his face was wet with sweat. Tom Fox, his hand on his gun, moved relentlessly closer to Booker.

"All right, then!" he screamed. "I did it! I killed Maclaren. Now, Sheriff, save me from this man!"

I relaxed at last, as Tharp put the handcuffs on Booker. As they were leaving I said, "What about Park? What happened to him?"

Tharp cleared his throat. "Morgan Park is dead. He was killed last night on the Woodenshoe."

*   *   *

We all looked at him, waiting. "That Apache of Pinder's killed him," Tharp explained. "Park ran for it after he busted out of jail. He killed his horse crossin' the flats an' he run into the Injun with a fresh horse. He wanted to swap, but the Apache wouldn't go for the deal, so Park tried to drygulch him. He should have knowed better. The Injun killed him an' lit out."

"You're positive?" D'Arcy demanded.

Tharp nodded. "Yeah, he died hard, Park did."

The door opened, and Jonathan Benaras was standing there. "Been scoutin' around," he said. "Bodie Miller's done took out. He hit the saddle about a half hour back an' headed north out of town."

Bodie Miller gone!

It was impossible. Yet, he had done it. Miller was gone! I got to my feet. "Good," I said quietly. "I was afraid there would be trouble."

Pinder got to his feet. "Don't you trust that Miller," he said grudgingly. "He's a snake in the grass. You watch out."

So there it was. Pinder was no longer an enemy. The fight had been ended, and I could go back to the Two Bar. I should feel relieved, and yet I did not. Probably it was because I had built myself up for Bodie Miller and nothing had come of it. I was so ready, and then it had all petered out to nothing at all.

Olga had the Bar M and her uncle to run it for her, and nobody would be making any trouble for Canaval. There was nothing for me to do but to go back home.

My horse was standing at the rail, and I walked out to him and lifted the stirrup leather to tighten the cinch. But I did not hurry. Olga was standing there in front of the restaurant, and the one thing I wanted most was to talk to her. When I looked up she was standing there alone.

"You're going back to the Two Bar?" Her voice was hesitant.

"Where else? After all, it's my home now."

"Have—have you done much to the house yet?"

"Some." I tightened the cinch and then unfastened the bridle reins. "Even a killer has to have a home." It was rough, and I meant it that way.

She flushed. "You're not holding that against me?"

"What else can I do? You said what you thought, didn't you?"

She stood there looking at me, uncertain of what to say, and I let her stand there.

She watched me put my foot in the stirrup and swing into the saddle. She looked as if she wanted to say something, but she did not. Yet when I looked down at her she was more like a little girl who had been spanked than anything else I could think of.

Suddenly, I was doing the talking. "Ever start that trousseau I mentioned?"

She looked up quickly. "Yes," she admitted, "but—but I'm afraid I didn't get very far with it. You see, there was—"

"Forget it." I was brusque. "We'll do without it. I was going to ride out of here and let you stay, but I'll be double damned if I will. I told you I was going to marry you, and I am. Now listen, trousseau or not, you be ready by tomorrow noon, understand?"

"Yes. All right. I mean—I will."

Suddenly, we were both laughing like fools and I was off that horse and kissing her, and all the town of Hattan's Point could see us. It was right there in front of the cafe, and I could see people coming from saloons and standing along the boardwalks all grinning.

Then I let go of her and stepped back and said, "Tomorrow noon. I'll meet you here." And with that I wheeled my horse and lit out for the ranch.

Ever feel so good it looks as if the whole world is your big apple? That was the way I felt. I had all I ever wanted. Grass, water, cattle, and a home and wife of my own.

The trail back to the Two Bar swung around a huge mesa and opened out on a wide desert flat, and far beyond it I could see the suggestion of the stones and pinnacles of badlands beyond Dry Mesa. A rabbit burst from the brush and sprinted off across the sage, and then the road dipped down into a hollow. There in the middle of the road was Bodie Miller.

He was standing with his hands on his hips, laughing, and there was a devil in his eyes. Off to one side of the road was Red, holding their horses and grinning too.

"Too bad!" Bodie said. "Too bad to cut down the big man just when he's ridin' highest, but I'll enjoy it."

This horse I rode was skittish and unacquainted with me. I'd no idea how he'd stand for shooting, and I wanted to be on the ground. Suddenly, I slapped spurs to that gelding, and when the startled animal lunged toward the gunman I went off the other side. Hitting the ground running I spun on one heel and saw Bodie's hands blur as they dove for their guns, and then I felt my own gun buck in my hand. Our bullets crossed each other, but mine was a fraction the fastest despite that instant of hesitation when I made sure it would count.

His slug ripped a furrow across my shoulder that stung like a thousand needles, but my own bullet caught him in the chest and he staggered back, his eyes wide and agonized. Then I started forward, and suddenly the devil was up in me. I was mad, mad as I had never been before. I opened up with both guns. "What's the matter?" I was yelling. "Don't you like it, gunslick? You asked for it. Now come and get it! Fast, are you? Why you cheap, two-bit gunman, I'll—"

But he was finished. He stood there, a slighter man than I was, with blood turning his shirtfront crimson, and with his mouth ripped by another bullet. He was white as death. Even his lips were gray, and against that whiteness was the splash of blood. In his eyes now there was another look. The killing lust was gone, and in its place was an awful terror, for Bodie Miller had killed, and enjoyed it with a kind of sadistic bitterness that was in him—but now he knew he was being killed, and the horror of death was surging through him.

"Now you know how they felt, Bodie," I said bitterly. "It's an ugly thing to die with a slug in you because some punk wants to prove he's tough. And you aren't tough, Bodie, just mean."

He stared at me, but he didn't say anything. He was gone, and I could see it. Something kept him upright, standing in that white-hot sun, staring at me, the last face he would ever look up.

"You asked for it. Bodie, but I'm sorry for it. Why didn't you stay to punching cows?"

Bodie backed up another step, and his gun slid from his fingers. He tried to speak, and then his knees buckled and he went down. Standing over him, I looked at Red.

"I'm ridin'," Red said huskily. "Just give me a chance." He swung into the saddle and then looked down at Bodie. "He wasn't so tough, was he?"

"Nobody is," I told him. "Nobody's tough with a slug in his belly."

He rode off, and I stood there in the trail with Bodie dead at my feet. Slowly, I holstered my gun and then led my horse off the trail to the shade where Bodie's horse still stood.

Lying there in the dusty trail, Bodie Miller no longer looked mean or even tough. He looked like a kid that had tackled a job that was too big for him.

There was a small gully off the trail. It looked like a grave, and I used it that way. Rolling him into it, I shoved the banks in on top of him and then piled on some stones. Then I made a cross for him and wrote his name on it, and the words: HE PLAYED OUT HIS HAND. Then I hung his guns on the cross and his hat.

It was not much of an end for a man, not any way you looked at it, but I wanted no more reputation as a killer—mine had already grown too big.

Maybe Red would tell the story, and maybe in time somebody would see the grave. But if Red's story was told it would be somewhere far away and long after, and that suited me.

A stinging in my shoulder reminded me of my own wound, but when I opened my shirt and checked my shoulder I found it a mere scratch.

Ahead of me the serrated ridges of the wild lands were stark and lonely along the sky, and the sun behind me was picking out the very tips of the peaks to touch them with gold. Somehow the afternoon was gone, and now I was riding home to my own ranch, and tomorrow was my wedding day.

SHOWDOWN ON THE HOGBACK

No man can be understood except against the background of his own time. The characters in "Showdown on the Hogback" lived in a time and place when workdays were long, living conditions were harsh, and the work itself was brutally hard. Yet they expected nothing more. At least, they had fresh air.

Conditions in eastern cities were worse in many respects. Trade unions either did not exist or were fighting for acceptance, and sweatshop conditions prevailed everywhere. Sanitary conditions were just as primitive as in the West, only with less clean air and sunlight.

The western man grew up fighting to protect the land he claimed and the cattle he drove. There was no policeman to call; he learned not to call for help because there was nobody to listen. He saddled his own broncs, and he fought his own battles.

Showdown on
the Hogback

I

Everything was quiet in Mustang. Three whole days had
passed without a killing. The townfolk, knowing their community, were not fooled, but had long since resigned themselves to the inevitable. They would, in fact, be relieved
when the situation was back to normal, with a killing every
day, or more on hot days. When there had been no killing for
several days, pressure mounted because no one knew who
would be next.

Moreover, with Clay Allison, who had killed thirty men,
playing poker over at the Morrison House, and Black Jack
Ketchum, who richly deserved the hanging he was soon to
get, sleeping off a drunk at the St. James, trouble could be
expected.

The walk before the St. James was cool at this hour, and
Captain Tom Kedrick, a stranger in town, sat in a well-
polished chair and studied the street with interested eyes.

He was a tall young man with rusty brown hair and
green eyes, quiet mannered and quick to smile. Women
never failed to look twice, and when their eyes met his their
hearts pounded, a fact of which Tom Kedrick was totally
unaware. He knew women seemed to like him, but it never
failed to leave him mildly astonished when they liked him
very much, which they often did.

The street he watched was crowded with buckboards,
freight wagons, a newly arrived stage, and one about to
depart. All the hitchrails were lined with saddled horses
wearing a variety of brands.

Kedrick was suddenly aware that a young man stood
beside him, and he glanced up. The fellow was scarcely more
than a boy and he had soft brown eyes and hair that needed

cutting. "Captain Kedrick?" he inquired. "John Gunter sent
me. I'm Dornie Shaw."

"Oh, yes!" Kedrick got to his feet smiling and thrust out
his hand. "Nice to know you, Shaw. Are you working for
Gunter?"

Shaw's long brown eyes were faintly ironic. "With him,"
he corrected. "I work for no man."

"I see."

Kedrick did not see at all, but he was prepared to wait
and find out. There was something oddly disturbing about
this young man, something that had Kedrick on edge and
queerly alert. "Where's Gunter now?"

"Down the street. He asked me to check an' see if you
were here an', if you were, to ask you to stick around close to
the hotel. He'll be along soon."

"All right. Sit down, why don't you?"

Shaw glanced briefly at the chairs. "I'll stand. I never sit in
no chair with arms on them. Apt to get in the way."

"In the way?" Kedrick glanced up, and then his eyes fell
to the two guns Shaw wore, their butts hanging wide. "Oh,
yes! I see." He nodded at the guns. "The town marshal
doesn't object?"

Dornie Shaw looked at him, smiling slowly. "Not to me,
he don't. Wouldn't do him no good if he did.

"Anyway," he added after a minute, "not in Mustang.
Too many hard cases. I never seen a marshal could make it
stick in this town."

Kedrick smiled. "Hickok? Earp? Masterson?"

"Maybe." Dornis Shaw was openly skeptical. "But I
doubt it. Allison's here. So's Ketchum. Billy the Kid's been
around, and some of that crowd. A marshal in this town
would have to be mighty fast an' prove it every day."

"Maybe you're right." He studied Shaw surreptitiously.
What was it about him that was so disturbing? Not the two
guns, for he had seen many men who wore guns, had been
reared among them, in fact. No, it was something else, some
quality he could not define, but it was a sort of lurking
menace, an odd feeling with such a calm-eyed young man.

"We've got some good men," Shaw volunteered, after a
minute. "Picked up a couple today. Laredo Shad's goin' to be
one of the best, I'm thinkin'. He's a tough hand an' gun wise
as all get out. Three more come in today. Fessenden, Poinsett,
an' Goff."

*   *   *

Obviously, from the manner in which he spoke, the names meant much to Shaw, but they meant exactly nothing to Kedrick. Fessenden seemed to strike some sort of a responsive note, but he could not put a finger on it. His eyes strayed down the street, studying the crowd. "You think they'll really fight?" he asked, studying the street. "Are there enough of them?"

"That bunch?" Shaw's voice was dry. "They'll fight, all right. You got some tough boys in that outfit. Injun scrappers an' such like. They won't scare worth a durn." He glanced curiously at Kedrick. "Gunter says you're a fighter."

Was that doubt in Shaw's voice? Kedrick smiled. And then shrugged. "I get along. I was in the Army, if that means anything."

"Been West before?"

"Sure! I was born in California, just before the rush. When the war broke out I was sixteen, but I went in with a bunch from Nevada. Stayed in a couple of years after the war, fighting Apaches!"

Shaw nodded, as if satisfied. "Gunter thinks well of you, but he's only one of them an' not the most important one."

A short, thickset man with a square-cut beard looking enough like General Grant to be his twin was pushing through the crowd toward them. He even smoked a thick black cigar.

The man walking beside him was as tall as Kedrick, who stood an easy inch above six feet. He had a sharply cut face and his eyes were cold, but they were the eyes of a man born to command, a man who could be utterly ruthless. That would be Colonel Loren Keith. That meant there was one, yet, whom he must meet—the man Burwick. The three were partners, and of the three, only Burwick was from the area.

Gunter smiled quickly, his lips parting over clenched white teeth that gripped his cigar. He thrust out his hand. "Good to see you, Kedrick! Colonel, this is our man! If there ever was a man born to ramrod this thing through, this is the one! I told you of that drive he made for Patterson! Took those cattle through without losing a head, rustlers an' Commanches be danged!"

Keith nodded, his cold eyes taking in Kedrick at a glance. "Captain—that was an Army title, Kedrick?"

"Army. The war between the states."

"I see. There was a Thomas Kedrick who was a sergeant in the fighting against the Apaches."

"That was me. All of us went down some in rank after the troops were discharged."

"How much time in the war?" Keith's eyes still studied him.

"Four years, and two campaigning in the Southwest."

"Not bad. You should know what to expect in a fight." His eyes went to Kedrick's, faintly supercilious. "I have twelve years, myself. Regular Army."

Kedrick found that Keith's attitude irritated him. He had meant to say nothing about it, but suddenly he was speaking. "My American Army experience, Colonel, was only part of mine. I was with Bazaine, at the defense of Metz, in the Franco-Prussian War. I escaped and was with MacMahon at the Battle of Sedan."

Keith's eyes sharpened and his lips thinned. Kedrick could feel the sharp dislike rising in the man. Keith was defiantly possessed of a strong superiority complex.

"Is that all?" he asked coolly.

"Why, no. Since you ask, it was not. I was with Wolseley in the second Ashanti war in Africa. And I was in the two-year campaign against the Tungans of northern Tien Shan—with the rank of general."

"You seem to get around a good bit," Keith said dryly. "A genuine mercenary!"

Kedrick smiled, undisturbed. "If you like. That's what you want here, isn't it? Men who can fight? Isn't it customary for some men to hire others to do their fighting for them?"

Colonel Keith's face flamed and then went white, but before he could speak, a big, square-faced man thrust himself through the crowd and stopped to face them. "You, is it, Gunter? Well, I've heard tell the reason why you're here, an' if you expect to take from hardworkin' men the land they've slaved for, you better come a-shootin'!"

Before anyone could speak, Dornie slid between Keith and Gunter and fronted the man. "You lookin' for trouble? You want to start your shootin' now?"

His voice was low, almost a purr, but Kedrick was startled by the shocked expression on the man's face. He drew back, holding his hands wide. "I wasn't bracin' you, Dornie! Didn't even know you was around!"

"Then get out!" Shaw snarled, passion suddenly breaking through his calmness—passion and something else, something Kedrick spotted with a shock—the driving urge to kill!

"Get out!" Shaw repeated. "An' if you want to live, keep goin'!"

Stumblingly, the man turned and ducked into the hastily assembled crowd, and Tom Kedrick, scanning their faces, found hard indifference there, or hatred. In no face did he see warmth or friendly feeling. He frowned thoughtfully and then turned away.

Gunter caught his arm, eager to take advantage of the break the interruption had made to bring peace between the two. "You see what we're up against?" he began. "Now that was Peters. He's harmless, but there's others would have drawn, and drawn fast! They won't be all like that! Let's go meet Burwick!"

Kedrick fell in beside Gunter, who carefully interposed himself between the two men. Once, Tom glanced back. What had become of Dornie Shaw he did not know, but he did know his second in command, which job was Shaw's, was a killer. He knew the type from of old.

Yet he was disturbed more than he cared to admit by the man who had braced them. Peters had the look of an honest man, even if not an intelligent one. Of course, there might be honest men among them, if they were men of Peters' stripe. He was always a follower, and he might follow where the wrong men led.

Certainly, if this land was going to Gunter, Keith, and Burwick through a government bill there could be nothing wrong with it. If the government sold the land to them, squatters had no rights there. Still, if there were many like Peters, the job was not going to be all he had expected.

Gunter stopped before a square stone house set back from the street. "This here's headquarters," he said. "We hole up here when in town. Come on in."

A wide veranda skirted the house, and as they stepped upon it they saw a girl in a gray skirt and white blouse sitting a few feet away with an open book in her lap. Gunter halted. "Colonel, you've met Miss Duane.

"Captain Kedrick, my niece, Consuelo Duane."

Their eyes met—and held. For a breathless moment, no voice was lifted. Tom Kedrick felt as though his muscles had gone dead, for he could not move. Her own eyes were wide, startled.

Kedrick recovered himself with a start. He bowed.

"Miss Duane!"

"Captain Kedrick." Somehow she was on her feet and moving toward him, "I hope you'll like it here!"

His eyes had not left hers, and now color was coming into her cheeks. "I shall!" he said gently. "Nothing can prevent me now."

"Don't be too sure of that, Captain!" Keith's voice was sharp and cold. "We are late for our visit. Let's be going. Your pardon, Connie. Burwick is waiting."

Kedrick glanced back as he went through the door, and the girl was still standing there, poised, motionless.

Keith's irritation was obvious, but Gunter seemed to have noticed nothing. Dornie Shaw, who had materialized from somewhere, glanced briefly at Kedrick, but said nothing at all. Coolly, he began to roll a smoke.

II

Burwick crouched behind a table. He was an incredibly fat man and incredibly dirty. A stubble of graying beard covered his jowls and his several chins, yet the eyes that measured Kedrick from beneath the almost hairless brows were sharp, malignant, and set close alongside a nose too small for his face. His shirt was open, and the edge of the collar was greasy. Rims of black marked each fingernail.

He glanced at the others and then back at Kedrick. "Sit down!" he said. "You're late! Business won't wait!" His bulbous head swung from Kedrick to Gunter. "John, this the man who'll ramrod those skunks off that land? This him?"

"Yes, that's Kedrick," Gunter said hastily. Oddly enough, he seemed almost frightened of Burwick. Keith had said nothing since they had entered the room. Quietly, he seemed to have withdrawn, stepped momentarily from the picture. It was, Kedrick was to discover, a faculty he had when Burwick was near. "He'll do the job, all right!"

Burwick turned his eyes on Kedrick. After a moment, he nodded. "Know a good deal about you, son!" His voice was almost genial. "You'll do if you don't get soft with them! We've no time to waste, you understand! They've had notice

to move! Give 'em one more notice. Then get 'em off or bury
'em! That's your business, not mine! I'll ask no questions," he
added sharply, "an' I'll see nobody else does! What happens
here is our business!"

He dismissed Kedrick from his mind and turned his
attention to Gunter. "You've ordered like I told you? Grub
for fifty men for fifty days? Once this situation is cleaned up I
want to get busy at once. The sooner we have work started,
the sooner we'll be all set. I want no backfiring on this job."

Burwick turned sharply at Tom Kedrick. "Ten days! I
give you ten days! If you need more than five, I'll be disap-
pointed! If you've not the heart for it, turn Dornie loose!
Dornie'll show 'em!" He cackled suddenly. "That's right!
Dornie'll show 'em!"

He sobered down, glanced at the papers on his desk,
and then spoke without looking up. "Kedrick, you can go.
Dornie, you run along, too!"

Kedrick hesitated and then arose. "How many of these
men are there?" he asked suddenly. "Have any of them
families?"

Gunter turned on him nervously. "I'll tell you all you
need to know, Tom. See you later!"

Kedrick shrugged and picking up his hat, walked out.
Dornie Shaw had already vanished. Yet when he reached the
veranda, Connie Duane still sat there, only now she was not
reading, merely staring over the top of her book at the dusty,
sun-swept street.

He paused, hat in hand. "Have you been in Mustang
long?"

She looked up, studying him for a long minute before
she spoke. "Why, no. Not long. Yet long enough to learn to
love and hate." She turned her eyes to the hills and then
back to him. "I love this country, Captain. Can you understand that?

"I'm a city girl, born and bred in the city, and yet when
I first saw those red rock walls, those lonely mesas, the desert, the Indian ponies—why, Captain, I fell in love! This is
my country! I could stay here forever!"

Surprised, he studied her again, more pleased than he
could easily have admitted. "That's the way I feel about it.
But you said to love and to hate. You love the country. Now
what do you hate?"

"Some of the men who infest it, Captain. Some of the

human wolves it breeds, and others, bred elsewhere, who
come to it to feed off the ones who came earlier and were
more courageous but are less knowing, less tricky."

More and more surprised, he leaned on the rail. "I don't
know if I follow you, Miss Duane. I haven't been here long,
this time, but I haven't met any of those you speak of."

She looked up at him, her eyes frank and cool. Slowly,
she closed her book, and turned toward the door. "You
haven't, Captain?" Her voice was suddenly cool. "Are you
sure? At this moment, I am wondering if you are not one of
them!" She stepped through the door and was gone.

Tom Kedrick stood for a moment, staring after her.
When he turned away it was with a puzzled frown on his
face. Now what did she mean by that? What did she know
about him that could incline her to such a view? Despite
himself, he was both irritated and disturbed. Coupled with
the anger of the man Peters, it offered a new element to his
thinking. Yet, how could Consuelo Duane, John Gunter's
niece, have the same opinion owned by Peters? No doubt
they stemmed from different sources.

Troubled, he walked on down to the street of the town
and stood there, looking around.

He had not yet changed into western clothes and wore a
flat-crowned, flat-brimmed black hat, which he would retain,
and a tailored gray suit with black western-style boots. Pausing on the corner, he slowly rolled a cigarette and lighted it.
He made a dashing, handsome figure as he stood there in his
perfectly fitted suit, his lean, bronzed face strong, intelligent,
and interesting.

Both men and women glanced at him and most of them
twice. His military erectness, broad shoulders, and cool self-
possession were enough to mark him in any crowd. His mind
had escaped his immediate problem now and was lost in the
never ending excitement of a crowded western street. Such
places held, all jammed together without rhyme or reason, all
types and manners of men.

For the west was, of all things, a melting pot. Adventur-
ers came to seek gold, new lands, and excitement. Gamblers,
women of the oldest and most active profession, thugs, gunmen, cow rustlers, horse thieves, miners, cowhands, freight-
ers, and just drifters, all crowded the street. That bearded
unshaven man in the sun-faded red wool shirt might, i

prompted, start to spout Shakespeare. The slender young man talking to the girl in the buckboard might have graduated from Oxford, and the white-faced gambler might be the scion of an old southern family.

There was no knowing in this strangest, most exciting and colorful of countries, during its most exciting time. All classes, types, and nationalities had come west, all looking for the pot of gold at the foot of any available rainbow, and most of them were more engrossed in the looking than the finding.

All men wore guns, most of them in plain sight. Few of them would hesitate to use them if need be. The man who fought with his fists was a rarity, although present.

A big man lurched from the crowd. Tom glanced at him, and their eyes met. Obviously, the man had been drinking and was hunting trouble, and as their eyes met, he stopped. Sensing trouble, other passersby stopped, too.

"So?" The big man stood wide-legged, his sleeves rolled above thick, hairy forearms. "Another one of them durn thieves! Land stealers!" He chuckled suddenly. "Well, your murderer ain't with you now to save your bacon, an' I aim to get my share of you right now! Reach!"

Kedrick's mouth was dry, but his eyes were calm. He held the cigarette in his right hand near his mouth. "Sorry, friend. I'm not packing a gun. If I were, I'd still not kill you. You're mistaken, man, about that land. My people have a rightful claim to it."

"Have they, now?" The big man came a step nearer, his hand on the butt of his gun. "The right to take from a man the land he's sweated over? To tear down his home? To run his kids out on the desert?"

Despite the fact that the man was drunk, Tom Kedrick saw beyond it a sullen and honest fury—and fear. Not fear of him, for this man was not afraid, nor would he be afraid of even Dornie Shaw. He was afraid for his family. The realization of that fact struck Kedrick and disturbed him anew. More and more he was questioning the course he had chosen.

The crowd murmured and was ugly. Obviously, their sympathies were with the big man and against Kedrick.

He heard a low murmur and then a rustling in the crowd, and suddenly, there was deathly silence. Kedrick saw the big man's face pale and heard someone whisper hoarsely, "Look out, Burt! It's Dornie Shaw!"

Kedrick was suddenly aware that Shaw had moved up

beside him. "Let me have him, Captain," Shaw's voice was low. "It's time this here was stopped."

Kedrick's voice was sharp, cold. "No! Move back, Shaw! I'll fight my own battles!"

"But you ain't got a gun!" Shaw's voice was sharper in protest.

Burt showed no desire to retreat. That the appearance of Shaw was a shock was evident, but this man was not Peters. He was going to stand his ground. His eyes, wary now, but puzzled, shifted from Shaw to Kedrick, and Tom took an easy step forward, putting himself almost within arm's length of Burt.

"Shaw's not in this, Burt," he said quietly. "I've no quarrel with you, man, but no man calls me without getting his chance. If you want what I've got, don't let the fact that I'm not armed stop you. I wanted no quarrel, but you do, so have at it!"

Suspicion was in the big man's eyes. He had seen guns come from nowhere before, especially from men dressed as this one did. He was not prepared to believe that Kedrick would face him unarmed. "You got a gun!" he snapped. "You got a hideout, you durned coyote!"

He jerked his gun from the holster, and in that instant, Tom Kedrick moved. The edge of his left hand chopped down on the rising wrist of the gun hand, and he stepped in, whipping up his right in an uppercut that packed all the power in his lean, whipcord body. The punch was fast and perfectly timed, and the crack of it on the corner of Burt's jaw was like the crack of a teamster's whip! Burt hit the walk just one split second after his gun, and hit it right on his shoulder blades.

Coolly then, Kedrick stooped and picked up the gun, an old 1851 model Navy revolver. He stood over the man, his eyes searching the crowd. Wherever he looked, there were hard, blank faces. He glanced down at Burt, and the big man was slowly sitting up, shaking his big head. He started to lift his right hand and gave a sudden gasp of pain. He stared at it and then looked up. "You broke my wrist!" he said. "It's busted! An' me with my plowin' to do!"

"Better get up," Kedrick said quietly. "You asked for it, you know."

When the man was on his feet, Kedrick calmly handed

him his six-shooter. Their eyes met over the gun and Kedrick smiled. "Take it. Drop it down in your holster an' forget it. I'm not worried. You're not the man to shoot another in the back."

Calmly, he turned his back and walked slowly away down the street. Before the St. James, he paused. His fingers trembled ever so slightly as he took out a paper and shook tobacco into it.

"That was slick." It was Dornie Shaw's soft voice. His brown eyes probed Kedrick's face curiously. "Never seen the like! Just slapped his wrist an' busted it!"

With Keith, John Gunter had come up, smiling broadly. "Saw it all, son! That'll do more good than a dozen killings! Just like Tom Smith used to do! Old Bear Creek Tom, who handled some of the toughest rannies that ever came over the trail with nothin' but his fists!"

"What would you have done if he had jerked that gun back and fired?" Keith asked.

Kedrick shrugged, wanting to forget it. "He hadn't time," he said quietly, "but there are answers to that, too!"

"Some of the boys will be up to see you tonight, Tom," Gunter advised. "I've had Dornie notify Shad, Fessenden, and some of the others. Better figure on a ride out there tomorrow. Makin' a start, anyway. Just sort of ride around with some of the boys to let 'em know we ain't foolin'."

Kedrick nodded and after a brief discussion went inside and to his room. Certainly, he reflected, the West had not changed. Things still happened fast out here.

He pulled off his coat, waistcoat, and vest, then his boots. Stripped to the waist, he sat down on the bed and dug into his valise. For a couple of minutes he dug around and then drew out two well-oiled holsters and gun belts. In the holsters were two .44 Russian pistols, Smith & Wesson guns manufactured on order for the Russian army and among the most accurate shooting pistols on the market up to that time.

Carefully, he checked the loads and then returned the guns to their holsters and put them aside. Digging around, he drew out a second pair of guns, holsters, and belts. Each of these was a Walch twelve-shot Navy pistol, caliber .36, and almost identical in size and weight to the Frontier Colt and the .44 Russian.

Rarely seen in the West and disliked by some, Kedrick

had used the guns on many occasions and found them always satisfactory. There were times when the added firepower was a big help. As for stopping power, the .36 in the hands of a good marksman lacked but little offered by the heavier .44 caliber.

Yet, there was a time and a place for everything, and these guns had an added tactical value. Carefully, he wrapped them once more and returned them to the bottom of his valise. Then he belted on the .44 Russians and digging out his Winchester, carefully cleaned, oiled, and loaded it. Then he sat down on the bed and was about to remove his guns again and stretch out, when there was a light tap at the door.

"Come in," said Kedrick, "and if you're an enemy, I'll be pleased to know you!"

The door opened and closed all in a breath. The man that stood with his back to it facing Kedrick was scarcely five feet four, yet almost as broad as he was tall. But all of it was sheer power of bone and muscle, with not an ounce of fat anywhere. His broad brown face might have been graved from stone, and the bristle of short-cropped hair above it was black as a crow's wing. The man's neck spread to broad, thick shoulders. On his right hip he packed a gun. In his hand he held a narrow-brimmed hard hat.

Kedrick leaped to his feet. "Dai!" The name was an explosion of sound. "Dai Reid! And what are you doing in this country?"

"Ah? So it's that you ask, is it? Well, it's trouble there is, boy, much of trouble! An' you that's by way of bringin' it!"

"Me?" Kedrick waved to a chair. "Tell me what you mean."

The Welshman searched his face and then seated himself, his huge palms resting on his knees. His legs were thick muscled and bowed. "It's the man Burwick you're with? An' you've the job taken to run us off the land? There is changed you are, Tom, an' for the worse!"

"You're one of them? You're on the land Burwick, Keith, and Gunter claim?"

"I am that. And a sight of work I've done on it, too. An' now the rascals would be puttin' me off. Well, they'll have a fight to move me, an' you, too, Tom Kedrick, if you're to stay one of them."

Kedrick studied the Welshman thoughtfully. All his doubts had come to a head now, for this man he knew. His own father had been Welsh and his mother Irish, and Dai Reid had been a friend to them both. Dai had come from the old country with his father, had worked beside him when he courted his mother, and although much younger than Gwilym Kedrick, had come West with him, too.

"Dai," he said slowly, "I'll admit that today I've been having doubts of all this. You see, I knew John Gunter after the war, and I took a herd of cattle over the trail for a friend of his. There was trouble that year, the Indians holding up every herd and demanding large numbers of cattle for themselves, the rustlers trying to steal whole herds, and others demanding money for passage across land they claimed. I took my herd through without paying anything but a few fat beefs for the Indians, who richly deserved them. But not what they demanded—they got what I wanted to give.

"Gunter remembered me from that and knew something of my war record, so when he approached me in New Orleans, his proposition sounded good. And this is what he told me.

"His firm, Burwick, Keith and Gunter, had filed application for the survey and purchase of all or parts of nearly three hundred sections of land. They made oath that this land was swampland or overflowed and came under the General Land Office ruling that it was land too wet for irrigation at seeding time, though later requiring irrigation, and therefore subject to sale as swamp.

"He went on to say that they had arranged to buy the land, but that a bunch of squatters were on it who refused to leave. He wanted to hire me to lead a force to see the land was cleared, and he said that as most of them were rustlers, outlaws, or renegades of one sort or another, there would be fighting, and force would be necessary."

Dai nodded. "Right he was as to the fighting, but renegades, no. Well," he smiled grimly past his pipe, "I'd not be saying that now, but there's mighty few. There are bad apples in all barrels, one or two," he said, "but most of us be good people, with homes built and crops in.

"An did he tell you that their oath was given that the land was unoccupied? Well, given it was! And let me tell you, ninety-four sections have homes on them, some mighty poor, but homes.

"Shrewd they were with the planning. Six months the

notices must be posted, but they posted them in fine print
and where few men would read, and three months are by
before anything is noticed, and by accident only. So now they
come to force us off, to be sure the land is unoccupied and
ready. As for swamp, 'tis desert now, and always desert.
Crops can only be grown where the water is, an' little enough
of that."

Dai shook his head and knocked out his short-stemmed
pipe. "Money we've none to fight them, no lawyers among
us, although one who's as likely to help. A newspaper man,
he is. But what good without money to send him to Washington?"

The Welshman's face was gloomy. "They'll beat us, that
we know. They've money to fight us with, and tough men,
but some of them will die on the ground and pay for it with
their red blood. And those among us there are who plan to
see 'tis not only the hired gunners who die, but the high an'
mighty. You, too, lad, if among them you stay."

Kedrick was thoughtful. "Dai, this story is different from
the one I've had. I'll have to think about it, and tomorrow we
ride out to look the land over and show ourselves."

Reid looked up sharply. "Don't you be one of them, boy!
We've plans made to see no man gets off alive if we can help
it."

"Look, man!" Kedrick leaned forward. "You've got to
change that! I mean, for now. Tomorrow it's mainly a show of
force, a threat. There will be no shooting, I promise you.
We'll ride out, look around, and then ride back. If there's
shooting, your men will start it. Now you go back to them
and stop it. Let them hold off, and let me look around."

Dai Reid got slowly to his feet. "Ah, lad! 'tis good to see
you again, but under happier circumstances I wish it were!
I'd have you to the house for supper and a gam, as in the old
days! You'd like the wife I have!"

"You? Married?" Kedrick was incredulous. "I'd never
believe it!"

Dai grinned sheepishly. "Married it is, all right, and
happy, Tom." His face darkened. "Happy if I can keep my
ground. But one promise I make! If your bloody riders take
my ground, my body will be there when they ride past, and
it will be not alone, but with dead men around!"

Long after the Welshman had gone, Tom Kedrick sat
silently and studied the street beyond the window. Was this

what Consuelo Duane had meant? Whose side was she on? First, he must ride over the land and see it for himself, and then he must have another talk with Gunter. Uneasily, he looked again at the faces of the men in his mind. The cold, wolflike face of Keith, the fat, slobby face of Burwick, underlined with harsh, domineering power, and the face of Gunter, friendly, affable, but was it not a little . . . sly?

From outside came the noise of a tinny piano and a strident female voice, singing. Chips rattled, and there was the constant rustle of movement and of booted feet. Somewhere a spur jingled, and Tom Kedrick got to his feet and slipped into a shirt. When he was dressed again, with his guns belted on, he left his room and walked down the hall to the lobby.

From a room beside his, a man stepped and stared after him. It was Dornie Shaw.

III

Only the dweller in the deserts can know such mornings, such silences, drowsy with warmth and the song of the cicadas. Nowhere but in the desert shall the far miles stand out so clearly, the mesas, towers, and cliffs so boldly outlined. Nowhere will the cloud shadows island themselves upon the desert, offering their brief respite from the sun.

Six riders, their saddles creaking, six hard men, each lost in the twisted arroyos of his own thoughts, were emerging upon the broad desert. They were men who rode with guns, men who had used their guns to kill and would use them so again. Some of them were already doomed by the relentless and ruthless tide of events, and to the others their time, too, would come.

Each of them was alone, as men who live by the gun are always alone, each man a potential enemy, each shadow a danger. They rode jealously, their gestures marked by restraint, their eyes by watchfulness.

A horse blew through his nostrils, a hoof clicked on a stone, someone shifted in his saddle and sighed. These were the only sounds. Tom Kedrick rode an Appaloosa gelding, fifteen hands even, with iron-gray forequarters and starkly white hindquarters splashed with tear-shaped spots of solid black—a clean-limbed horse, strong and fast, with quick, intelligent eyes and interested ears.

When they bunched to start their ride, Laredo Shad stopped to stare at the horse, walking around it admiringly. "You're lucky, friend. That's a horse! Where'd you find him?"

"Navajo remuda. He's a Nez Perce war horse, a long ways off his reservation."

Kedrick noticed the men as they gathered and how they all sized him up carefully, noting his western garb and especially the low-hung, tied-down guns. They had seen him yesterday in the store clothes he had worn from New Orleans, but now they could size him up better, judge him with their own kind.

He was tall and straight, and of his yesterday's clothing only the black, flat-crowned hat remained, the hat and the high-heeled rider's boots. He wore a gray wool shirt now and a black silk kerchief around his neck. His jeans were black, and the two guns rode easily in position, ready for the swing of his hand.

Kedrick saw them bunch, and when they all were there, he said simply, "All right, let's go!"

They mounted up. Kedrick noted slender, wiry Dornie Shaw; the great bulk of Si Fessenden; lean, bitter Poinsett; the square, blond Lee Goff; sour-faced Clauson, the oldest of the lot; and the lean Texan, Laredo Shad. Moving out, he glanced at them. Whatever else they might be, they were fighting men. Several times Shaw glanced at his gun.

"You ain't wearin' Colts?"

"No. Forty-four Russians. They are a good gun, one of the most accurate ever built." He indicated the trail ahead with a nod. "You've been out this way before?"

"Yeah. We got quite a ride. We'll noon at a spring I know just over the North Fork. There's some deep canyons to cross and then a big peak. The Indians an' Spanish called it the Orphan. All wild country. Right beyond there we'll begin strikin' a few of 'em." He grinned a little, showing his white, even teeth. "They are scattered all over hell's half acre."

"Dornie," Goff asked suddenly, "you figure on ridin' over to the malpais this trip?"

Clauson chuckled. "Sure, he will! He should've give up long ago, but he's sure hard to whip! That girl has set her sights higher than any west-country gunslinger."

"She's shapely, at that!" Goff was openly admiring. "Right shapely, but playin' no favorites."

"Maybe they're playin' each other for what they can get," Poinsett said, wryly. "Maybe that's where he gets all the news he's tellin' Keith. He sure seems to know a sight of what's goin' around."

Dornie Shaw turned in his saddle, and his thin features had sharpened. "Shut up!" he said coldly.

The older man tightened, and his eyes blazed back with genuine hate. Yet he held his peace. It was educational to see how quickly he quieted down; for Poinsett, a hard, vicious man with no love for anybody or anything, obviously wanted no part of what Shaw could give him.

As the day drew on, Kedrick studied the men and noticed they all avoided giving offense to Shaw, even the burly Fessenden, who had killed twenty men, and was the only one of the group Kedrick had ever seen before. He wondered if Fessenden remembered him and decided he would know before the day was out.

Around the noon camp, there was less friendly banter than in a cow camp. These men were surly and touchy. Only Shad seemed to relax much, but everything came easily for him. Clauson seemed to take over the cooking job by tacit consent, and the reason was soon obvious. He was really an excellent cook.

As he ate, Tom Kedrick studied his situation with care. He had taken this job in New Orleans, for at the time he had needed money badly. Gunter had put up the cash to get him out here, and if he did back out, he would have to find a way to repay him. Yet the more he looked over this group, the more he believed that he was into something that he wanted out of, but fast.

He had fought as a soldier of fortune in several wars. War had been his profession, and he had been a skilled fighting man almost from the beginning. His father, a one-time soldier, had a love for tactics, and Tom had grown up with an interest in things military. His education had mostly come from his father and from a newspaper man who lived with them for a winter and helped to teach the boy what he could.

Kedrick had grown up with his interest in tactics and had entered the Army and fought through the war between the states. The fighting had given him a practical background to accompany his study and theory, but with all his fighting and the killing it had entailed, he had not become callous.

To run a bunch of renegades off the land seemed simple enough, and it promised action and excitement. It was a job he could do. Now he was no longer sure it was a job he wanted to do, for his talk with Dai Reid, as well as the attitude of so many of the people in Mustang, had convinced him that all was not as simple as it had first appeared. Now, before taking a final step, he wanted to survey the situation and see just whom he would be fighting, and where. At the same time he knew the men who rode with him were going to ask few questions. They would do their killing, collect their money, and ride on.

Of them all, only Shad might think as he did, and Kedrick made a mental note to talk with the Texan before the day was over, to find out where he stood and what he knew. He was inclined to agree with Shaw's original judgment, that Shad was one of the best of the lot with a gun. The man's easy way was not only natural to him. He was simply confident with that hard confidence that comes only from having measured his ability and knowing what he could do when the chips were down.

After Kedrick finished his coffee he got to his feet and strolled over to the spring, had a drink, and then arose and walked to his horse, tightening the cinch he had loosened when they stopped. The air was clear, and despite their lowered voices, he could catch most of what was said.

The first question he missed, but Fessenden's reply he heard. "Don't you fret about him. He's a scrapper from way back, Dornie. I found that out. This here ain't our first meetin'."

Even at this distance and with his horse between him and the circle of men, Kedrick could sense their attention.

"Tried to finagle him out of that Patterson herd, up in Injun territory. He didn't finagle worth a durn."

"What happened?" Goff demanded. "Any shootin'?"

"Some. I was ridin' partners with Chuck Gibbons, the Llano gunman, an' Chuck was always on the prod, sort of. One, two times I figured I might have to shoot it out with him my own self, but wasn't exactly honin' for trouble. We had too good a thing there to bust it up quarrelin'. But

Chuck, he was plumb salty, an' when Kedrick faced him an' wouldn't back down or deliver the cattle, Chuck called him."

Fessenden sipped his coffee while they waited impatiently. When they could stand the suspense no longer, Goff demanded, "Well, what happened?"

The big man shrugged. "Kedrick's here, ain't he?"

"I mean—what was the story?"

"Gibbons never cleared leather. None of us even seen Kedrick draw, but you could have put a half dollar over the two holes in Chuck's left shirt pocket."

Nobody spoke after that. Tom Kedrick took his time over the cinch, and then with his horse between them, he walked away further and circled, scouting the terrain thoughtfully.

He was too experienced a man to fail to appreciate how important is knowledge of terrain. All this country from Mustang to the territory line would become a battleground in the near future, and a man's life might depend on what he knew, so he wasted no opportunity to study the country or ask questions.

He had handled tough groups before, and he was not disturbed over the problem they presented, although in this case he knew the situation was serious. In a group they would be easier to handle than separately, for these men were individualists all and without any group loyalty. They had faith in only two things in the last analysis, six-gun skill and money. By these they lived and by these they would die.

That Fessenden had talked was pleasing, for it would settle the doubts of some of them, at least. Knowing him for a gunhand, they would more willingly accept orders from him, not because of fear, but rather because they knew him for one of their own and not some stranger brought in for command.

When they moved out, taking their time, the heat had increased. Not a thing stirred on the wide, shallow face of the desert but a far and lonely buzzard that floated high and alone over a far-off mesa. Tom Kedrick's eyes roamed the country ceaselessly, and yet from time to time his thoughts kept reverting to the girl on the veranda. Connie Duane was a beautiful girl—Gunter's niece, but apparently not approving all he did.

Why was she here? What was her connection with Keith? Kedrick sensed the animosity of Keith and welcomed it. A quiet man, Keith was slow to anger, but tough, and when pushed, a deep-seated anger arose within him in a black tide that made him a driving fury. Knowing this rage that lay dormant within him, he rode carefully, talked carefully, and held his temper and his hand.

Dornie Shaw drew up suddenly. "This here is Canyon Largo," he said, waving his hand down the rift before them. "That peak ahead an' on your right is the Orphan. Injuns won't let no white man up there, but they say there's a spring with a good flow of water on top.

"Yonder begins the country in the Burwick, Keith and Gunter buy. They don't have the land solid to the Arizona border, but they've got a big chunk of it. The center of the squatters is a town called Yellow Butte. There's maybe ten, twelve buildin's there, among 'em a store, a stable, corrals, a saloon, an' a bank."

Kedrick nodded thoughtfully. The country before him was high desert country and could under no circumstances be called swamp. In the area where he stood there was little growth, a few patches of curly mesquite grass of black grama, with prickly pear, soapweed, creosote bush, and catclaw scattered through it. In some of the washes he saw the deeper green of piñon and juniper.

They pushed on, entered the canyon, and emerged from it, heading due west. He rode warily, and once, far off on his left, he glimpsed a horseman. Later, seeing the same rider, nearer than before, he deduced they were under observation and hoped there would be no attack.

"The country where most of the squatters are is right smack dab in the middle of the range the company is after. The hombre most likely to head 'em is Bob McLennon. He's got him two right-hand men name of Pete Slagle an' Pit Laine. Now, you asked me the other day if they would fight. Them three are shinnery oak. Slagle's an oldish feller, but McLennon's in his forties an' was once a cow-town marshal. Laine, well, he's a tough one to figure, but he packs two guns an' cuts him a wide swath over there. I hear tell he had him some gun trouble up Durango way an' he didn't need no help to handle it."

From behind him Kedrick heard a low voice mutter, "Most as hard to figure as his sister!"

*   *   *

Dornie's mouth tightened. He gave no other evidence that he had heard, but the comment added a little to Kedrick's information. Obviously, Dornie Shaw had a friend in the enemy's camp, and the information with which he had been supplying Keith must come from that source. Was the girl betraying her own brother and her friends? It could be, but could Shaw come and go among them without danger? Or did he worry himself about it?

There had been no mention of Dai Reid, yet the powerful little Welshman was sure to be a figure wherever he stood, and he was definitely a man to be reckoned with.

Suddenly, a rider appeared from an arroyo not thirty yards off and walked her horse toward them. Dornie Shaw swore softly and drew up. As one man, they all stopped.

The girl was small, well made, her skin as brown as that of an Indian, her hair coal black. She had large, beautiful eyes and small hands. Her eyes flashed from Dornie to the others and then clung to Tom Kedrick, measuring him for a long minute. "Who's your friend, Dornie?" she said. "Introduce me."

Shaw's eyes were dark and hard as he turned slightly. "Captain Kedrick, I want you to meet Sue Laine."

"Captain?" She studied him anew. "Were you in the Army?"

"Yes," he said quietly. Her pinto was not the horse of the rider who had been observing them; therefore, there was another rider out there somewhere. Who was he?

"You're ridin' quite a ways from home, Sue," Shaw interrupted. "You think that's wise?"

"I can take care of myself, Dornie!" Her reply was cool, and Kedrick saw blood rise under Shaw's skin. "However, I came to warn you, or Captain Kedrick, if he is in charge. It won't be safe to ride any further. McLennon called a meeting this morning, and they voted to open fire on any party of surveyors or strange riders they see. From now on, this country is closed. A rider is going to Mustang tonight with the news."

"There she is," Goff said dryly. "They are sure enough askin' for it! What if we ride on anyway?"

Sue glanced at him. "Then there will be fighting," she said quietly.

"Well," Poinsett said impatiently, "what are we talkin'

for? We come here to fight, didn't we? Let's ride on an' see how much battle they got in them."

Tom Kedrick studied the girl thoughtfully. She was pretty, all right, very pretty. She lacked the quiet beauty of Connie Duane, but she did have beauty. "Do they have scouts out?" he asked.

She glanced at him. "Not yet, but they will have." She smiled. "If they had, I'd never have dared ride to warn you."

"Whose side are you on, Miss Laine?" Kedrick asked.

Dornie's head came around sharply, and his eyes blazed. Before he could speak, Sue Laine answered for herself. "That decision I make for myself. My brother does not make it for me, nor any one of them. They are fools! To fight over this desert!" Contemptuously, she waved a hand at it. "There's no more than a hare living on it, anyway! If they lose, maybe we can leave this country!"

She swung her horse abruptly. "Well, you've had your warning. Now I'll go back."

"I'll be ridin' your way," Shaw interposed.

Her eyes swung back to him. "Don't bother!" Then she turned her attention deliberately to Kedrick and measured him again with her cool eyes, a hint of a smile in them now. "If anybody comes, let Captain Kedrick come. They don't know him!"

Somebody in the group chuckled, and Dornie Shaw swung his horse, his face white as death. His teeth were bared, his right head poised. "Who laughed?" he said, his voice almost trembling.

"Miss Laine," Kedrick said quietly, "I think Dornie Shaw could make the trip better than I. He knows the country."

Shaw's eyes glittered. "I asked—*who laughed?*"

Kedrick turned his head. "Forget it, Shaw." His voice was crisp. "There'll be no fighting with other men in this outfit while I'm in command!"

For an instant, Dornie Shaw held his pose. Then his eyes, suddenly opaque as a rattler's, swung toward Kedrick. "You're tellin' *me?*" Incredulity mixed with sarcasm.

Tom Kedrick knew danger when he saw it, but he only nodded. "You or anybody, Dornie. We have a job to do. You've hired on for that job as much as any man here. If we begin to fight among ourselves we'll get nothing done, and right now we can't afford to lose a good man.

"I scarcely think," he added, "that either Keith or Burwick would like the idea of a killing among their own men."

Shaw's eyes held Kedrick's, and for as instant there was no sound. A cicada hummed in the brush, and Sue Laine's horse stamped at a fly. Tom Kedrick knew in that instant that Dornie Shaw hated him, and he had an idea that this was the first time Shaw had ever been thwarted in any purpose he held.

Then Shaw's right hand slowly lowered. "You got me on that one, Captain," his voice was empty, dry. "I reckon this is too soon to start shootin'—an' old man Burwick is right touchy."

Sue Laine glanced again at Kedrick, genuine surprise and not a little respect in her eyes. "I'll be going. Watch yourselves!"

Before her horse could more than start, Kedrick asked, "Miss Laine, which of your outfit rides a long-legged grula?"

She turned on him, her face pale as death. "A—a grulla?"

"Yes," he said. "Such a rider has been watching us most of the morning, and such a rider is not over a half mile away now. Also," he added, "he has a field glass!"

Fessenden turned with an oath, and Poinsett glared around. Only Shaw spoke. His voice was strained and queer. "A grulla? Here?"

He refused to say more, but Kedrick studied him, puzzled by the remark. It was almost as if Shaw knew a grulla horse, but had not expected it to be seen here. The same might be true of Sue Laine, obviously upset by his comment. Long after they rode on, turning back toward the spring on the North Fork, Kedrick puzzled over it. This was an entirely new element that might mean anything or nothing.

There was little talking on the way back. Poinsett was obviously irritated that they had not ridden on in, yet he seemed content enough to settle down into another camp.

IV

Dornie Shaw was silent, saying nothing at all. Only when Tom Kedrick arose after supper and began to saddle his horse did he look up. Kedrick glanced at him. "Shaw, I'm ridin' to Yellow Butte. I'm going to look that setup over at first hand. I don't want trouble an' I'm not huntin' any, but I want to know what we're tacklin'."

Shaw was standing, staring after him, when he rode off. He rode swiftly, pushing due west at a good pace to take advantage of the remaining light. He had more than one reason for the ride. He wanted to study the town and the terrain, but also he wanted to see what the people were like. Were they family men? Or were they outlaws? He had seen little thus far that tended to prove the outlaw theory.

The town of Yellow Butte lay huddled at the base of the long, oval-shaped mesa from which it took its name. There, on a bit of flat land, the stone and frame buildings of the town had gathered together. Most of them backed against the higher land behind them and faced toward the arroyo. Only three buildings and the corrals were on the arroyo side, but one thing was obvious. The town had never been planned for defense.

A rifleman or two on top of Yellow Butte could cover any movement in the village, and the town was exposed to fire from both the high ground behind the town and the bed of the arroyo, where there was shelter under its banks. The Butte itself was scarcely one hundred and fifty feet higher than the town and looked right down the wide street before the buildings.

Obviously, however, some move had been made toward defense, or was in the process of being made, for there were some piles of earth, plainly from recent digging, near several of the buildings. He studied them, puzzled over their origin and cause. Finally, he gave up and scouted the area.

He glanced at the butte thoughtfully. Had they thought of putting their own riflemen up there? It would seem the obvious thing, yet more than one competent commander had forgotten the obvious at some time during his career, and it might also be true of these men. The top of the butte not only commanded the town, but most of the country around. It was the highest point within several miles.

That could come later. Now Kedrick turned his palouse down the hill toward the town, riding in the open, his right hand hanging free at his side. Yet, if he was seen, nothing was done to disturb him. How would it have been if there were more than one rider?

He swung down before the Butte Saloon and tied his horse at the rail. The animal was weary, he knew, and in no shape for a long ride, but he had made his own plans, and they did not require such a ride.

The street was empty, so he stepped up on the walk and pushed through the swinging doors into the bright lights of the interior. A man sitting alone at a table saw him, scowled and started to speak, and then went on with his solitaire. Tom Kedrick crossed to the bar. "Rye," he said quietly.

The bartender nodded and without looking up, poured the drink. It was not until Kedrick dropped his coin on the bar that he looked up. Instantly, his face stiffened. "Who're you?" he demanded. "I never saw you before!"

Kedrick was aware that men had closed in on both sides of him, both of them strangers. One was a sharp-looking, oldish man, the other an obviously belligerent redhead. "Pour a drink for my friends, too," he said, and then he turned slowly, so they would not mistake his intentions, until his back was to the bar. Carefully, he surveyed the room.

There were a dozen men here, and all eyes were on him. "I'm buying," he said quietly. "Will you gentlemen join me?"

Nobody moved, and he shrugged. He turned back to the bar. His drink was gone.

Slowly, he lifted his eyes to the bartender. "I bought a drink," he said quietly.

The man stared back at him, his eyes hard. "Never noticed it," he said.

"I bought a drink and paid my money, and I want my drink."

All was still. The men on either side of him leaned on the bar, ignoring him.

"I'm a patient man," he persisted. "I bought a drink, an' I want it—now."

"Mister," the bartender thrust his wide face across the bar, "we don't serve drinks to your kind here. Now get out before we throw you out!"

Kedrick's forearms were resting on the edge of the bar, and what happened was done so swiftly that neither man beside him had a chance to move.

Tom Kedrick's right hand shot out and grabbed the bartender by the shirt collar under his chin. Then he turned swiftly, back to the bar, and heaved! The bartender came over the bar as if greased and hit the floor with a crash.

Instantly, Kedrick spun away from the two men beside him
and stood facing the room, gun in hand.

Men had started to their feet, and several had moved
toward him. Now they froze where they were. The .44 Russian had appeared as if materialized from thin air.

"Gentlemen," Kedrick said quietly, "I did not come here
hunting trouble. I have been hired for a job, as all of you, at
some time or another, have been hired for a job. I came to
see if you were the manner of men you have been represented as being. Evidently your bartender is hard of hearing
or lacking in true hospitality. I ordered a drink.

"You," Kedrick gestured at the man playing solitaire,
"look like a man of judgment. You pour my drink and put it
on the end of the bar nearest me. Then," his eyes held the
room, "pour each of these gentlemen a drink." With his left
hand he extracted a gold eagle from his pocket slapped it on
the bar. "That pays."

He took another step back, and then coolly, he holstered
his gun. Eyes studied him, but nobody moved. The redhead
did not like it. He had an urge to show how tough he was,
and Kedrick could see it building. "You!" Kedrick asked
quickly. "Are you married? Children?"

The redhead stared at him, and then said, his voice surly.
"Yeah, I'm married, an' I got two kids. What's it to you?"

"I told you," Kedrick replied evenly, "I came to see
what manner of men you are."

The man who was pouring the drinks looked up. "I'll
answer your questions. I'm Pete Slagle."

"I've heard of you."

A slight smile came to Slagle's mouth. "Yeah," he said,
"an' I've heard of you."

Nobody moved or spoke while Slagle calmly poured the
drinks. Then he straightened and glanced around the room.
"Men," he said, "I reckon there's no use goin' off half cocked
an' gettin' somebody killed. Let's give this man a chance to
speak his piece. We sure don't have to buy what he wants to
sell us if we don't like his argument."

"Thanks, Slagle." Kedrick studied the room. Two of the
faces seemed hard, unrelenting. Another was genuinely interested, but at the door in the rear, a man loitered who had
shifty eyes and a sour face. He could have been, in disposition at least, a twin brother to the former outlaw Clauson.

"The land around here," Kedrick said quietly, "is about to be purchased from the government by the firm who have employed me. The firm of Burwick, Keith and Gunter. In New Orleans, where I was hired, I was told that there were squatters on the land, a bunch of outlaws, renegades, and wasters, and that they would resist being put off and would aim to keep the badlands for themselves. My job was to clean them out, to clear the land for the company. I have come here for that purpose."

There was a low murmur from the back of the room. Kedrick took time to toss off his drink and then calmly began to roll a smoke. To his right, the door opened and two men came in. One of these was as tall as himself with coal black hair turning gray at the temples. His eyes were gray and cold, his face firmly cut. He glanced sharply around the room and then at Kedrick.

"Captain Tom Kedrick, Bob," Slagle said quietly, "speakin' his piece. He's just explained that we've been represented as a bunch of renegades."

"That sounds like Burwick," McLennon said. "Get on with it, Kedrick."

"I've little to say but this. Naturally, like any good fighting man, I wanted to look over the terrain. Moreover, since arriving in Mustang certain rumors and hints have reached me that the picture is not one-sided. I have come out here to look you over, to see exactly what sort of people you are and if you are the outlaws and wasters you have been represented to be. Also, I would like to have a statement from you."

Red's face was ugly. "We got nothin' to say to you, Kedrick," he said harshly, "nothin' at all! Just you come down here with your killers an' see how many get away alive!"

"Wait a minute, Red!" Slagle interrupted. "Let Bob have his say."

"Aw, why bother?" Red said roughly. "The man is scared, or he'd never have come huntin' information!"

Kedrick's eyes held Red's thoughtfully, and he said slowly, "No, Red, I'm not scared. If I decide the company is right and you are to be run off, that is exactly what I'll do. If the men I have are not enough, I'll get more. I'm used to war, Red, I've been at it all my life, and I know how to win. I'm not here because I'm scared. I have come simply because I make a pass at being a just man. If you have a just claim to your places here and are not as represented, I'll step out of this.

"Naturally," he added, "I can't speak for the others, but I will advise them as to my conclusions."

"Fair enough," McLennon agreed. "All right, I'll state our case. This land is government land like all of it. The Navajos an' Utes claim some of it, an' some of us have dickered with them for land. We've moved in an' settled on this land. Four or five of us have been here upward of ten years. Most of us have been here more than three.

"We've barns built, springs cleaned out, and some fences built. We've stocked some land and lived through a few bad summers and worse winters. Some of us have wives, an' some of us children. We're makin' homes here. The company is tryin' to gyp us.

"The law says we were to have six months' notice. That is, it was to be posted six months before the sale by the government to the company. This land, as we understand it, is supposed to be unoccupied. Well, it ain't. We live on it. Moreover, that notice was posted five months ago, stuck around in out-of-the-way places, in print so fine a man can scarcely read it without a magnifyin' glass.

"A month ago one of the boys read it, but it took him a few days to sort the meanin' out of the legal phrasin', an' then he hightailed it to me. We ain't got the money to send a man to the government. So all we can do is fight. That's what we figure on. If the company runs us off, which I don't figure you or nobody can do, they'll buy ever' inch of it with their blood, believe me."

A murmur of approbation went through the room, and Kedrick scanned their faces thoughtfully. Dornie Shaw had judged these men correctly. They would fight. Moreover, with men like McLennon and Slagle to lead them, they would be hard to handle.

Legally, the company seemed to be in the better position. Also, the squatters were bucking a stacked deck. From here, it would take a man all of two weeks, and possibly three, to even get to Washington, let alone cut through all the government red tape to get to the men who could block the sale—if it could be blocked.

"This here's a speculation on their part," McLennon stated. "There's rumors this here land is goin' into an Injun reservation, an' if it does, that means they'll stick the government a nice price for the land."

"Or you will," Kedrick replied. "Looks like there's two sides to this question, McLennon. The company has an argument. If the federal government does make this a reservation, you'll have to move, anyway."

"We'll face that when it comes," Slagle said. "Right now we're buckin' the company. Our folks aren't speculators. We aren't gunmen, either."

Another man had entered the room, and Kedrick spotted him instantly. It was Burt, the big man he had whipped in the street fight. The man stopped by the wall and surveyed the room.

"None of you?" Kedrick asked gentle. "I have heard some stories about Pit Laine."

"Laine's a good man!" Red burst out heatedly. "He'll do to ride any river with!"

Neither McLennon nor Slagle spoke, and the latter shifted his feet uneasily. Evidently, there was a difference of opinion here. He made a note to check on Laine, to find out more about him.

"Well," he said finally, "I reckon I'll study on it a little. In the meantime, let's keep the peace. I'll keep my men off if you will do likewise."

"We aren't huntin' trouble," McLennon said. "As long as there's no shootin' at us, an' as long as the company men stay off our land, there'll be no trouble from us."

"Fact is," Slagle said, "we sent Roberts ridin' in with a message to Burwick to that effect. We ain't huntin' for no trouble."

Kedrick turned toward the door, but the bartender's voice stopped him. "You forgot your change," he said dryly.

Kedrick glanced at him, grinned, and then picked it up. "Be seein' you," he said, and stepped to the door. At that instant, the door burst open and a man staggered into the room, his arm about another man, whom he dropped to the floor. "Roberts!" the man said. "He's been murdered!"

All eyes stared at the man on the floor. That he had been shot many times was obvious. He had also been ridden over, for his body was torn and beaten by the hoofs of running horses. Tom Kedrick felt his stomach turn over. Slick with pity and shock, he lifted his eyes.

He looked up into a circle of accusation. McLennon,

shocked and unbelieving. Slagle, horrified. Red and the others, crowding closer. "Him!" Red pointed a finger that trembled with anger. "While he stands an' talks to us, his outfit murders Bob!"

"Get him!" somebody yelled. "Get him! I got a rope!"

Kedrick was standing at the door, and he knew there was no reasoning with these men. Later, they might think, and reason that he might have known nothing about the killing of Roberts. Now, they would not listen. As the man yelled, he hurled himself through the swinging doors and jerking loose his reins, hit the saddle of the palouse. The startled horse swung and lined out, not down the street, but between the buildings.

Behind him, men shouted and cursed. A shot rang out, and he heard a bullet clip past his head as he swung between the buildings. Then he knew his escape had driven him into a cul-de-sac, for he was now facing, not more than two hundred yards away, the rim around the flat where the town lay. Whether there was a break in that wall he could not guess, but he had an idea both the route upstream and that downstream of the arroyo would be covered by guards, so he swung his horse and charged into the darkness toward Yellow Butte itself.

As he had come into town, he had seemed to see a V-shaped opening near its base. Whether there was a cut through the rim there he did not know. It might only be a box canyon and a worse trap than the one into which he had run on his first break.

He slowed his pace, knowing that silence was the first necessity now, for if they heard him, he could easily be bottled up. The flat was small, and aside from crossing the arroyo, there were but two routes of escape, and both would be watched, as he had first surmised. The butte towered high above him now, nd his horse walked softly in the abysmal darkness at its foot. His safety was a matter of minutes, for they must know they had him.

The palouse was tired, he knew, for he had been going all day, and the day was warm and he was a big man. He was in no shape for a hard run against fresh horses, so the only possible escape lay in some shrewd move that would have them guessing and give him time. Yet he must be gone before daylight or he was through. By day they would comb this area and surely discover him.

Now the canyon mouth yawned before him. The walls were not high but were steep enough to allow no escape on horseback, at least.

The shouts of pursuit had stopped now, but he knew they were hard at work to find him. By now they would know from the guards on the stream that he was still on the flat and had not escaped. Those guards might be creatures of his own imagination, but knowing the men with whom he dealt, he was shrewd enough to realize that if they had not guarded the openings before his arrival, they certainly would have been sent guards out at once.

The canyon was narrow and he rode on, moving with extreme caution. Yet when he had gone but a short distance he saw the end of the canyon rising above him, black and somber.

His throat tightened and his mouth went dry. The palouse stopped and Tom Kedrick sat silent, feeling the labored breathing of the horse and knowing this was an end. He was trapped, fairly trapped!

Behind him, a light flared briefly and then went out, but there was a shout. That had been a struck match, somebody looking for tracks. And they had found them. In a few minutes more, for they would move cautiously, they would be here.

There would be no reasoning with them now. They had him. He was trapped.

V

Captain Tom Kedrick sat very still, listening. He heard some gravel stir, and a stone rattled down the canyon. Every move would count now, and he must take no unnecessary chance. He was cornered, and while he did not want to kill any of these men, he had no intention of being killed.

Carefully, he dismounted. As his boot touched the sand he tested it to make sure no sound would result when his weight settled. Haste now was his greatest danger. There might be nothing he could do, but he was a man of many experiences, and in the past there had always been a way out. Usually there was, if a man took his time and kept his head.

Standing still beside the Appaloosa, he studied the situation. His eyes had grown accustomed to the darkness under the bulk of Yellow Butte. He stared around, seeing the faint gray of sand underfoot, the black bulk of boulders and the more ragged bulk of underbrush. Leading his horse, he followed a narrow strip of gray that showed an opening between boulders.

Scarcely wide enough to admit his horse, the opening led back for some twenty feet and then widened. These were low boulders, rising scarcely above his waist, with the brush somewhat higher. The horse seemed to sense the danger, for it, too, walked quietly, almost without sound.

Literally, he was feeling his way in the dark, but that trail of sand must come from somewhere, for water had run here, and that water might spill off the cliff edge or might come through some opening. Walking steadily, he found himself going deeper into a tangle of boulders, weaving his way along that thin gray trail, into he knew not what.

Twice he paused and with his hat, worked back along the path, brushing out the tracks. He could not see how good a job he was doing, but the opening was narrow enough to give him a good chance of success. When he had pushed back into the tangle for all of ten minutes, he was brought up sharply by the cliff itself. He had found his way up the slope, through the talus, brush, and scattered boulders, to the very face of the rock.

Above him, and apparently out of reach, was a notch in the cliff, and this was probably the source of the sandy trail he had followed. Worried now, he ground hitched the palouse and moved along the cliff, feeling his way along the face, searching each crack.

To his left, he found nothing. Several times he paused to listen, but no sound came from down the canyon. If this was a box canyon, with no exit, they would probably know it and make no attempt to close it until daylight. In the darkness a man could put up quite a fight in here. Yet, because of their eagerness to avenge the dead man, they might push on.

Speaking softly to the horse, he worked his way along the face to the right, but here the pile of talus fell off sharply and he dipped into a hollow. It was cool and the air felt damp. There might even be a spring there, but he heard no water running.

Despite the coolness, he was sweating, and he paused,

mopping his face and listening. As he stood there he felt a faint breath of wind against his cheek!

He stiffened with surprise. Then with a sudden surge of hope, he turned and eagerly explored the rocky face, but could find no source for that breeze. He started on, moving more cautiously. Then the talus began to steepen under his feet, so he worked his way up the cliff alone. He carried with him his rifle.

At the top he could turn and glance back down the canyon, and the faint grayness in the distance indicated the way he had come. Here the canyon turned a bit, ending in a sort of blind alley on an angle from the true direction of the canyon. There, breaking the edge of the cliff above him, was a notch, and a steep slide led to the top!

It must have been some vague stirring of wind from up there on the rim that had touched his cheek, but the slide was steeper than a stairway and might start sliding under foot. Certainly, the rattle would give away his attempt, and it would be the matter of a few minutes only for them to circle around. As far as that went, they could even now be patrolling the rim above him.

Turning, his foot went from under him, and only a frenzied grasp at some brush kept him from falling into whatever hole he had stumbled upon. Scrambling back to good footing, he dropped a pebble and heard it strike some fifteen or twenty feet down. Working his way along the edge, he reached the foot of the slide, or nearly there, and knew what he had come upon.

Water, flooding down that slide during heavy rains, had struck a soft stratum of sand or mud at this point, and striking it with force, had gouged out a deep hole that probably ran back into the canyon itself. There was always a chance that deep within this crack there might be some hiding place, some concealment. Turning abruptly, he returned for his horse.

The slide continued steeply to the bottom of the crevasse scooped from the earth, and when they reached bottom, he glanced up. He was walking, leading the horse, but the opening of the hole in which he stood was at least fifteen feet above him and not more than seven or eight feet in width. He moved on into it, and after only a short distance it was

almost covered on top by a thick growth of brush growing on
the surface or from the sides near the top.

It was cool and still down here, and he pushed on until
he found a spot where the rush of water had made a turn and
had gouged deeply under the bank, making a sort of cave
beneath the overhang. Into this he led his horse, and here he
stopped. A little water stood at the deepest part of the turn,
and he allowed the palouse to drink. When the horse had
finished, the shallow pool was gone.

Kedrick tried the water in his canteen and then stripped
the saddle from the horse and rubbed him down with a
handful of coarse grass. Then he tied the horse and spreading
his blanket, rolled up in it. He was philosophical. He had
done what he could. If they found him now, there was
nothing to do but shoot it out where he was.

Surprisingly, he slept, and when he awakened it was the
startled breathing of the palouse that warned him. Instantly,
he was on his feet, speaking in a whisper to the horse and
resting his hand on its shoulder. Day had come, and somewhere above them, yet at some distance, there were voices!

The cave in which he stood was sandstone, no more than
fifteen feet in depth and probably eight feet high at the
opening. Kedrick moved to the mouth and studied the crevasse down which he had come. It was as he had supposed, a
deeply cut watercourse from the notch in the cliff. Evidently,
during heavy rains this roared full of water, almost to the
brim.

At the place where he now stood the brush on either side
almost met over the top, and at one point a fallen slab
bridged the crack. Glancing back the way he had come,
Kedrick saw that much of it was also covered by brush, and
there was a chance that he would not be found—a very, very
slim chance, but a chance. He could ask for no more.

He wanted to smoke, but dared not, for the smell of it
might warn them of his presence. Several times he heard
voices, some of them quite near. He glanced toward the back
of the cave and saw the gelding drinking again. Evidently
water had seaped through during the night, even though not
much. His canteen was over half full, and as yet water was
not a problem.

His rifle across his knees, he waited, from time to time
staring down the crevasse in the direction he had been going.

Where did this water flow? It must flow into the arroyo below, near town, and in that case they would certainly know of it. The men and women of the town might not know of it, but the children would without doubt. Trust them to find every cave, every niche in the rock, within miles!

Yet as the morning wore on, although he heard occasionally the sound of voices, nobody approached his place of concealment, nor did they seem aware of it. Once, he ventured out into the crevasse itself and pulled a few handfuls of grass growing on a slight mound of earth. This he fed to the horse, who ate gratefully. He dug some jerky from his own pack and chewed on it, wishing for a cup of coffee.

Later, he ventured farther down the crevasse, which seemed to dip steeply from where he was. Hearing no voices, he pushed on, coming to a point where the crevasse turned sharply again. The force of the water had hollowed out a huge cave like a bowl standing on edge, and then the water had turned and shot down an even steeper declivity into the black maw of a cavern!

Having come this far, he took a chance on leaving his horse alone and walked on down toward the cave. The entrance was high and wide, and the cave extended deep into the mountain, with several shelfs or ledges that seemed to show no signs of water. There was a pool in the bottom, and apparently the water filled a large basin, but lost itself through some cracks in the bottom of the larger hollow.

He penetrated no great distance and could find no evidence of another outlet, nor could he feel any motion of air. Yet, as he looked around him, he realized that with some food a man might well hide in this place for weeks, and unless they went to the foot of the slide and found the opening into the crevasse, this place might never be discovered.

The runoff from the cliff, then, did not go to the arroyo, but ended here, in this deep cavern.

The day wore on slowly, and twice he walked back down to the cavern to smoke, but left his horse where it was, for he had an idea he could escape later. Yet when dusk came and he had worked his way back up the crevasse slide and crawled out on the edge where he could look toward the entrance, he saw two men squatting there beside a fire, with rifles under their hands.

They believed him concealed inside and hoped to starve him out.

By this time Dornie Shaw must have returned to Mustang with news of his disappearance and probably of their murder of the messenger, for Kedrick was sure that it had been his own group who had committed the crime. It was scarcely possible that Gunter or Keith would countenance such a thing near town, where it could not fail to be seen and reported upon by unfriendly witnesses.

Returning, he studied the slide to the rim. It was barely possible that a horse might scramble up there. It would be no trick for an active man, and the palouse was probably a mountain horse. It was worth a gamble, if there was no one on top to greet him. Pulling an armful of grass from near the brush and boulders, he returned to the horse and watched it gratefully munch the rich green grass.

Connie Duane was disturbed. She had seen the messenger come to her uncle and the others and had heard their reply. Then, at almost noon the following day, Dornie Shaw and the others had come in, and they had returned without Tom Kedrick.

Why that should disturb her she could not have said, but the fact remained that it did. Since he had stepped up on the veranda she had thought of little else, remembering the set of his chin, the way he carried his shoulders, and his startled expression when he had seen her. There was something about him that was different, not only from the men around her uncle, but from any man she had known before.

Now, when despite herself she had looked forward to his return, he was missing.

John Gunter came out on the veranda, nervously biting the end from a cigar. "What happened?" she asked. "Is something wrong? Where's Captain Kedrick?"

"Wish I knew!" His voice was sharp with anxiety. "He took a ride to look over those squatters an' never came back. I don't trust Shaw, no matter how much Keith does. He's too bloodthirsty. We could get into a lot of trouble here, Connie. That's why I wanted Kedrick. He has judgment, brains."

"Perhaps he decided he wanted no part of it, Uncle. Maybe he decided your squatters were not outlaws or renegades."

Gunter glanced at her sharply. "Who has been talking to you?" he demanded.

"No one. It hasn't been necessary. I have walked around

town, and I've seen that some of these outlaws, as you call then, have wives and children, that they buy supplies and look like nice, likeable people. I don't like it, Uncle John, and I don't like to think that my money may be financing a part of it."

"Now, now! Don't bother your head over it. You may be sure that Loren and I will do everything we can for your best interests."

"Then drop this whole thing!" she pleaded. "There's no need for it. I've money enough, and I don't want money that comes from depriving others of their homes. They all have a right to live, a chance."

"Of course!" Gunter was impatient. "We've gone over all this before! But I tell you most of those people are trash, and no matter about that, they all will be put off that land, anyway. The government is going to buy out whoever has control. That will mean us, and that means we'll get a nice, juicy profit."

"From the government? Your own government, Uncle?" Connie studied him coolly. "I fail to understand the sort of man who will attempt to defraud his own government. There are people like that, I suppose, but somehow I never thought I'd find one in my own family."

"Don't be silly, child. You know nothing of business. You aren't practical."

"I suppose not. Only I seem to remember that a lot of worthwhile things don't seem practical at the moment. No," she got to her feet, "I believe I'll withdraw my investment in this deal and buy a small ranch somewhere nearby. I will have no part in it."

"You can't do that!" Gunter exploded impatiently. "Your money is already in, and there's no way of getting it out until this business is closed. Now, why don't you trust me like a good girl? You always have before!"

"Yes, I have, Uncle John, but I never believed you could be dishonest." She studied him frankly. "You aren't very happy about this yourself. You know," she persisted, "those people aren't going to move without a fight. You believed they could be frightened. Well, they can't. I've seen Bob McLennon, and he's not the kind of a man who can be frightened, even by that choice bunch of murderers Loren has gathered together."

"They aren't that. Not murderers," Gunter protested

uneasily, but refused to meet her eyes. "Reckless, yes. And temperamental. Not murderers."

"Not even Dornie Shaw? The nice-looking, boyish one who has killed a dozen men and is so cold-blooded and fiendish at times that others are afraid of him? No, Uncle, there is no way you can sidestep this. If you continue you are going to countenance murder, the killing of innocent people.

"Loren doesn't care. He has always been cold-blooded. You've wondered why I wouldn't marry him. That's why. He has the disposition of a tiger. He would kill anything or anyone that stood in his way. Even you, Uncle John."

He started and looked at her uneasily. "Why do you say that?"

"Because it's true. I know our tall and handsome man. He will allow nothing to come between him and what he desires. You've chosen some choice companions." She got to her feet. "If you hear anything of Captain Kedrick, let me know, will you?"

Gunter stood still for a long time after she left. He swore bitterly. Connie was like her mother. She always had the faculty for putting her finger on the truth, and certainly she was right about this. It was beginning to look ugly, but away down deep in his heart, he was upset less over Keith than over Burwick. That strange, fat, and dirty man was a thing of evil, of corruption. There was some evil thing within him, something cold and vicious as a striking snake.

Connie Duane was not the only person who was disturbed over the strange disappearance of Tom Kedrick.

Bob McLennon, unofficial commander of the forces for defense, sat in his rambling ranch house on the edge of Yellow Butte. Pete Slagle, Burt Williams, Dai Reid, and Pit Laine were all gathered there. With them was Sue Laine, keeping to the background. Her dark, lovely eyes were stirring from one to the other, and her ears were alert for every word.

"Blazes, man!" McLennon said irritably. "Where could he have gone? I'd have sworn he went into that box canyon. There was no other place for him to go, unless he took wings and flew! He had to go in there!"

"You looked yourself," Slagle said dryly. "Did you see him? He just ain't there, that's all! He got plumb away!"

"He probably did that," Dai Reid commented. "A quick man, that Tom Kedrick. Hand or mind, he's quick." He drew out his pipe and stoked it slowly. "You shouldn't have jumped him," he continued. "I know that lad, an' he's honest. If he said that was what he come for, it was the truth he told. I'd take my oath he'd no knowledge of the killin'!"

"I'd like to believe that," McLennon agreed. "The man impressed me. We could use an honest man on the other side, one who would temper the wind a bit or get this thing stopped."

"It won't be that Shaw who stops. He's a murderin' little devil," Slagle said. "He'll kill like a weasel in a chicken pen until there's nought left to kill."

"Kedrick fought me fair," Williams said. "I'll give him that."

"He's a fair man," Dai persisted. "Since a lad I've known him. I'd not be wrong. I'd give fifty acres of my holdin' for the chance to talk to him."

Daylight brought the first attack. It came swiftly, a tight bunch of riders who exploded from the mouth of the arroyo and hit the dusty street of Yellow Butte on a dead run, pistols firing. Then came the deep, heavy concussion of dynamite. As suddenly as they had come, they were gone. Two men sprawled in the street.

Peters, the man Shaw had faced down in the streets of Mustang, was one of them. He had taken three .44 slugs through the chest and died before he hit the ground. He had made one final effort to win back his self-respect. He had seen Dornie Shaw in the van of the charging riders and rushed into the street to get him. He had failed to get off a single shot.

The second man down was shot through the thigh and arm. He was a Swede who had just put in his second crop.

The riders had planned their attack well. They had worked near enough to the guards at the mouth of the arroyo and had come at a time when no attack was expected. The one guard awake was knocked down by a charging horse, but miraculously suffered only bruises. Two bundles of dynamite had been thrown. One had exploded against the door of the general store, smashing it off its hinges and tearing up the porch. The second had exploded harmlessly between the buildings.

The first rattle of rifle fire brought Tom Kedrick to an observation point. He had saddled his horse, hoping for a break, and instantly, he saw it. The two guards had rushed to the scene of action, and he led his horse out of the crevasse and rode at a canter to the canyon's mouth. Seeing dust over the town, he swung right and, skirting close to the butte, slipped out into the open, a free man once more!

VI

Kedrick did not return toward Mustang. He had come this far for a purpose, and he meant to achieve it. Turning west and north, he rode upstream away from Yellow Butte and Mustang. He wanted actually to see some of the homes of which so much had been said. By the way these people lived he could tell the sort they were. It was still and warm in the morning, and after the preliminary escape, he slowed his horse to a walk and studied the terrain.

Certainly, nothing could be farther from swampland, and in that at least, the company had misrepresented. Obviously, they had misrepresented in maintaining that the land was vacant, but if the squatters were a shiftless lot, Kedrick knew he would continue his job. Already he was heartily sick of the whole mess, yet he owed Gunter money, and now to pay it back was a big problem. And then, although the idea lurked almost unthought in the back of his consciousness, there was Connie Duane.

In his fast-moving and active life he had met many women, and a few had interested him, but none so much as this tall girl with the quiet, interested eyes. His desire to get back to Mustang had nothing to do with the company, but only with her. At the same time, Dornie Shaw had acted without his orders, had slain the messenger and attacked the town. Of course, they might think him dead.

Turning due north he rode through the sagebrush and catclaw toward two towering blue mountains that stood alone on this side of the rim that bordered the country to the north. On his left, he saw broken land and what was evidently a deep arroyo. He swung the Appaloosa over and headed it toward the canyon. Suddenly, he reined in.

On the ground before him were the tracks of a trotting horse, and he recognized them. They were the same tracks left by the strange rider on the grulla mustang who had scouted their approach to Yellow Butte. The tracks were fresh.

Riding more slowly, he came to the edge of the canyon and looked down at a long green meadow, fenced and watered by a small stream. At the far side, tucked in a corner, was a stone cottage, at once more attractive and better built than any other he had seen in this section. Ahead of him a trail turned down, so without delay, he rode down it and walked his horse across the meadow by a narrow lane, toward the house.

It was a pleasant place of sandstone blocks and a thatched roof. Shade trees sheltered the yard, and there were a half dozen hens pecking about. In the corral, there were several horses. His heart jumped as he saw the grulla, saddled and waiting.

He drew up in the dooryard and swung down, trailing his reins. The door opened, and a girl came out with a pan of water. She started as she saw him, and he recognized her instantly. It was Sue Laine, the girl of the trail, the girl in whom Dornie was reputed to be interested.

"You!" she gasped as she stared at him. "They told me you were dead!"

He shrugged. "Not dead, just hungry. Could you feed a man?"

She studied him a minute and then nodded. "Come in. Better tie your horse, though. He'll head for that meadow if you don't. And," her voice was dry, "you may need him. This isn't exactly friendly country."

He tied his horse near the grulla and followed her inside. "Isn't it?" he said. "Somehow I gathered you weren't exactly an enemy to the company."

"Don't say that!" she flared. "Don't ever say that!" Her voice lowered. "Not around here, anyway! If my brother ever heard!"

So Pit Laine and his sister did not see alike? That was an interesting point. He bathed his hands and face in the basin she gave him, and then combed his hair. Ruefully, he rubbed his chin. "Your brother got a razor? I hate to go unshaven."

She brought a razor without comment, and he shaved and then dried his face and hands and walked into the house. It was amazingly neat, and on a side table there were several books. Flowered curtains hung at the windows, and several copper dishes were burnished to brightness. He sat down and she brought him food, beef, eggs, and homemade bread with honey.

"Everybody's looking for you," she said. "Where have you been?"

He accepted the statement and ignored the question. "After that messenger was killed, I had to get out of Yellow Butte. I did. What's been happening?"

"Keith served a final ultimatum. We either move, or they run us out. McLennon refused."

"He did right."

She turned on him, her eyes questioning. "You think that? I thought you were their man?"

He looked up from his food and shook his head. "I don't know where I stand, but I don't go for murder or for running people out of their homes."

"They can't stay, anyway. If this land becomes a reservation they will all be moved off. We will, too. They are foolish to fight."

"At least, the government will buy their land and pay for their investment. In any event, the company has misrepresented things."

"Does it matter?" She sat down opposite him. "They will win. They have money, influence, and power. The settlers here have nothing." She looked around her bitterly. "Perhaps you think I am going against my own people, but that's not true. These aren't my people. Pit and I don't belong here and we never have, although Pit won't see it. Do you think I want to slave my life away on this desert?"

She leaned toward him. "Look, Captain Kedrick, you're one of them, not just working for them, not just a hired gunman like Dornie Shaw. You can lead the men you have to, and I wouldn't be surprised but what you could even handle Keith. You could be a big man in this country or any country.

"Why be foolish and start thinking like you are? These farmers and ranchers can do nothing for you. They can't even help themselves. The company will win, and if you are one of them, you will have a share in the winning. Don't be foolish, Captain. Stay with them, and do what you have to do."

"There are things more important than money. There's self-respect."

She stared at him, her eyes widening. "You don't really believe that. Try buying supplies with it sometime. You won't get anyplace. But that isn't the point. You'll do what you want, but I want a man who will take me out of this desert." She got up quickly and came around the table. "You could do it, Captain. You could become rich, right here."

He smiled at her. "Ambitious, aren't you?"

"Why not? Being a rancher's wife doesn't appeal to me. I want to get away from here, go someplace, be something, and enjoy life." She hesitated, studying him. "You could edge Gunter out of it, and Keith—maybe even Burwick. But the first two would be easy, and I know how."

"You do?" He looked up at her. She stood very close to him, and she was smiling down at him. She was, he had to admit, a lovely girl and an exciting one—too exciting for comfort right now, and that was a fact she understood completely. "How?"

She shook her head. "Oh, no! That I'd tell you only if you threw in with me, joined me. But this much I'll tell you—John Gunter is small potatoes. They needed money, and he had that girl's money, so they roped him in. Keith is dangerous because he is ambitious and unscrupulous, but the man to reckon with is Burwick. He will be top man when this thing is over, and you can bank on it. He has a way figured, all the time."

"You seem to know a great deal."

"I do. Men like me, and men talk. They don't have any idea how much I lead them to say or how much I remember."

"Why tell me all this?"

"Because you're the man who can do what has to be done. You could whip that bunch into line. All of them would listen to you, even Dornie Shaw—and he's suspicious of you."

"Of me? Why?"

"He saw Dai Reid come from your room. He was watching you."

So that was it? He had suspected that Shaw had something on his mind. But why had Shaw been watching? What was the little gunman thinking of? And had he reported that conference to Keith?

Kedrick finished his meal and lighted a cigarette. Ever since their first meeting in the desert, this girl had puzzled him. He was inclined to doubt any girl, reared as she must have been, could be so sincerely disdaining of all loyalty and so plainly self-seeking. And this girl was scarcely more than a child, slim, brown, and lovely, with her quick, measuring eyes and her soft lips.

Now she seemed to have selected him for the man who was to take her away from the desert. But how many others held the same idea? And then, he had no idea of leaving the desert.

"Your brother around?" he asked.

Her glance was a quick flash of alarm. "You don't want to see him or talk to him! You'd better get out of here!"

"On the contrary, Sue. I'd like to talk to Pit. I've heard about him, and I'd like to know him."

"You'd better go!" she warned. "He'll be back soon, and some of that yellow Butte crowd may be with him."

"You mean he's not here? Then whose horse is that out there—that grulla?"

Her face was strange as she shook her head. "You'll think I'm a liar, but I don't know. I never saw the rider."

His eyes searched hers. He could see nothing but sincerity there, sincerity and a little fear. "You mean that horse showed up there, tied like that? And you never saw the rider?"

"That's right. I looked out this morning, shortly after Pit left, and he was tied right there. This isn't the first time! He has been here twice before when Pit was gone, and some others have seen him, most of them women when their husbands are away. Mrs. Burt Williams said he was tied to her corral for three or four hours one day."

"But surely someone sees the rider come and mount up?"

"Never. He'll be out there like he is now—he's gone!"

Kedrick came to his feet with a start and stared out the door. Sue was right. The mouse-colored horse was gone. His own palouse stood where he had been left, but the grulla had disappeared.

Walking out into the yard, he looked around very carefully, but there was nothing in sight on the plain or the hills. The horse, and he was positive he had seen it only a few minutes before, was gone! He looked at her and saw the strained expression on her face. Then he walked out to the Appaloosa. Pinned to his saddle was a note. He took it down and glanced at it and then passed it to Sue, who had come up beside him.

STAY AWAY.

Kedrick shrugged. "Your brother do this?"

"Oh, no! I told him about the horse, and he knew no more about it than I. Besides, he didn't print that. He couldn't. Pit never learned to either read or write."

Long after he had left the Malpais Arroyo behind, he was puzzling over the strange horse. Somebody was seriously trying either to puzzle or frighten the squatters, yet it was an action unlike the company. Moreover, it must be somebody who had a lot of time to spend.

Kedrick rode north toward Blue Hill and then swung east, crossing the Old Mormon Trail and skirting the rim.

This was good grazing land. There was an abundance of rough forage here, and a good herd of cattle could fatten on this range without trouble. Moreover, the herding problem was solved in part by the rim, which provided a natural drift fence beyond which the cattle could not go. When he reached Salt Creek he turned down the creek toward the river, but then swung east again. Passing near Chimney Rock, he rode southeast until he struck the Hogback Trail. Once over that ridge, he headed due east for Mustang.

Yet as always, his eyes were alive and alert. He loved this land, harsh though it might be at some times. He loved the dim purples and blues, the far-flung mists, and, morning and night, the gray-green of the sagebrush and the rust-red of the sandstone. It was a good country and there was room for all if it were left open for settlement.

His own mind was not yet resolved. The problem of his debt to Gunter weighed heavily upon him, and there were other considerations. He wanted no trouble, and to withdraw now might mean plenty of it, particularly if he remained in the country, which he had every reason to do. He would try to talk the company out of withdrawing, but knew that would fail.

Just where, in all this, did Connie Duane actually stand? Was she involved more deeply than he believed? Or was it only what had been implied, that her uncle had invested her money in the land speculation? If such was the case, it might be difficult or impossible to get out at this stage—even if they would allow it.

Burwick puzzled him. Obviously the controlling power, he gave no evidence of where that power came from aside from some native shrewdness. Yet there might be much more to the man, and evidently was, for that Keith and Gunter deferred to him was obvious.

Purposely, Kedrick had said nothing of his hideaway near Yellow Butte when talking to Sue. That young lady already knew more than was good for her, and that spot might again become useful. It was something to know.

Mustang was asleep when he rode into the town and headed for the stable. He put his horse up and rubbed it down thoroughly, gave it a good bait of corn, and forked down some hay. Then he made his way quietly to the St. James. As he neared the hotel a tall, lean figure arose from the chair where he himself had been sitting a few days before. The build and the broad hat, the very hang of the guns, left no mistake. It was Laredo Shad.

"Captain?" The voice was low. "You all right?"

"Yes, and you?"

Shad chuckled. "Don't worry none about Shad! I stay healthy." He motioned to a chair. "You better sit down. I've been hopin' you'd show up."

"What's the talk?" Did they think I was dead or skipped the country?"

"Some of both, I reckon. Keith was fit to be tied. He wants to see you as soon as you show—no matter when."

"He'll wait. I'm tired."

Shad nodded and then lighted his cigarette, which had gone out. "You know, I ain't right sure about this business."

Kedrick nodded. "I know what you mean. I'm not the man to run folks out of their homes."

"You quittin'?"

"Not yet. I'll talk to 'em first."

"Won't do no good. They are mighty bloodthirsty. It was Poinsett shot that messenger. Dornie put him up to it. Poinsett killed him, an' then four, five of those rannies shot up the body. I don't think Fessenden shot any, an' maybe Goff didn't. You can lay your last peso I didn't shoot none. It was mighty raw, Captain, mighty raw!"

"They'll pay for it. Were you on the Yellow Butte raid?"

"Uh-huh, but I didn't shoot nobody. I'm no Bible packer, Captain, but I do figure a fightin' man shouldn't tackle folks who can't fight back, an' I ain't the man to be firin' on no women or kids."

"What are they talkin' up now? Any plans you know of?"

Shad hesitated, and then shrugged. "Reckon you'd better talk that out with them, Captain. I may know somethin', but I ain't tellin', not yet."

The Texan sat silent for a few minutes while both men smoked, and then he waved an impatient hand. "Captain, I hired on as a gunhand, an' such I am, but I didn't figure on this sort of thing. Some of those hombres on the other side of this shindig look a durned sight more human than some on our own side. I'm gettin' shut of the whole shebang."

"Uh-huh"— surprisingly, Kedrick found resolution coming to him—"I know how you feel, but my own way will be different. I think if I can't talk Gunter an' the rest of them out of that I'll change sides."

Shad nodded. "I've thought of it. I sure have."

Kedrick turned suddenly and found Dornie Shaw standing not twenty feet behind them. Slowly, he got to his feet, and Laredo Shad did likewise. Shaw's eyes avoided Kedrick. "If you figure on leavin' us, Shad, you better figure on killin' me first."

"If I have to," Laredo said quietly, "then I reckon you can die as simple as any other man. Want to try it now?"

"That's enough, Shad!" Kedrick's voice was sharp. "I've said there would be no more fighting! Not in this outfit!"

Dornie Shaw turned his head slowly and smiled at Kedrick. "Still like to give orders, do you? Maybe that'll be changed."

"Maybe." Tom Kedrick shrugged. "That will be time enough for me to stop giving orders. I'm turning in."

"Keith wants to see you."

"He can wait. I've had a rough time. There's nothing he wants won't wait."

"Shall I tell him that?"

"If you like."

Shaw smiled again. "You must carry a lot of weight where you come from Kedrick, but don't forget it ain't here. Keith is a bad man to buck. So's Burwick."

Kedrick shrugged again. "I've bucked worse. But at the

moment, I'm bucking nobody. I need sleep, and by the Lord Harry, sleep is what I'll get. Whatever Keith has on his mind can wait until daylight. I'll be up then."

Shaw started to go and then hesitated, unable to restrain his curiosity. "What happened to you? We figured you were dead or taken prisoner when you didn't come back."

For the first time Kedrick began to wonder. Had Shaw wanted the messenger killed for that very reason. Had he deliberately moved that way hoping the enraged settlers would kill Kedrick? It was most likely. "It doesn't matter," he said, passing off the remark casually. "I found a way to keep out of sight."

Shaw turned away, and when he had gone only a few steps, Tom Kedrick spoke up suddenly. "By the way, Dornie. Know anybody who rides a grulla mustang?"

Shaw stopped abruptly, but he did not turn. His whole body had seemed to stiffen. Then he started on. "No," he said gruffly, "I sure don't."

Laredo Shad stared after him. "You know, pardner, you'll either kill that hombre someday or you'll be killed."

"Uh-huh," Kedrick said quietly, "I've the same feeling."

VII

Keith was pacing the floor in the office at the gray stone building when Kedrick walked in. He stopped and turned swiftly. "Shaw tells me you came in after midnight. Why didn't you come to me according to my orders?"

"Frankly, I was tired. Furthermore," Kedrick returned Keith's look, "I'd nothing to report that wouldn't keep."

"You were hired to do a job, and you haven't done it." Keith stood with his hands on his hips. "Where've you been?"

Briefly and clearly, Kedrick explained, omitting only the visit to Laine's and the story of the hideout. "Frankly," he said, "having looked the situation over, I'd say you had small chance of driving those people off. Also, you and Gunter misrepresented things to me and the government. That land is occupied not by renegades and outlaws, but by good, solid people. You can't get away with running them off."

Keith smiled contemptuously. "Gettin' scared? You were supposed to be a fighting man! As for what we can do or can't do, let me tell you this, Kedrick! We've started to run those people off, and we'll do it! With or without you! Hiring you was Gunter's idea, anyway."

"That's right, it was." Gunter walked into the room followed by Burwick, and he glanced swiftly from Kedrick to Keith. "If you're complainin' about his going to look over that country, you can stop. I sent him."

"Did you tell him to come back scared to death? Saying we can't swing it?"

Burwick had been silent, but now he moved to the big chair behind the desk and dropped into it. He sighed heavily and wiped the back of his hand across his mouth. Then he glanced at Kedrick keenly. "What did you find out?"

"That they are determined to fight. I talked to Bob McLennon and to Slagle. There's no quit in those men. They'll fight at the drop of a hat, and to the last ditch. Right now, at this minute, they are ready for anything. Your raid killed one man, and wounded another. The dynamite blasted a door loose and blew a hole in the porch."

Burwick turned swiftly and glared at Keith. "You told me three men dead and a building destroyed! Hereafter you be sure reports to me are accurate." He swung back to Kedrick. "Go on. What happened to you? You got away?"

"I'm here."

Their eyes met and held for a long time, Burwick's stone cold and hard, examining, probing.

"What do you think of the deal?" he asked finally.

"The fight," Kedrick replied carefully, "will raise a stink clear to Washington. Remember the Lincoln County War? We'll have us another general down here, and you know how much profit you'll make out of that place then!"

Burwick nodded his huge head. "Sensible, that's sensible! Have to think our way around that. At least," he glared again at Keith and Gunter, "this man can bring in some sensible ideas and make a coherent report. You two could learn from him."

He looked up at Kedrick. "Anything else?"

"A couple of things. There's a mysterious rider out on those plains. Rides a mouse-colored horse, and he's got those folks more jittery than all your threats."

"Hah?" Burwick was uninterested. He shuffled papers on his desk. "What's this I hear about you quittin'?"

"I won't be a party to murder. These people aren't

outlaws, but good, substantial folks. I'd say buy them out or leave them alone."

"You aren't running this affair!" Keith replied coldly. "We will decide what is to be done."

"Nobody quits," Burwick said quietly, his eyes on Kedrick's, "unless I say so!"

Tom Kedrick smiled suddenly. "Then you'd better say so, because I've quit, as of now!"

"Tom!" Gunter protested. "Let's talk this over!"

"What of the money you owe the firm?" Keith demanded, unpleasantly. "You can repay that, I suppose?"

"There's no need."

They all turned at the voice. Connie Duane stood in the door. "You have money of mine in this project. When Uncle John got it from me he told me it was a real estate speculation. His other activities have been honest and practical, so I did not investigate. Now I have. I shall withdraw my money, and you can pay me less the sum advanced to Captain Kedrick. He may repay me when circumstances permit it."

All in the room were still. Gunter's face was pale, and Keith looked startled and then angry. He started to protest, but he was too slow. Burwick turned on Gunter. "You!" he snorted angrily. "You told me that was your money! You fool! What do you mean, bringing a woman into a deal like this? Well, you brought her in. Now you manage her or I shall!"

"Nobody," Connie replied, "is managing me or my affairs from now on. I'll handle them myself!" She turned to Kedrick. "I'm glad, Captain, that you've made this decision. I am sure you'll not be sorry for it."

Kedrick turned to follow her from the room, but Burwick's voice stopped him. "Captain!"

He turned. Keith's eyes were ugly, and Gunter's face was haunted by doubt and fear. "Captain Kedrick," Burwick said, "I believe we are all being too hasty. I like your caution in this matter. Your suggestion that cleaning out those people might make trouble and cause talk in Washington is probable. I had considered that, but not knowing McLennon, had considered the chance negligible.

"Slagle," he added, "I know. McLennon I do not know. Your suggestion eliminates a frontal attack. We must try some other means. Also," he added, "I believe that your presence has some claim on that of Miss Duane. Consequently, as we can brook no failure now, I have a proposition for you. How would you like to come into the firm? As a silent partner?"

Keith's face flushed angrily, but Gunter looked up, his eyes suddenly hopeful. Burwick continued. "We could give you a fifteen percent interest, which believe me, will be adequate. I believe you could keep Miss Duane in line, and with you at the helm we might straighten this whole thing out—without bloodshed."

Kedrick hesitated. The money was a temptation, for he had no desire to be indebted to Connie, yet the money alone would mean nothing. It was that last phrase that gripped his attention and made him incautious. "Without bloodshed," he repeated. "On those terms, I accept. However, let's discuss this matter a bit further."

Keith spun on his heel. "Burwick, this doesn't make sense! You know the only way we'll get those people off is by driving them off! We agreed on that before. Also, this man is not reliable. I happen to know that he has friends on the other side and has actually been in communication with them."

"So much the better." Burwick pursed his fat lips and mopped perspiration from his face. "He'll have a contact he can use then to make a deal." He chuckled. "Suppose you two run along and let me talk to Captain Kedrick?"

Hours later, Tom Kedrick paused on the street and studied it with care. Burwick had been more than reasonable, and little as he was able to trust him, yet he thought it possible that Burwick was sincere in his agreement to buy off a few of them and to try to convince others. Certainly, if the government moved in they would have to move anyway. With McLennon and Slagle out of the picture, the chances were there would be no fight, for the others lacked leadership. No fighting meant no deaths, and the settlers would come out of it with a little money at least.

He paced the street irritably, avoiding company. Burwick stank of deceit, but the man was a practical man, and he should realize that a sudden mess of killings preceding the sale of the land would create a furor that might cause them to lose out all around. At least, trouble had been avoided for the time, and even Connie was hopeful that something might be done. Tomorrow he was returning again to try to make some deal with McLennon and Slagle. A neutral messenger was leaving tonight.

"They won't come to town," Burwick had agreed, "so why not pick some intermediate point? Meet them, say, at Largo Canyon or Chimney Rock? Have your talk there, and I'll come with you. Just you and me, McLennon, and Slagle. We can talk there and maybe make peace. Ain't it worth a try?"

It was only that chance for peace that had persuaded him and helped him to persuade Connie. She had listened in silence as he explained the situation. Then she had turned to him frankly. "Captain, you don't trust them, and neither do I. Uncle John has never been this way before, and I believe somehow he has fallen under the domination of those other men. However, I think that if Burwick is willing to talk, we should at least agree. I'll stand by you in this, and we'll hope something can come of it that will prevent trouble."

Kedrick was less hopeful than he had let it appear, and now he was studying the situation from every angle. As things stood, it was a stalemate. He was confident that with McLennon and Slagle to lead them, the settlers could manage a stiff defense of their town and their homes. Certainly, they could prevent the survey being completed and prevent any use being made of their lands.

Yet there were fiery elements on both sides, and Keith did not like the turn things had taken. Colonel Loren Keith had from the beginning planned on striking fast and wiping out the opposition. It would be merely another unsolved mystery of the West. Kedrick resolved to keep an eye on the man and be prepared for anything.

He returned to the St. James and to bed. He awakened early and was surprised to see Keith mounted and riding out of town at daybreak.

With a bound he was out of bed and dressing. Whatever Keith had in mind, he meant to know. Swiftly, he descended the stairs and went to the livery stable. Mounted, he headed out of town, found Keith's tracks with ease, and followed them. Keith had turned off the trail and headed west and slightly north, but after a few miles, Kedrick lost the trail and took a wide swing to try and cut it again, but Keith had vanished somewhere in the vicinity of Largo Canyon.

Returning to the hotel, he found a message from Bob McLennon. He and Slagle would meet with Burwick and Kedrick at Chimney Rock at three in the afternoon on Wednesday. It was now Monday, and a whole day lay between. Yet during the remainder of Monday he saw nothing of Dornie Shaw, although Laredo Shad appeared a couple of times and then vanished into one of the saloons.

At midnight the door of his room opened slowly and Tom Kedrick sat up, gun in hand. It was Laredo Shad.

"Somethin's up," he said, dropping on the bed, "an' she looks mighty peculiar. Couple of hours ago Poinsett an' Goff showed up an' said they had quit. No fightin' here, so they were pullin' out for Durango. About a half hour later they mounted up an' took out."

"What's peculiar about that?" Kedrick inquired, building a smoke. "That's in line with Burwick's talk with me."

"Yeah," Shad replied dryly, "but both of them came in here with a good deal of gear. They lost their packhorses somewheres and went out only with what they could carry on the one horse, and durned little of that."

"What about Fessenden?"

"Ain't seen him."

"Any of the others gone?"

"Clauson is. At least, he ain't around in sight. I ain't seen him since morning."

That left Shaw, who had been around little himself, and Fessenden, if he was still in town. Despite himself, Kedrick was disturbed, but if Burwick's was getting rid of his warriors it was a good sign. Probably he, Tom Kedrick, was getting too suspicious. Nothing, Shad said, had been said to him about quitting. "In fact," he said dryly, "the Mixus boys pulled in this morning, an' they went right to Burwick."

"Who are they?"

"Killers. Drygulchers, mostly. Bean an' Abe Mixus. They were in that Sandoval affair. Couple of men died awful opportune in that affair, an' come to think of it, Burwick was around. Fact is, that was where I met him."

"Were you in that?"

"Uh-uh. I was in town, though, an' had me a run-in with Roy Gangle. Roy was a mighty tough ranny who'd been ramroddin' a big spread down thataway, an' when he got into the war he went bad, plumb bad. We'd had trouble over a steer, an' he braced me. He was a mite slow."

It made no sense—gunmen leaving, but others arriving. Of course, the Mixus boys could have been spoken to before the change of plans. That must be it. He suggested as much to Laredo, and the Texan nodded dubiously. "Maybe. I don't trust that hombre none. Your man Gunter is in over his head, Keith, well, he's all around bad when it comes to that, but neither of them can hold a candle to that Burwick."

Study the situation as he would, Tom Kedrick could see no answer to it, and the fact remained that they were to meet Slagle and McLennon for a peace conference. Out of that, anything might come, and he had no real cause to distrust Burwick.

Morning was bright and clear, with the sun promising a hot day. Yet it was still cool when Kedrick appeared on the street and crossed to the little restaurant where he ate in silence. He was on his second cup of coffee when Connie came in.

Her face brightened with a smile as she saw him, and she came over to his table. "You know, you're the one bright spot in this place! I'm so tired of that old stone house and seeing that dirty old man around that I can scarcely stand it. I'll be glad when this is all over."

He studied her. "What will you do then?"

"You know, I've not really thought of that. What I want to do is to get a ranch somewhere, a place with trees, grass, and some running water. It doesn't have to be a big place."

"Cattle?"

"A few, but horses are what I want. Horses like that one of yours, I think."

"Good idea. It takes less land for horses, and there's always a market for good stock." He studied the beauty of her mouth, the quietness and humor of her eyes. "Somehow I'm glad to think you're staying. It wouldn't be the same without you. Not now."

She looked at him quickly, her eyes dancing with laughter, but with the hint of a question in their depths. "Why, Tom! That sounds almost like gallantry! Like you were trying to make love to me, like all the cowboys!"

"No, Connie," he said quietly, "when I make love to you there won't be any doubt about it. You'll know, and I won't be fooling."

"Somehow I think you're right. You wouldn't be fooling."

"Over west of here," he said, "west and south, there's a great rim that stretches for miles across the country, and a splendid pine forest atop it. There's trees, water, game, and some of the finest mountain meadows a man ever saw. I know a place over there where I camped once, a good spring, some tall trees, graceful in the wind, and a long sweep of land clear to the rim's edge, and beyond it miles upon miles of rolling, sweeping range and forest."

"It sounds fascinating, like what I've been wanting ever since I came west."

He pushed back his chair. "Maybe when this is over, you'd ride over that way with me? I'd like to show it to you."

She looked up at him. "All right, Tom. We'll look at it together."

He paused, hat in hand, staring out the door. "Together," he mused. Then he glanced down at her. "You know, Connie, that's the most beautiful word in the language— together."

He walked away then, pausing to pay his check and hers and then stepping outside into the warmth of the street. A buckboard had stopped and a man was getting out of it, a man who moved warily and looked half frightened. He glanced around swiftly and then ducked through the door into the store.

VIII

Two men crossed the street suddenly. One of them was a man Kedrick had never seen before; the other was the sly-looking loafer he had seen hanging around the back door in the saloon at Yellow Butte. The loafer, a sour-faced man called Singer, was talking. They stopped, and he indicated the buckboard to the man with him. "That's him, Abe," Singer was saying. "He's one of that crowd from across the way. He's brother-in-law to McLennon."

"This is a good place to start," Abe replied shortly, low voiced. "Let's go!"

Tom Kedrick turned on his heel and followed them. As they stepped into the door, he stepped after and caught it before it slammed shut. Neither man seemed to be aware of his presence, for they were intent on the man at the counter.

"Hello, Sloan!" Singer said softly. "Meet Abe Mixus!"

The name must have meant something to Sloan, for he turned, his face gray. He held a baby's bottle, which he was in the act of buying, in his right hand. His eyes, quick and

terror stricken, went from one to the other. He was frightened, but puzzled, and he seemed to be fighting for self-
control. "You in this squabble, Singer? I figured you to be
outside of it."

Singer chuckled. "That's what I aim for folks to think."

Mixus, a lean, stooped man with yellow eyeballs and a
thin-cheeked face drew a paper from his pocket. "That's a
quitclaim deed, Sloan," he said. "You can sign it an' save
yourself trouble."

Sloan's face was gray. His eyes went to the deed and
seemed to hold there. Then, slowly, they lifted. "I can't do
that. My wife's havin' a child in the next couple of days. I
worked too hard on that place to give it up. I reckon I can't
sign."

"I say you better." Mixus's voice was cold, level. The
storekeeper had vanished, and the room was empty save for
the three and for Tom Kedrick, standing in the shadows near
some hanging jeans and slickers. "I say you better sign because you don't own that prop'ty anyhow. Want to call me a
liar?"

Sloan's face was gray, and yet resolution seemed to have
overcome his immediate fear. He was a brave man, and
Kedrick knew that whatever he said now, he would die. He
spoke first.

"No, Abe," he said softly, "I'll call you a liar!"

Mixus stiffened as if struck. He was a killer and dangerous, but he was a smart, sure-thing killer, and he had believed himself alone but for Singer. Now somebody was behind
him. He stood stock-still and then started to turn. Singer had
fallen back against the wall, his eyes staring to locate Kedrick.

"It's Kedrick!" he said. "The boss gunman!"

Mixus scowled. "What's the matter?" he said irritably.
"What yoo buttin' in for?"

"There's to be no more killing, Abe." Kedrick held his
ground. "We're havin' a peace conference tomorrow. This
killing is over."

"Got my orders," Mixus persisted. "You talk to Burwick."

There was a movement from Sloan, and he whirled on
him. "You stand still!" he barked.

"You can go, Sloan," Kedrick said. "Get in your outfit an'
head back an' tell McLennon my word is good. You'd better
stop thinking about him, Abe. You're in trouble, and I'm the
trouble."

Mixus was confused. He knew Kedrick was ramrodding the gunmen for the company, and he was puzzled. Had he been about to do the wrong thing? But no, he had—"You fool!" His confusion burst into fury. "Keith tol' me to get him!"

"Shut up!" Singer yelled. "Dang it! You—!"

Abe Mixus was a cold-blooded killer and no heavyweight mentally. Orders and counterorders had come to him, and worked up to a killing pitch he had been suddenly stopped in the middle of it and switched off into this back trail, where he floundered hopelessly. Now Singer seemed to be turning on him, and he swung toward him, his teeth bared, his face vicious.

"Don't you tell me, you white-livered coyotte!" he snarled.

One hand hung over a gun, and Singer, frightened, grabbed for his own gun. Instantly, Mixus whipped out his .44, and flame stabbed at Singer. The renegade turned on his heel. His knees slowly bucked and he slid to the floor, his head against a sack of flour, blood welling from his mouth.

Mixus stared down at him, and then slowly, he blinked and then blinked again. Awareness seemed to return to him, and his jittery nerves calmed. He stared down at Singer almost unbelieving. 'Why, I—I—killed Singer!" he said.

"That's right," Kedrick was watching him, knowing now upon what a slender thread of irritation this man's muscles were poised. "What will Keith say to that?"

Cunning came over Abe's horselike face. "Keith? What give you the idea he had anythin' to do with this?" he demanded.

Slowly, attracted by the shooting and made confident by its end, people were gathering in front of the door. The storekeeper had come into the room and stood watching, his face drawn and frightened.

Tom Kedrick took a slow step back as Abe's eyes turned toward the front of the store. Putting the slickers between them, Kedrick moved on cat feet to the opening between the counters and slid through into the living quarters and out into the alley behind the store.

Crossing the street below the crowd, he wound up in front of the St. James, pausing there. Laredo Shad materialized beside him. "What happened?" he asked swiftly.

Kedrick explained. "I don't get it," he said. "Keith may

be moving on his own but Burwick was to hold off until we had our talk—and I know Keith didn't like that. He spoke right up about it."

"Ain't Singer supposed to be a settler?" Shad asked. "Won't this serve to get 'em all riled up? Who knew that Singer was with Keith an' the company?"

"You've a point there," Kedrick said thoughtfully. "This may be the very thing that will blow the lid off."

"Both of them were mighty jumpy. It looked like they had Sloan marked because he was McLennon's relative. I sprung a surprise on them, an' Mixus just couldn't get himself located."

The crowd separated and then gathered in knots along the street to discuss the new event. Shad loitered there beside him and was standing there when Loren Keith came up. He glanced sharply at Shad and then at Kedrick. "What's happened over there?"

He kept his eyes on Kedrick as he spoke, and Kedrick shrugged. "Shooting, I guess. Not unusual for Mustang from what I hear."

"Mixus was in there," Shad commented. "Wonder if he had a hand in it?"

Keith turned and looked at Laredo, suspicion in his eyes. "Who was shot?" he inquired, his eyes going from one to the other.

"Singer, they tell me," Shad said casually. "I reckon Mixus killed him."

"Mixus? Kill Singer?" Keith shook his head. "That's preposterous!"

"Don't know why," Laredo drawled. "Mixus come here to fight, didn't he? An' ain't Singer one of them settlers?"

Colonel Keith hesitated, his sharp, hard features a picture of doubt and uncertainty. Watching him, Kedrick was amused and pleased. The storekeeper had not seen him, and it was doubtful if anyone had but Mixus, the dead man, and the now missing Sloan.

What Abe Mixus would offer as an explanation for shooting Singer, Tom couldn't conceive, but a traitor had died and the enemy was confounded. Little as it might mean in the long run, it was for the moment a good thing. The only fly in the ointment was the fact that Singer had been a squatter and that few if any knew of his tie-up with Keith and the company.

Watching the crowds in the street, Tom Kedrick began

to perceive a new element shaping itself. Public opinion was a force Burwick had not reckoned with, and the faces of the men talking in the streets were hard and bitter.

These were mostly poor men who had made their own way or were engaged in making their way, and they resented the action of the company. Few had known Singer well, and those few had little use for the man, but the issue, from their viewpoint, was not a matter of personalities, but a matter of a bunch of hardworking men against the company, an organization largely of outsiders seeking to profit from the work of local people. Furthermore, whatever Singer was, he was not a gunman, and he was a local man. Abe Mixus was a known killer, a gunman whose gun was for hire.

Tom Kedrick nodded toward the street. "Well, Colonel," he said, "you'd better start thinking about that unless you want to stretch hemp. That bunch is sore."

Keith stared at them nervously and then nodded and hurried away toward headquarters. Shad watched him go and turned toward Kedrick. "You know, we're sort of tied in with the company, an' I don't aim to hang for 'em. Let's light a shuck out of here an' stick in the hills a few days!"

"Can't. I've got to make that meeting with Burwick. But you might get out of town, anyway. Scout around and see what you can find of Goff and them—if they really left the country or not. Meet me at Chimney Rock about five tomorrow evening—make it later, about sundown."

Leaving Shad, Kedrick hurried to his room in the St. James and bundled his gear together. He carried it down to the livery stable and saddled the palouse. When that was done, staying off the main street, he headed for headquarters. Yet it was Connie Duane he wanted to see, and not Burwick or Keith.

There was no sign of any of them. Gunter was not around, and Burwick and Keith seemed to have vanished. Idling in the office, Tom heard a slight movement upstairs. He called out. Feet hurried along the floor above him, and then Connie was at the stair head. "Yes?" recognizing him, she hurried down. "Is something wrong?"

Swiftly, he explained, holding nothing back. "Nothing may come of it, although it wouldn't take much to start it, and they all know that the company's gunmen are mostly out of town. Burwick, Keith, and your uncle must have lit out."

"Uncle John hasn't been around all day. I saw him at breakfast, and then he diappeared."

"I'll look around. Do you have a gun?" He shook his head then. "Don't much think you'll need it, most of them like you around here, and you've been pretty outspoken. But stay close to your room. The lid's going to blow off."

He turned away, but she called to him, and he turned again when he reached the door. "Tom?" He seemed to see pleading in her eyes. "Be careful, Tom."

Their eyes held for a long moment, and then he nodded. "I will—if I can."

He went out and paused on the steps. Burwick and Keith might get out of the way, but whatever else Gunter might be, he was scarcely the man to leave his niece behind at a time of danger. Puzzled that he should be thus inconsistent, Kedrick paused and looked around him. The back street was bare and empty. The white powdery dust lay thickly and had sifted into the foliage of the trees and shrubs.

Kedrick hitched his guns into place and walked slowly around the house. The stable lay behind it, but it was usually filled with horses. Now it seemed empty. He strode back, his spurs jingling a little and tiny puffs of dust rising from his boots as he walked.

Once, nearly to the stable, he paused by a water trough and listened for noise from the town. It was quiet, altogether too quiet. He hesitated, worrying about Connie again, but then went on and into the wide door that gave entrance to the shadowed coolness of the stable.

The stalls were empty, all save one. He walked back, then paused. The chestnut was Gunter's horse, and his saddle lay nearby. Could he be somewhere around town? Kedrick considered that and then dismissed it. He removed his hat, wiped the band with his kerchief, then replaced it. His face was unusually thoughtful, and he walked to the far end of the stable, examining every stall as he walked back.

Nothing.

Puzzled, he stepped out into the bright glare of the sun and heard no sound anywhere. He squinted his eyes around and then saw the ramshackle old building that had done duty for a stable before the present large one had been built. He stared at it and then turned in that direction. He had taken scarcely a step when he heard a rattle of hoofs. He swung swiftly around, half crouched, his hands wide.

Then he straightened. Sue Laine slid from her horse and ran to him. "Oh, I've found you, Tom!" she cried, catching him by the arms. "Tom, don't go to that meeting tomorrow. There's going to be trouble!"

"You mean, McLennon's framed something?"

"McLennon?" For an instant she was startled. "Oh, no! Not Mac!" Her expression changed. "Come home with me, Tom. Please do! Let them have this out and get it over with! Come home with me!"

"Why all this sudden worry about me?" He was sincerely puzzled. "We've only met once, and we seem to have different ideas about things."

"Don't stand here and argue! Tom, I mustn't be seen talking to you—not by either side. Come with me and get away from here until this is all over. I've seen Dornie, and he hates you, Tom! He hates you."

"He does, does he?" He patted her arm. "Run along home now. I've things to do here."

"Oh?" Her eyes hardened a little. "Is it that woman? That Duane girl? I've heard all about her, how beautiful she is, how— how she—what kind of girl is she?"

"She's a lovely person," he said gravely. "You'd like her, Sue."

Sue stiffened. "Would I? I wonder how much you know about women, Tom? Or do you know anything about them? I could never like Connie Duane!"

She shook his arm. "Come, if you're coming. I just heard this last night, and I can't—I won't see this happen."

"What? What's going to happen?"

She stamped her foot with impatience. "Oh, you fool, you! They plan to kill you, Tom! Now, come on!"

"Not now," he said quietly, "I've got to get this fight settled first. Then maybe I'll ride your way. Now run along, I've got to look around."

Impatiently, she turned and walked to her horse. In the saddle she glanced back at him. "If you change your mind—"

"Not now," he repeated.

"Then be careful. Be careful, Tom."

He watched her go and then happened to glance toward the house. Connie Duane stood in the window, looking down at him, but as he looked up, she turned sharply away. He started for the house, but then hesitated. There was nothing

he could say now, nothing that would have any effect or do
any good at all.

He started toward the front of the house again and then
stopped. On an impulse he turned and walked swiftly back to
the little old building and caught the latch. The door was
weathered and gray. It creaked on rusty hinges and opened
rheumatically. Inside, there was the musty odor of decay.
Kedrick stood there for a minute watching the sunlight filter
through the cobwebbed window and fall in a faint square
upon the ancient straw that littered the earthen floor. Then
he stepped forward, peering around the corner of the nearest
stall.

John Gunter lay sprawled upon his face, his head pillowed upon one forearm, the back of his shirt covered with a
dark, wide stain. Kedrick knelt beside him.

Connie's uncle had been stabbed in the back. Three
powerful blows, from the look of the wounds, had been
struck downward— evidently while he sat at a desk or table.

He had been dead for several hours.

IX

Alton Burwick, for all his weight, sat his saddle easily and
rode well. His horse was a blood bay, tall and long limbed.
He walked it alongside Tom Kedrick's palouse, and from time
to time he spurred it to a trot and then eased down. On this
morning, Burwick wore an ancient gray felt hat, torn at the
flat crown, and a soiled neckerchief that concealed the greasy
shirt collar.

His shirt bulged over his belt, and he wore one gun, too
high on his hip for easy use. His whiskers seemed to have
neither grown nor been clipped. They were still a rough
stubble of dirty mixed gray. Yet he seemed unusually genial
this morning.

"Great country, Kedrick! Country for a man to live in! If
this deal goes through, you should get yourself a ranch. I aim
to."

"Not a bad idea." Kedrick rode with his right hand
dangling. "I was talking about that yesterday, with Connie
Duane."

The smile vanished from Burwick's face. "You talked to
her yesterday? What time?"

"Afternoon." Kedrick let his voice become casual, yet he was alert to the change in Burwick's voice. Had Burwick murdered Gunter? Or had it been one of the squatters? With things as they were, it would be difficult or impossible to find out. "We had a long talk. She's a fine girl."

Burwick said nothing, but his lips tightened. The red canyon walls lifted high above them, for along here they were nearly five hundred feet above the bottom of Salt Creek. There was but little farther to go, he knew, and he was puzzled by Burwick's increased watchfulness. The man might suspect treachery, but he had said nothing to imply anything of the kind.

Tom's mind reverted to Sue's warning of the previous day—they intended to kill him—but who were "they"? She had not been specific in her warning, except to say that he should not keep this rendezvous today. Kedrick turned the idea over in his mind, wondering if she were deliberately trying to prevent a settlement or if she knew something and was genuinely worried.

Pit Laine, her gunslinging brother, was one element in the situation he could not estimate. Laine had not been mentioned in any of the discussions. He seemed always just beyond reach, just out of sight, yet definitely in the background, as was the mysterious rider of the mouse-colored horse. That whole story seemed fantastic, but Kedrick did not think Sue was inclined to fall for tall stories.

The canyon of Salt Creek widened out, and several branch canyons opened into it. They left the creek bed and rode closer together to the towering cliffs, now all of seven hundred feet above the trail. They were heading south, and Burwick, mopping his sweaty face from time to time with a dirty handkerchief, was no longer talking.

Kedrick pushed back his hat and rolled a smoke. He had never seen Burwick so jittery before, and he was puzzled. Deliberately, he had said nothing to any of the company about Gunter, although he had arranged with some of the townspeople to have the body moved. Tom was afraid it might precipitate the very trouble he was trying to end, and bring the fight into open battle. Moreover, he was not at all sure of why Gunter had been killed or who had done it. That it could be retaliation for Singer's death was an answer to be considered, but it might have been done by either Keith or Burwick.

He drew up suddenly, for a horse had left recent tracks coming in alone from the northwest. Burwick followed his eyes, studying the tracks. "I've seen those tracks before," Tom Kedrick said. "Now whose horse is that?"

"We better step it up," Burwick said, impatiently. "They'll be there before us."

They pushed on into the bright, still morning. The sky overhead was a vast blue dome scattered with fleecy puffballs of clouds, like bolls of cotton on the surface of a lake of pure blue. The red cliffs towered high on their left, and the valley on their right swept away in a vast, gently rolling panorama. Glancing off over this sagebrush-dotted valley, Tom knew that lost in the blue haze some seven or eight miles away was Malpais Arroyo and Sue Laine.

Was she there this morning? Or was she riding somewhere? She was strangely attractive, that slim, dark-haired, dark-eyed girl with her lovely skin, soft despite the desert sun and desert wind. She had come to him, riding all that distance to bring him a warning of danger. Why? Was it simply that she feared for him? Was she in love with him? He dismissed that idea instantly, but continued to wonder. She was, despite her beauty, a hard, calculating little girl, hating the country around and wanting only to be free of it.

Heat waves danced out over the bottomland, and shadows gathered under the red wall. A dust devil lifted and danced weirdly across the desert and then lost itself among the thick antelope brush and the catclaw. Tom Kedrick mopped his brow and swung his horse farther east, the tall spire of Chimney Rock lifting in the distance, its heavier-shouldered companion looming beside and beyond it.

"Look!" Burwick's voice held a note of triumph. "There they come!"

To the south, and still three or four miles off, they could see two riders heading toward Chimney Rock. At this distance they could not be distinguished, but their destination was obvious.

"Now that's fine!" Burwick beamed. "They'll be here right on time! Say"—he glanced at his heavy gold watch—"tell you what. You'll be there a shade before them, so what say you wait for them while I have me a look at a ledge up in the canyon?"

In the shadow of the rock, Kedrick swung down. There

was a small pool of water there. He let the palouse drink and ground hitched him deeper in the shade, near some grass. Then he walked back and dropping to the ground lit a smoke. He could see the two riders nearing now. One was on a fast-stepping chestnut, the other a dappled gray.

They rode up and swung down. The first man was Pete Slagle, the second a stranger whom Kedrick had not seen before. "Where's McLennon?" he asked.

"He'll be along. He hadn't come in from the ranch, so I came on with Steelman here. He's a good man, an' anything he says goes with all of us. Bob'll be along later, though, if you have to have his word."

"Burwick came. He's over lookin' at a ledge he saw in the canyon over there."

The three men bunched, and Steelman studied Kedrick. "Dai Reid tells me you're a good man. Trustworthy, he says."

"I aim to be." He drew a last drag on his cigarette and lifted his head to snap it out into the sand.

For an instant, he stood poised, his face blank. Then realization hit him. "Look out!" he yelled. "Hit the dirt!"

His voice was drowned in a roar of guns, and something smashed him in the body even as he fell. Then something else slugged him atop the head, and a vast wave of blackness folded over him, pushing him down, down, down, deeper and deeper into a swirling darkness that closed in tightly around his body, around his throat. And then there was nothing, nothing at all.

Alton Burwick smiled and threw down his cigar. Calmly, he swung into the saddle and rode toward the four men who were riding from behind a low parapet of rocks near the chimney. As he rode up they were standing, rifles in hand, staring toward the cluster of bloody figures sprawled on the ground in the shade. "Got 'em!" Shaw said. His eyes were hard. "That cleans it up, an' good!"

Fessenden, Clauson, and Poinsett stared at the bodies, saying nothing. Lee Goff walked toward them from his vantage point, where he had awaited anyone who might have had a chance to escape. He stooped over the three.

Slagle was literally riddled with bullets, his body smashed and bloody. Off to one side lay Steelman, half the top of his head blown off. Captain Kedrick lay sprawled deeper in the shadow, his head bloody, and a dark stain on his body.

"Want I should finish 'em off for sure?" Poinsett asked.

"Finish what off?" Clauson sneered. "Look at 'em—shot to doll rags."

"What about Kedrick?" Fessenden asked. "He dead for sure?"

"Deader than Columbus," Goff said.

"Hey!" Shaw interrupted. "This ain't McLennon! This here's that Joe Steelman!"

They gathered around.

"Sure is!"

Berwick swore viciously. "Now we're in trouble! If we don't get McLennon, we're—" His voice trailed away as he looked up at Dornie Shaw. The soft brown eyes were bright and boyish.

"Why, Boss," he said softly, dropping his cigarette and rubbing it out with his toe, "I reckon that's where I come in. Leave McLennon to me. I'll hunt him down before sun sets tomorrow!"

"Want company?" Poinsett asked.

"Don't need it," Shaw said, "but come along. I hear this Bob McLennon used to be a frontier marshal. I never liked marshals no way."

They drifted to their horses and then moved slowly away—Dornie Shaw, Poinsett, and Goff toward the west and Bob McLennon. Alton Burwick, his eyes thoughtful, rode toward the east and Mustang. With him rode the others. Only Fessenden turned nervously and looked back. "We should have made sure they were dead."

"Ride back if you want," Clauson said. "They are dead all right. That Kedrick! I had no use for him. I aimed my shot right for his smart skull."

Afternoon drew on. The sun lowered, and after the sun came coolness. Somewhere a coyote lifted his howl of anguish to the wide white moon, and the desert lay still and quiet beneath the sky.

In the deeper shadow of the towering chimney and its bulkier neighbor, there was no movement. A coyote, moving nearer, scented the blood, but with it there was the dreaded man smell. He whined anxiously, drew back, and then trotted slowly off, turning only once to look back. The palouse, still ground hitched, walked along the grass toward the pool and then stopped, nostrils wide at the smell of blood.

It had been well down behind some rocks and brush,

and the shooting had only made it lift its head. Then it had returned to cropping the thick green grass that grew in the tiny subirrigated area around the chimney. Nothing more moved. The coolness of the night stiffened the dried blood and stiffened the bodies of the men who lay sprawled there.

Ten miles north, Laredo Shad, late for his meeting with Kedrick, limped along the trail leading a badly lamed horse. Two hours before, the trail along an arroyo bank had given way and the horse had fallen. The leg was not broken, but was badly injured. Shad swore bitterly and walked on, debating as he had for the past two hours on the advisability of camping for the night. But remembering that Kedrick would be expecting him, he pushed on.

An hour later, still plodding and on blistered feet, he heard a horse's hoofs and drew up, slipping his rifle into his hands. Then the rider materialized from the night, and he drew up also. For a long minute no word was said. Then Shad spoke. "Name yourself, pardner."

The other rider also held a gun. "Bob McLennon," he said. "Who are you?"

"Laredo Shad. My horse lamed hisself. I'm headed for Chimney Rock. Supposed to meet Kedrick there." He stared at the rider. "Thought you was to be at the meetin'? What happened?"

"I didn't make it. Steelman an' Slagle went. I'm ridin' up here because they never come in."

"What?" Shad's exclamation was sharp. "McLennon, I was right afeared of that. My bet is there's been dirty work. Never trusted that there Burwick, not no way."

McLennon studied the Texan, liking the man, but hesitant. "What's your brand read, Laredo? You a company man?"

Shad shook his head. "Well, now, it's like this. I come in here drawin' warrior pay to do some gunslingin', but I'm a right uppity sort of a gent about some things. This here didn't size up right to me or to Kedrick, so we been figurin' on gettin' shut of the company. Kedrick only stayed on hopin' he could make peace. I stayed along with him."

"Get up behind me," McLennon said. "My horse will carry double, an' it ain't far."

X

His eyes were open a long time before realization came. He was lying in a clean, orderly place with which he was totally unfamiliar. For a long time he lay there, searching his memory for clues to tie all this together. He, himself, was Captain Tom Kedrick—he had gone west from New Orleans—he had taken on a job—then he remembered.

There had been a meeting at Chimney Rock, and Steelman had come in place of McLennon, and then he had thrown his cigarette away and had seen those men behind the rocks, seen the sunlight flashing on their rifle barrels, actually. He had yelled and then dropped, but not fast enough. He had been hit in the head, and he had been hit in the body at least once.

How long ago was that? He turned his head and found himself in a square stone room. One side of the room was native rock, as was part of another side. The rest had been built up from loose stones gathered and shaped to fit. Besides the wide bed on which he lay, there was a table and a chair. He turned slightly, and the bed creaked. The door opened, and he looked up into the eyes of Connie Duane!

"Connie?" he was surprised. "Where is this place? What's happened?"

"You've been unconscious for days," she told him, coming to the bedside. "You have had a bad concussion, and you lost a lot of blood before Laredo and Bob McLennon found you."

"What about the others?"

"Both of them were dead, and by all rights, you should have been."

"But where are we? What is this place?"

"It's a cliff dwelling, a lonely one and very ancient. It is high up in the side of the mountain called Thieving Rock. McLennon knew where it was, and he knew that if word got out that you were alive they would be out to complete the job at once, so they brought you here. McLennon did, with Shad."

"Are they still here?"

"Shad is. He hunts and goes to Yellow Butte for supplies, but he has to be very careful because it looks like they are beginning to get suspicious."

"McLennon?"

"He's dead, Tom. Dornie Shaw killed him. He went to Mustang to find a doctor for you and encountered Dornie on the street. Bob was very fast, you know, but Dornie is incredible! He killed Bob before he could get a shot off."

"How did you get here?"

"Bob McLennon and Shad had talked about it, and they knew I was against the company and also that Uncle John had been killed. So they came to me, and I came out here right away. I knew a little about nursing, but not much. Laredo has been wonderful, Tom. He's a true friend."

Kedrick nodded. "Who did the shooting? I thought I saw Poinsett."

"He was one of them. I heard them talking about it, but was not sure until later. Poinsett was there, with Goff, Fessenden, Clauson, and Shaw."

"Anything else happened?"

"Too much. They burned Yellow Butte's saloon and livery stable, and they have driven almost half the people off the land. Their surveyors are on the land now, checking the survey they made previously. A handful of the squatters have drawn back into the mountains somewhere under Pit Laine and that friend of yours, Dai Reid. They are trying to make a stand there."

"What about Sue?"

She looked at him quickly. "You liked her, didn't you? Well, Sue has taken up with Keith. They are together all the time. He's a big man, now. They've brought in some more gunmen, and the Mixus boys are still here. Right now, Alton Burwick and Loren Keith have this country right under their thumbs. In fact, they even called an election."

"An election?"

"Yes, and they counted the ballots themselves. Keith was elected mayor, and Fessenden is sheriff. Burwick stayed out of it, of course, and Dornie Shaw wouldn't take the sheriff's job."

"Looks like they've got everything their own way, doesn't it?" he mused. "So they don't know I'm alive."

"No. Shad went back there and dug three graves. He buried the other two and then filled in the third grave and put a marker over it with your name on it."

"Good!" Kedrick was satisfied. He looked up at the girl.

"And how do you get out here and back without them becoming curious?"

She flushed slightly. "I haven't been back, Tom. I stayed here with you. There was no chance of going back and forth. I just left everything and came away."

"How long before I can be up?"

"Not long, if you rest. And you've talked enough now."

Kedrick turned over the whole situation in his mind. There could be no more than a few days before the sale of the land would come off, and if there was one thing that mattered, it was that the company not be permitted to profit from their crookedness. As he lay there resting, a plan began to form in his mind, and the details supplied themselves one by one as he considered it.

His guns hung on a nail driven into the wall close to his hand. His duffle, which he had brought away from the St. James, lay in the corner. It was almost dark before he completed his planning, and when Laredo came in he was ready for him.

"Cimarron?" Shad nodded. "Bloomfield would be nearer. How's that?"

"Good!" Kedrick agreed. "Make it fast."

"That ain't worryin' me," Laredo said, rolling his tobacco in his jaws. "They've been mighty suspicious lately. Suppose they trail this place down while I'm gone?"

"We'll have to chance that. Here's the message. Hurry it up!"

The sun was bright in the room when Connie came through the door with his breakfast. She turned, and her face went white. "Oh, you're up!"

He grinned shakily. "That's right. I've laid abed long enough. How long has it been?"

"Almost two weeks," she told him, "but you mustn't stand up. Sit down and rest."

There was a place by a window where he had a good view of the trail below. At his request, Connie brought the Winchester to him, and her own rifle. He cleaned them both, oiled them carefully, and placed them beside his window. Then he checked his guns and returned them to their holsters, digging the two Walch Navy pistols from his duffle and checking them also.

Thoughtfully, he considered. It was late to do anything now, but it was a wonder he had not thought of Ransome before. No more able legislator existed in Washington than Frederic Ransome, and the two had been brother officers in the war between the states, as well as friends in France during the Franco-Prussian War, when Ransome had been there as an observer. If anybody could block the sale to the company, he could, even on such short notice.

His telegram would be followed by a letter supplying all the details, and with that to go on, Ransome might get something done. He was a popular and able young senator with good connections and an affable manner. Moreover, he was an excellent strategist. It would make all the difference in this situation.

The cliff dwelling was built well back from the face of the cliff, and built evidently with an eye toward concealment as well as defense. They had called this, Connie told him, Thieving Rock long before the white man appeared, and the Indians who lived here had been notorious thieves. There was a spring, so water was not a worry, and there were supplies enough for immediate purposes.

Two days dragged slowly by. On the morning of the third, Kedrick was resuming his station by the window when he saw a rider coming into the narrow canyon below.

The man was moving slowly and studying the ground as he came, although from time to time he paused and searched the area with careful eyes. Kedrick pushed himself up from his chair and taking the Winchester, worked his way along the wall to the next room.

"Connie?" he called softly. There was no reply, and after a minute, he called a second time. Still no answer.

Worried now, he remembered she had said something about going down below to gather some squaw cabbage to add greens to their diet.

Back at the window, he studied the terrain carefully, and then his heart gave a leap, for Connie Duane was gathering squaw cabbage from a niche in the canyon wall, not fifty yards from the unknown rider!

Lifting his rifle, Kedrick checked the range. It was all of four hundred yards and a downhill shot. Carefully, he sighted on the rider but then relaxed. He was nearer the girl now, and a miss might ricochet and kill the girl, for the canyon wall would throw any bullet he fired back into the canyon itself, and it might even ricochet several times in the close confines.

Yet, somehow, she had to be warned. If the rider saw her tracks, he would find both the girl and the hideout. Suddenly, the ears of his horse came up sharply, and the rider stiffened warily and looked all around. Carefully, Kedrick drew a bead on the man again. He hated to kill an unwarned man, but if necessary he would not hesitate.

Connie was standing straight now and appeared to be listening. Tense in every fiber, Tom Kedrick watched and waited. The two were now within fifty feet of each other, although each was concealed by a corner of rock and some desert growth, including a tall cottonwood and some cedars.

Still listening, both stood rigid, and Kedrick touched his lips with the tip of his tongue. His eyes blurred with the strain, and he brushed his hand across them.

The rider was swinging to the ground now, and he had drawn a gun. Warily, he stepped out from his ground-hitched horse. Shifting his eyes to Connie, Tom saw the girl wave, and lifting his hand, he waved back and then lifted the rifle. She waved a vigorous negation with her arm, and he relaxed, waiting.

Now the man was studying tracks in the sandy bottom of the wash, and as he knelt, his eyes riveted upon the ground, a new element entered the picture.

A flicker of movement caught the tail of Kedrick's eye, and turning his head he saw Laredo Shad riding into the scene. He glared swiftly at the window and waved his hand. Then he moved foreward and swung to the ground.

From his vantage point Kedrick could hear nothing, but he saw Laredo approach, making heavy going of it in the thick sand, and then, not a dozen yards from the man, he stopped.

He must have spoken, for the strange rider stiffened as if shot and then slowly got to his feet. As he turned, Tom saw his face full in the sunlight. It was Clauson!

What happened then was too fast for the eye to follow. Somebody must have spoken, but who did not matter. Clauson's gun was drawn, and he started to swing it up. Laredo Shad in a gunman's crouch, flashed his right-hand gun. It sprang clear, froze for a long instant, and then just as Clauson fired, Shad fired—but a split second sooner!

Clauson staggered a step back, and Shad fired again. The outlaw went down slowly, and Laredo walked forward and stripped his gun belts from him. Then from his horse he took his saddlebags, rifle, and ammunition. Gathering up the dead man and working with Connie's help, they tied him to the saddle and then turned the horse loose with a slap on the hip.

Connie Duane's face was white when she came into the room. "You saw that?"

He nodded. "We didn't dare to let him go. If we had, we would all have been dead before noon tomorrow. Now," he said with grim satisfaction, "they'll have something to think about!"

Shad grinned at him when he came in. "I didn't see that gun he had drawed," he said ruefully. "Had it layin along his leg as he was crouched there. Might've got me."

He dropped the saddlebags. "Mite of grub," he said, "an' some shells. I reckon we can use 'em even though I brought some. The message got off, an' so did the letter. Fellow over to the telegraph office was askin' a powerful lot of questions. Seems like they've been hearin' about this scrap."

"Good! The more the better. We can stand it, but the company can't. Hear anything?"

"Uh-huh. Somebody from outside the state is startin' a row about Gunter's death. I hear they have you marked for that. That is, the company is sayin' you did it."

Kedrick nodded. "They would try that. Well, in a couple of days I'll be out of this, and then we'll see what can be done."

"You take some time," Shad said dubiously. "That passel of thieves ain't goin' to find us. Although," he said suddenly, "I saw the tracks of that grulla day afore yesterday, an' not far off."

The grulla again!

Two more days drifted by, and Tom Kedrick ventured down the trail and the ladders to the canyon below with Laredo and visited their horses, concealed in a tiny glade not far away. The palouse nickered and trotted toward him, and Kedrick grinned and scratched his chest. "How is it, boy? Ready to go places?"

"He's achin' for it," Shad said. He lighted a smoke and squinted his eyes at Kedrick. "What you aim to do when you do move?"

"Ride around a little. I aim to see Pit Laine, an' then I'm goin' to start huntin' up every mother's son that was in that drygulching. Especially," he added, "Dornie Shaw."

"He's bad," Laredo said quietly. "I never seen it, but
you ask Connie. Shaw's chain lightnin'. She seen him kill
Bob."

"So one of us dies," Kedrick said quietly. "I'd go willing
enough to take him with me, an' a few others."

"That's it. He's a killer, but the old bull of that woods is
Alton Burwick. Believe me, he is. Keith is just right-hand
man for him, an' the fall guy if they need one. Burwick's the
poison mean one."

With Connie they made their start three days later and
rode back trails beyond the rim to the hideout Laine had
established. It was Dai Reid himself who stopped them, and
his eyes lighted up when he saw Kedrick.

"Ah, Tom!" His broad face beamed. "Like my own son,
you are. We'd heard you were killed dead."

Pit Laine was standing by the fire, and around him on
the ground were a dozen men, most of whom Kedrick recognized. They sat up slowly as the three walked into the open
space, and Pit turned. It was the first time Kedrick had seen
him, and he was surprised.

He was scarcely taller than his sister, but wide in the
shoulders and slim in the hips. When he turned, he faced
them squarely, and his eyes were sharp and bitter. This was a
killing man, Kedrick decided, as dangerous in his own way as
that pocket-sized devil Dornie Shaw.

"I'm Kedrick," he said, "and this is Connie Duane. I
believe you know Shad."

"We know all of you." Laine watched them, his eyes
alert and curious.

Quietly and concisely, he explained, and ended by saying,
"So there it is. I've asked this friend of mine to start an
investigation into the whole mess and to block the sale until
the truth is clear. Once the sale is blocked and that investigation started, they won't be with us long. They could get away
with this only if they could keep it covered up, and they had
a fair chance of doing that."

"So we wait and let them run off?" Laine demanded.

"No," Tom Kedrick shook his head decidedly. "We ride
into Mustang—all of us.

"They have the mayor and the sheriff, but public opinion
is largely on our side. Furthermore," he said quietly, "we
ride in the minute they get the news the sale is blocked.

Once that news is around town, they will have no friends. The bandwagon riders will get off, and fast."

"There'll be shootin'," one old-timer opined.

"Some," Kedrick admitted, "but if I have my way, there'll be more of hanging. There's killers in that town, the bunch that drygulched Steelman and Slagle. The man who killed Bob McLennon is the man I want."

Pit Laine turned. "I want him."

"Sorry, Laine. He killed Bob, an' Bob was only in town to get a doc for me. You may," he added, "get your chance, anyway."

"I'd like a shot at him my own self," Laredo said quietly, "but somethin' else bothers me. Who's this grulla rider? Is he one of you?"

Laine shook his head. "No, he's got us wonderin', too."

"Gets around plenty," the old-timer said, "but nobody ever sees him. I reckon he knows this here country better than any of us. He must've been around here for a long time."

"What's he want?" Shad wondered. "That don't figure."

Kedrick shrugged. "I'd like to know." He turned to Dai. "It's good to see you. I was afraid you'd had trouble."

"Trouble?" Dai smiled his wide smile. "It's trouble, you say? All my life there's been trouble. Where man is, there will be trouble to the end of time, if not of one kind, then another. But I take my trouble as it comes, boy."

He drew deeply on his short-stemmed pipe and glanced at the scar around Kedrick's skull. "Looks like you'd a bit of it yourself. If you'd a less hard skull you'd now be dead."

"I'd not have given a plugged peso for him when I saw him," Laredo said dryly. "The three of them were just lyin' there, bloody an' shot up. We thought for sure they was all dead. This one, he'd a hole through him, low down an' mean, an' that head of his looked like it had been smashed, until we moved him. He was lucky as well as thick skulled."

Morning found Laredo and Kedrick once more in the saddle. Connie Duane had stayed behind with some of the squatters' women. Together, they were pushing on toward Mustang, but taking their time, for they had no desire to be seen or approached by any of the company riders.

"There's nothing much we can do," Kedrick agreed, "but I want to know the lay of the land in town. It's mighty important to be able to figure just what will happen when the news hits the place. Right now, everything is right for them. Alton Burwick and Loren Keith are better off than they ever were.

"Just size it up. They came in here with the land partly held by squatters with a good claim on the land. That land they managed to get surveyed, and they put in their claim to the best of it, posted the notices, and waited them out. If somebody hadn't seen one of those notices and read it, the whole sale might have gone through and nobody the wiser. Somebody did see it, and trouble started. They had two mighty able men to contend with, Slagle and McLennon.

"Well, both of them are dead now. And Steelman, another possible leader, is dead too. So far as they are aware, nobody knows anything about the deaths of those men or who caused them. I was the one man they had learned they couldn't depend on, and they think I'm dead. John Gunter brought money into the deal, and he's dead and out of the picture completely.

"A few days more and the sale goes through and the land becomes theirs, and there isn't any organized opposition now. Pit Laine and his group will be named as outlaws and hunted as such, and believe me, once the land sale goes through, Keith will be hunting them with a posse of killers."

"Yeah," Laredo drawled, "they sure got it sewed up, looks like. But you're forgettin' one thing. You're forgettin' the girl. Connie Duane."

"What about her?"

"Look," Shad said, speaking around his cigarette, "she sloped out of town right after McLennon was killed. They thought she had been talking to you before, and she told 'em off in the office, said she was gettin' her money out of it. All right, so suppose she asks for it and they can't pay?"

"Suppose," he added, "she begins to talk and tells what she knows, and they must figure it's plenty. She was Gunter's niece, and for all they know he told her more than he did tell her."

"You mean they'll try to get hold of her?"

"What do you think? They'll try to get hold of her, or kill her."

Tom Kedrick's eyes narrowed. "She'll be safe with Laine," he said, but an element of doubt was in his voice. "That's a good crowd."

Shad shrugged. "Maybe. Don't forget that Singer was

one of them, but he didn't hesitate to try to kill Sloan or to point him out for Abe Mixus. He was bought off by the company, so maybe there are others."

At that very moment, in the office of the gray stone building, such a man sat opposite Alton Burwick, while Keith sat in a chair against the wall. The man's name was Hirst. His face was sallow, but determined. "I ain't lyin'!" he said flatly. "I rode all night to get here, slippin' out of camp on the quiet. She rode in with that gunman, Laredo Shad, and this Kedrick hombre."

"Kedrick! Alive?" Keith sat forward, his face tense.

"Alive as you or me! Had him most of the hair clipped on one side of his head, an' a bad scar there. He sort of favored his side, too. Oh, he'd been shot all right, but he's ridin' now, believe me!"

The renegade had saved the worst until last. He smiled grimly at Burwick. "I can use some money, Mr. Burwick," he said, "an' there's more I could tell you."

Burwick stared at him, his eyes glassy hard. Then he reached into a drawer and threw two gold eagles on the desk. "All right! What can you tell me?"

"Kedrick sent a message to some hombre in Washington name of Ransome. He's to block the sale of the land until there's a complete investigation."

"What?"

"Keith came to his feet, his face ashen. This was beyond his calculations. When the idea had first been brought to his attention, it had seemed a very simple, easy way to turn a fast profit. He had excellent connections in Washington through his military career, and with Burwick managing things on the other end and Gunter with the money, it seemed impossible to beat it. He was sure to net a handsome sum, clear his business with Gunter and Burwick, and then return east and live quietly on the profits. That it was a crooked deal did not disturb him, but that his friends in the East might learn of it did!

"Ransome!" His voice was shocked. "Of all people!"

Frederic Ransome had served with him in the war, and their mutual relationship had been something less than friendly. There had been that episode by the bridge. He flushed at the thought of it, but Ransome knew, and Ransome would use it as a basis for judgment. Kedrick had no way of knowing just how fortunate his choice of Ransome had been.

"That does it!" He got to his feet. "Ransome will bust this wide open, and love it!"

He was frightened, and Burwick could see it. He sat there, his gross body filling the chair, wearing the same soiled shirt. His eyes followed Keith with irritation and contempt. Was Keith going bad on him now?

"Get back there," Burwick said to Hirst, "and keep me informed of the movements. Watch everything closely now, and don't miss a trick. You will be paid."

When Hirst had gone, Burwick turned to Keith and smiled with his fat lips. "So does it matter if they slow it up a little? Let them have their investigation. It will come too late."

"Too late?" Keith was incredulous. "With such witnesses against us as Kedrick, Shad, Connie, and the rest of them?"

"When the time comes," Burwick said quietly, "there will be no witnesses! Believe me, there won't be!"

XI

Keith turned on Burwick, puzzled by the sound of his voice. "What do you mean?" he asked.

Burwick chuckled and rolled his fat lips on his cigar. There was malice and some contempt in the look he gave Keith. How much better, he thought, had Kedrick not been so namby-pamby. He was twice the man Keith was, for all the latter's commanding presence.

"Why," he said, "if there's no witnesses, there'll be no case. What can these people in town tell them? What they suspect? Suspicions won't stand in a court of law, or with that committee. By the time they get here, this country will be peaceful and quiet, believe me."

"What do you mean to do?" Keith demanded.

"Do? What is there to do? Get rid of Kedrick, Laredo Shad, and that girl. Then you'll take a posse and clean out that rat's nest back of the rim. Then who will they talk to? Gunter might have weakened, but he's dead. With the rest of them out of it—"

"Not Connie!" Keith protested. "Not her! For heaven's sake, man!"

Burwick snorted, and his lips twisted in an angry sneer as he heaved his bulk from the chair. "Yes, Connie!" he said. "Are you a complete fool, Keith? Or have you gone soft? That girl knows more than all of them! Suppose Gunter talked to her, and he most likely did? She'll know everything, everything, I tell you!"

He paced back across the room, measuring Keith. The fool! He was irritated and angry. He couldn't understand the sort of men they made these days, a weak and snivelling crowd. Keith had played out his time. If he finished this job alive— Dornie didn't like Keith. Burwick chuckled suddenly. Dornic! Now there was a man! The way he had killed that Bob McLennon!

"Now get this. Get the boys together. Get Fessenden, Goff, Clauson, Poinsett, and the Mixus boys and send them out with Dornie. I want those three killed, you hear me? I want them dead before the week is out. And no bodies, understand?"

Keith touched his dry lips, his eyes haunted. He had bargained for nothing like this. It had all seemed such an easy profit, with only a few poverty-stricken squatters to prevent them from acquiring wealth in a matter of a few months. And everything had started off just as Burwick had suggested; everything had gone so well. Gunter had provided the money, and he had fronted for them in Washington.

Uneasily now, Keith realized that if trouble was made over this, it would be he, himself, upon whom the blame would rest. Burwick somehow had been in the background in the East as much as he, Keith, had been kept in the background here. Yet it would be his guilt if anything went wrong. And with Ransome investigating, everything had gone wrong.

Of course, he sighed deeply, Burwick was right. There was only one thing to do now. At least, Dornie and the others would not hesitate. Suddenly, he remembered something.

"You mentioned Clauson. He's out of it, Burwick. Clauson came in last night, tied to his horse. He had been dead for hours."

"What?" Burwick stopped his pacing and walked up to Keith. "You just remembered?" He held his face inches away from Keith's and glared. "Is anybody backtracking that horse? You blithering idiot! Clauson was dynamite with a gun, so if he's dead, shot, it had to be by one of three men, and you know it!"

Burwick's face was dark with passion, and he wheeled and walked the length of the room, swearing in a low, violent voice that shocked Keith with its deep, underlying passion. When he turned again, Burwick's eyes were ugly with fury. "Can't you realize," he demanded hoarsely, "those men are dangerous?

"Don't you see that every second they are alive we are in danger? You have seen Dornie in action. Well, believe me, I'd sooner have him after me than Kedrick. I know Kedrick! He's a former Army officer—that's what you're thinking all the time—an officer and a gentleman!

"But he's something more, do you hear? He's more. He's a gentleman—that's true enough—but the man's a fighter. He loves to fight! Under all that calmness and restraint, there's a drive and power that Dornie Shaw could never equal. Dornie may be faster, and I think he is, but don't you forget for one instant that Kedrick won't be through until he's down, down and dead!"

Loren Keith was shocked. In his year's association with Burwick he had never seen the man in a passion and had never heard him speak with such obvious respect and even— yes—even fear, of any man. What had Alton Burwick seen that he himself had not seen?

He stared at Burwick, puzzled and annoyed, but some of the man's feeling began to transmit itself to him, and he became distinctly uneasy. He bit his lips and watched Burwick pacing angrily.

"It's not only him, but it's Shad, that cool, thin-faced Texan. As for Laine"—Burwick's eyes darkened—"he may be the worst of the lot. He thinks he has a personal stake in this."

"Personal?" Keith looked inquiringly at the older man. "What do you mean?"

Burwick dismissed the question with a gesture. "No matter. They must go, all of them, and right now." He turned and his eyes were cold. "Keith, you fronted for us in Washington. If this thing goes wrong, you're the one who will pay. Now go out there and get busy. You've a little time, and you've the men. Get busy!"

When he had gone, Burwick dropped into his chair and

stared blindly before him. It had gone too far to draw back now even if he was so inclined, and he was not. The pity of it was that there had been no better men to be had than Keith and Gunter.

Yet, everything could still go all right, for he would know how to meet any investigating committee, how to soft-pedal the trouble and turn it off into a mere cow-country quarrel of no moment and much exaggerated. The absence of any complaining witness would leave them helpless to pro-ceed, and he could make it seem a mere teapot tempest. Keith was obviously afraid of Ransome. Well he was not.

Burwick was still sitting there when the little cavalcade of horsemen streamed by, riding out of town on their blood trail. The number had been augmented, he noticed, by four new arrivals, all hard, desperate men. Even without Keith they might do the job. He heaved himself to his feet and paced across the room, staring out the window. It went badly with him to see Connie Duane die, for he had plans for Connie—maybe. His eyes narrowed.

Out on the desert the wind stirred restlessly, and in the brassy sky above, a lone buzzard circled as if aware of the creeping tension that was slowly gripping the country be-neath it.

Far to the north, toward Durango, a cattle buyer pulled his team to a halt and studied the sky. There was no hint of storm, yet he had felt uneasy ever since leaving town on his buying trip down to Yellow Butte and Mustang. There had been rumors of trouble down that way, but then, there had been intermittent trouble down there for some time, and he was not alarmed. Yet he was somehow uneasy, as though the very air carried a warning.

South of him, and below the rim, Laredo Shad and Kedrick turned aside from the Mustang trail and headed toward Yellow Butte. It was only a little way out of their line of travel, but both men wanted to see what had happened there. Yet when they approached the town, aside from the blackened ruins of the destroyed buildings, everything seemed peaceful and still. Eight or ten families had moved back into the town, and a few had never left. They looked up warily as the two riders drew near. Then they nodded a greeting.

They knew now that these two were siding with them against the company, but hardship and struggle had wearied them, and they watched the two enter the settlement without excitement. The saloon had opened its doors in the large, roomy office of the livery stable, and they went there now. A couple of men leaned on the bar, and both turned as they entered, greeted them, and returned to their conversation.

It was growing cool outside, and the warmth of the room felt good. Both men stepped to the bar, and Kedrick ordered and paid. Shad toyed with his drink. He seemed uneasy, and finally he turned to Tom. "I don't like it," he said, low voiced. "Somehow or other Burwick is goin' to know about Ransome, an' he'll be in a sweat to get Connie out of the way, an' you an' me with her."

Kedrick agreed, for his own mind had been reading sign along the same trail. The only way out for the company now was to face the committee, if Ransome managed one, with a plausible tale and an accomplished fact and then let them make the most of it.

"Burwick's a snake," Shad commented. "He'll never quit wigglin' until the sun goes down for the last time. Not that one. He's in this deep, an' he ain't the man to lose without a fight."

Horses' hoofs sounded on the road outside, and when they turned, Pit Laine and Dai Reid were dismounting before the door. They walked in, and Laine looked at Kedrick and then moved on to the bar. Dai looked worried, but said nothing. After a minute, Laine turned suddenly and went outside. "What's the matter?" Kedrick asked.

"It be worry, boy, and some of it shame, an' all for that sister of his. Who would think it of her? To go over to the other side? He's that shy about it, you would scarce believe. When a man looks at him, he thinks it's his sister they are thinkin' on and how she sold out to that traitor to mankind, that rascal Keith."

Kedrick shrugged. "Ambition and money do strange things. She has the makings of a woman, too."

Laine opened the door. "Better come out," he said. "We've got trouble."

They crowded outside. Men were hurrying toward the houses, their faces grave. "What is it?" Kedrick asked quickly.

"Burt Williams signaled from the top of the butte. There's riders coming from Mustang, a bunch of them."

As they looked, the small dark figure of a man appeared on the edge of the mesa once more. This time they saw his arm wave, once—twice—three times, and continue until he had waved it six times. When he had completed, he gestured to the southeast. Then he signaled four more times from the southwest.

"Ten riders," Laine spat. "Well, we've got more than that here, but they aren't as salty as that crowd."

Burt Williams, favoring his broken arm, knelt behind a clump of brush on top of Yellow Butte and studied the approaching horsemen through the glass. He knew all in this group by sight but not by favor. One by one he named them off to himself, "Keith, Dornie Shaw, Fessenden an' Goff—Poinsett." He scowled. "No, that ain't Poinsett. That's one of the Mixus boys. Yep, an' there's the other."

He swung his glass. The four riders, spaced well apart, were approaching at a steady pace. None of their faces were familiar. He stared at them a while, but finally placed only one of them, a bad man from Durango who ran with Port Stockton and the Ketchum outfit. His name was Brokow.

Stirred, he searched the country all around the town for other movement. Then he turned back to the larger cavalcade of riders. Had he held on a certain high flat a minute longer he would have seen two unmounted men cross it at a stooping run and drop into the wide arroyo northeast of town.

As it was, he had been studying the approaching group for several minutes before he realized that Poinsett was not among them. He was with neither group.

Worried, Williams squinted his eyes against the sun, wondering how he could apprise them of the danger down below, for the absence of Poinsett disturbed him. The man was without doubt one of the most vicious of the company killers, a bitter man, made malignant by some dark happening in his past, but filled now with a special sort of venom all his own. Williams would have worried even more had he seen Poinsett at that moment.

The attack had been planned carefully and with all of Keith's skill. He surmised who they would be looking for and hoped their watcher would overlook the absence of Poinsett, for it was he whom Keith wanted in the right position, for Poinsett was unquestionably the best of the lot with a rifle.

At that moment, not two hundred yards from town, Poinsett and his companion, Alf Starrett, were hunkered down in a cluster of brush and boulders at one side of the arroyo. Poinsett had his Spencer .56 and was settling into position for his first shot. Starrett, with a fifteen-shot Henry .44, was a half dozen yards away.

Poinsett pulled out a huge silver watch and consulted it. "At half after two, he says. All right, that's when he'll get it." With utmost composure he began to roll a smoke, and Alf Starrett, a hard-faced and wizened little man, noticed that his fingers were steady as he sifted tobacco into the paper.

Bob McLennon had planned the defense of Yellow Butte, if such a defense became necessary, and while Bob had been something of a hand with a gun, he definitely had not been a soldier or even an Indian fighter. Moreover, they had not expected an all-out battle for the town. Whatever the reason, he had committed a fatal error, for that pile of boulders and brush offered perfect concealment and almost perfect cover while affording complete coverage of the town, its one street, and the back as well as front of most of the buildings.

Keith had been quick to see this on his earlier visits to the town and had planned to have Poinsett and Starrett approach the place some time before the main force moved in. In this, owing to their own experience, they had been successful.

Poinsett finished his cigarette and took up his rifle. Then he settled down to careful watching and checking of the time. He had his orders, and they were explicit. He was to fire on the first target offered after half past two—and his first shot must kill.

Shad and Kedrick had returned to the saloon, and Pit Laine was loitering in front. Dai had gone across the street. Laine was in a position out of sight of Poinsett, but the latter had glimpsed Dai. The Welshman, however, offered only a fleeting target and Poinsett did not consider firing. His chance came at once, however.

The door of one of the nearest shacks opened and a man came out. He wore a broad-brimmed gray hat, torn at the crown, and a large checked shirt tucked into jeans supported by suspenders. He turned at the door and kissed his wife. Poinsett took careful aim with his .56, choosing as his aiming point the man's left suspender buckle. Taking a good deep breath, he held it and squeezed off his shot.

The big bullet struck with a heavy thump. The man took a heavy lurch sidewise, tried to straighten, and then went down. His wife ran from the door, screaming. Up the street a door banged, and two men ran into the street, staring. Starrett's first shot knocked the rifle from the hand of one, splintering the stock. Poinsett dropped his man, but the fellow began to drag himself, favoring one leg, which even at this distance they could see covered with a dark blotch at the knee.

Poinsett was a man without mercy. Coolly and carefully, he squeezed off his second shot. The man stiffened, jerked spasmodically, and lay still.

"Missed my man," Alf said, apologetically, "but I ruined his shootin' iron."

Poinsett spat, his eyes cold. "Could happen to anybody," he said, philosophically, "but I figured you burnt him anyways."

Within the saloon, Kedrick had a glass half to his mouth when the shot boomed, followed almost at once by two more, their reports sounding almost as one.

"Blazes!" Shad whirled. "They ain't here yet?"

"They've been here," Kedrick said with quick realization. He swung to the door, glancing up the street. He saw the body of the last man to fall, and leaning out a bit, glimpsed the other. His lips tightened, for neither man was moving.

"Somebody is up the draw," he explained quickly. "He's got the street covered. Is there a back door?"

Kedrick dove for the door, followed by the others as the bartender indicated the way and then caught up his shotgun. His pockets were already stuffed with shells. At the door Kedrick halted. Then, flattening against the wall, he stared up the draw. From here he could see the edge of the bunch of boulders and guessed the fire came from there. "Pinned down," he said. "They are up the draw."

Nobody moved. His memory for terrain served him to good purpose now. Recalling the draw, he remembered that it was below the level of the town beyond that point, but right there the boulders offered a perfect firing point.

Scattered shots came from down the draw, and nobody spoke. All knew that the three men down there could not long withstand the attack and would fall back on the town to be taken in the rear.

XII

Kedrick made up his mind quickly. Defense of the town was now impossible, and they would be wiped out or burned alive if they attempted to remain here. "Shad," he said quickly, "get across the street to Dai and Pit. Yell out to the others and get them to fall back, regardless of risk, to the canyon at the foot of Yellow Butte."

He took a step back and glanced at the trapdoor to the roof. The bartender saw the intent and shook his head. "You can't do it, boy. They'd get you from down the creek."

"I'm going to chance it. I think they are still too far off. If I can give you folks covering fire you may make it."

"What about you," Shad demanded.

"I'll make it. Get moving!"

Laredo wheeled and darted to the door, paused an instant, and lunged across the street. The bartender hesitated, swore softly, and then followed. Kedrick picked up a bottle of the liquor and shoved it into his shirt. Then he jumped for the edge of the trapdoor, caught it and pulled himself through into the small attic. Carefully, he studied the situation.

Hot firing came from downstream, and evidently the killers were momentarily stopped there. He hoisted himself through, swung to the ridge of the roof, and carefully studied the boulders. Suddenly, he caught a movement, and knew that what he had first believed to be a gray rock was actually a shirt. He took careful aim with his Winchester and then fired.

The gray shirt jumped, and a hand flew up and then fell loose. Instantly, a Spencer boomed and a bullet tore a chunk from the ridge near his face and splattered him with splinters. Kedrick moved down the roof a bit. Then, catching the signal from the window across the street, he deliberately shoved his rifle and head up and fired four fast shots, and then two more.

Ducking his head, he reloaded the Winchester. Another bullet smashed the ridgepole, and then a searching fire began, the heavy slugs tearing through the roof about three to four inches below the top.

Kedrick slid down the roof and hesitated at the edge of the trapdoor. Seeing a distant figure circling to get behind the men in the wash, he took careful aim and squeezed off his shot. It was all of five hundred yards, and he had only a small bit of darkness at which to aim.

The shot kicked up sand short of the mark by a foot or more as nearly as he could judge, and he knew he had missed, but the would-be sniper lost his taste for his circling movement and slid out of sight. Kedrick went down the trap and dropped again into the saloon. Regretfully, he glanced at the stock of whiskey and then picked up two more bottles and stuffed them into his pockets.

Hesitating only a second, he lunged across the street for the shelter of the opposite building. The Spencer boomed, and he knew that the hidden marksman had been awaiting this effort. He felt the shock of the bullet, staggered, but kept going.

Reaching the opposite side, he felt the coldness of something on his stomach and glanced down. The bottle in his shirt had been broken by the bullet, and he smelled to high heaven of good whiskey. Picking the glass out of his shirt, he dove for the livery stable and swung into the saddle on the palouse.

The Spencer boomed again and again as he hit the road riding hard, but he made it. The others cheered as he rode pell mell through the canyon mouth and swung to the ground.

"This is no good," Laine said. "They can get behind us on the ridge."

Two men limped in from the draw, having withdrawn from boulder to boulder. Kedrick glanced around. There were fourteen men and women here who were on their feet. One man, he who had had the rifle knocked from his hand, had a shattered arm. The others were slightly wounded. Of them all, he had only seven men able to fight.

Quickly, he gave directions for their retreat. Then, with Dai and Shad to hold the canyon mouth and cover them, they started back up the canyon.

Tom Kedrick measured his group thoughtfully. Of Laredo, Dai, and Laine, he had no doubts at all. Of the others, he could not be sure. Some of them were good men, and one or two were obviously frightened. Nobody complained, however, and one of the men whose face was pale took a wounded man's rifle and gave him a shoulder on which to lean. He led them to the crevasse and down into it.

Amazed, they stared around. "What do you know?" The

bartender spat. "Been here nigh seven year an' never knowed of this place!"

There were four horses in the group, but they brought them all into the cave. One of the men complained, but Kedrick turned on him. "There's water, but we may be glad to eat horsemeat." The man swallowed and stared.

Laine pointed at Kedrick's shirt. "Man, you're bleedin'!"

Kedrick grinned. "That isn't blood, it's whiskey! They busted one of the bottles I brought away!"

Pit chuckled. "I'd most as soon it was blood," he said. "Seems a waste of good liquor."

The seven able men gathered near the escape end of the crevasse, and one of them grinned at Kedrick. "I wondered how you got away so slick. Is there another way out down there?"

He shook his head. "If there is, I don't know it. I waited and got out through the canyon when it wasn't watched."

Laine's face was serious. "They could hold us in here," he said, anxiously. "We'd be stuck for sure."

Kedrick nodded. "I'm taking an extra canteen and some grub. Then I'm going atop the Butte to join Burt Williams. I'd like one man with me. From up there we can hold them off, I think."

"I'm your man," Laredo said quietly. "Wait'll I get my gear."

A rifle boomed, and then Dai Reid joined them. "They are comin' up," he said. He glanced at Kedrick. "One man dead in the boulders. I got the look of him by my glass. It was Alf Starrett. Poinsett was the other."

"Starrett was a skunk," Burnett, one of the settlers said. "A low-down skunk. He killed a man up Kansas way, an' a man disappeared from his outfit once that occasioned considerable doubt if he didn't get hisself another."

Kedrick turned to Pit Laine. "Looks like your show down here," he said. "Don't open fire until you have to; don't fire even one shot unless it's needed. We'll be on top."

He led the way out of the crevasse and into the boulders and brush behind it. There was no sign of the attackers, and he surmised they were holed up awaiting the arrival of some supporting fire from the rim back of the canyon.

Tom glanced up at the towering Butte. It reared itself all of a hundred and fifty feet above him and most of it totally without cover. As they waited, a rifle boomed high above them and there was a puff of dust in the canyon mouth. Burt Williams had opened up.

Yet their first move toward the Butte drew fire, and Laredo drew back. "No chance. We'll have to wait until dark. You reckon they'll hit us before then?"

"If they do, they won't get far." Tom Kedrick hunkered well down among the slabs of rock at the foot of the Butte. "We've got us a good firing point right here." He rolled a smoke and lit up. "What are you planning when this is over, Shad? Do you plan to stay here?"

The tall Texan shrugged. "Ain't pondered it much. Reckon that will take care of itself. What you aimin' to do?"

"You know the Mogollons southwest of here? I figured I'd go down there and lay out a ranch for myself." He smoked thoughtfully. "Down in East Texas, before I came west, a fellow arrived there named Ikard. Had some white-faced cattle with him, and you should see 'em! Why, they have more beef on one sorry critter than three longhorns. I figured a man could get himself a few Hereford bulls and start a herd. Might even buy fifty or sixty head for a beginning, and let 'em mix with the longhorns if they like."

"I might go for somethin' like that," Laredo said quietly, "I always wanted to own a ranch. Fact is, I started one once, but had to get shut of it."

He studied the end of his cigarette. "That was in the Texas Panhandle, a ways south of Tascosa. Quite a ways. It was rough country. I mean rough to live in, not rough like this is. Why, you could stand on your own front step down thataway an' see straight ahead for three days! Coyotes? Why, you should see 'em! They'd whip a grizzly, or near it, an' make these coyotes around here look like jackrabbits."

He stared down the canyon toward the mouth, his rifle across his knees. He did not look at Kedrick, but he commented casually. "We need luck, Captain, plenty of luck."

"Uh-huh." Kedrick's face was sober. "Right now we're bottled up, and believe me, Burwick will stop at nothing. I wonder who was on watch up the canyon? Or supposed to be?"

"Somebody said his name was Hirst. Sallow-faced hombre."

"We'll have to talk to him. Was he down below?"

"Come to think of it, he wasn't. He must have hid out back there."

"Or sold out. Remember Singer? He wouldn't have been the only one."

Laredo rubbed out the last of his cigarette. "They'll be makin' their play soon. You know, Kedrick, I'd as soon make a break for it, get a couple of horses, an' head for Mustang. When we go we might as well take Keith an' that dirty Burwick with us."

Kedrick nodded agreement, but he was thinking of the men below. There were at least four good men aside from Shad, Laine, and Dai Reid. That left the numbers not to unevenly balanced. The fighting skill and numbers were slightly on the enemy's side, as they had at least twelve men when the battle opened, and they had lost only Starrett. That made the odds eleven to eight unless they had moved up extra men, which was highly probable. Still, they were expecting defense, and an attack—?

He studied the situation. Suddenly, a dark figure loomed on the rim of the canyon some hundred and fifty yards off and much higher. He lifted his rifle and fired even as both Shad and Kedrick threw down on him with rifles, firing instantly. The man vanished, but whether hit or not they could not tell.

Desultory firing began, and from time to time they caught glimpses of men advancing from the canyon mouth, but never in sight long enough to offer a target, and usually rising from the ground some distance from where they dropped. The afternoon was drawing on, however, and the sun was setting almost in the faces of the attackers, which made their aim uncertain and their movements hesitant. Several times Shad or Kedrick dusted the oncoming party, but got in no good shots. Twice a rifle boomed from the top of the butte, and once they heard a man cry out as though hit.

"You know, Laredo," Kedrick said suddenly, "it goes against the grain to back up for those coyotes. I'm taking this grub up to Burt, an' when I come back down, we're going to move down that canyon and see how much stomach they've got for a good scrap."

Shad grinned, his eyes flickering with humor. "That's ace high with me, pardner," he said dryly. "I never was no hand for a hole, an' the women are safe."

"All but one," Kedrick said. "That Missus Taggart who lives in that first house. Her husband got killed and she wouldn't leave."

"Yeah, heard one of the womenfolks speak on it. That Taggart never had a chance. Good folks, those two."

Colonel Loren Keith stared gloomily at the towering mass of Yellow Butte. That man atop the Butte had them pinned down. Now if they could just get up there. He thought of the men he had commanded in years past and compared them with these outside—a pack of murderers. How had he got into this, anyway? Why couldn't a man know when he took a turning where it would lead him? It seemed so simple in the beginning to run off a bunch of one-gallused farmers and squatters.

Wealth—he had always wanted wealth, the money to pay his way in the circles where he wanted to travel, but somehow it had always eluded him, and this had seemed a wonderful chance. Bitterly, he stared at the butte and remembered the greasy edge of Burwick's shirt collar and the malice in his eyes. Burwick used men as he saw fit, and disposed of them when he was through.

In the beginning it hadn't seemed that way. His own commanding presence, his soldier's stride, his cold clarity of thought, all these left him despising Gunter as a mere businessman and Burwick as a conniving weakling. But then suddenly Burwick began to show his true self, and all ideas of controlling the whole show left Keith while he stared in shocked horror as the man unmasked. Alton Burwick was no dirty weakling, no mere ugly fat man, but a monster of evil, a man with a brain like a steel trap, stopping at nothing, and by his very depth of wickedness startling Keith into obedience.

Gunter had wanted to pull out. Only now would Keith admit even to himself the cause of Gunter's death, and he knew he would die as quickly. How many times had he not seen the malevolence in the eyes of Dornie Shaw, and well he knew how close Shaw stood to Burwick. In a sense, they were of a kind.

His feeling of helplessness shocked and horrified Keith. He had always imagined himself a strong man and had gone his way, domineering and supercilious. Now he saw himself as only a tool in the hands of a man he despised, yet unable to escape. Deep within him, there was the hope that they still would pull their chestnuts from the fire and take the enormous profit the deal promised.

One man stood large in his mind, one man drew all his anger, hate, and bitterness. That man was Tom Kedrick.

From that first day Kedrick had made him seem a fool. He, Keith, had endeavored to put Kedrick firmly in his place, speaking of his rank and his twelve years of service, and then Kedrick had calmly paraded an array of military experiences that few men could equal, and right before them all. He had not doubted Kedrick, for vaguely now, he remembered some of the stories he had heard of the man. That the stories were the truth and that Kedrick was a friend of Ransome's infuriated him still more.

He stepped into the makeshift saloon and poured a drink, staring at it gloomily. Fessenden came in, Goff with him.

"We goin' to roust them out of there, Colonel?" Goff asked. "It will be dark, soon."

Keith tossed off his drink. "Yes, right away. Are the rest of them out there?"

"All but Poinsett. He'll be along."

Keith poured another stiff shot and tossed it off as quickly. Then he followed them into the street of Yellow Butte.

They were all gathered there but the Mixus boys, who had followed along toward the canyon, and a couple of the newcomers, who had circled to get on the cliff above and beyond the boulders and brush where the squatters had taken refuge.

Poinsett was walking down the road in long strides. He was abreast of the first house when a woman stepped from the door. She was a square-built woman in a faded blue cotton dress and man's shoes, run down at the heel. She held a double barreled shotgun in her hands, and as Poinsett drew abreast of her, she turned on him and fired.

She fired both barrels at point-blank range, and Poinsett took them right through the middle. Almost torn in two, he hit the ground, gasping once, his blood staining the gray gravel before their shocked eyes.

The woman turned on them, and they saw she was no longer young. Her square face was red, and a few strands of graying hair blew about her face. As she looked at them, her work-roughened hands still clutching the empty shotgun, she motioned at the fallen man in the faded check shirt.

In that moment the fact that she was fat and growing old and that her thick legs ended in the grotesque shoes seemed to vanish, and in the blue eyes were no tears, only her chin trembling a little, as she said, "He was my man. Taggart never give me much, an' he never had it to give, but in his own way, he loved me. You killed him—all of you. I wish I had more shells."

She turned her back on them and without another glance, went into the house and closed the door behind her.

They stood in a grim half circle then, each man faced suddenly with the enormity of what they were doing and had done.

Lee Goff was the first to speak. He stood spraddle-legged, his thick hard body bulging all his clothes, his blond hair bristling. "Anybody bothers that woman," he said, "I'll kill him."

XIII

Keith led his attack just before dusk and lost two men before they withdrew, but not before they learned of the hole. Dornie Shaw squatted behind the abutment formed by the end wall of the canyon where it opened on the plain near the arroyo. "That makes it easy," he said. "We still got dynamite."

Keith's head came up, and he saw Shaw staring at him, his eyes queerly alight. "Or does that go against the grain, Colonel? About ten sticks of dynamite dropped into that crevasse, an' Burwick will get what he wants—no bodies."

"If there's a cave back there," Keith objected, "they'd be buried alive!"

Nobody replied. Keith's eyes wandered around to the other men, but their eyes were on the ground. They were shunning responsibility for this, and only Shaw enjoyed it. Keith shuddered. What a fool he had been to get mixed up in this!

A horse's hoof struck stone, and as one man they looked up. Saddle leather creaked, although they could not see the horse. A spur jingled, and Alton Burwick stood among them.

Loren Keith straightened to his feet and briefly explained the situation. Burwick nodded from time to time and then added, "Use the dynamite. First thing in the morning. That should end it, once and for all."

He drew a cigar from his pocket and bit off the end. "Had a wire. That committee is comin' out, all right. Take them a couple of weeks to get here, an' by that time folks should be over this an' talkin' about somethin' else. I'm figurin' a bonus for you all."

He turned back toward his horse. Then he stopped and catching Dornie Shaw's eye, jerked his head.

Shaw got up from the fire and followed him, and Keith stared after them, his eyes bitter. Now what? Was he being left out of something else?

Beyond the edge of the firelight and beyond the reach of their ears, Burwick paused and let Shaw come up to him. "Nice work, Dornie," he said. "We make a pair, you an' me."

"Yeah," Dornie nodded. "An' sometimes I think a pair's enough."

"Well," Burwick puffed on his cigar, "I need a good man to side me, an' Gunter's gone—at least."

"That company of yours," Dornie was almost whispering, "had too many partners, anyway."

"Uh-huh," Burwick said quietly. "It still has."

"All right, then." Dornie hitched his guns into a firmer seating on his thighs. "I'll be in to see you in a couple of days at most."

Burwick turned and walked away, and Dornie saw him swing easily to the saddle, but it was all very indistinct in the darkness. He stayed where he was, watching the darkness and listening to the slow steps of the horse. They had a funny sound—a very funny sound.

When he walked back to the campfire, he was whistling "Green Grow the Lilacs, O."

The attack came at daybreak. The company had mustered twenty men, of whom two carried packages of dynamite. This was to be the final blow, to wipe out the squatters once and for all.

Shortly before Burwick's arrival, Keith and Dornie Shaw, with Fessenden accompanying them, made a careful reconnaissance of the canyon from the rim. What they found pleased them enormously. It was obvious, once the crevasse had been located, that not more than two men could fire from it at once, and there was plenty of cover from the scattered boulders. In fact, they could get within throwing distance without emerging in the open for more than a few seconds at a time. Much of the squatters' field of fire would be ruined by their proximity to the ground and the rising of the boulders before them.

The attack started well, with all the men moving out, and they made twenty yards into the canyon, moving fast. Here, the great slabs fallen from the slope of Yellow Butte crowded them together. And there the attack stopped.

It stopped abruptly, meeting a withering wall of rifle fire, at point-blank range!

Tom Kedrick knew a thing or two about fighting, and he knew full well that his hideout would in the long run become a deathtrap. He put himself in Keith's place and decided what that man would do. Then he had his eight men, carrying fourteen rifles, slip like Indians through the darkness to carefully selected firing positions far down the canyon from where Keith would be expecting them.

Five of the attackers died in that first burst of fire, and as the gunhands broke for cover, two more went down, and one dragged himself to the camp of the previous night with a shattered kneecap.

He found himself alone.

The wife of Taggart had begun it—the mighty blast of rifle fire completed it.

The company fighters got out of the canyon's mouth, and as one man they moved for their horses, Keith among them and glad to be going. Dornie Shaw watched him mount up and swung up alongside him. Behind them, moving carefully, as if they were perfectly disciplined troops, the defenders of the canyon moved down, firing as they came. A horse dropped, and a man crawled into the rocks and then jumped up and ran. Dai Reid swung wide of the group and started after him. Another went down before they got away, and Kedrick turned to his group. "Get your horses, men. The women will be all right. This is a job that needs finishing now."

A quarter of a mile away, Brokow spotted a horse standing alone and started for it. As he arose from the rocks, a voice called out from behind. "A minute!"

Brokow turned. It was only one man approaching him, the Welshman, Dai Reid. He stared at the man's Spencer, remembering his own gun was empty. He backed up slowly, his eyes haunted.

"My rifle's empty," he said, "an' I've lost my Colt."

"Drop the rifle, then," Dai said quietly. "This I've been wanting, for guns be not my way."

Brokow did not understand, but he dropped his rifle. He was a big man, hulking and considered powerful. He watched

in amazement as Reid placed his Spencer carefully on the
ground and then his gun belt. With bowlegged strides, the
shorter man started for Brokow.

The outlaw stared and then started forward to meet Dai.
As they drew near, he swung. His rocklike fist smashed Dai
Reid flush on the chin. Reid blinked only and then lunged.
Twice more Brokow swung, blows filled with smashing panic
born of the lack of effect of that first punch. Dai seemed
unable to avoid them, and both connected solidly, and then
his huge, big-knuckled hand grasped Brokow's arm and jerked
him near.

The hand slipped to the back of his head and jerked
Brokow's face down to meet the rising of the Welshman's
head. Stars burst before Brokow's eyes, and he felt the bone
go in his nose. He swung wildly, and then those big hands
gripped his throat and squeezed till Brokow was dead. Then
Dai Reid dropped the outlaw to the sand, and turning, he
walked away. He did not notice the horse that stood waiting.
It was a grulla.

In the headlong flight that followed the debacle in the
canyon's mouth, only Lee Goff had purpose. The hard-bitten
Montana gunman had stared reality in the face when Taggart's
wife turned on him. It was only coincidence that she so
resembled his own mother, long since dead of overwork in
rearing seven boys and five girls on a bleak Montana ranch.

He headed directly for Yellow Butte and the Taggart
home. He did not dismount, only he stopped by the door and
knocked gently. It opened, and he faced Mrs. Taggart, her
eyes red now from weeping. "Ma'am," he said, "I guess I
ain't much account, but this here's been too much. I'm driftin'.
Will you take this here—as a favor to me?"

He shoved a thick roll of bills at her, his face flushing
deep red. For an instant, she hesitated, and then she accepted the money with dignity. "Thanks, son. You're a good
boy."

The Old Mormon Trail goes across northern New Mexico
into Colorado and Utah. Lee Goff's bald-faced sorrel stirred
the dust on that road all the way across two states before its
rider began to look the country over.

Behind him, had he known, Tom Kedrick was riding to
Mustang. With him were Laredo Shad, Pit Laine, Dai Reid,
Burt Williams, and the others. They made a tight, grim-faced

little cavalcade, and they rode with their rifles across their saddle forks.

Due west of them, had they only known, another little drama was taking place, for the riders they followed were not all the riders who had abandoned the fight in the canyon. Two of them, Dornie Shaw and Colonel Loren Keith, had headed due west on their own. Both men had their own thoughts and their own ideas of what to do, and among other things, Keith had decided that he had had enough. Whether the others knew it or not, they were through, and he was getting out of the country.

There was some money back there in Mustang, and once he had that, he was going to mount up and head for California. Then let Ransome investigate. After a few years he would return to the East, and if the subject ever came up, would swear he had had nothing to do with it, that he only represented them legally in the first steps of the venture.

What Dornie Shaw was thinking nobody ever guessed, and at this moment, he had no thought at all in his mind. For his mind was not overly given to thought. He liked a few things, although he rarely drank and seemed never to eat much. He liked a good horse and a woman with about the same degree of affection, and he had liked Sue Laine a good bit. But the woman who really fascinated him was Connie Duane, who never seemed aware that he was even alive.

Most of all he liked a gun. When cornered or braced into a fight, he killed as naturally and simply as most men eat. He was a creature of destruction, pure and simple. Never in his life had he been faced with a man who made him doubt his skill. He had never fought with anything but guns, and he vowed he never would.

The two rode rapidly and both were mounted well, so by the time Kedrick was leaving Yellow Butte and lining out for town, they had reached the bank of Salt Creek Wash. Here Keith swung down to tighten his saddle cinch while his horse was drinking. After a moment, Dornie got down, too.

Absently, Keith asked, "Well, Dornie, this breaks it, so where do you think you'll go now?"

"Why, Colonel," Shaw said softly, in his gentle, boy's voice, "I don't know exactly where I'm goin', but this here's as far as you go."

It took a minute for the remark to sink in, and then Keith turned, his puzzled expression stiffening into blank horror and then fear. Dornie Shaw stood negligently watching him, his lips smiling a little, his eyes opaque and empty.

The realization left Loren Keith icy cold. Dornie Shaw was going to kill him.

He had been an utter fool ever to allow this to happen. Why had he left the others and come off with Shaw? Why hadn't he killed him long since, from behind if need be, for the man was like a mad dog. He was insane, completely insane.

"What's on your mind, Shaw?" Without realizing it, he spoke as he might to a subordinate. Shaw was not conscious of the tone. He was looking at Keith's belt line. The colonel, he reflected, had been taking on a little weight here lately.

"Why, just what I say. You've come as far as your trail takes you, Colonel. I can't say I'm sorry."

"Burwick won't like this. We're two of the men on whom he relies."

"Uh-huh, that's the way it was. It ain't now. Back yonder," he jerked his head toward the butte, "he sort of implied he'd got hisself one too many partners." He shoved his hat back a little. "You want to try for your gun? It won't help you none, but you can try."

Keith was frightened. Every muscle within him seemed to have tightened until he could not move, yet he knew he was going to. But at the last, he had something to say, and it came from some deep inner conviction. "Kedrick will kill you, Dornie. He's going to win. He'll beat Burwick, too."

Suddenly, he remembered something. It had been only a fleeting expression on Dornie Shaw's face, but something. "Dornie!" he shot the word out with the force of desperation. "There behind you! The grulla!"

Shaw whirled, his face white, an almost animallike fury on it. As he turned, Keith, gasping hoarsely and triumphantly, grabbed for his gun. He got it, and the gun swung up, but he had never coped with a fighter like Shaw. In the flashing instant that he whirled and found nothing behind him, Dornie hurled himself backward. Keith's shot split wide the air where he had stood an instant before, and then Dornie himself fired from the ground, fired once and then a second time.

Keith caught the bullet through the midsection, right where that extra weight had been gathering, and he took the second one in the same place.

He fell, half in the trickle of water that was Salt Creek. Feeding shells into his gun, Dornie Shaw stared down at the glazing eyes. "How did you know?" he asked sullenly. "How did you know?"

XIV

Fessenden rode well forward in the saddle, his great bulk carried easily with the movement of the horse. His wide face was somber with thought and distaste. Like the others, the wife of Taggart had affected him as nothing else could have. He was a hard man who had done more than his share of killing, but he had killed men ruthlessly, thoughtlessly, in mortal combat where he himself might die as easily.

Several times before he had hired his gun, but each time in cattle or sheep wars or struggles with equals, men as gun wise as he himself. Never before had he actually joined in a move to rob men of their homes. Without conscience in the usual sense, he had it in this case, for the men who moved west, regardless of their brand, were largely men in search of homes. Before, he had thought little of their fight. Several times he had helped to drive nesters from cattle range, and to him that was just and logical, for cows needed grass, and people lived on beef, and most of the range country wasn't suited to farming, anyway.

But in this case there was a difference, he now realized, thinking of it for the first time. In this case men were not being driven off for cattle, but only for profit. To many, the line was a fine one to draw; to Fessenden and his like, once the matter was seen in its true light, that line became a gap, an enormous one.

Actually he rode in a state of shock. The victory Keith had wanted had seemed so near. The taking of the few left in the canyon had seemed simple. His qualms against the use of dynamite he had shrugged off, if uncomfortably. He had gone into the canyon with the others to get the thing over with, to get his money and get out. And then, long before they expected it, came that smashing, thunderous volley, made more crashing by the close canyon walls, more destructive by the way the attackers were channeled by the boulders.

Shock started the panic, and distaste for the whole affair kept some of them, at least, on the move. Yet it was hard to

believe that Clauson and Poinsett were dead, that Brokow
had vanished, that Lee Goff was gone. For alone of the
group, Goff had told Fessenden he was leaving. He had not
needed to tell him why.

Behind him rode the Mixus boys, somber with disap-
pointment at the failure of the attack. They had no qualms
about killing and no lines to draw even at the killing of
women. They were in no true sense fighting men; they were
butchers. Yet even they realized the change that had come
over the group. What had become of Brokow or Goff they did
not know, only that disintegration had set in and that these
men had turned into a snarling pack of wolves venting their
fury and their hatred on each other.

Mustang lay quiet when they rode into town. It was the
quiet before the storm, and the town, like that cattle buyer,
who had turned back to Durango, sensed the coming fury of
battle. No women were on the street, and only a few hardy
souls loitered at the bars or card tables. The chairs before the
St. James were deserted, and Clay Allison had ridden back to
his home ranch, drunk and ugly.

An almost Sunday peace lay over the town when Fessenden drew up before the Mustang Saloon and swung down
from his weary horse. Slapping his hat against his leg to beat
off the dust, Fessenden stood like a great shaggy bull and
surveyed the quiet of the street. He was too knowing a
western man not to recognize the symptoms of disaster.
Clapping his hat all awry upon his shaggy head, he shoved his
bulk through the doors and moved to the bar.

"Rye," he said, his voice booming in the cavernous interior. His eyes glinted around the room and then back to the
bartender.

That worthy could no longer restrain his curiosity. "What's
happened?" he asked, swallowing.

A glint of irony came into the hard eyes of the gunman.
"Them squatters squatted there for keeps," he said wryly,
"an' they showed us they aim to stay put." He tossed off his
drink. "All Hades busted loose." Briefly he explained. "You'd
have figured there was a thousand men in that neck of the
rocks when they opened up. The thing that did it was the
unexpectedness of it, like steppin' on a step in the dark when
it ain't there."

He poured another drink. "It was that Kedrick," he said

grimly. "When I seen him shift to the other side I should've lit a shuck."

"What about Keith?"

"He won't be back."

They turned at the new voice and saw Dornie Shaw standing in the doorway, smiling. Still smiling he walked on in and leaned against the bar. "Keith won't be back," he said. "He went for his gun out on Salt Creek."

The news fell into a silent room. A man at a table shifted his feet, and his chair creaked. Fessenden wet his lips and downed his second drink. He was getting out of town, but fast.

"Seen that girl come in, short time back," the bartender said suddenly, "that Duane girl. Thought she'd gone over to the other side."

Dornie's head lifted. His eyes brightened and then shadowed. He downed his own drink and walked jauntily to the door. "Stick around, Fess. I'll be back." He grinned. "I'll collect for both of us from the old man."

The bartender looked at Fessenden. "Reckon he'll bring it if he does?"

The big gunman nodded absently. "Sure! He's no thief! Why, that kid never stole a thing in his life. He don't believe in it. An' he won't lie or swear—but he'll shoot the heart out of you an' smile right in your face while he's doing it."

The show had folded. The roundup was over. There was nothing to do now but light out. Fessenden knew he should go, but a queer apathy had settled over him, and he ordered another drink, letting the bartender pour it. The liquor he drank seemed now to fall into a cavern without bottom, having no effect.

On the outskirts of town, Tom Kedrick reined in. "We'll keep together," he said quietly. "We want Keith, Shaw, Burwick, the Mixus boys, and Fessenden. There are about four others that you will know whom I don't know by name. Let's work fast and make no mistakes.

"Pit, you take Dai and two men and go up the left side of the street. Take no chances. Arrest them if you can. We'll try them, and," his face was grim, "if we find them guilty they'll have just two sentences—leave the country or hang. The Mixus boys and Shaw," he said, "will hang. They've done murder."

He turned in his saddle and glanced at the tall Texan. "Come on, Shad," he said quietly. "We'll take two men and the right side of the street, which means the livery stable, the St. James and the Mustang."

Kedrick glanced over at Laine. "Pit," he said, "if you run into Allison or Ketchum, better leave 'em alone. We don't want 'em."

Laine's face was grave. "I ain't huntin' 'em," he said grimly, "but if they want it, they can have it."

The parties rode into town and swung down on their respective sides of the street. Laredo grinned at Kedrick, but his eyes were sober. "Nobody wants to cross Laine today," he said quietly. "The man's in a killin' mood. It's his sister."

"Wonder what will happen when they meet?"

"I hope they don't," Shad said, "she's a right pretty sort of gal, only money crazy."

The two men with them stood hesitant, waiting for orders. Both were farmers. One carried a Spencer .56, the other a shotgun. Shad glanced at them. "Let these hombres cover the street, Tom," he suggested. "You take the St. James, an' I'll take the stable."

Kedrick hesitated. "All right," he agreed finally. "But take no chances, boy."

Laredo grinned and waved a negligent hand and walked through the wide door of the stable. Inside, he paused, cold and seemingly careless, actually as poised and deadly as a coiled rattler. He had already seen Abe Mixus' sorrel pony and guessed the two drygulchers were in town. He walked on in a step and saw the barrel of a rifle push through the hay.

He lunged right and dove into a stall, drawing his gun as he went, and ran full tilt into the other Mixus! Their bodies smashed together, and Mixus, caught off balance, went down and rolled over. He came up clawing for a gun. Laredo kicked the gun from under his hand and sent it spinning into the wide open space between the rows of stalls.

With a kind of whining cry, Bean Mixus sprang after it, slid to his knees, and got up, turning. Laredo Shad stood tall and dark, just within the stall, and as Mixus turned like a cornered rat and swung his gun around, Laredo Shad fired, his two shots slamming loud in the stillness of the huge barn. Bean Mixus fell dead.

The rifle bellowed, and a shot ripped the stall stanchion

near his head. Laredo lunged into the open, firing twice more at the stack of straw. The rifle jerked and then thundered again, but the shot went wild. Laredo dove under the loft where Abe Mixus was concealed and fired two more shots through the roof over his head where he guessed the killer would be lying.

Switching his guns, he holstered the empty one and waited. The roof creaked some distance away, and he began to stalk the escaping Mixus, slipping from stall to stall. Suddenly, a back door creaked and a broad path of light shot into the darkness of the stable. Laredo lunged to follow—too late.

The farmer outside with the shotgun was the man Sloan. As Abe Mixus lunged through the door to escape, they came face to face, at no more than twenty feet of distance. Abe had his rifle at his hip, and he fired. The shot ripped through the water trough beside Sloan, and the farmer squeezed off the left-hand barrel of his shotgun.

The solid core of shot hit Mixus in the shoulder and neck, knocking him back against the side of the door, his long face drawn and terror stricken, his neck and shoulder a mass of blood that seemed to well from a huge wound. He fought to get his gun up, but Sloan stepped around, remembering Bob McLennon's death and the deaths of Steelman and Slagle. The other barrel thundered, and a sharp blast of flame stabbed at Abe Mixus.

Smashed and dead, the killer sagged against the doorjamb, his old hat falling free, his face pillowed in the gray, blood-mixed dust.

Silence hung heavy in the wake of the shots. Into that silence Laredo Shad spoke. "Hold it, Sloan!" He stepped through the door, taking no glance at the fallen man. "The other one won't hang, either," he said. "They were both inside."

The two men drew aside, Sloan's face gray and sick. He had never killed a man before and wanted never to again. He tried to roll a smoke, but his fingers trembled. Shad took the paper and tobacco from him and rolled it. The farmer looked up, shamefaced. "Guess I'm yellow," he said. "That sort of got me."

The Texan looked at him gloomily. "Let's hope it always does," he said. He handed him the cigarette. "Try this," he told him. "It will make you feel better. Wonder how Kedrick's comin'?"

"Ain't heard nothin'!"

Pit Laine stood in a door across the street. "Everythin' all right?" he called.

"Yeah," the other farmer called back, "only you don't have to look for the Mixus boys no more. They ain't gonna be around."

Captain Tom Kedrick had walked up the street and turned into the door of the St. James Hotel. The wide lobby was still, a hollow shell, smelling faintly of old tobacco fumes and leather. The wrinkled clerk looked up and shook his head. "Quiet today," he said. "Nobody around. Ain't been no shootin' in days."

Guns thundered from down the street, then again and again. Then there was silence and then the two solid blasts of the shotgun.

Both men listened, and no further sound came. A moment later Pit Laine called out and the farmer answered. The clerk nodded. "Same town," he said. "Last couple of days I been wonderin' if I wasn't back in Ohio. Awful quiet lately," he said, "awful quiet."

Tom Kedrick walked down the hall and out the back door. He went down the weathered steps and stopped on the grass behind the building. There was an old, rusty pump there, and the sun was hot on the backs of the buildings. He walked over to the pump and worked the handle. It protested, whining and groaning at the unaccustomed work and finally, despairing of rest, threw up a thick core of water that splashed in the wooden tub. When he had pumped for several minutes, Kedrick held the gourd dipper under the pump and let it fill. The water was clear and very cold. He drank greedily, rested, and then drank again.

Far up the backs of the buildings, at the opposite end of town, a man was swinging an ax. Kedrick could see the flash of light on the blade and see the ax strike home, and a moment later the sound would come to him. He watched and then wiped the back of his hand across his mouth and started along in back of the buildings toward the Mustang.

He moved with extreme care, going steadily, yet with every sense alert. He wore his .44 Russians and liked the feel of them, ready to his hands. The back door of the Mustang was long unpainted and blistered by many hot suns. He glanced at the hinges and saw they were rusty. The door would squeak. Then he saw the outside stair leading to the second floor, and turning, he mounted the stairs on tiptoe, easing through that door and walking down the hall.

In the saloon below, Fessenden had eliminated half a bottle of whiskey without destroying the deadening sense of futility that had come over him. He picked up a stack of cards and riffled them skillfully through his fingers, and there was no lack of deftness there. Whatever effect the whiskey had had, it was not on his hands.

Irritated, he slammed the cards down and stared at the bartender. "Wish Dornie'd get back," he said for the tenth time, "I want to leave this town. She don't feel right today."

He had heard the shots down the street, but had not moved from the bar. "Some drunk cowhand," he said irritably.

"You better look," the bartender suggested, hoping for no fights in the saloon. "It might might be some of your outfit."

"I got no outfit," Fess replied shortly. "I'm fed up. That stunt out there to Yellow Butte drove me off that range. I'll have no more of it."

He heard the footsteps coming down the hall from upstairs and listened to their even cadence. He glanced up, grinning. "Sounds like an Army man. "Listen!"

Realization of what he had said came over him, and the grin left his face. He straightened, resting his palms on the bar. For a long moment, he stared into the bartender's eyes. "I knew it! I knew that hombre would—" He tossed off his drink. "Aw, I didn't want to leave town, anyway!"

He turned, moving back from the bar. He stood spraddle-legged, like a huge grizzly, his big hands swinging at his hips, his eyes glinting upward at the balcony and the hall that gave onto it. The steps ceased, and Tom Kedrick stood there, staring down at him.

Neither man spoke for a full minute, while suspense gripped the watchers, and then it was Fessenden who broke the silence. "You lookin' for me, Kedrick?"

"For any of your crowd. Where's Shaw? And Keith?"

"Keith's dead. Shaw killed him back up on the Salt after you whipped us in the canyon. I dunno where he is now."

Silence fell once more, and the two men studied each other. "You were among them at Chimney Rock, Fessenden,"

Kedrick said. "That was an ambush—drygulcher's stunt, Fess."
Kedrick took another step forward. Then he sidestepped
down the first step of the stairs that ran along the back wall
until about six steps from the bottom. Then, after walking
across a landing, he came down facing the room.

Fessenden stood there, swaying slightly on his thick,
muscular legs, his brutal jaw and head thrust forward. "Aw,
hell!" he said, and grabbed iron.

His guns fairly leaped from their holsters spouting flame.
A bullet smashed the top of the newel-post at the head of the
stairs and then ricocheted into the wall. Another punctured a
hole just behind Kedrick's shoulder. Tom Kedrick stepped
down another step and then fired. His bullet turned Fessenden,
and Kedrick ran lightly down four steps while Fessenden
smashed two shots at him.

Kedrick dove headlong for the landing, brought up hard
against the wall, and smashed another shot at the big man. It
knocked a leg from under him and he rolled over on his feet,
colliding with the bar.

He had been hit twice, but he was cold sober and deadly.
He braced himself and with his left hand clinging to the bar,
lifted his right and thumbed back the hammer. Kedrick fired
two quick shots with his left gun. One ripped a furrow down
the bar and hit Fessenden below the breast bone, a jagged,
tearing piece of metal when it struck.

Fessenden fired again, but the bullet went wild, and his
sixth shot was fired in desperation as he swung up his left-
hand gun, dropping the right into his holster. Taking his
time, feeling his life's blood running out of him, he braced
himself there and took the gun over into his right hand. He
was deliberate and calm. "Pour me a drink," he said.

The bartender, lying flat on his face behind the bar,
made no move. Tom Kedrick stood on the edge of the landing now, staring at Fessenden. The big gunman had been hit
three times, through the shoulder, the leg and the chest,
and he still stood there, gun in hand, ponderous and
invulnerable.

The gun came up, and Fessenden seemed to lean forward with it. "I wish you was Dornie," he said.

Kedrick triggered. The shot nailed Fessenden through
the chest again. The big man took a fast step back and then
another. His gun slipped from his hand, and he grabbed a

glass standing on the bar. "Gimme a drink!" he demanded. Blood bubbled at his lips.

Tom Kedrick came down the steps, his gun ready in his hand and walked toward Fessenden. Holding his gun level and low down with his right hand, Kedrick picked up the bottle with his left and filled the empty glass. Then he pulled over another glass and poured one for himself.

Fessenden stared at him. "You're a good man, Kedrick," he said, shaping the words patiently. "I'm a good man, too—on the wrong side."

"I'll drink to that." Kedrick lifted his glass. They clicked them, and Fessenden grinned crookedly over his.

"You watch that Dornie," he advised, "he's rattler—mean." The words stumbled from his mouth and he frowned, lifting the glass. He downed his drink, choked on it, and started to hold out his big hand to Kedrick. Then he fell flat on his face. Holstering his gun, Tom Kedrick leaned over and gripped the big right hand. Fessenden grinned and died.

XV

Connie Duane had reached Mustang only a short time before the survivors of the fight at Yellow Butte began to arrive. Restless, after the leaving of the men for their return to the squatters' town, she had begun to think of what lay ahead, of Fred Ransome and the impending investigation and of her uncle's part in it.

All his papers as well as many of her own remained under lock in the gray stone house in Mustang, but if she was to get her own money back from Burwick or was to clear any part of the blame from her uncle, she knew it must be done with those papers. Mounting her horse she left the camp beyond the rim and striking the Old Mormon Trail, headed south. She was on that trail when the sun lifted, and she heard the distant sound of shots.

Turning from the trail she reined her horse into the bed of Salt Creek and rode south, passing the point where only a short time later Loren Keith was to meet his death at the hands of Dornie Shaw. Once in town, she believed, she would be safe, and she doubted if anyone would be left in the gray house unless it was Burwick, and she knew that he rarely left his chair.

Arriving in Mustang, she rode quickly up the street and then cut over behind the stone house and dismounted. She went into the house through the back door and went very quietly. Actually, she need not have bothered, for Alton Burwick was not there. Making her way up the old stairs, she unlocked the door to the apartment she had shared with her uncle and closed the door behind her.

Nothing seemed to have been disturbed. The blinds were drawn as she had left them, and the room was still. A little dust had collected, and the light filtering in around the blinds showed it to her. Going to her trunk, she opened it and got out the ironbound box in which she carried her own papers. It was intact and showed no evidence of having been tampered with. From the bottom of the trunk she took an old purse in which there were two dozen gold eagles, and these she changed to the purse she was now carrying.

Among other things, there was an old pistol there, a huge, cumbersome old thing. This she got out and laid on the table beside her. Then she found a derringer seven-shot .22 caliber pistol her father had given her several years before he died, and she put it in the pocket of her dress.

Hurrying across the room, she went into the next room and began to go through her uncle's desk, working swiftly and surely. Most of his papers were readily available, and apparently nobody had made any effort to go through them, probably believing they contained nothing of consequence or that there would be plenty of time later. She was busy at this when she heard a horse walk by the house and stop near the back steps.

Instantly she stopped what she was doing and stood erect. The window here was partly open and she could hear the saddle creak very gently as whoever it was swung down. Then a spur jingled, and there was a step below, then silence.

"So? It's you."

Startled by the voice, Connie turned. Sue Laine stood behind her, staring with wide eyes. "Yes," Connie replied, "I came for some things of mine. You're Sue, aren't you?"

Without replying to the question, the girl nodded her head toward the window. "Who was that? Did you see?"

"No. It was a man."

"Maybe Loren has come back." Sue studied her, unsmiling. "How are they out there? Are they all right? I mean—did you see Pit?"

"Yes. He's unhappy about you."

Sue Laine flushed, but her chin lifted proudly. "I suppose he is, but what did he expect? That I was going to live all my life out there in that awful desert? I'm sick of it! Sick of it, I tell you!"

Connie smiled. "That's strange. I love it. I love it, and every minute I'm there, I love it more. I'd like to spend my life here, and I believe I will."

"With Tom Kedrick?"

Sue's jealousy flashed in her eyes, yet there was curiosity, too. Connie noticed how the other girl studied her clothes, her face.

"Why—I—where did you ever get that idea?"

"From looking at him. What girl wouldn't want him? Anyway, he's the best of the lot."

"I thought you liked Colonel Keith?"

Sue's face flushed again. "I—I—thought I did, too. Only part of it was because Tom Kedrick wouldn't notice me. And because I wanted to get away from here, from the desert. But since then—I guess Pit hates me."

"No brother really hates his sister, I think. He'd be glad to see you back with him."

"You don't know him. If it had been anybody but someone associated with Alton Burwick, why—"

"You mean, you knew Burwick before?"

"Knew him?" Sue stared at her. "Didn't you know? Didn't he tell you? He was our stepfather."

"Alton Burwick?" Connie stared in amazement.

"Yes, and we always suspected that he killed my father. We never knew, but my mother suspected later, too, for she took us and ran away from him. He came after us. We never knew what happened to mother. She went off one night for something and never came back, and we were reared by a family who just took us in."

A board creaked in the hall, and both girls were suddenly still, listening.

Guns thundered from the street of the town, and both girls stared at each other, holding their breath. There was a brief silence and then a further spattering of shots. Then the door opened very gently and Dornie Shaw stood there facing the two girls.

He seemed startled at finding the girls together and

looked from one to the other, his brown eyes bright, but now confused.

Then he centered his eyes on Sue Laine. "You better get out," he said. "Keith's dead."

"Dead?" Sue gasped, horrified. "They—they killed him?"

"No. I did. Up on the Salt. He drew on me."

"Keith—dead." Sue was shocked.

"What about the others? Where are they?" Connie asked quickly.

Dornie turned his head sharply around and looked hard at her, a curious, prying gaze as if he did not quite know what to make of her. "Some of 'em dead," he said matter of factly. "They whipped us. It was that Kedrick," he spoke without emotion or shadow of prejudice, as though completely indifferent. "He had 'em set for us, an' they mowed us down." He jerked his head toward the street. "I guess they are finishin' up now. The Mixus boys an' Fessenden are down there."

"They'll be coming here," Connie said with conviction. "This is the next place."

"I reckon." He seemed indifferent to that, too. "Kedrick'll be the first one. Maybe," he smiled, "the last one."

He dug out the makings, glancing around the room and then back at Sue. "You get out. I want to talk to Connie."

Sue did not move. "You can talk to us both. I like it here."

As he touched his tongue to the paper his eyes lifted and met hers. They were flat, expressionless. "You heard me," he said. "I'd hate to treat you rough."

"You haven't the nerve!" Sue flashed back. "You know what would happen to you if you laid hands on a woman in this country! You can get away with killing me, but this country won't stand for having their women bothered, even by a ratty little killer like you!"

Connie Duane was remembering the derringer in her pocket and lowered her hand to her hip within easy grasp of the gun.

A sudden cannonade sounded and then a scattering of more shots. At that moment Kedrick was finally shooting it out with Fessenden. Dornie Shaw cocked an inquisitive ear toward the sound. "Gettin' closer," he said. "I ain't really in no hurry until Kedrick gets here."

"You'd better be gone before he does come." Connie was surprised at the confidence in her voice. "He's too much for you, and he's not half frightened like these others are. He'll kill you, Dornie."

He stared at her and then chuckled without humor. "Him? Bah! The man doesn't live who can outdraw Dornie Shaw! I've tried 'em all! Fess? He's supposed to be good, but he don't fool with Dornie! I'd shoot his ears off."

Calmly, Connie dropped her right hand into her pocket and clutched the derringer. The feel of it gave her confidence. "You had better go," she said quietly. "You were not invited here, and we don't want you."

He did not move. "Still playin' it high an' mighty, are you? You've got to get over that. Come on, you're coming with me."

"Are you leaving?" Connie's eyes flashed. "I'll not ask you again!"

Shaw started to speak, but whatever it was he planned to say never formed into words, for Connie had her hand on the derringer, and she fired from her pocket. Ordinarily, she was a good shot, but had never fired the gun from that position. The first bullet burned a furrow along Dornie Shaw's ear, notching it at the top, the second stung him along the ribs, and the third plowed into the table beside him.

With a grunt of surprise, he dove through the door into the hall. Sue was staring at Connie. "Well, I never!" Her eyes dropped to the tiny gun that Connie had now drawn from her pocket. "Dornie Shaw! And with that! Oh, just wait until this gets around!" Her laughter rang out merrily, and despite herself, Connie was laughing, too.

Downstairs near the door, Dornie Shaw clutched his bloody ear and panted as though he had been running, his face twisting as he stared at his blood. Amazed, he scarcely noticed when Kedrick came up the steps, but as the door pushed open, he saw him. For a fatal instant, he froze. Then he grabbed for his gun, but he had lost his chance. In that split second of hesitation, Kedrick jumped. His right hand grasped Dornie's gun wrist, and Kedrick swung the gunman bodily around, hurling him into the wall. Shaw's body hit with a crash, and he rebounded into a wicked right to the wind.

Shaw was no fighter with his hands, and the power of that blow would have wrecked many a bigger man. As it was, it knocked every bit of wind from the gunman's body, and then Kedrick shoved him back against the wall. "You asked me what I'd do, once, with a faster man. Watch this, Dornie!"

Kedrick lifted his right hand and slapped the gunman across the mouth. Crying with fury, Shaw fought against the bigger man's grip while Kedrick held him flat against the wall, gripping him by the shirt collar, and slapped him, over and back. "Just a cheap killer!" Kedrick said calmly. "Somebody has already bled you a little. I'll do it for good."

He dropped a hand to Dornie's shirt and ripped it wide. "I'm going to ruin you in this country, Dornie. I'm going to show them what you are—a cheap, yellow-bellied killer who terrorizes men better than himself." He slapped Dornie again and then shoved him into the wall once more and stepped back.

"All right, Shaw! You got your guns! Reach!"

Almost crying with fury, Dornie Shaw grabbed for his guns, but as he whipped them free, all his timing wrecked by the events of the past few minutes, Kedrick's gun crashed and Shaw's right-hand gun was smashed from his hand. Shaw fired the left-hand gun, but the shot went wild, and Kedrick lunged, chopping down with his pistol barrel. The blow smashed Dornie Shaw's wrist and he dropped the gun with a yelp.

He fell back against the wall, trembling and staring at his hands. His left wrist was broken and his right thumb was gone, and where it had been, blood was welling.

Roughly, Kedrick grabbed him and shoved him out the door. He stumbled and fell, but Kedrick jerked him to his feet, unmindful of the gasps of the onlookers attracted by the sounds of fighting. In the forefront of the crowd were Pit Laine, Dai Reid, and Laredo Shad, blinking with astonishment at the sight of the most feared gunman in the country being treated like a whipped child.

Shaw's horse stood nearby, and Kedrick motioned to him. "Get on him—backwards!"

Shaw started to turn and Kedrick lifted his hand and the gunman ducked instinctively. "Get up there! Dai, when he's up, tie his ankles together."

Dornie Shaw, befuddled by the whipping he had taken, scarcely aware of what was happening, lifted his eyes. Only he saw the grulla tied near the stone house. It was the last straw; his demoralization was complete.

Feared because of his deadly skill with guns and his love

of killing for the sake of killing, he had walked a path alone, avoided by all or catered to by them. Never in his life had he been manhandled as he had been by Tom Kedrick. His ego was shattered.

"Take him through the town." Kedrick's voice was harsh. "Show them what a killer looks like. Then fix up that thumb and wrist and turn him loose."

"Turn him loose?" Shad demanded. "Are you crazy?"

"No, turn him loose. He'll leave this country so far behind nobody will ever see him again. This is worse than death for him, believe me. He shrugged. "I've seen them before. All they need, that kind, is for somebody to face them once who isn't afraid. He was fast and accurate with his guns, so he developed the idea he was tough.

"Other folks thought the same thing. He wasn't tough. A tough man has to win and lose, he has to come up after being knocked down, he has to have taken a few beatings and know what it means to win the hard way.

"Anybody," he said dryly, "can knock a man down. When you've been knocked down at least three times yourself and then got up and floored the other man, then you can figure you're a tough hombre. Those smoke poles of Shaw's greased his path for him. Now he knows what he's worth."

The crowd drifted away, and Connie Duane was standing in the doorway. Tom Kedrick looked up at her, and suddenly he smiled. To see her now, standing like this in the doorway, was like life-giving rain upon the desert, coming in the wake of many heat-filled days.

She came down the steps to him and then looked past him at Pit. "Your sister's upstairs, Pit. You'd better talk to her."

Laine hesitated; then he said stiffly, "I don't reckon I want to."

Laredo Shad drew deep on his cigarette and squinted through the smoke at Laine. "Mind if I do?" he asked. "I like her."

Pit Laine was astonished. "After this?"

Shad looked at the fire end of his cigarette. "Well," he said, speaking seriously, "the best cuttin' horse I ever rode was the hardest to break. Them with lots of get up an' go to 'em often make the best stock."

"Then go ahead." Pit stared after him. Then he said, "Tell her I'll be along later."

XVI

For three weeks, there was no sign of Alton Burwick. He seemed to have vanished into the earth, and riders around the country reported no sign of him.

At the end of that time three men got down from the afternoon stage and were shown to rooms in the St. James. An hour later, while they were at dinner, Captain Tom Kedrick pushed open the door and walked into the dining room. Instantly, one of the men, a tall, immaculate young man whose hair was turning gray at the temples, arose to meet him, hand outstretched. "Tom! Say, this is wonderful! Gentlemen, this is Tom Kedrick, the man I was telling you about. We served together in the war between the states! Tom—Mr. Edgerton and Mr. Cummings."

The two men, one a pudgy man with a round, cheerful face, the other as tall as Frederic Ransome, with gray muttonchop whiskers, acknowledged the introduction. When Kedrick had seated himself, they began demanding details. Quietly, and as concisely as possible, he told them his own story from his joining the company in New Orleans.

"And Burwick's gone?" Edgerton asked. He was the older man with the muttonchop whiskers. "Was he killed?"

"I doubt it, sir," Kedrick replied. "He simply vanished. The man had a faculty for being out of the way when trouble came. Since he left, with the aid of Miss Duane's and her uncle's papers, we've managed to put together most of the facts. However, Burwick's papers have disappeared, or most of them."

"Disappeared?" Edgerton asked. "How did that happen?"

"Miss Duane tells me that when she entered the house before the final trouble with Shaw, she passed the office door and the place was undisturbed and the desk all in order. After the crowd had gone and when we returned, we saw that somebody had been rifling the desk and the safe."

"You imply that Burwick returned? That he was there then?"

"He must have been. Connie—Miss Duane—tells me that only he had the combination and that he kept all the loose ends of the business in his hands."

Cummings stared hard at Kedrick. "You say that this

Shaw fellow killed Keith? How do we know that you didn't? You admit to killing Fessenden."

"I did kill him. In a fair fight before witnesses. I never even saw Keith's body after he was killed."

"Who do you think killed John Gunter?" Cummings demanded.

"My guess would be Burwick."

"I'm glad you're not accusing Keith of that," Cummings replied dryly.

"Keith wouldn't have used a knife," Kedrick replied quietly. "Neither would he have attacked him from behind, as was obviously the case."

"This land deal, Kedrick," Ransome asked. "Where do you stand in it?"

"I? I don't stand at all. I'm simply not in it."

Cummings looked up sharply. "You don't stand to profit from it at all? Not in any way?"

"How could I? I own nothing. I have no holdings or claim to any."

"You said Burwick promised you fifteen percent?"

"That's right. But I know now that it was merely to appease me long enough to get me on the spot at Chimney Rock, where I was to be killed along with the others. Burwick got me there and then rode off on the pretext that he wanted to look at a mineral ledge."

"How about this girl? The Duane girl?" Cummings asked sharply. "Does she stand to profit?"

"She will be fortunate to get back her money that her uncle invested."

"See, Cummings?" Ransome said. "I told you Kedrick was honest. I know the man."

"I'll give my opinion on that later, after this investigation is completed. Not now. I want to go over the ground and look into this matter thoroughly. I want to investigate this matter of the disappearance of Alton Burwick, too. I'm not at all satisfied with this situation."

He glanced down at the notes in his hand and then looked up. "As to that, Kedrick, wasn't Fessenden a duly elected officer of the law when you shot him? Wasn't he the sheriff?"

"Elected by a kangaroo election," Kedrick replied, "where the votes were counted by the two officials who won. If that is a legal election, then he was sheriff."

"I see. But you do not deny that he had authority?"

"I do deny it."

Connie Duane was awaiting him when he walked back to his table. She smiled as he sat down, and listened to his explanation. She frowned thoughtfully. "Cummings? I think there is something in Uncle John's papers about him. I believe he was acting for them in Washington."

"That explains a lot then." Kedrick picked up his coffee cup and then put it down abruptly, for Laredo Shad had come into the room, his face sharp and serious. He glanced around and sighting Kedrick, hurried toward him, spurs jingling. Kedrick got to his feet. "What's wrong? What's happened?"

"Plenty! Sloan was wounded last night and Yellow Butte burned!"

"What?" Kedrick stared.

Shad nodded grimly. "You shouldn't have turned that rat loose. That Dornie Shaw."

Kedrick shook his head irritably. "I don't believe it. He was thoroughly whipped when he left here. I think he ran like a scared rabbit when he left, and if he did want revenge, it would be after a few months, not so soon. No, this is somebody else."

"Who could it be?"

His eyes met Connie's and she nodded, her eyes frightened. "You know who it could be, Tom. It could be Burwick."

Of course, that was what he had been thinking. Burwick had bothered him, getting away scot-free, dropping off the end of the world into oblivion as he had. Remembering the malignant look in the man's eyes, Kedrick was even more positive. Burwick had counted on this land deal. He had worked on it longer than any one of them, and it meant more to him.

"Shad," he said suddenly, "where does that grulla tie in? It keeps turning up, again and again. There's something more about all this than we've ever known, something that goes a lot deeper. Who rides the grulla? Why is it he has never been seen? Why was Dornie so afraid of it?"

"Was he afraid of the grulla?" Shad asked, frowning. "That doesn't figure."

"Why doesn't it? That's the question now. You know, that last day when I had Shaw thoroughly whipped, he looked up and saw something that scared him, yet something that I think he more than half expected. After he was gone down the street, I looked around, and there was nothing there. Later, I stumbled across the tracks of the grulla mustang. That horse was in front of the house during all the excitement!"

Frederic Ransome came into the room again and walked to their table. "Cummings is going to stir up trouble," he said, dropping into a chair. "He's out to get you, Kedrick, and if he can, to pin the killing of Keith on you, or that of Burwick. He claims your story is an elaborate buildup to cover the murder of all three of the company partners. He can make so much trouble that none of the squatters will get anything out of the land and nothing for all their work. We've got to find Burwick."

Laredo lit a cigarette. "That's a tough one," he said, "but maybe I've got a hunch."

"What?" Kedrick looked up.

"Ever hear Burwick talk about the grulla?"

"No, I can't say that I did. It was mentioned before him once that I recall, and he didn't seem interested."

"Maybe he wasn't interested because he knowed all about it," Shad suggested. "That Burwick has me puzzled."

Connie looked up at him. "You may be right, Laredo, but Pit and Sue Laine were Burwick's stepchildren, and they knew nothing about the horse. The only one who seemed to know anything was Dornie Shaw."

Tom Kedrick got up. "Well, there's one thing we can do," he said. "Laredo, we can scout out the tracks of that horse and trail it down. Pick up an old trail, anything. Then just see where it takes us."

On the third day it began to rain. All week the wind had been chill and cold, and clouds had hung low and flat across the sky from horizon to horizon. Hunched in his slicker, Laredo slapped his gloved hands together and swore. "This finishes it!" he said with disgust. "It will wipe out all the trails for us!"

"All old anyway," Kedrick agreed. "We've followed a dozen here lately, and none of them took us anywhere. All disappeared on rock or were swept away by wind."

"Escavada's cabin isn't far up this canyon," Shad suggested. "Let's hit him up for chow. It will be a chance to get warm, anyway."

"Know him?"

"Stopped in there once. He's half Spanish, half Ute. Tough old blister, an' been in this country since before the grass came. He might be able to tell us something."

The trail into the canyon was slippery, and the dull red of the rocks had turned black under the rain. It slanted across the sky in a drenching downpour, and when they reached the stone cabin in the corner of the hills, both men and horses were cold, wet, and hungry.

Escavada opened the door for them and waved them in. He grinned at them. "Glad to have company," he said. "Ain't seen a man for three weeks."

When they had stripped off their slickers and peeled down to shirts, pants, and boots, he put coffee before them and laced it with a strong shot of whiskey. "Warm you up," he said. "Trust you ain't goin' out again soon. Whiskey's mighty fine when a body comes in from the cold, but not if he's goin' out again. It flushes the skin up, fetches all the heat to the surface, and then gives it off into the air. Man freezes mighty quick, drinkin' whiskey."

"You ever see a grulla mustang around, Escavada?" Laredo asked suddenly, looking up at the old man.

He turned on them, his eyes bright with malicious humor. "You ain't some of them superstitious kind, be you? Scared of the dark like? An' ghosts?"

"No," Kedrick said, "but what's the tie-up?"

"That grulla. Old story in this here county. Dates back thirty, forty years. Maybe further than that. Sign of death or misfortune, folks say."

Laredo looked inquiringly at Kedrick, and Kedrick asked, "You know anything about it? That horse is real enough. We've both seen the grulla."

"So've I," the old man said. He dropped into a chair and grinned at them. His gray hair was sparse, but his eyes were alive and young. "I seen it many times, an' no misfortune come my way. Not unless you call losin' my shovel a misfortune."

He hitched his chair nearer the woodpile and tossed a couple of sticks on the fire. "First I heard of it was long ago. Old folks used to tell of a Spanish man in armor, ridin' a mouse-colored horse. He used to come an' go about the hills, but the story back of it seems to be that a long time back some such fellow was mighty cruel to the Injuns. That story sort of hung around an' a body heard it every now and again until about fifteen, sixteen years back. Since then, she's been mighty lively."

"You mean, you heard the story more since then?" Kedrick asked.

"Uh-huh. Started with a wagon train wiped out by Injuns up on the Salt. Every man jack of them killed dead—womenfolks, too, the story was. There was a youngster come off scot-free, boy about five or six years old. He crawled off into the brush, an' after, he swore them Injuns was led by a white man on a grulla horse, a white man in armor!"

"Wild yarn," Shad said, "but you can't blame the kid, imaginin' things after what he must've seen."

"He said that hombre in the armor went around with a long knife, an' he skewered every one of the bodies to make sure they was real dead. He said once that hombre looked right square at him, layin' in the brush, an' he was scared like all get-out, but must've been he wasn't seen, 'cause he wasn't bothered."

"An' this grulla has been seen since?" Shad asked. "Regular?"

"Uh-huh, but never no rider close enough to say who or what. Sometimes off at a distance, sometimes just the horse, standin'. Most folks get clear off when they see that horse."

He got up and brought back the coffeepot. "Right odd you should ask me about him now," he commented. "Right odd."

Both men looked at him, and sensing their acute interest, he continued. "Been huntin' here lately. Caught me a few bees off the cactus an' mesquite, figurin' to start a bee line. Well, I got her started, all right, an' I trailed them bees to a place far south of here.

"South an' west, actually. Most of this country hereabouts is worked out of bees. I been at it too long, so I was workin' a good ways off. Well, my bee line took me over toward the Hogback. You know that place?

"She's a high curvin' ridge maybe five or six hundred feet at the crest, but she rises mighty close to straight up for four hundred feet. Crawlin' up there to locate the cave them bees was workin' out of, I come on a cave like a cliff dwellin', only it wasn't. She was manmade, an' most likely in the past twenty years or so.

"What started me really lookin' was my shovel—the one I lost. She was right there on that ledge, so I knowed it hadn't been lost, but stole off me, so I began huntin' around. I found back inside this place it was all fixed up for livin'. Some grub there, blankets, a couple of guns, an' under some duffle in the corner, an old-time breastplate an' helmet."

"You're serious?" Kedrick demanded incredulously.

"Sure as I'm alive! But," Escavada chuckled, "that ain't the best of it. Lyin' there on the floor, deader than last years hopes, was a young fellow. He had a knife, old-time Spanish knife that a fellow in armor might have carried, an' it was skewered right through him!"

"A young man—dead?" Kedrick suddenly leaned forward. "Anything odd about him? I mean, was he missing a thumb?"

Escavada stared. "Well, now, if that don't beat all! He was missin' a thumb, an' he was crippled up mighty bad in the other arm. Carried her in a sling."

"Dornie Shaw!" Laredo leaped to his feet. "Dornie Shaw, by all that's holy!"

"Shaw?" Escavada puckered his brows, his old eyes gleaming. "Now that's most odd, most odd! Shaw was the name of that boy, the one who didn't get killed with the wagon train!"

Kedrick's face was a study. Dornie Shaw—dead! But if Dornie had been the boy from the wagon train, that would account for his superstitious fear of the grulla mustang. But to suppose that after all these years Dornie had been killed by the same man, or ghost if you believed in ghosts, that killed the rest of them so many years before was too ridiculous. It was, he thought suddenly, unless you looked at it just one way.

"Man can't escape his fate," Escavada said gloomily. "That boy hid out from that knife, but in the end it got him."

Kedrick got up. "Could you take us to that place, Escavada? Down there on the Hogback?"

"I reckon." He glanced outside. "But not in this rain. Rheumatiz gets me."

"Then tell me where it is," Kedrick said, "because I'm going now!"

They were crossing the head of Coal Mine Creek when Laredo saw the tracks. He drew up suddenly, pointing at the tracks of a horse, well shod. "The grulla!" Kedrick said grimly. "I'd know those tracks anywhere!"

They pushed on. It was very late, and the pelting rain still poured down upon their heads and shoulders. The trails were slippery, and dusk was near. "We'd better find us a hole to crawl into," Shad suggested. "We'll never find that horse in this weather!"

"By morning the tracks will be gone, and I've a hunch we'll find our man right in that cliff dwelling where Escavada saw Dornie's body!"

"Wonder how Dornie found the place?"

"If what I think is right," Kedrick replied, wiping the rain from his face, "he must have run into an old friend and been taken there to hide out. That old friend was the same rider of the grulla that killed his family and friends with the wagon train, and when he saw that armor, he knew it."

"But what's it all about?" Shad grumbled. "It don't make sense! An' no horse lives that long."

"Sure not. There may have been a half dozen grullas in that length of time. This man probably tried to capitalize on the fears of the Indians and Mexicans who live up that way to keep them off his trail. We'll probably find the answer when we reach the end of our ride!"

The Hogback loomed black and ominous before them. The trail, partly switchback and partly sheer climb, led over the sharp, knifelike ridge. They mounted, their horses laboring heavily at the steep and slippery climb. Twice, Tom Kedrick saw the tracks of the grulla on the trail, and in neither case could those tracks have been more than an hour old.

Kedrick glanced down when they saw the opposite side and then dismounted. "This one is tricky," he said grimly. "We'd better walk it."

Halfway down, lightning flashed, and in the momentary brightness, Laredo called out, "Watch it, Tom! High, right!"

Kedrick's head jerked around just as the rifle boomed. The bullet smacked viciously against the rock beside him, spattering his face with splinters. He grabbed for his gun, but it was under his slicker. The gun boomed again, five fast shots, as fast as the marksman could work the lever of his rifle.

Behind Tom Kedrick, the anguished scream of a wounded horse cut the night, and Shad's warning yell was drowned in the boom of the gun again. Then he flattened against the rock barely in time to avoid the plunging, screaming horse!

His own Appaloosa, frightened, darted down the trail with the agility of a mountain goat. The rifle boomed again, and he dropped flat.

"Shad? You all right?"

There was a moment before the reply, and then it was hoarse, but calm. "Winged me, but not bad."

"I'm going after him. You all right?"

"Yeah. You might help me wrap this leg up."

Sheltered by the glistening, rain-wet rock, with gray mist swirling past them on the high ridge of the Hogback, Kedrick knelt in the rain. Shielding the bandage from the rain with a slicker, he bound the leg. The bullet had torn through the flesh, but the bone was not broken.

XVII

When the wound was bandaged, Kedrick drew back into the shelter of the slight overhang and stared about. Ahead and below them was a sea of inky blackness. Somewhere down that mountain would be their horses, one probably dead or dying, the other possibly crippled.

Around them all was night and the high, windy, rain-wet rocks. And out there in the darkness a killer stalked them, a killer who could at all of three hundred yards spot his shots so well as to score two hits on a target seen only by a brief flash of lightning. Next time, those shots could kill. And there was no doubt about it. Now the situation was clear. It was kill or be killed.

"Sure," Laredo said dryly, "you got to get him, man. But you watch it. He's no slouch with that Spencer!"

"You've got to get off this ridge," Kedrick insisted. "The cold and rain up here will kill you!"

"You leave that to me," Shad replied shortly. "I'll drag myself down the trail an' find a hole to crawl into down on the flat below this Hogback. Might even find your palouse down there. You got grub an' coffee in those saddlebags?"

"Yeah, but you'd better not try a fire until I come back."

Shad chuckled. "Make sure you come back. I never did like to eat alone!"

Slipping his hands under his slicker through the pockets,

Tom gripped his guns. His rifle, of course, was in his saddle scabbard. He was going to have to stalk a skilled killer, a fine marksman, on his own ground in absolute darkness with a handgun! And the killer had a Spencer .56!

Lightning flashed, but there was no more shooting. Somewhere out there the killer was stalking them. He would not give up now or retreat. This, for him, was a last stand unless he killed them both. His hideout now was known, and if they escaped he would no longer be safe. That he did not intend to be driven from the country was already obvious by the fact that he had stayed this long.

Kedrick crawled out, using a bush to cover his movement, and then worked along the windy top of the ridge toward a nest of boulders he had seen ahead of him by the lightning flash. The wind whipped at his hat and flapped the skirt of his slicker. His right-hand gun was drawn, but under the slicker.

He crawled on. Lightning flashed and he flattened out on the rocks, but the Spencer bellowed, the bullet smashing his eyes and mouth full of gravel. Rolling over, he held his fire, spitting and pawing desperately at his blinded eyes.

There was no sound but the wind and rain. Then, in the distance, thunder roared and rumbled off among the peaks, and when the lightning flashed again he looked out along the high ridge of the Hogback. Lashed by the driving rain, its rocks glistened like steel under clouds that seemed a scarce arm's length above Kedrick's head. Mist drifted by him, touching his wet face with a ghostly hand, and the weird white skeletons of long-dead pines pointed their sharp and bony fingers toward the sky.

Rain pelted against his face, and he cowered, fearing the strike of a bullet at each flash of lightning, smelling the brimstone as the lightning scarred the high ridge with darting flame. He touched his lips with his tongue and stared until his eyes ached with strain.

His mouth was dry and his stomach empty, and something mounted within him. Fear? Panic? He could stay still no longer. With infinite patience, he edged forward, working his way a little over the edge of the ridge toward the hulking black clumps of some juniper, ragged trees, whipped to agonized shapes by generations of wind.

There was no sound but the storm, no sight of anything. He moved on, trying to estimate how far away the cliff house would be, to guess if he could reach it first or get between it and the killer out there. Flame stabbed the night, and something burned sharply along his shoulders. He let go everything and rolled, crashing down a dozen feet before he brought up in a tangle of dead limbs.

But the killer was not waiting. He loomed suddenly, dark on the crest; and crouching like a hunted animal, every instinct alert, Kedrick fired!

The dark figure jerked hard, and then the Spencer bellowed. The bullet plastered a branch near him, and Kedrick knew that only his own shot had saved his life. He fired again and then deliberately hurled himself backward into the night, falling, landing, crawling. He got to his feet and plunged into the absolute darkness, risking a broken limb or a bad fall, anything to get the distance he needed. Then lightning flashed, and as if by magic the Spencer boomed. How the man had followed his plunging career he could not know, but he felt the stab and slam of the bullets as they smashed about him! This man was shooting too close! He couldn't miss long!

His shoulders burned, but whether that shot had been a real wound or a mere graze he did not know. Something fluid trickled down his spine, but whether it was rainwater through the slit coat or his own blood, he could not guess.

He moved back, circling. Another shot, but this slightly to his left. Quickly he moved left, and a shot smacked right near where he had been standing. The killer was using searching fire now, and he was getting closer.

Kedrick moved back, tripped, and fell, and bullets laced the air over him. Evidently the man had a belt full of ammunition, or his pockets stuffed.

Kedrick started to rise, but his fingers had found a hard smoothness, not of rock, but of earth and gravel! Carefully, he felt about in the darkness.

The path! He was on a path, and no doubt the path to the cliff house!

He began to move along it, feeling his way carefully. Once, off to his left, he heard a rock roll. He took a chance and fired blind and then rolled over three times and felt the air split apart as the shots slammed the ground where he had been. He fired again and then again, always moving.

Lightning flashed, and he saw a hulking thing back on the trail the way he had come, a huge, glistening thing, black and shining. Flame sprang from it, and he felt the shock of the bullet. Then he steadied himself and fired again.

Deliberately, then, he turned and worked his way down the path. Suddenly, he felt space before him, and found the path here took a sharp turn. Another step and he might have plunged off! How near was his escape he knew in another instant when lightning flashed and he saw far below him the gray-white figure of the Appaloosa standing in the rain!

He worked his way down the cliff. Then he found a ledge, and in a moment, his hands found the crude stone bricks of the cliff house. Feeling his way along it, he felt for the door, and then pushing it open he crawled into the inner darkness and pushed the door shut behind him.

After the lashing of wind and rain the peace seemed a miracle. Jerking off his soaking hat he tossed it aside and threw off the slicker. There was a chance the killer would not guess that he knew of this place, and undoubtedly had he not known he would have passed it by in the darkness and storm.

Working his way along the floor, he found a curtain dividing this from an inner room. He stepped through it and sat down hard on the bunk. Feeling for his left-hand gun he found the holster empty, and he had fired five shots with his right gun. Suddenly, the curtain stirred and there was a breath of wind. Then it vanished. The killer was in the other room! He had come in!

Kedrick dared not rise, for fear the bed would creak, but he heard a match strike, and then a candle was lighted. Feet shuffled in the other room. Then came a voice. "I know you're in there, Kedrick. There's water on the floor in here. I'm behind a piece of old stone wall that I use for a sort of table. I'm safe from your fire. I know there's no protection where you are. Throw your guns out and come with your hands up! If you don't, I'm going to open fire an' search every inch of that room!"

Over the top of the blanket curtain, which was suspended from a pole across the door, Tom Kedrick could see the roof in the other room. The cave house was actually much higher than need be. Evidently the killer had walled up an overhang or upper cave. Kedrick could see several heavy cedar beams that had served to support a ceiling, now mostly gone. If that was true in the other room, it might be true in his also.

He straightened to his feet, heard a sudden move, and then fired!

From the other room came a chuckle. "Figured that would draw fire! Well, one gun's empty. Now toss out the other an' come out. You haven't a chance!"

Kedrick did not reply. He was reaching up into the darkness over his head, feeling for the beams. He touched one, barely touched it, and then reached up with both hands, judging the distance he had to jump by the width of the beams in the other room.

What if it were old and would not support his weight? He had to chance that.

He jumped. His fingers hooked well over the edge, and soundlessly he drew himself up. Now Kedrick could see into the lighted room, but he could not locate the killer. The voice spoke again. "I'm giving you no more time, Kedrick. Come out or I start to shoot! Toss that other gun first!"

Silence lay in the room, a silence broken by the sudden bellow of a gun! The killer fired, emptied a six-gun, and then emptied another. Tom Kedrick waited, having no idea how many guns the man had or what he might have planned for. Then six more carefully spaced shots were fired. One of them ricocheting dangerously close to Kedrick's head.

There was a long pause and then a sound of movement. "All right, if you're alive in there now, you got a shot comin', but if you want to give up, you can. I sort of want you alive."

Suddenly the blanket was jerked from its moorings and Alton Burwick stood in the opening, a gun gripped in his fist, ready to fire.

Kedrick made no sound, and the man stared and then rushed into the room. Almost whining with fury, he jerked Kedrick's hat from the bed and then the slicker. As the latter fell to the floor, with it fell Kedrick's other pistol, which falling from the holster had hooked into a tear in the slicker. He stared at it furiously and then jerked the bed aside. Almost insane with fury, he searched, unbelieving and whining like an angry hound on a trail.

He stopped, his pent-up fury worn away, and stood there, his chest heaving with his exertions, his fist still gripping the pistol. "Gone! Gone!" he cried, as if bereft. "When I had him right here!"

Kedrick's fingers had found a tiny sliver of wood, and

deliberately, he snapped it against Burwick's cheek. The fat man jerked as if stung and then looked up. Their eyes met, and slowly he backed away, but now he was smiling. "Oh, you're a smart one, Kedrick! Very smart! Too bad it couldn't have been you with me instead of that weakling Keith! All front and show, but no bottom to him, no staying quality!

"But," he sighed, "I've got you anyway, and you'll suffer for what you've done." He scooped Kedrick's other pistol from the floor and backed away. "All right, get down!"

Kedrick dropped to the floor, and the fat man waved irritably at the gun he clutched. "No use to bluff. That's empty. Throw it down!"

"What's it all about, Burwick?" Tom asked suddenly. "Why this place? The armor? What about Dornie Shaw?"

"Ah? How did you know about that? But no matter, no matter!" He backed to the wall, watching Kedrick and holding the gun. "Why, it was gold, boy! Gold and lots of it! It was I stirred those Indians up to attacking that caravan! I wanted the gold they carried, and most of it belonging to Dornie's pa!

"I knew about it! Followed them from Dodge. Knew when they drew it from the bank there, and how much!

"They fooled me though. When the Indians hit, they'd buried it somewhere. It could have been a lot of places. That was the trouble. They might have buried it sooner, but somewhere along the trail. I've dug and I've hunted, but I've never found it. Maybe I will someday, but nobody else is going to!

"Wondered why I wanted the land? Profit, sure! But I wanted this piece, a couple of sections in here, all for myself. Figured on that, working it out somehow. The gold's somewhere between here and Thieving Rock. Has to be."

Kedrick nodded. "That clears up a lot of things. Now you drop that gun, Burwick, and come as my prisoner."

Burwick chuckled fatly. "Try to bluff me? I'd of expected that from you! Nervy one, huh? Bet you got that Connie Duane, too! By the Lord Harry, there's a woman! No scare to her! Not one bit! Drop your gun, boy, or I'll put my first bullet through your kneecap!"

He was going to shoot, and Tom Kedrick knew it. Coolly, he squeezed off his own shot, an instant faster. He shot for the gun hand, but the bullet only skinned the thumb knuckle and hit Burwick in the side.

The fat man jerked and his face twisted, and he stared at the gun, lifting his own. Coolly, Kedrick fired again and then again. The bullets struck with an ugly smack, and Burwick wilted, the gun going from his limp fingers to the floor. Kedrick stepped in and caught him, easing him down. The flabby cheeks were suddenly sagging and old. Bitterly, the man stared upward at him. "What happened? That—that—?"

"The gun was a Walch twelve-shot Navy pistol," Tom explained. "I started carrying them a few days ago, replacing the .44 Russians."

Burwick stared at him, no hatred in his eyes. "Smart!" he said. "Smart! Always one trick better than me, or anybody! You'll—do, boy!"

On the streets of Mustang the sun was warm after the rain. Tom Kedrick, wounded again but walking, stood beside Connie Duane. Shad was grinning at them. "Look mighty fine in that tailored suit, Tom. You goin' to be gone long?"

"Not us! We'll be married in Santa Fe, and then we're headin' for the Mogollons and that ranch."

"Seems a shame not to hunt for that gold," Laredo complained. "But anyway, the real treasure was that box full of Burwick's papers. Sure made Cummings hunt his hole. But I do regret that gold."

"I don't," Connie replied. "It's caused too much trouble. Alton Burwick spent his life and a good many other lives after it. Let it stay where it is. Maybe a better man will find it, who needs it more than we do!"

"Gosh!" Laredo said suddenly. "I got to light a shuck! I'm late to meet Sue! So long, then!" They watched him go, waiting for the stage.

Everything was quiet in Mustang—three whole days without a killing.

ABOUT LOUIS L'AMOUR

"I think of myself in the oral tradition—as a troubador, a village taleteller, the man in the shadows of the campfire. That's the way I'd like to be remembered—as a storyteller. A good storyteller."

It is doubtful that any author could be as at home in the world re-created in his novels as Louis Dearborn L'Amour. Not only could he physically fill the boots of the rugged characters he writes about, but he has literally "walked the land my characters walk." His personal experiences as well as his lifelong devotion to historical research have combined to give Mr. L'Amour the unique knowledge and understanding of the people, events, and challenge of the American frontier that have become the hallmarks of his popularity.

Of French-Irish descent, Mr. L'Amour can trace his own family in North America back to the early 1600s and follow their steady progression westward, "always on the frontier." As a boy growing up in Jamestown, North Dakota, he absorbed all he could about his family's frontier heritage, including the story of his great-grandfather who was scalped by Sioux warriors.

Spurred by an eager curiosity and desire to broaden his horizons, Mr. L'Amour left home at the age of fifteen and enjoyed a wide variety of jobs including seaman, lumberjack, elephant handler, skinner of dead cattle, assessment miner, and officer on tank destroyers during World War II. During his "yondering" days he also circled the world on a freighter, sailed a dhow on the Red Sea, was shipwrecked in the West Indies and stranded in the Mojave Desert. He has won fifty-one of fifty-nine fights as a professional boxer and worked as a journalist and lecturer. A voracious reader and collector of rare books, Mr. L'Amour's personal library of some 10,000 volumes covers a broad range of scholarly disciplines including many personal papers, maps, and diaries of the pioneers.

Mr. L'Amour "wanted to write almost from the time I could walk." After developing a widespread following for his many adventure stories written for the fiction magazines, Mr. L'Amour published his first full-length novel, *Hondo*, in 1953. Mr. L'Amour is now one of the four bestselling living novelists in the world. Every one of his more than 85 novels is constantly in print and every one has sold more than one million copies, giving him more million-copy bestsellers than any other living author. His books have been translated into more than a dozen languages, and more than thirty of his novels and stories have been made into feature films and television movies.

Among Mr. L'Amour's most popular books are *The Lonesome Gods, Comstock Lode, The Cherokee Trail, Flint, Son of a Wanted Man, The Shadow Riders, Silver Canyon, Bowdrie, The Walking Drum*, his historical novel of the 12th century, and his series of novels which tells the continuing saga of the Sackett family, the latest of which is the bestseller *Jubal Sackett*.

The recipient of many great honors and awards, in 1983 Mr. L'Amour became the first novelist ever to be awarded a Special National Gold Medal by the United States Congress in honor of his life's work. In 1984 he was also awarded the Medal of Freedom by President Ronald Reagan.

Mr. L'Amour lives in Los Angeles with his wife, Kathy, and their two children, Beau and Angelique.

LOUIS L'AMOUR
BANTAM BOOKS
SHORT STORY CHECKLIST

Be Careful.

The only authorized Louis L'Amour short story collections are published by Bantam Books. All Bantam paperbacks have a rooster trademark on their upper or lower left corners and on their spines. If a L'Amour short story book does not carry the rooster logo it is unauthorized and may contain stories you already own in Bantam editions.

For your protection, you may want to detach and save this L'Amour short story list, checking off the box as you read each story.

DETACH AND SAVE

1. ☐ WAR PARTY
☐ Trap of Gold. ☐ One for the Pot ☐ War Party ☐ Get Out of Town ☐ Booty for a Badman ☐ The Gift of Cochise ☐ A Mule for Santa Fe ☐ Alkali Basin ☐ Men to Match the Hills ☐ The Defense of Sentinel

2. ☐ THE STRONG SHALL LIVE
☐ The Strong Shall Live ☐ One Night Stand ☐ Trail to Squaw Springs ☐ Merrano of the Dry Country ☐ The Romance of Piute Bill ☐ Hattan's Castle ☐ Duffy's Man ☐ Big Man ☐ The Marshal of Sentinel ☐ Bluff Creek Station

3. ☐ YONDERING
☐ Where There's Fighting ☐ The Dancing Kate ☐ Glorious! ☐ Dead-End Drift ☐ Old Doc Yak ☐ Survival ☐ Thicker Than Blood ☐ The Admiral ☐ Shanghai Not Without Gestures ☐ The Man Whole Stole Shakespeare ☐ A Friend of the General ☐ Author's Tea ☐ A Man of the Trees Broken By Snow

4. ☐ BUCKSKIN RUN
☐ The Ghosts of Buckskin Run ☐ No Trouble for the Cactus Kid ☐ Horse Heaven ☐ Squatters on the Lonetree ☐ Jackson of Horntown ☐ There's Always a Trail ☐ Down the Pogonip Trail ☐ What Gold Does to a Man

5. ☐ BOWDRIE
☐ Bowdrie Rides a Coyote Trail ☐ A Job for a Ranger ☐ Bowdrie Passes Through ☐ A Trail to the West ☐ More

Bowdrie (Con't)
Brains Than Bullets ☐ Too Tough to Brand ☐ The Thriller
From the Pecos

6. ☐ THE HILLS OF HOMICIDE
☐ The Hills of Homicide ☐ Unguarded Moment ☐ Dead
Man's Trail ☐ With Death in His Corner ☐ The Street of
Lost Corpses ☐ Stay Out of My Nightmare ☐ Collect
From a Corpse ☐ I Hate to Tell His Widow

7. ☐ BOWDRIE'S LAW
☐ McNelly Knows a Ranger ☐ Where Buzzards Fly ☐ Case
Closed—No Prisoners ☐ Down Sonora Way ☐ The Road
to Casa Piedras ☐ A Ranger Rides to Town ☐ South of
Deadwood ☐ The Outlaws of Poplar Creek ☐ Rain on
the Mountain Fork ☐ Strange Pursuit

8. ☐ LAW OF THE DESERT BORN
☐ Law of the Desert Born ☐ Riding On ☐ The Black
Rock Coffin Makers ☐ Desert Death Songs ☐ Ride, You
Tonto Raiders! ☐ One Last Gun Notch ☐ Death Song of
the Sombrero ☐ The Guns Talk Loud ☐ Grub Line
Rider ☐ The Marshal of Painted Rock ☐ Trap of Gold

9. ☐ RIDING FOR THE BRAND
☐ Riding for the Brand ☐ Four-Card Draw ☐ His
Brother's Debt ☐ A Strong Land Growing ☐ The Turkey-
feather Riders ☐ Lit a Shuck for Texas ☐ The Nester and
the Piute ☐ Barney Takes a Hand ☐ Man Riding West
☐ Fork Your Own Broncs ☐ Home in the Valley ☐ West
is Where the Heart Is

10. ☐ DUTCHMAN'S FLAT
☐ Dutchman's Flat ☐ Keep Travelin' Rider ☐ Trail to
Pie Town ☐ Mistakes Can Kill You ☐ Big Medicine
☐ Man From Battle Flat ☐ West of the Tularosas ☐ McQueen
of the Tumbling K ☐ The One for the Mohave Kid ☐ The
Lion Hunter and the Lady ☐ A Gun for Kilkenny

11. ☐ THE RIDER OF THE RUBY HILLS
☐ The Rider of the Ruby Hills ☐ Showdown Trail ☐ A
Man Called Trent ☐ The Trail to Peach Meadow Canyon

12. ☐ THE TRAIL TO CRAZY MAN
☐ The Trail to Crazy Man ☐ Riders of the Dawn ☐ Showdown on the Hogback